DRAGON'S BREATH

FRANK SMITH
Dragon's Breath

Nelson Foster & Scott
A Division of General Publishing Co. Ltd.,
Don Mills, Canada

First published in 1980 by
Nelson Foster & Scott
a division of
General Publishing Co. Ltd.,
30 Lesmill Road,
Don Mills, Ontario

First printing

Canadian Cataloguing in Publication Data

Smith, Frank A.
    Dragon's Breath

ISBN 0-919324-46-0

I. Title

PS8587.M474D72   C813'.54   C80-094376-7
PR9199.3.S573D72

ISBN 0-919324-46-0

Cover Design: Maher & Murtagh

Printed and bound in the United States

Acknowledgments

My thanks to Audrey De Baghy of the Banff Springs Hotel

and

Sergeant William J. McCoy of the Banff RCMP

who generously gave of their time, and patiently answered my questions.

Also to the management and staff of the Banff Springs Hotel, and to the experts who gave me help and information, particularly Harry Pringle and Jim Davies of Banff, Peter Fuhrmann of Canmore, and Art Reimer, Bill Lyndon, and Francis Shen of Edmonton.

Prologue

Wang Lu-chi pressed his face hard against the porthole, straining to catch one last glimpse of the supply ship as it slowly dropped astern. The rusting bow lifted to the long, rolling swell of the North Atlantic, then slid ponderously into a deep, gray trough until only the mast was visible. A curtain of rain swept in from the west, peppering the surface of the sea like buckshot, and the supply ship disappeared from view.

The link, tenuous as a cobweb, was broken. Wang Lu-chi stared disconsolately at the lowering clouds and thought of home. Four more weeks of crushing boredom before he would leave behind this cold and dreary patch of ocean. Two, perhaps three more months before he would see his wife and newborn son. He made a wry grimace. Newborn son, indeed. His son would be at least five months old by the time he arrived home again. He continued to watch the rain, remembering another such day. It seemed like a century ago, but it had rained just like this. He remembered standing there outside their new apartment, soaking wet and embarrassed because Liu Tsia had run down the steps and flung her arms around him as he crossed to the waiting car. He felt again her long, slender fingers clinging to his own as she pleaded with him to stay, not caring that the others, technicians like himself, were watching from the car. Even now he could feel the silent censure in their eyes because he could not control the actions of his young wife.

He remembered, too, how roughly he had pulled away from her, and the shock in her eyes as he turned to go. He looked back as the car drove away but Liu Tsia was nowhere to be seen. For a moment, just a fleeting, frozen instant of time, Wang Lu-chi thought he saw her face, her eyes still moist with tears, then realized it was his own reflection mirrored in the glass. He turned away and searched the room with a sullen gaze as if seeking an escape, but nothing had changed.

It was a cold room, not cold in the physical sense, for the temperature was maintained at precisely 22°C, humidity at 38 percent, but it was cold and white and featureless with glistening paint on every metal wall. Even the seal around the door was white. Pervasive ocean salt and particles of dust were scoured from the air by filters working tirelessly around the clock, and the lighting level never varied no matter what the hour. The console was not white, but there was no warmth to be found there. Aluminum and steel, black plastic knobs, and switches gleamed dully beneath banks of fluorescent lights. Full spectrum tubes, of course; for health, they said. Seemingly endless rows of blank gray panels stretched out on either side. His fingers brushed the burnished metal as Wang Lu-chi slid automatically into the padded chair and waited for the order to resume the operation. He stared at darkened screens and softly winking lights, but his inner eye saw only his wife and son. They would be asleep now, safe and snug in the new apartment. Irrationally, he suddenly resented the very comfort which, but a moment before, had comforted him.

"At least they don't have to put up with being tossed around in a battered old ship twenty-four hours a day," he muttered resentfully.

He passed a hand wearily over his face and wondered why the order had not come. He scanned the surface screen and saw that the supply ship had set a course southwest by west, and was moving steadily away. And there, as if glued to the face of the screen, were the seven sister ships locked into a preset course by a matrix of navigational beams. His hand hovered over the controls, waiting.

The generators were always shut down when the supply ship came, and, of course, when any other vessel approached to within 2,000 meters. Not that they would come to any harm, but it was best not to take any chances. Ships out here were few and far between, and with the exception of the occasional, small, Icelandic fishing boat ranging far to the west of the main fleet, they had seen nothing for almost three weeks.

The speaker above his head crackled into life and the order he had been expecting came. Wang Lu-chi responded automatically, but his mind was only partly on the job. His senses registered the pulse of the five huge generators as they surged to full operating speed, but his thoughts were still very far away in China. His eyes flicked to the temperature gauges as he cut in the generators one by one. The needles rose swiftly to settle against the green mark on each scale, and he grunted softly with approval.

Mechanically, he pushed COMPUTER ON. The screen filled up with information, but his well-trained fingers were already on the switch marked MATRIX POWER LOCK. The switch snapped down even as the message on the screen began to register in his brain.

Too late his eyes found the unexpected blip on the sonar screen. Sweat broke into glistening beads across his brow. He felt the tremor beneath his feet as something brushed against the giant cables trailing from the underwater ports beneath the stern. His outstretched fingers grasped the main power switch, only to be jerked away again as he was flung hard against the console.

The sea convulsed. The metal deck beneath his feet slammed upward. The lights went out, and with them went the life of Wang Lu-chi.

Chapter 1

Tai Ling shrugged out of his heavy overcoat and shook the melted snow from it before handing it to the waiting girl. He tucked his gloves neatly into one of the pockets, then carefully smoothed the wrinkles from his jacket while she hung the coat on a wooden peg. Tai Ling was a slim, spare man whose elbows never quite seemed to tuck in properly. His face was long and lean, made narrower by ears that, like his elbows, stuck out at an awkward angle. Deep-set eyes looked out gravely on the world; and when he was nervous, as he was now, a tic caused his right eyelid to twitch spasmodically.

He glanced around, expecting to see others there. The girl read his glance and shook her head. "You are the first to arrive," she told him. "I am instructed to tell you that the minister has been delayed. He will be here as soon as possible. Please be seated."

The room was sparsely furnished, but mercifully warm. A damp, faintly unpleasant smell rose from the uneven wooden floor bleached almost white from years of constant scrubbing. Six thinly padded chairs were set around an oval conference table made of oak, its scarred but gleaming surface marred only by the thick red folders that lay unopened before each empty chair. Faded, sepia-colored photographs of hydro installations hung on sepia-colored walls, reminding him that the building had at one time housed a British engineering firm. No one, it seemed, had thought to change the decor since the early 1930s.

"No, no, not there!" the girl said sharply as he made to take a seat at the table. She indicated a padded bench beside the window; he moved obediently toward it, but, perversely, remained standing. The girl disappeared behind a screen in one corner of the room, reappearing a moment later to offer him a steaming cup of fragrant tea. He sipped it eagerly, as grateful for the warmth of the cup in his hands as for the tea itself. He smiled across the cup and said, "It's very good. Thank you very much."

The girl did not speak, but inclined her head in brief acknowledgment before retiring behind the screen once more. She wore, he noted approvingly, a white, high-necked blouse and dark blue skirt, a welcome relief from the shapeless semi-uniforms one saw by the countless thousands every day.

His eyes were thoughtful as he sipped his tea. The winds of change blew softly but insistently across the land. Mao's memory had been laid to rest. Adherents of the Gang of Four were in disarray, purged, or in hiding. The gates that had been so tightly shut against the outside world were being cautiously unbarred. The young were restless, flexing muscles that had, in the older generation, all but atrophied. To the old, the Long March was still a vivid, living memory; to the young it was but another page of history. The old looked back with pride upon the years of selfless sacrifice; the young looked only to the future, impatient to be recognized.

And in the middle ground of life, Tai Ling often felt uneasy.

He moved closer to the window and stood looking down at the people in the street below. Two weeks ago, clad in summer cotton, they had celebrated the warmest National Day on record; now they braced themselves against the bite of driving snow, hands thrust deep inside their padded winter coats. A wry smile touched his lips. It was ironic, he thought, considering the purpose of the meeting here today.

His slender fingers gripped the cup a little tighter, seeking warmth and, quite unreasonably, comfort. The cup was cold.

The door behind him opened, and he turned to see the girl go forward to usher in a small, wraith of a man whose shoulders sagged beneath the weight of a winter coat far too big for him. A woolen scarf beaded with melting snow was wound around his head. His face looked gray and pinched as he peered through winter-misted glasses. He puffed and grunted as he struggled from the heavy coat.

"Such a day!" he panted as the coat came free. "If this is the best Peking has to offer, the sooner I can return to the sunny south, the happier I shall be."

The girl smiled mechanically. "You are the second to arrive," she told him as if reciting. "The minister has instructed me to tell you that he will be detained. He will be here as soon as he is free. Will you take some tea?" Without waiting for a reply, she made her way to the table behind the screen and began to fill another cup. Her duties, Tai Ling decided, did not extend to introductions.

He moved forward hesitantly. There was something familiar about the newcomer, who removed his glasses and wiped them absently on the corner of his loose-fitting jacket, then set them back in place again. "Ah, that's much better!" he exclaimed to no one in particular. He peered short-sightedly across the room, moving his head from side to side as if he knew someone was there but couldn't see them properly.

If doubt still lingered in Tai Ling's mind, the well-remembered gesture banished it completely. He moved across the room, hand extended.

"Doctor Kuan Lo!" he exclaimed delightedly. "It's so good to see you here. I had no idea . . . I've often thought of you, but I certainly didn't expect to see you here today. You won't remember me. My name is . . ."

"Tai Ling," the little man broke in, and laughed at the startled look on Tai Ling's face. His thin, bony fingers gripped the hand of the younger man and held it firmly.

"Bu—but that's incredible!" Tai Ling stammered. "It's been years, and you must have seen thousands of students. Surely you don't remember them all?"

"Only the exceptional ones," Kuan Lo smiled. He became serious. "But, in this case, I must confess I knew you would be here. Ah, the tea." He turned to the girl who·had appeared at his elbow. "Thank you very much, my dear," he said. He sipped the liquid noisily and nodded his approval.

"It is *Comrade* Pi Hsia," she said with emphasis. She turned and walked stiffly back to her corner.

Kuan Lo made a wry face. "I wonder if it was the 'my dear' she so objected to, or your use of the title 'Doctor'? " he said with mock gravity.

Tai Ling looked disconcerted. His eyelid twitched. "It was the way we used to address you," he said. "It just slipped out . . . I apologize. It was a social error for which I must take full responsibility. I shall choose my words with more care in future."

Kuan Lo's eyebrows drew together as he regarded his former pupil over the rim of the cup, but he made no comment. He moved to the window and shivered. "Abominable weather," he muttered. "Absolutely abominable!"

Tai Ling remained in the middle of the room until he felt the muscles in his quivering eyelid ease. He set his empty cup aside and joined Kuan Lo at the window. The snow was thickening. At first, he had not recognized his former teacher. And it wasn't just the passage of time; after all, fifteen years wasn't that much. No, it was more than that. More than the simple loss of hair; more, even, than the rounded shoulders and the obvious loss of weight. A great deal of weight. It seemed to Tai Ling that Kuan Lo had become little more than a shell of his former self. He seemed almost to have shrunk, and looked like an old man though he was scarcely more than in his early fifties. Tai Ling stared at the falling snow. The silence was becoming uncomfortable.

"You went to Canton after you left Shanghai," he said abruptly.

Kuan Lo nodded but continued to watch the slanting snow. It was as if he had withdrawn to some distant place. "Yes," he said at last. "I was born there, you know." He pulled a face. "I would prefer to be there now. It was beautiful when I left."

"You have just arrived, then? I mean you came up for this conference?"

Again Kuan Lo nodded without taking his eyes from the snow. "It's about the only thing that would make me leave Canton. I've never been fond of Peking. It's too cold, too flat and open, too . . . impersonal."

"You'll be happy to return to your family, then," Tai Ling said. "I remember your wife very well," he went on. "She helped me with my English when," he glanced around and theatrically lowered his voice, "it wasn't very popular. I admired her very much. She . . ."

"My wife is dead," Kuan Lo said harshly. "And," he went on as if to cut off further intrusions into his private life, "so is my daughter." He turned on his heel and walked across the room in search of another cup of tea.

Tai Ling was stunned. He vividly remembered Kuan Lo's wife. A lovely, gentle woman who seemed always to be pleased when students came to the house to ask her husband about some problem or other. He wondered, now, if she had ever guessed that often it was her they really came to see because they were fascinated by her flaxen hair. She was the only fair-haired European woman they had ever seen. No, not European; American, that was it. She had been born in China of American parents, but something had happened to them when she was just a child. He couldn't remember the details;

perhaps it was during the time of the floods, but he knew that she had been orphaned and brought up by a Chinese family as one of their own. For a time — several months in fact, Tai Ling remembered painfully — he had secretly admired her. Even now, after all these years, he flushed as he recalled the fantasies he used to weave. Perhaps, despite what had happened later, it was just as well that he had met Sung S'u-mah when he did.

Kuan Lo reappeared at his side, and gently placed a hand on Tai Ling's arm. "I'm sorry," he apologized. "You could not know. It happened suddenly . . . ten years . . ." He sipped his tea and turned his eyes to the window.

"And you, my friend," he went on at last. "How did you enjoy your last two summers tossing about on the open sea? It must have been a new experience for you, eh?" He appeared not to see the startled look on Tai Ling's face. "And why," he went on in a quiet voice, "did the data stop so suddenly? Why is everyone so nervous when I ask about what happened out there?" He turned to regard Tai Ling over the top of his glasses. There was no sign of short-sightedness in his level stare.

Tai Ling dropped his eyes and looked away. "That subject is forbidden," he whispered fiercely.

Kuan Lo's hand rested lightly on Tai Ling's sleeve. "There is no need for alarm," he said gently. "The data you sent back was coming directly to me for evaluation. I, too, am part of *Dragon's Breath*." He grimaced as he said the words, and then observed sourly, "Not very enigmatic, but appropriate enough, I suppose." He turned his attention to his tea once more.

Before Tai Ling could gather his thoughts together, the girl reappeared with two men. The first, Tai Ling recognized immediately; the second he knew only by reputation.

Wu Tan was squat and almost obscenely obese. He struggled out of his overcoat while the second man literally danced attendance, brushing snow from the coat with quick, nervous gestures, and shaking it carefully before handing it to the girl. Even from across the room, Tai Ling could hear the labored, asthmatic breathing of Wu Tan. It sounded worse than he remembered it. The fat man tugged his cotton jacket down over his bulging belly as he advanced into the room. His broad, pumpkin face creased into a smile that lost its way in the pallid folds of flesh long before it reached his eyes. A nauseous mixture of acrid body odor combined with peppermint preceded him. The man sucked incessantly on mints. Tai Ling repressed a shudder even as he arranged his own features into a smile of welcome.

"Comrade Wu Tan, this is indeed an unexpected surprise," he murmured. "May I introduce a former teacher of mine, Comrade Kuan Lo of Canton." He turned to the little man and went on, "Comrade Wu Tan is the Chairman of the Revolutionary Committee for Meteorological Studies, North and Eastern Sectors," he explained. "I'm sure you must have heard of him and of his work."

Kuan Lo inclined his head. "You are known by reputation even in Canton," he replied urbanely.

Wu Tan's eyes narrowed, but he jerked his head in curt acknowledgment.

"Of course," Tai Ling rushed on, sensing the antagonism between the two men, "Comrade Kuan Lo is renowned for his advanced work in core studies. I'm sure you must be familiar with the studies he . . ."

"Indeed?" Wu Tan wheezed. "How interesting." He regarded Tai Ling distastefully. He didn't need to be reminded, no matter how obliquely, and least of all by Tai Ling, that his own appointment had been largely, if not entirely, political.

"I was not aware that you were in Peking," he observed with some asperity. His obsidian eyes gleamed malevolently. "An official inquiry, perhaps? I should have thought that after that incident at sea last year . . ." He finished the sentence with a shrug.

"A technician made an unfortunate error," Tai Ling said carefully, avoiding Wu Tan's belligerent stare. He could feel the rush of blood to his face and knew his discomfort showed.

"But it was *your* technician," Wu Tan said with finality.

The second man, almost hidden by Wu Tan's enormous girth, appeared at the fat man's elbow. He carried two cups of tea, one of which he offered deferentially to Wu Tan. He waited until Wu Tan had tasted the tea and nodded his approval before turning his attention to Tai Ling. He ignored Kuan Lo completely.

"We have not met before," he annouced in a thin, high-pitched voice. "I replaced you when you left the hurricane study" — he sipped his tea carefully as if he feared it would be too hot — "unfinished. I, too, have the honor of serving on the Revolutionary Committee. I am Yeung Chao."

A real charmer, this one, Tai Ling thought. He made serving on the Revolutionary Committee sound as if it were something very special instead of mandatory. A fitting companion for Wu Tan. He met the insolent stare with stony silence.

"The study has been completed now, of course." Yeung Chao tossed back an unruly lock of cascading hair with a practised gesture. Younger than Tai Ling, he exuded self-confidence. Even by the way he held his head, like an actor making the most of the light before the cameras, it was evident that he held himself in high esteem. "There can be no true achievement without correct thought," he added smugly. "It might have been completed much earlier if the records had been . . . ." He shrugged, a mannerism so like that of his superior, Wu Tan, that it had to have been deliberately copied.

"Please take your seats. The minister is here." The girl's voice cut sharply across the room.

They took their places, Tai Ling and Kuan Lo on one side of the table, Wu Tan and Yeung Chao on the other. The fat man's chair creaked ominously as he settled into it and eyed the two men across the table with obvious displeasure. As if to emphasize the point, a gusty belch erupted from his throat and burst obscenely in the quiet room. Kuan Lo was bad enough, he ruminated sullenly, a provincial nobody, an academic of no political distinction whatsoever, and worse, an intellectual, but even that unsavory combination was preferable to the likes of Tai Ling, a self-confessed deviationist. And, as if that were not enough, the man was clearly culpable in the North Atlantic disaster. Obviously, there had been a mistake. The very idea of Tai Ling as a member of his delegation was intolerable. There would have to be a clear understanding with the minister.

Across the table Tai Ling sat staring at the folder in front of him, his fingers plucking nervously at the cover. There were six of them; six folders and six chairs. One for the minister, of course, and one . . .

His thoughts were interrupted as Chiang Feng-wei, clad in an immaculate, tailored uniform, entered the room. He was exceptionally tall for one of his race, and he carried himself well, despite his age. His back was ramrod straight, his gray hair cropped close to his head. He sat down with his back to the window and surveyed each one of them in turn. When, at last, he spoke, it was without preamble or apology.

"Comrades, you have been brought together for the first time as members of a delegation chosen to attend the international seminar known as the Global Atmospheric Research Seminar. It arises, as I'm sure you are all aware, out of the studies that have been conducted throughout the world during the past ten or twelve years under the Global Atmospheric Research Programme — acronym, GARP. Your submissions, that is to say your position papers, have been studied for technical accuracy, academic theory, and correct thought. You are to be congratulated. Only minor revisions will be necessary." Chiang paused and leaned back in his chair, letting his eyes dwell on each of them in turn.

Beside him Tai Ling heard the faintest of sighs; a

long, carefully controlled release of breath. It was as if
Kuan Lo had been holding it in ever since Chiang Feng-
wei had entered the room. He stole a swift glance at his
companion, but Kuan Lo's face gave nothing away.

The minister was speaking again. "The chairman of
this delegation will be Comrade Wu Tan. And, since they
are already working together, it has been suggested that
Comrade Yeung Chao be elected to the position of
secretary. Are there any objections?"

No one spoke. Yeung Chao inclined his head
deferentially, but he could not hide the gleam of triumph
in his eyes.

Chiang rubbed his hands together slowly as if
disposing of an unpleasant piece of business he was glad
to have behind him. "Now, let us begin with the agenda
on page nine . . ."

"A moment, please, Comrade Minister," Wu Tan
broke in. "Am I to understand that the membership of
this delegation is fixed? That I, as chairman, will have
no voice in the choice of suitable delegates?" The
emphasis on the word 'suitable' was slight but sufficient.

The minister regarded Wu Tan with thinly concealed distaste. "I had *no* choice in the selection of
delegates," he said. "The composition of this delegation
was decided at the highest level. You have the right to
appeal, of course . . ." The ball was in Wu Tan's court.

The fat man spread his hands, and his face assumed a
mask of shocked surprise. "I sought only to clarify my
position, Comrade Minister," he wheezed. "Who am I to
challenge such an . . ."

"Who, indeed?" said the minister curtly. He turned
his attention to the folder in front of him while Wu Tan
fumed inwardly.

A muffled figure entered the room and began to
divest itself of a bulky anorak, but Chiang Feng-wei did
not appear to be surprised by the interruption. He waited
patiently until the newcomer was seated at the table. Tai
Ling sucked in his breath, a sharp, involuntary gasp that

drew a questioning look from Kuan Lo. He felt the blood drain from his face, and he barely heard the words spoken by the minister.

"Comrades, this is Sung S'u-mah. Some of you will have met her in the course of your work. She is, as I'm sure you know, a meteorologist of some repute, and she will be joining you at the seminar. However," he paused and glanced around the table to make sure he had their undivided attention, "Comrade Sung S'u-mah will have the added responsibility of Political Advisor while you are out of the country. I am sure you will all give her your complete support and cooperation."

For the first time since he had entered the room, Chiang Feng-wei smiled.

Chapter 2

Roy Guthrie stepped inside the office of the Director of Operations - Planning, and closed the door. The world became muted in soft, hushed tones of brown and beige. Walls, carpets, drapes, chairs, and even the blotter in the center of the desk were color-coordinated. It was a room designed by a committee. It was, thought Guthrie, the ultimate compromise; a world of halftones where nothing was defined. He wondered if it were symbolic. The man behind the desk motioned him to a chair. He sank slowly into a sea of crushed vinyl. It was like drowning in sepia.

Sam Stauffer was a big man. He looked strangely out of place in this quiet retreat of ordered tranquility. Ten years ago he would have been described as rangy; now he was heavy jowled and running to fat. Thick, straggling eyebrows and a florid complexion contrasted oddly with the skull-like whiteness of his bald head. The late February sunlight slanting through the window gave it a pale, lumpy appearance that reminded Guthrie of the dough his mother used to pummel into buns. Stauffer butted a half-smoked cigarette in an ashtray already full, and lit another.

Guthrie waited. He was used to waiting and he did it well. Shorter than Stauffer by half a head, he was slim and compact, a distance runner who knew the importance of pace. His sandy hair was thinning out on top, but the soft coloring of his skin made him look younger than his forty-two years. He looked relaxed and comfortable. In fact he was neither. The summons to appear in the director's office had been abrupt and unexpected.

"Search me," Bronson had growled irritably in answer to Guthrie's question. "I don't know what he wants any more than you do." His eyes narrowed as he regarded Guthrie over the top of his half-glasses. "You sure *you* don't know what it's about? Something you left out of your report . . . ?"

Guthrie shook his head impatiently. "What about the rumor mill?" he persisted.

Bronson chewed on the plastic cap of his pen. "I heard he's been pulling blues and operational records all week," he said at last. He gazed at a spot above Guthrie's head. "Caracas's open for a deputy chief of station." He didn't sound convincing.

Guthrie made a face. "After five years in South East Asia? That wouldn't make much sense."

Bronson shrugged. "Who says it's gotta make sense?" He picked up the telephone and began to stab buttons with the pen. "Better get up there," he advised. He's waiting for you."

Guthrie nodded and made for the door.

"Oh, and Guthrie," Bronson was leaning back in his chair, the phone wedged between his ear and his shoulder while he stared at his new digital watch, "let me know what the hell it's all about, will you?" he said plaintively. "You are supposed to be working for me."

As the door closed behind him, Guthrie heard Bronson drop the phone back in place. "Goddam watch lost another tenth of a second!" he muttered. The door clicked shut.

Now, from the depths of the vinyl-covered chair, Guthrie's pale eyes held steady under Stauffer's scrutiny, while the director tried to match the things he'd read in the files and field reports with this quiet, almost timid-looking man. He looked, Stauffer thought, like an underpaid accountant. Except for the eyes.

"Why did we lose the pipeline in Manila?" he asked abruptly. His voice was surprisingly soft for such a big man. "What happened to Litkov? He was sending through top-grade stuff. Then nothing. What happened?"

Guthrie steepled his fingers beneath his chin. So that was why he was here. Litkov. Imperceptibly, he allowed himself to relax. In the case of Litkov, Guthrie had made a field decision, and he was quite prepared to defend it, even to the director. But why hadn't Bronson known? There had to be something else, some other reason for Stauffer to have taken a personal interest.

"I assume you've read the file?" His words were mild, unhurried.

"Assume nothing," Stauffer told him. "Just tell me what happened."

Guthrie nodded and settled himself more comfortably in the chair. "I spent almost a year setting up Litkov," he began, "but it was well worth the time in the end. His control was one of my own people, a woman, code name Blue Willow. She's in your files."

Stauffer grunted. It might have been an acknowledgment.

"Everything was working just fine. Litkov was sending through material that was making everyone all the way up the line delirious. They couldn't get enough of it." He sighed and shook his head as if he'd just heard something sad. "Unfortunately, Litkov fell in love with Blue Willow and wanted to come over. He figured he'd paid his dues; now he wanted out. Blue Willow came to see me. She asked me if it could be arranged. She had no idea how valuable the material was that Litkov had been passing through her. I told her flatly, no. Absolutely no way. She was to find a way, any way to play him along; stall for as much time as possible. We needed that information." Guthrie's eyes met Stauffer's across the desk. "That's when she told me that she was in love with him," he said quietly.

Stauffer nodded for him to continue.

"We argued, but it was clear they'd made up their

minds. The girl was really in love with Litkov; I'm
convinced of that. She threatened to go over to their side
if I wouldn't bring him over. She was to meet him that
same night to give him my answer." Guthrie paused, his
eyes looking beyond Stauffer as if visualizing the scene.
"My prime concern was to salvage what I could," he
went on at last. "I had to protect the pipeline, and Litkov
was the pipeline. The break had to be quick, and it had to
be permanent. They were to meet in a park that evening.
Blue Willow was crossing the road when a van came out
of traffic and knocked her down. Litkov was waiting for
her; he saw it all. She was DOA at the hospital, and they
never did find the van."

Stauffer eyed him narrowly. "And Litkov?"

"Got the hell out of there before the police arrived.
There was a call made to the hospital about an hour later,
inquiring about the girl. It had to be him."

Smoke flowed gently from Stauffer's nostrils.
"What if he'd gone to pieces or made a run for it on his
own?" he challenged.

Guthrie shook his head. "The risk was minimal, in
my opinion," he said with finality. "Litkov didn't have
anywhere to run, and he knew what would happen to him
if he bared his soul to his own people. Give him another
six months, if he's still in Manila, and I think we could
run him again. He has a weakness for the women there."

"Not if he suspects . . ." Stauffer let the sentence
hang.

"He doesn't suspect a thing," Guthrie said quietly.
"Believe me, I'd know."

Stauffer glanced up sharply. "You've got another
line on him?"

"You'll have your material within six months, I'm
sure of it," Guthrie said, closing the subject.

Stauffer leaned forward across the desk and pointed
his cigarette accusingly at Guthrie. "This girl, Blue
Willow, appears in the file, but she's never been associated
with Litkov," he said. "Why?"

Guthrie smiled. "You know what Manila's like," he

said easily. "Security there is like a sieve. I couldn't afford to have anyone connect Blue Willow with him. It was too dangerous. I have to protect my people."

Stauffer leaned back. Cold-blooded bastard! He'd been right about the eyes. But just the man he was looking for. "What did Bronson tell you?" he asked.

"Just to report to you, nothing more."

Stauffer jerked his head. "Good. And, when you leave here, that's exactly what you'll tell him. Nothing. Understand? From this moment on you'll take orders from me; you'll report only to me, and you'll tell no one — I repeat, no one — of our conversation. Is that clear?"

"And if you get hit by a truck? What then?" Guthrie's voice was pitched low, mild, inquiring.

Stauffer glowered but his eyes met an unwavering stare. "There is a record," he conceded grudgingly. "Buried deep. I'll give you a reference number, but it's only to be used if something should happen to me. And it's to be given only to the Security Committee. One man on that committee knows the meaning of that number. He won't identify himself in committee, but he'd contact you afterward. Satisfied?"

"It's . . . unusual," Guthrie said noncommittally.

Stauffer's head jerked one more. "Damned right it is. It has to be. You'll see why. I'll run through it once, then you can ask all the questions you like. Then, we'll take it a step at a time until we're both satisfied." He raised a quizzical eye in Guthrie's direction.

Guthrie nodded. "Go ahead."

Stauffer grunted. He turned his chair toward the window, taking time to marshal his thoughts. He needed no file to prompt him, but he found it hard to begin; hard to share with someone else a secret that had been almost exclusively his for so many years. Ash spilled down his tie. He ground out his cigarette and began to talk.

"Several years ago, we put a deep-cover agent into Red China. When I say deep-cover, I mean *deep*! At that time no one knew when we might find ourselves at war with them; no one knew what our future needs would be. But we did know that we had almost no direct sources of hard intelligence. You've been in the East long enough to know how hard it is to get a reliable agent in there. Well, we did it. Never mind how; just take my word for it. We put one in there without so much as a ripple. That was the tough part. Once in, all he had to do was dig himself in deeper, work hard, advance as far up the ladder as possible, and wait. That's all, just wait."

Stauffer fell silent as if remembering something from a long time ago. "It could be five, ten, even twenty years," he went on at last. "And during that time we would stay completely clear. No contact, nothing. We wouldn't ask for a thing. But, when we did, it would be the most important thing he'd ever do in his life. The reason for his very existence. Hell! I don't have to explain it to you. You've been around long enough to know the meaning of deep-cover." Stauffer's hand slid across the desk feeling for the open packet of cigarettes. The lighter clicked and smoke billowed around his head like a ragged halo in the fading sunlight.

"So," he continued, "the last thing we expected was to hear from him. Naturally, we had a channel open, but it was a one-way channel. Little more than a monitor, really. No one ever expected to use it because the agent was in place and inactive." Stauffer paused, and Guthrie sensed that he was having difficulty in finding the words to go on. "I guess we got a little careless." The director's voice was harsh. He turned to face Guthrie, his eyes bleak behind the curl of smoke. "The point is," he said, jabbing the cigarette in Guthrie's direction, "he did contact us." Ash spilled across the desk and settled on the color-coordinated blotter. "No codes. At least, nothing fancy. Just one fast message in the clear."

"And you're sure it's genuine," Guthrie said. He stared at the fallen ash reprovingly.

Stauffer shrugged. "There's always room for doubt," he rumbled. "But in this case we can't see any reason for the Chinese to send us a message like this one if they have uncovered the agent."

"Unless," Guthrie said, "they know or suspect that an agent exists but they don't know who it is. They may want you to lead them to him."

"Good point," Sauffer agreed, "but invalid. The ID codes were correct in every detail. If they have those, they have our man. No, we're pretty sure the message is genuine. We think our agent has stumbled across something so important that, in his estimation, anyway, it's worth risking his cover to let us know."

Guthrie nodded. He could see the way it was shaping up. "You need someone to go in and get the information out, right?"

To his surprise, Stauffer shook his head. "It isn't quite that simple," he said quietly. "Our agent is coming here — well, not exactly here — to a seminar up in Canada. A little place called Banff. It's a resort town in the Rockies."

"Banff?" Guthrie repeated. "I used to ski up there as a kid. We used to hit all those places; Whitefish in Montana, Banff and Lake Louise up in Alberta."

Again Stauffer grunted. He looked for a place to butt his cigarette, and, finding none, picked up the overflowing ashtray and dumped it in the plastic-shrouded wastebasket. With deliberate care, he ground out the cigarette while a mantle of ash settled like snow around the wastebasket.

"In something less than three months time," Stauffer went on, "in May, there will be a Global Atmospheric Research Seminar, GARS for short. As the name implies, it's an international affair. All the big-name meteorologists, hydrologists, and other scientists will be there, including those from mainland China and the USSR. They've spent some ten or twelve years evaluating material gathered in the late 'Sixties. You may remember that; they had a big staging point with ships and planes going every which way off Dakar. Now, they're going to sit down and talk about their findings and plan the next phase of the program. Our agent will attend as a bona fide member of the Chinese delegation. Your job will be to set up a cover that will allow us to debrief our agent without anyone even suspecting that he's been in contact with us. Debriefing could take from six to eight hours, according to his estimation, and he wants experts from several scientific disciplines to be on hand for the debriefing. Needless to say, none of our people are to know who it is they're talking to."

Guthrie pursed his lips in a silent whistle, his mind already grappling with the obstacles.

Stauffer's voice broke in harshly on his thoughts. "There is one more thing you should know," he said. He paused as if reluctant to go on. "The channel our agent used to let us know he's coming was penetrated. Not by the Chinese; by the Russians."

"Oh, Judas!" Guthrie groaned softly.

"Yeah, it's screwed up, all right," Stauffer admitted baldly. "But we think it's still salvageable." He drew another cigarette from the pack and pointed it at Guthrie. "I'll level with you, Guthrie," he said deliberately, as if doing him a favor. "We were gambling and we lost." He lit the cigarette. "We've known for some time that one of our agents has been turned by the Russians. Things were pretty quiet; nothing was going to break. Or so we thought. We gave him some rope so we could find out to whom he was passing information, and maybe feed in a little disinformation before we cut him out."

Stauffer grimaced. "Our timing wasn't worth a shit. We have to assume the Russians know just as much as we do."

The sigh that escaped Guthrie was barely audible. "And just how much is that?" he asked.

Stauffer stared at the man across the desk for several seconds before replying. "They know he's an accredited delegate, but they don't know who he is. The double agent who handled the message knows only that it came from inside China. He doesn't know who it is, but you can bet on it that he's passed along the full text of the message to the Moscow Center. They'll have a reception committee waiting for him in Banff. They'll try to spot our people first, then let us lead them to the agent. Then they'll move in."

Guthrie frowned but remained silent.

Stauffer nodded as if a question had passed between them. "They want to know what's in his head because they know it's just as important to them as it is to us. Maybe more important."

"Then your deep-cover agent must have given some clue as to the kind of information he has," Guthrie reasoned. There was an edge to his voice. He wished Stauffer would come to the point.

But the director would not be rushed. "In a way," he said. "He gave us a set of numbers. It didn't take us too long to figure them out, and it won't take the Russians long to do the same."

"Do they know you're on to their informant?"

"Not a chance," Stauffer said with certainty. Guthrie decided privately that he wouldn't like to take bets on it.

"That's one of the things we do have going for us," the director continued. "They don't know that we'll be watching for them. They'll be covering the Chinese delegation like a blanket, and they'll be waiting for us to make our move. We've got to distract them, draw them away so they won't know that the debriefing has taken place."

"To say nothing of keeping the Chinese from missing one of their own delegates for some eight hours," Guthrie added sarcastically. "You mentioned a set of numbers," he went on before Stauffer could respond. "They have to be the heart of the message. What do they represent?"

Stauffer hesitated, and Guthrie thought he was going to refuse to be drawn. But the director nodded.

"There's no reason why you shouldn't know," he conceded. "He gave us these figures." He pulled a pad toward him and wrote down a string of numbers. He turned it so that Guthrie could see what he had written.

54252440480

Guthrie looked up, puzzled. "That's it?"

"That's it." Stauffer smiled tightly. "It didn't make a hell of a lot of sense to us, either, until we fed it into the computer and asked for every possibility associated with that sequence of numbers. You wouldn't believe the number of things a set of digits like that can mean. We got a pile of paper half the height of this desk. Then the analyzers took over, and they came up with this." He scribbled on the pad once more, splitting the numbers into groups.

54 25 24   40 48 0

"Now, if you add a couple of things, it reads like this."

Latitude 54 25' 24" N

Longitude 40 48' 0" W

Guthrie eyed the figures. "There have to be several possible combinations even when you introduce latitude and longitude," he said. "I take it this particular one has some special significance."

"Damned right it's significant," Stauffer said. He leaned back in his chair and jabbed his cigarette at Guthrie again. "Last September, there was an accident, or what we thought was an accident at the time, about four hundred miles off the southern tip of Greenland. A Russian sub, nuclear powered, was on its last leg of a four-month cruise. It was one of the newest ones out, so we were tracking it. It's a game Navy plays on both sides. Well, the goddam thing blew up. And I mean *blew*! No warning, nothing. It just went up. The whole area was contaminated; fish catches had to be destroyed; fishermen had to be isolated and checked for contamination. There was a hell of a lot of noise going on between governments."

Stauffer glanced at the closed file on his desk. "I guess you wouldn't have heard much about it where you were," he observed, "but take my word for it, it was messy. The only thing that saved us from getting the blame was that the Russians knew that we'd quit tracking them a couple of days before the sub blew up. They knew as well as we did that our sub had dropped back and, in fact, was on its way home. We'd reverted to standard satellite tracking for the rest of the cruise, because by that time we'd learned just about everything we were going to learn; so it was strictly a monitor job. But the Russians were puzzled. They refused to believe that their sub had blown up due to a malfunction. They had no warning. She just went up like she'd been torpedoed. There were a few freighters in the general area but they got the hell out of there as fast as they could. Apparently none were sunk because no one reported a loss. The only odd thing was that a few pieces of wreckage were picked up that didn't seem to tie in with the sub, but they could have come from anywhere. The Russians combed the area for weeks, but so far as we could tell, came up empty.

"Those figures," Stauffer tapped the sheet in front of him, "represent the exact latitude and longitude of that explosion. So you can see why our friends in Moscow would be most interested in talking to our man. If they think he holds the key to what happened to their sub out there, they'll stop at nothing to get their hands on him. It will be your job to see that they don't."

Roy Guthrie remained silent, his fingers steepled as he thought about the situation. If Stauffer's information was reliable, the Chinese didn't know about the deep-cover agent, but they would maintain tight security around their own people while they were on foreign soil just as a matter of course. To spirit one of their delegates away for some eight hours without their knowledge would take some doing. It wouldn't be good enough to fake some sort of accident; they mustn't even suspect that they'd lost track of him at all.

"Okay," he said at last. "I think you'd better tell me the ground rules. For instance, is it absolutely necessary that this be a face-to-face debriefing? I mean, could it be done over a secure radio channel or phone line?"

"Too risky," Stauffer said promptly. "If someone should get on to it, we'd never even know. It has to be done in a way that will allow us to control the situation. Naturally, the agent has to be hidden from the debriefing team, and the voice has to be masked or disguised so they won't know whom they're talking to."

"What about these scientists? Are they company men? Outsiders?"

"Don't worry about them," Stauffer told him. "We can arrange to handle them so there won't be any leaks."

Guthrie sighed, but he let it pass. "All right, then, what about me? Is there any way that the Russians can know about me?"

The director shook his head emphatically. "They don't know whom the message was intended for in the company. But they'll be expecting someone to show up; in fact they'll be counting on it, so you'd better be damned careful."

Guthrie eyed the man behind the desk. "And what about the name of the agent? I'll have to know which delegate I'm to snatch so that I can plan ahead and get information to him. I need to know his capabilities. It could take a lot of cooperation on his part too, you know."

Stauffer thrust out his lower lip and shook his head emphatically. "No way," he said. "That secret stays here until you have a need to know. All I'm going to tell you at this time is that our agent is capable of almost everything from parachuting to deep-sea diving. No handicaps. I'll assign a number to each delegate before you go. When it's time, you can contact me and I'll give you the number assigned to our agent."

It was no more than Guthrie expected. The mission was in jeopardy as matters stood; Stauffer was right to protect what little security there was left. But he couldn't do it alone. "I'll need a team," he said. "I don't know how this is going to be done, but I can't set up something like this without a team. That could very well mean that some members of the team will have to meet the agent face-to-face."

Stauffer nodded. "I've given that a lot of thought," he said. "I can help you there. Work out your plan, then let me know the absolute minimum number of people you'll need. I have final say on anyone selected. If you have to make use of local help, they're not to be told anything about the overall operation. They mustn't even suspect what's going on. I want our agent protected at all times." He stared across the desk as if willing Guthrie to fully understand what he was about to say.

"*There will be no loose ends,*" he stated quietly. "None. Understand?"

The muscles around Guthrie's mouth tightened. "I understand."

Stauffer gave a grunt of satisfaction. He reached into a drawer from which he pulled a file. "You'll find all the details of the seminar in there," he said as he shoved it across the desk. "The names of the delegates and the latest information we have on all of them is on top. Read it. Memorize it, because that folder will not leave this room."

Guthrie opened the file and skimmed through the names. Part way through, he stopped. "One of the delegates is a woman," he observed. Stauffer said nothing. The lighter clicked once more and a fresh cloud of smoke enveloped him. "You've been referring to the agent as a male," Guthrie went on, choosing his words carefully. "I know it's standard terminology for agents, but in this case I'd like to be sure. Can we eliminate the woman?"

The director rose from his chair and stretched. "You read everything contained in that file," he advised. "You're going to need to know every detail about those people." He walked over to the window and stood looking out across the river to where the sun had set behind a heavy bank of clouds.

"Your mission starts now," he said in a low voice. Guthrie didn't hear him. He was already deeply absorbed in the contents of the file.

Chapter 3

It was snowing as Bill McCrimmon backed the metallic brown Malibu out of the garage behind his apartment. Huge, wet flakes settled on the windshield and slid lazily down the glass, melting by the time they hit the bottom. It wouldn't last. Already patches of blue sky were appearing over Mt. Norquay and Cascade. He rolled the window down. The air felt soft and moist against his face. He tasted it, savoring it on his tongue like wine. Winter had been long and spiteful, but now, at last, it seemed to be losing its icy grip.

He turned south into Banff Avenue. There was little traffic. It was the in-between season. The skiers, finally conceding that winter was over, had packed up their gear and gone; the summer crowd had not yet begun to arrive. McCrimmon grimaced at the thought. Banff was quiet now, but in another month when the schools disgorged impatient children and thankful teachers, the annual migration to the mountains would begin. It was hard to believe that, in just a few short weeks, Banff's population would leap from some 5,000 people to close to 30,000.

A siren started up behind him. He saw the flashing light, heard the screech of tires as the police car gathered speed, shot past him, and headed south. Instinctively he moved over to let the police car by, then tramped the pedal hard and fell in behind the blue and white. Within seconds he saw the accident ahead. A car, Corvette by the look of it, had jumped the curb and rammed into the railings on the bridge. Smoke billowed from beneath the mangled hood, and a girl was tearing at the twisted door, trying to reach the driver.

The police car swerved across the road, blocking traffic from the south. McCrimmon swung his car broadside to the traffic coming up behind. He tore the fire extinguisher from the clips beneath the dash, and was out and running toward the Corvette almost before his own car had come to rest. The driver of the police car was there ahead of him, wrenching at the door, trying to force it open to get at the driver wedged behind the steering wheel.

"Get away from the car," he warned the girl. "It could explode." She shook her head, and forced her slender fingers through the gap between the door and metal post. Together, they pried the door open inch by inch. Inside, the driver was slumped across the wheel, unconscious, a livid gash across his forehead oozing blood. McCrimmon forced the nozzle of the extinguisher beneath the mangled hood and pulled the trigger. The thick, black smoke slowly changed to gray, then faded into white. By the time the driver's door was completely open, it had stopped altogether. He turned to help the constable. Between them they eased the driver out and carried him well clear of the car before lowering him carefully to the ground.

"Thanks, Sarge," the young policeman said. He peeled off his jacket and draped it over the recumbent form. "You want to check him out while I call for an ambulance?"

"Go ahead," McCrimmon told him.

The unconscious man was young, no more than twenty if McCrimmon were any judge. He probed the wound with careful fingers, then lifted the jacket and examined the young man's chest. No sign of blood. He pulled the shirt open and probed with gentle fingers. It didn't feel as if there were any bones broken despite the clear marks of the steering wheel on the skin. He dropped the jacket back in place.

The girl appeared beside him. "Will he be all right?" she asked anxiously. Her eyes were dark and luminous as she looked earnestly for reassurance.

"He's going to have a hell of a bruise tomorrow," McCrimmon told her, "but apart from that I think he's going to be all right. His breathing sounds all right, and his pulse is strong and regular. The wound on his head is superficial. You a friend of his?"

She shook her head. "I was waiting at the lights," she indicated the traffic lights at the south end of the bridge, "when I saw him take the corner. He was going much too fast. He couldn't make it, jumped the curb, and hit the railings. I just jumped out of my car and ran along to help. I was afraid when I saw the smoke . . . I thought he might be trapped . . . the car might explode . . ."

"Too bad more people don't react like that," McCrimmon said. "It isn't often . . ." He stopped abruptly as he saw the blood trickling from her fingers. "Is that his or yours?" he asked sharply.

"It's nothing," she protested quickly. "I think I must have cut it on the door; I really don't remember doing it." She pressed a Kleenex against the gash but it continued to bleed. A second police car pulled up behind them, and, right behind, an ambulance. McCrimmon rose to his feet to let in the new arrivals.

"Your suit!" the girl exclaimed as he took her arm and steered her toward his car. He glanced down and saw the mud stains on the knees.

"Never mind the suit," he told her firmly. "It can be cleaned. Let's take a look at that hand before we do anything else. That's quite a gash. The hospital is just around the corner. Perhaps . . ."

"I'm certainly not going to any hospital for a little

thing like that," the girl replied indignantly, and, suddenly he liked her.

"Okay, but let's have a look at it anyway. I think you'll agree that it does need attention. At least let me clean it so it doesn't become infected." He opened the door on the passenger's side and took a first aid kit from the glove compartment. "Now, just sit there and let me have a look at it."

She slid into the seat and looked up at him demurely. "Yes, Doctor," she said with mock solemnity. Then, "Do you order everyone around like this?"

He grinned and took her hand. For the first time since they'd met, he really looked at her. She took his breath away. Sunlight glancing through the windshield threw highlights on blue-black hair that fell softly to her shoulders. Her eyes were dark and serious, with just a hint of laughter tucked almost out of sight, and high, broad cheekbones gave her face a slightly oriental look. McCrimmon caught his breath, and the faint scent of jasmine teased his senses. He became conscious of her eyes upon him, and dropped his gaze to her hand. His own seemed to be big and clumsy against the small, cool, slender fingers of the girl.

The wound ran in a jagged line from the base of the little finger, across her palm, and ended just below the thumb. It did not appear to be very deep, but it continued to bleed profusely. "Just hold it there with the thumb of your other hand," he instructed her. "Now, press down gently. Ah, that's got it. Just hold it there for a minute." The blood slowed, then stopped completely. He cleaned the wound and put a dressing on it before making it secure with a bandage.

"There, I think that's got it," he told her, smoothing the creases out of the bandage and tying it at the wrist. He released her hand reluctantly. "I'm not so sure that it shouldn't have a couple of stitches." She jerked her hand away as if she expected him to do it right there and then.

"Okay, okay," he laughed, "I guess it will mend without them. It's just that it's going to hurt for a while when you use your hand. I'm pretty sure it'll be all right, but if it starts to give you trouble, promise me that you'll see a doctor. Okay?"

She smiled and nodded quickly. "I'm sure it won't be any trouble," she told him. "I'm really very grateful. Thank you . . .?" Her voice was soft and warm and mellow, and McCrimmon caught himself staring once again.

"Oh! Oh, yes, my name's Bill. Bill McCrimmon," he told her. "And," he added quickly, "I'll need your name," he nodded in the direction of the Corvette, "as a witness, of course."

"Of course," she said solemnly, amusement in her eyes. "My name is Jacintha Lee."

He liked the sound of it, especially the way she said it. "And your address, Miss Lee?"

She didn't contradict the 'Miss', and he'd observed no rings except for an amethyst on her right hand, but she dropped her eyes to the bandage and began to gently smooth the folds. "I can't give you that, I'm afraid," she said in a low voice. "You see, I just arrived in Banff this morning, and I haven't had time to look for accommodation yet."

"I know just about all the accommodation going," McCrimmon said. "Perhaps I can help."

"Oh, no, that's quite all right," the girl broke in hastily. "I—I'd rather take my time, look around and see where everything is before settling on a place." Her voice precluded argument. She glanced across the road to where the police were trying to pull the Corvette away from the railings. Traffic was beginning to move across the bridge, and a tow truck was backing toward the damaged car. "I'd better move my car," she said. "I left it at the lights; it'll be blocking traffic."

He nodded, reluctant to end this unexpected interlude. "I'll drive you there," he said.

"But it's only a few yards away," she protested. He grinned and firmly closed the door, then went around the other side and got in behind the wheel.

"You've been injured," he told her lightly. "The least I can do is take you back to your car."

"You are being very kind," she said seriously.

"And you," he returned, just as seriously, "were very kind to that young man. He could have been seriously injured or even killed. That car could have exploded, you know."

"I know," she said gravely. "I'm glad you came along. You and that policeman."

Her eyes did strange things to his pulse. "Look, Miss Lee — ah, Jacintha — if you don't mind me calling you that. Would you, I mean, since you're new to Banff, maybe . . ." God! He was stammering like an idiot. He took a deep breath. "I'd like to take you to dinner," he said with a rush. He stared straight ahead as if intent upon his driving while, inwardly, he held his breath. He knew she was searching for a tactful way to tell him to get lost.

"I—I think I'd like that Bill." She spoke his name hesitantly as if testing it on her tongue.

He turned to stare at her. "You will?" he said unbelievingly.

She nodded. "Although you've already been much too kind to me. Thank you very much. Is it all right if I telephone you when I know where I'll be staying?"

"Great," McCrimmon said, "and it's my pleasure." He turned the corner at the lights and stopped the car. Across the road a yellow Datsun was parked tight against the curb. Drivers honked their horns as they negotiated the narrow space between the Datsun and the Malibu, but McCrimmon barely heard them. He took a notebook from his pocket, scribbled down his name and number, tore out the page and gave it to the girl. "You can call that number anytime, and they'll see that I get the message," he told her. "Would seven be all right?"

"Seven will be fine," she agreed. She took the slip of

paper, glanced briefly at it, then put it in the pocket of her jacket. A driver leaned on his horn and glared at them as he thundered past.

"I'd better get my car out of the way," she said tactfully. "And thank you once again." She slipped from the car, closed the door, and was running across the road almost before he knew it.

He rolled the window all the way down and leaned out. "You're sure you'll be all right?" he shouted, then felt like a fool. She'd only cut her hand.

"I'll be fine," she shouted back. "See you at seven." The car started, the lights changed, and she was gone.

Still thinking of Jacintha Lee, McCrimmon drove the short distance along Spray Avenue to the hotel. The sky was clearing; the clouds were breaking up. Splashes of dazzling white stood out sharply against a sky of cerulean blue, like ice flows drifting in a summer sea. Spring, albeit belatedly, was in the air. The shadow of the huge hotel loomed high above the trees. Handhewn blocks of weathered Rundle limestone rose tier on massive tier, and green, steep-hipped dormered roofs thrust even higher as if to challenge the very peaks around them.

McCrimmon parked his car and made his way inside, conscious of the curious stares of passersby as his mud-soaked pants flapped inelegantly around his legs. There was little he could do about that; he was already twenty minutes late, and the Iron Duke was not noted for his tolerance. He was, of course, the last to arrive.

The special security team from Calgary had taken up positions on the far side of the long, oak table, while members of the hotel security team sat opposite them. Paul Cavanna, chief of hotel security, sat at one end, while at the other sat Inspector Arthur Wellington, RCMP, known throughout K Division as the Iron Duke. He did not look pleased. A rule-book policeman, rigid, and demanding, Wellington sat with hands clasped beneath his chin, supporting a thin, ascetic face devoid of color. Thin strands of Brylcreamed hair were combed carefully over a high, balding dome. His pale gray eyes flicked from face to face as if expecting to catch someone doing something he shouldn't. His eyes settled on McCrimmon reprovingly.

"My apologies, gentlemen," McCrimmon said as he took the only vacant seat. "I was delayed by a traffic accident down by the bridge."

"Anyone hurt?" The question came from Cavanna at the far end of the table.

"A young guy driving a Corvette," McCrimmon replied. "Luckily, he hit the bridge and not another car. I don't think his injuries are too serious."

Only slightly mollified, Wellington, who had been following the exchange, nodded curtly, grudgingly accepting the explanation. A redheaded girl sitting across the table from McCrimmon dropped one eyelid behind her granny glasses in a slow and saucy wink. A smile tugged at McCrimmon's mouth, but with the Iron Duke's gaze still full on him, he didn't return the wink. Cavanna shuffled the papers on the table before him and began to speak again. Very different from Inspector Wellington, he had an easygoing manner that belied the tremendous energy he poured into his job. Two years McCrimmon's senior, at thirty-four he was one of the youngest security chiefs in the hotel chain, and in McCrimmon's estimation, one of the best. He had to be. You just didn't make it in a hotel like the Banff Springs unless you were.

"So, gentlemen," he was saying, "I think we might . . ."

"May I interrupt for just a moment?"

Cavanna stopped and looked inquiringly at the Iron Duke. "Of course," he conceded, but there was a question in his voice.

"Before we continue," Wellington said ponderously, "I think we would all agree," he favored them each in turn with an acerbic stare that dared them to refute his words, "that this room is far too small to permit indiscriminate pollution by smoking. With your permission," he went on, nodding in Cavanna's direction, "I'd like to suggest that this room be declared a no smoking area, not only for this meeting, but for all future meetings."

McCrimmon smiled to himself while others grimaced and dutifully stubbed out their cigarettes. Wellington's aversion to smoking in any form was widely known, but they had counted on the fact that he was outside his own territory, and would be too polite to say anything. Those who thought that didn't know Wellington very well.

"Perhaps, Miss Graham, you could open one of the windows," Cavanna suggested to the redheaded girl. Obediently, she left the table and opened a casement window directly behind the Iron Duke, then returned to her seat. McCrimmon could feel the cool air from where he sat, but the inspector gave no sign that he was aware of it.

"Thank you, Miss Graham," Cavanna said, and tried again, this time without interruption.

"As I was about to say when Sergeant McCrimmon came in, for those of you who don't know me, my name is Paul Cavanna, chief of security in this hotel. My job is to make sure that our guests have a pleasant, trouble-free stay, whether they be weekend skiers or heads of state. In this particular case, of course, we will be dealing with the rather special conditions surrounding the international seminar which starts two days from now. There will be close to two hundred accredited delegates from twenty-three different countries. They will be accompanied by aides and secretaries who will swell the total to something like four hundred and sixty people. The seminar will continue for one week. During that time, not only are there many interlocking meetings and working sessions in various rooms throughout the hotel, but there will be the usual tours, cocktail parties hosted by one delegation or another, and probably a few things we haven't even heard about yet. My staff, augmented by security men from other hotels, will be covering all the activities here, extending, of course, to security on the golf course. There will be at least one man, hotel security or RCMP, assigned to every tour originating at the hotel. My staff will also take care of international press coverage, radio and TV interviews, and we have done all the screening of associated personnel; technicians, cameramen, etcetera.

"You are all familiar with the drill, I think, although you may not have worked this hotel before. All my men are fully trained, some of them by your own force, and the hotel is our home territory. We'll handle everything at this end. For those of you who are unfamiliar with the hotel, you will find floor plans in the folders in front of you, together with a complete schedule of events. The schedule, you will note, is subject to change, and you can count on it that it will be changed. If there is one thing I've learned over the years it's that schedules are made to be changed, so be prepared. Again, for those unfamiliar with the hotel, there will be a guided tour after lunch. This room will be available to us for the duration of the seminar, and all future briefings will be held here." Cavanna paused and glanced down at the notes in front of him.

"Before Inspector Wellington takes over," he continued, "I'd like to mention one more thing. The young lady seated next to the inspector is my secretary and invaluable assistant, Sylvia Graham. She will be taking minutes of the meeting, and she will maintain the records associated with each event. If there is a change in schedule, Sylvia will know it. If, for example, CBC decides to send in a couple of new technicians at the last minute, she will arrange the clearance." He paused and looked around the table. "And that goes for *any* changes," he emphasized. "Every officer assigned to duties associated with this seminar will be required to carry his photo-ID. If someone goes sick and has to be replaced, the replacement must be cleared through my office.

Remember, no matter how small the change, call Sylvia.
Her business number is listed in the folder." He grinned.
"I said her *business* number. You'll have to do your own
investigating if you want her private number."

An appreciative murmur rippled through the police
ranks while Wellington looked pained. The girl acknowledged the introduction with a cheery wave of her hand,
but her smile was strictly professional. So long as Paul
Cavanna was around they could investigate all they liked,
but it would do them no good, McCrimmon knew.

"And now I'll turn you over to Inspector Wellington of the Calgary CIB," Cavanna said formally.

Wellington rose to his feet, placed his hands behind
his back, and looked at each face in turn to make sure he
had their undivided attention. Informality was an art the
inspector had never learned. Humor, at least on the job,
was something he didn't understand at all.

"Thank you, Mr. Cavanna," he said stiffly, "but,
before I continue, I would like to have the minutes
ammended to read CID rather than CIB." He paused to
make sure that Sylvia Graham was giving him her full
attention. "Unfortunately, far too many of our own
people persist in using the term, referring, presumably,
to the time when we used to be known as the Criminal
Investigation Branch. The correct name, of course, is
Criminal Investigation Directorate, or CID if you must
abbreviate." He bared his teeth in what he believed to be
a paternalistic smile. "Is that quite clear, my dear?"

Sylvia Graham nodded solemnly. "Oh, very clear,
Inspector," she said. She had the distinct feeling that he
would have patted her on the head had she been seated
within reach.

Wellington rubbed his hands together briskly.
"Good. Then I will continue." He shifted his gaze and
stared hard at one of Cavanna's men while he marshaled
his thoughts. The men stirred uneasily. For those
unfamiliar with Wellington's little mannerisms, his
pauses could be disconcerting. "As some of you already

know," he said, "I have been here for some time now, acquainting myself with the schedule of events, the security system employed within the hotel, and, of course, the information supplied by the Banff Detachment. I have spent some time with Mr. Cavanna, and I must say I'm impressed with the internal security of the hotel."

McCrimmon and Paul Cavanna exchanged glances. This was praise indeed from the Iron Duke. Perhaps, McCrimmon thought irreverently, the inspector had heard that the hotel was picking up the tab for lunch.

"However," Wellington continued, "a large number of the events of concern to us will take place outside the hotel, and it will take all of our combined resources to make sure that a reasonable level of security is maintained. This is a scientific seminar, not a First Ministers' conference, so our role will be that of unobtrusive protective policing. We will remain in the background as much as possible." The inspector's eye fell on a constable from Calgary. "That doesn't mean that you can regard this as some kind of holiday," he warned. Color rose in the young constable's face, but Wellington had already shifted his gaze.

"Some of the delegates will have their own security people with them," he went on. "Some of them will identify themselves to us, but there will be others who will prefer to be annonymous. They will not be here so much to protect their delegates as to use the seminar as a cover to gather information. We have been through the lists sent to us in advance, and we've been able to identify some of them. They're listed as aides, secretaries, or assistants, although one," the inspector permitted himself a thin smile, "is listed as a travel director. Naturally, we'll keep an eye on these people simply because they are officially part of the group, but their activities will be more closely watched by members of the Security Service who, for rather obvious reasons, are not here with us today. Remember," he warned sternly, "our job is to see that the seminar runs smoothly. I don't want any of you meddling in affairs best left to the cloak-and-dagger squad. Understood?" He glared at the young constable who nodded vigorously.

Wellington seemed suddenly to remember that half the people in the room were civilians. "I'm speaking, of course," he said, with a nod to Cavanna, "for the benefit of our own people. I'm sure you understand?"

"Of course," Cavanna acknowledged.

"Good." Wellington picked up the thread once again. "The Banff Detachment will look after local affairs. I've had a word with Staff Sergeant Beech, and he's agreed to cooperate in any way he can. For example, we know that there are at least two groups planning demonstrations. One has to do with civil liberties for the Latvian people and the other is for the release of Soviet dissidents." Wellington grimaced. He disliked anything that wasn't orderly. He particularly disliked demonstrations. "The local force is best left to look after such things," he said, dismissing the subject.

"And speaking of the local force, Sergeant McCrimmon here is not only assigned to our team, but will provide the necessary liaison with the Banff Detachment. It will be his responibility to see that we get local support if and when we need it."

Wellington tapped the folder in front of him. "You will see in here there are many tours laid on for the various delegations. The Upper Hot Springs, the chair lift on Mount Norquay, the gondola on Sulphur, sightseeing by helicopter, weather permitting, a luncheon at the Timberline, a bus trip to the Columbia Icefield — the usual Cook's tour, in fact." The inspector's face took on an even bleaker expression as his eyes swept around the table. "And every damned delegate will want to stop and take pictures, wander away from the group, or get stoned out of his mind because he thinks the liquor's free."

He sat down abruptly and opened the folder.

"Now," he sniffed, "let's take a look at each day and each activity step by step. Turn to page three; list of delegates, time and manner of arrival . . ."

Chapter 4

Wu Tan watched with sullen eyes the progress of the stewardess as she served the drinks. He watched the amber liquid splashing into plastic glasses; watched the man across the aisle set his drink casually aside, untouched, while he finished reading an article in a magazine. Drink it! Wu Tan commanded silently, but the man remained oblivious to the telepathic order. Wu Tan squirmed in his seat, wedged as he was into a space designed for someone half his weight and girth. The stewardess moved the trolley closer, bringing with it the tantalizing smell of rum. His thickened tongue tried to moisten lips as coarse and dry as desert sand. He tasted salt, the salt of his own sweat. The trolley stopped beside him, the prepoured drinks just inches from his nose. His mouth was dry; his throat was parched; the sugared smell of sweet, dark rum filled his senses. He closed his eyes and fought the craving down, wrestling with the agony as fiercely in his mind as with some monster from the Stygian deep. Down, down, and further down into the deepest reaches of his mind. As always, in this waking nightmare, he struggled with a door, pushing against an unseen force. The door clanged shut. Once more the terror was subdued and safely locked away. Until next time.

"And what will you have, sir?" The stewardess

smiled mechanically, trying to ignore the noxious, acrid smell emanating from this passenger. A sheen of perspiration glistened wetly on his face. She wondered whether he was ill, and decided not to ask in case he was.

Wu Tan opened his eyes and looked directly at the tray of drinks without emotion. Another battle won. He could say the word that meant so much; he could say 'no' and mean it. He deliberately held it back, savoring the moment before speaking.

Yeung Chao stirred beside him. "The chairman does not drink alcoholic beverages," he told the stewardess in his piping, reedy voice. "And I want nothing, thank you." He sat back in his seat and folded his arms primly.

Blood pounded in Wu Tan's ears. Color rose in purple fury in his face as he curtly shook his head at the waiting stewardess. He didn't trust himself to speak. She moved away. The trolley disappeared. The pounding in his head subsided. He took a peppermint from his pocket and clamped it between his teeth, then slumped down in his seat to sulk in brooding, angry silence. Beside him, overshadowed by the chairman's massive bulk, Yeung Chao smiled and composed himself for sleep.

Two seats behind, Tai Ling shook his head when the stewardess offered him a drink, and continued to stare morosely at the seat in front of him. Whether by accident or design, Sung S'u-mah was seated next to him, and he was acutely conscious of her presence. A magazine lay open on her lap, but she appeared to have fallen asleep. He stole a glance at her. Despite himself his pulses quickened as, with his eyes, he traced the outline of her cheek in silhouette, and the well-remembered softness of her lips. A strand of hair had strayed across her cheek; his fingers itched to stroke it gently back in place. Even now she still looked so young, so very vulnerable in response. Memories flooded in on him; haunting, bitter memories and he turned angrily away.

Out there, in the North Atlantic, he had all but forgotten Sung S'u-mah. Or so he had believed. But now, the very air between them seemed charged, brittle to the point of shattering; the breathless hush when birds stop singing before the breaking of a summer storm. His fingers hurt. He looked down to find them curled tightly round the armrest as if trying to leave their imprint on the metal tips. He stared at them, then grinned self-consciously at his self-imposed discomfort. He forced the tightened muscles in his belly to relax. He expelled the air held captive in his lungs in a long and thankful sigh.

The woman stirred beside him. "That's better, isn't it?" she murmured very quietly; so quietly, in fact, that he wondered if he'd heard the words at all or if his mind were playing tricks on him. And yet he should have been prepared, for hadn't she always had the uncanny knack of knowing what he thought almost before he knew himself?

He felt the muscles start to knot again. "I thought you were asleep," he said, not knowing what else to say.

"Daydreaming," she said. He remained silent but was conscious of her eyes upon him. "Don't you think it's time we talked about it?" she suggested carefully. Her voice was deliberately neutral but he detected tension beneath the surface.

And somehow that surprised him, for it suddenly occurred to him that perhaps, just perhaps, she might have suffered too. It turned his own thoughts upside down. It would take time to get used to such a new idea. "It was a long time ago," he answered, just as carefully. Out of the corner of his eye he saw her nod her head very slowly.

"And yet no more than yesterday in our hearts."

He turned to look at her and found her eyes full on him. His mouth was dry as he nodded in return. "No more than yesterday," he acknowledged quietly. He ran his tongue across his lips but no moisture came. "Why?" he said. The question that had burned inside him, tortured him throughout the lonely, silent years. "Why?" he repeated fiercely. "Why?"

Her fingers touched his hand, then quickly retreated as if afraid he would pull away. She avoided his eyes. "I was very young," she said softly. "Very idealistic. I wanted so much to be a part of the revolution, to help pluck out the cancers of deviation and self-interest. I was proud of our profession, yours and mine."

He bridled at that. "And what was that if not self-interest?" he challenged harshly. "You condemned me to three years as an outcast to satisfy *your* self-interest. "Aahyieee!" he breathed. "We were to be married, and yet you . . ." He broke off and shook his head in bleak rememberance.

Sung S'u-mah shook her head in vehement denial. "I did not know that you would try to defend Lin Yeh-Kuo," she burst out. "He was a traitor to the revolution; he openly advocated a return to the profit structure and personal incentives, to the old ways of the tyrant, Chiang Kai'shek. He was . . ."

"He was a good man," Tai Ling put in quietly. "A shy man, a lonely man, and a very honest man who felt deeply about people. No, not just *the masses*, that somehow inhuman conglomerate we always talk about, but people, individuals, each with his own peculiar set of needs and wants, hopes and dreams." Tai Ling shook his head and seemed to bring himself back from some distant point. "We didn't share each other's views," he went on. "In fact, we used to sit up half the night trying to convince the other that he was wrong. You see, I too was a revolutionary at that time, or so I fondly thought. But we harmed no one, neither did we intend to. He was a gentle man." There was pain in Tai Ling's eyes as he looked directly at Sung S'u-mah. "You were not content with your position as a meteorologist, were you? You wanted more." His voice hardened. "You sold yourself to Wang Chen-yin," he said deliberately. "And you helped destroy a brilliant man." The words were spoken bitterly. They were meant to hurt.

Sung S'u-mah did not flinch, but anguish like a

restless ghost lurked just below the surface of her eyes. There was a brittle edge to her voice when at last she spoke.

"Please do me the courtesy of listening to the truth," she said with fierce intensity. "I did not sell myself to anyone, least of all to Wang Chen-yin. It's true that I work for him, but I was recruited long ago, long before I met you. I had the honor of meeting Wang Chen-yin several years ago. He is a selfless, dedicated man whose only interest is to serve the People's Revolution. I was proud to be asked to serve." Her chin went up defiantly. "I'm still proud to serve in any way I can."

He made as if to say something, but she raised her hand in silent rebuke. "Please hear me out. I could not tell you of my work. I sought permission because I knew that you should be told. I wanted no secrets between us when—when we were married. But I was told that I must wait." She looked down at her hands before going on. "I was doing my job," she said stubbornly, as if justifying to herself the events she had set in motion. "I couldn't know that you would associate yourself with Lin Yeh-kuo." She looked up, frowning. "They told me that you could have saved yourself a lot of trouble, but you kept right on defending him even after you'd admitted he was wrong. Why?"

"It was persecution for the sake of persecution," Tai Ling answered. His eyes became blank as he turned them inward and looked backward in time.

"There *were* excesses; we know that now," Sung S'u-mah admitted grudgingly. She shrugged helplessly, and continued in a voice so quiet that he had to strain to hear her. "I left Shanghai. I was reassigned to a weather station in Kansu; then, later, to Peking. Permission to marry was, of course, withdrawn. Later, when I heard you were back after rehabilitation, it seemed better to try to forget the past."

"Can we ever forget the past?" Tai Ling challenged. "Are you not here, advisor to this seminar, because of me? I wonder, sometimes, why they let me come at all."

Sung S'u-mah shook her head impatiently. "You give yourself too much credit," she told him. "You forget that I, too, have a modest reputation as a meteorologist. I, too, have a paper to present. The fact that I am also charged with ensuring the political integrity of this delegation has nothing to do with you personally." She reached out and touched his hand. "You are not a dissident, Tai Ling," she said softly. "You are a good man, a good meteorologist; that's why you're here. But should we not protect our future? You and others like you *are* our future. So much, so very much depends upon each and every one of you." She stopped abruptly. There was something in his eyes that made her feel uneasy. A frown plucked at her brow.

"Our future?" he echoed hollowly. "What kind of future do we have when you consider the kind of work I've been doing recently? Eh? You must know what I've been doing out there in the . . ."

Her fingers suddenly tightened on his. "It is not something we should be talking about," she cut in. "It is sufficient to know that it is necessary. We need time; time to train our people, to . . ."

"Time." He repeated the word almost sadly. "It is always time, isn't it? But does anyone stop to count the cost?" He sighed and gently removed his hand from hers. "Survival," he observed enigmatically, "is such a relative term, isn't it?"

Their eyes met. The years of bitterness melted away. So strange, he thought. It was as if those years had never been. The summer storm had broken; behind it came the faintest stirrings of hope on a freshening breeze.

The meeting broke up shortly after three-thirty. While those who were unfamiliar with the hotel were being escorted through the labrynthine structure, Mc-Crimmon, Cavanna, and his secretary, Sylvia Graham, made their way to the lobby. Bellmen, their carts loaded high with luggage, swept past on their way to the elevators while incoming guests trailed in their

wake. Business in the main lobby was brisk. People of
every size, shape, and description crowded against the
dark panels of the reservation desk where three girls were
taking care of registration. The trio stood and watched as
the girls deftly matched names to reservations, handed
out keys, signaled for more bellmen, answered innumer-
able questions, and welcomed guests to the hotel. As each
new guest moved away, another took his place.
Throughout it all the three girls smiled, sometimes,
perhaps a little fixedly, but smiled nevertheless.

McCrimmon shook his head admiringly. "I don't
know how they manage to keep it up," he said, voicing
the thought shared by all of them. "Look at that guy over
there." A tall man, wearing a heavy overcoat and ragged
scarf around his neck, was waving his arms about and
shaking his finger under the nose of a pretty brunette.
The girl seemed unperturbed by it all, and waited politely
until he had finished. She smiled disarmingly, asked a
question, then wrote something on a card in front of her.
The man stood there uncertainly for a moment, then,
with a grudging nod, shambled away from the desk.

Cavanna shook his head. "The girls are selected very
carefully for that job," he said. "They have to be pretty
unflappable. You have to remember that most people
arrive here after a long journey. They're usually tired
and, more often than not, bitchy. If there's even the
slightest thing wrong, they take it out on the girls. Come
on," he went on, "it seems to be thinning out a bit. Let's
find out how things are going."

He led the way across the lobby to where the
brunette was busy completing the card. She looked up
and smiled at the security chief, and glanced past to where
the others stood. "Oh, oh," she said in mock alarm.
"What did I do? I see you've got the fuzz with you."
She flashed a smile in McCrimmon's direction. "Hi, Bill,"
she greeted him. "How've you been?"

"Do you know every girl in town?" Sylvia Graham

asked with a quizzical grin. "Judy's only been with us a few weeks."

"All part of the job," McCrimmon assured her with studied seriousness. "We have to keep a sharp eye out for the young, criminal types that start drifting into town at the beginning of the season." He moved up to the desk. "Hi, Judy," he greeted the girl. "Sorry, but we haven't found your camera yet. I'm afraid you're going to have to write it off. It's probably long gone by now; even if we found it there's no way of proving it's yours unless you can come up with that serial number from home."

The girl nodded. "I guess you're right," she agreed. "I should have written down the number."

"I take it you two have met," Cavanna said unnecessarily. "What happened, Judy?"

"I guess it was my fault, really," the girl told him. "It was when I first arrived in town by bus. I set my camera down with my suitcase while I went to make a phone call. Pretty stupid, eh? It got ripped off."

"You're lucky you didn't lose your suitcase as well," Cavanna told her. "How much was the camera worth?"

"About a hundred bucks, I think. My brother bought it for me when he found I was coming out here to work. That's why I don't want to write home for the serial number. I haven't told him yet."

McCrimmon shook his head. "They're easy to steal and even easier to sell," he observed. "They have to be the number one item in any tourist town. You wouldn't believe the number of people who leave them on the seat of their car and go away without even locking the doors. And then, of course, it's tape decks, radios, and . . ."

"Okay, okay," the girl said hastily. "Honest, I'll take better care of my stuff next time." She turned to Cavanna. "Is there something I can do for you?"

"Just wondered how we're doing on the GAR seminar," he said. "Some of the delegates should have arrived by now."

The girl nodded. "Some of them have arrived. I took the group from Denmark this morning. The Canadian delegates have been arriving for the past couple of days. Most of them have their wives with them. I guess they're making a holiday out of it."

The girl next to Judy turned to them. The name tag on her lapel announced that she was Chris. "The Australians are here," she told Cavanna with a grin. She was a pretty girl with red hair and freckles. Her eyes danced. "They wanted to know where they could find a beer, and whether we would go out with them tonight; in that order, incidentally. And that was before they even had rooms assigned."

"Sounds like the Aussies," Cavanna said. "Anyone else?"

Chris reached for a book and ran her finger down the pages. "Yes, France and Japan are in. The Russians are due this evening. The delegates from the U.K. are supposed to arrive in the morning. Most of the Americans are here; there are four more to come." She riffled the pages once more. "The members from Iraq arrived very early this morning. Senegal, Spain, China, and all the South American countries are due in either late tonight or tomorrow." She closed the book with a snap. "They should all be here by tomorrow afternoon. The ice-breaker is set for eight tomorrow evening."

"Ah, yes. The official welcoming cocktail party hosted by the Province of Alberta," Cavanna said. "Any problems so far?" he asked the girls.

They both shook their heads. "Nothing out of the ordinary," the girl named Chris told him. "Just the usual juggling of rooms; you know the sort of thing." She chuckled impishly and rolled her eyes. "And you should get a load of some of those 'secretaries'. Wow! You know, the ones who simply have to have connecting rooms in case their master calls for them to take a memo in the middle of the night."

"You're jumping to conclusions, Chris," Cavanna told her. His face was grave but a smile tugged at the corners of his mouth. "They're probably just trying to do their job."

"You can say that again," the girl agreed. "Some job!"

Cavanna turned to go. "Thanks, girls," he said. "Let me know if you have any trouble." He stopped in mid-stride and turned back to Judy. "What was the matter with the tall guy with the scarf?" he asked. "He looked as if he was giving you a bad time."

The brunette smiled. "We had given him a room with a double bed. He was some upset. Said he hadn't slept with *that woman* for twenty years and he didn't intend to start now. "She noted Cavanna's quizzical look, and shrugged. "Maybe she chews garlic," she offered. "I didn't think it was a good idea to ask. I've arranged with the housekeeper on that floor to have the double removed and two singles put in."

"They're a good bunch of girls," Cavanna said with quiet pride as they moved away from the desk.

McCrimmon agreed. "I'd better be getting back," he told the security chief. "See you tomorrow, Paul. You, too, Sylvia. Take care."

"You will be here early, won't you?" Cavanna said. "I'd like to go over the routes with you. Old Wellington is pretty good, but he doesn't know Banff like you do. I'd appreciate it if you could be there."

"I'll be there," McCrimmon assured him. "By personal invitation from the Iron Duke himself." A startled look crossed his face. "Oh, God!" he groaned. "I completely forgot. I was supposed to make a reservation for two in the Rob Roy Room for this evening. It slipped my memory completely. It'll be full, now." He looked hopefully at Cavanna. "Do you have any pull with the dining room staff, Paul?"

"For you and Wellington?" Cavanna seemed startled by the idea.

"God, no! It's for — well, I met this girl this morning. She's new in town and . . ."

"You felt obliged to show her around and take her

out for dinner," Cavanna finished for him. He turned to Sylvia Graham. "Pretty tough, wouldn't you say, Syl?"

"Almost impossible," she replied, deadpan. Her eyes grew thoughtful. "Of course, for a price . . ." She eyed the sergeant hopefully, then appeared to relent. "All right," she sighed. "What time?"

McCrimmon leaned over and pecked her on the cheek. "Thanks Sylvia," he said. "You may have just saved my life. Make it seven-thirty, will you?"

"The Rob Roy Room, eh? She must be something special, Bill. Or did you just get a raise?"

To her surprise, the sergeant appeared to give her offhand comment serious consideration. "She is," he said at last. "Do you know, Sylvia, I really think she is."

Cavanna exchanged glances with his secretary, but something in McCrimmon's manner prevented them from probing deeper.

Sylvia Graham turned to leave. "I'll take care of that for you, Bill," she called over her shoulder. Then, to Cavanna, "I'll be in the office if you need me, Paul. 'Bye, Bill. Have a pleasant evening." She moved off with a long swinging step. Cavanna stared after her.

"Best damned secretary I ever had," he told McCrimmon. "I've quit trying to keep track of all the time I owe her."

"She's a very special girl," the sergeant agreed. "Why don't you take her out to dinner some evening and tell her how much you appreciate her?"

Cavanna looked startled. "Sylvia? Oh, she's not interested in anything but the work here," he said. "She hardly ever leaves the place."

"Are you sure it's the place?"

The security chief stared at McCrimmon for several seconds, then laughed; but the sound was tinged with uncertainty. He turned to look after the girl who had by then disappeared beyond the corner. "It's a thought," he said brusquely. He glanced at his watch. "Sorry, Bill, but I've got to go." He turned abruptly and walked rapidly away.

As McCrimmon left the building and made his way to his car, a small, compact man with sandy hair folded his paper and rose from the couch in the center of the lobby. Roy Guthrie was in a thoughtful mood as he wandered outside. He stood at the parapet overlooking the valley of the Bow, and thought about the days that lay ahead.

McCrimmon drove back to the Detachment, his mind still preoccupied with the forthcoming seminar. It should be a simple assignment. After all, it wasn't as if these people were heads of state; they were scientists getting together to talk about the most innocuous subject in the world — the weather. What could go wrong with that? He parked the car behind the building and made his way to his office. He stopped in the doorway and grinned at the sight before him. Corporal Quinn sat hunched over the desk, a piece of paper in one hand, the remains of a sandwich in the other. The scowl on his face would have curdled milk. He looked up and saw the sergeant watching him.

"How come I get stuck with all this crap while you get to mingle with the international set?" he asked by way of greeting. The scowl still creased his brow as he leaned back and almost casually devoured the remains of the sandwich. He was a big man, square and solid. The chair creaked ominously beneath his weight.

"Charm and personality," McCrimmon said promptly. "I've got it; you haven't." He nodded in the direction of the paper Quinn held. "Problems?" he asked.

Quinn shook his head. The scowl dissolved. "Not really," he admitted. "It has to do with your seminar. The Russian delegation landed at the Calgary International airport a couple of hours ago, and they ran head on into a demonstration. I guess it was peaceful enough until one guy broke through and ran at them waving a big cylinder. One of the Russians decked him. Like out cold. They took him to hospital. He could have a broken jaw. They found out afterward that the guy was carrying a scroll, a list of names of people who have been prevented from joining their families outside the Soviet Union. I guess the crowd got pretty mad when the Russian hit him. Anyway," he concluded, "they've decided to give the Russian delegation an escort as far as the park gates. We'll pick'em up and escort them the rest of the way. Okay?"

"Fine," McCrimmon agreed. "Anything else on GARS?"

Quinn shook his head. "But I've got a message for you from your landlady. You know a girl by the name of Lee?"

McCrimmon nodded.

"Good, because she wants you to pick her up in the lobby of the Cascade Inn at seven. Does that make sense?"

"Sure does," the sergeant told him. He glanced at the time and turned to go. "I've got a few things to do before then, so I'll see you tomorrow," he told the corporal.

"Hold it," Quinn called after him. McCrimmon turned. "I don't remember anyone by the name of Lee." Quinn squinted at McCrimmon and scratched vigorously at his crew-cut head as if trying to stir his memory. "Lee . . ." he repeated. "Who is she, Bill?"

McCrimmon grinned. "None of your damned business," he said, and disappeared from view.

"Hey! Wait a minute," Quinn bellowed after him. "What am I going to tell Ellie? She likes to be kept up-to-date, you know. How be if the two of you come over for dinner, Sunday . . . ?" He was talking to himself and the sound of McCrimmon's rapidly retreating footsteps.

Chapter 5

It was a few minutes after six when Roy Guthrie parked the navy blue Mercedes just south of the Presbyterian Church. He remained in the car, idly watching the traffic and the thin but steady stream of tourists shuffling from store to store along the length of Banff Avenue. He saw nothing to arouse his suspicions, but he sat there for a few more minutes just to be sure. At six-thirty he left the car, carefully locking the doors before crossing the street and strolling back toward the river. Like other tourists, he looped from store to store, sometimes contenting himself with window shopping, sometimes going in. His eyes were never still. And keeping the air of a man who doesn't quite know what to take back for the kids, he strolled into Kirby Lane, a narrow arcade of shops that led to the lane behind the buildings on Banff Avenue. He turned at the far end and surveyed the narrow mall. He saw no one who should not be there; no movement out of place. He stepped out into the back lane.

A Chevy Nova, gray and faded, was parked in the third row back in the public parking lot. Guthrie unlocked the door and slid inside. A golf jacket and bright red cap lay on the seat, and he quickly exchanged them with the tweed jacket and shapeless fedora he'd been wearing. Still watchful, he drove out of the parking lot and turned right on Bear. No one was paying any attention. Guthrie settled back to concentrate on his driving, for Banff, like Paris or Montreal, seemed to attract drivers who lacked even the basic instincts of survival.

It took no more than a few minutes to reach the house. Gravel crunched softly beneath the tires as the car came to a halt beside the old, rambling wooden structure tucked beneath a stand of fir and pine that all but blocked the fading sunlight. High hedges at the front and side made it invisible from the road. The back garden halted abruptly at what amounted to the western flank of Tunnel Mountain. Guthrie left the car and mounted the steps to the front door. It opened before he had a chance to knock, and he was quickly drawn inside. The door snapped shut behind him. The man who stood before him in the dimly lighted hall was a tall, loose-limbed, shambling figure whose hair was tinged with gray, and whose eyes were tinged with sadness. The eyes and mouth crinkled at the corners and the sadness disappeared behind a toothy grin.

"Right on time," he said happily, tapping his watch for emphasis.

Guthrie nodded. Kellerman was so anxious to please that it was almost embarrassing. "How's it going, Norman?" he asked.

"Fine, fine," said Kellerman enthusiastically. "Come see for yourself." He led the way down the short hallway and opened a door on the right. He stood aside to allow Guthrie to enter first.

With the exception of an old, massive sideboard, the room had been cleared of furniture. A long, modern-looking conference table was in the process of being assembled, and stood in three sections propped against the wall. No chairs were evident, but they would be brought in later, after certain modifications had been made to what had once been a combined living and dining room. Equipment was strewn all over the floor. There were microphones and minispeakers, switches, panels, and even TV cameras mounted high up on the walls. A spaghetti-like jumble of cables snaked across the floor to disappear into a hole beside the sideboard. A man sat cross-legged on the floor, hunched in earnest concentration over a wiring diagram. He didn't even glance up as the two men entered.

Guthrie was used to the taciturn technician. "How's it coming, Stu?" he asked. "Will it be ready in time?"

"No sweat." The pudgy, red-faced man still didn't look up. Long, limp hair hung like a yellow curtain in front of his eyes, but it didn't seem to bother him. "It'll be ready."

Guthrie's eyes swept the room. "I'm glad it's you who has to sort out this mess," he observed. "How long will it be?"

"Should be ready to test by tomorrow night," he told him. "I'll need another day to check for bugs; maybe make a couple of modifications, but that should be about it."

Guthrie nodded. "Sounds good. Where are the tape recorders?"

"They're in the room next door," he was told. "I put an extra backup set in the basement. We're running out of space. All the rest of the rooms are stacked with furniture."

"Except for that one." Guthrie jerked his thumb in the direction of the wall behind the sideboard.

Stu nodded. "It's all set up with the TV monitors and the control panels. Want to take a look?" Without waiting for a reply, he scrambled to his feet and led the way to the room next door. It, too, had been cleared of everything but essential furniture. The video monitors were set out in a row on what appeared to be a kitchen table. A padded swivel chair sat before the table so that an operator could reach the control panel with ease. The panel itself, complete with microphone, speaker, and its own video monitor, sat in the middle of the table.

"Is it operational?" Guthrie asked.

"Sure is." The man flipped the switch to ON and the screens began to flicker. Sharp-focused images sprang to life, and Guthrie could see every part of the room next door on one or another of the monitors. Stu moved a control, and the cameras in the next room began to sweep through an arc of, perhaps, thirty degrees. He flipped another switch. "Go stick your head in the other room and say something, Norm," he told Kellerman who had been watching the demonstration in silence. Kellerman left the room and, a moment later, they saw him on the screens as he entered the room next door.

"Speak to me," Stu said into the microphone.

Kellerman waved self-consciously, and said, "One-two-three-four-five. Do you read me, Stu?"

"Loud and clear." He turned to Guthrie. "Okay?"

"Excellent!" Guthrie approved. "It's exactly what I want." A frown creased his brow. "What about the scrambling system?" he wanted to know. "It *has* to work. It's the key."

Again, the red-faced man shook his head. "No sweat," he assured Guthrie. "It's all in here." He patted a small, gray, metal box that stood beside the control panel. "Don't worry," he went on as Guthrie continued to look doubtful. "It'll be ready."

"What about backup?"

"There're two spares, for Christ's sake. Quit worrying. It'll work, take my word for it."

Guthrie appeared to relax. "Good," he said. "You've done a good job, Stu. A real good job."

The man shrugged deprecatingly. "Okay, Norm," he said into the mike, and snapped the switches to the OFF position.

"Any trouble with the neighbors?" Guthrie inquired as they left the room. "Anyone been snooping around?"

Kellerman met them in the hallway and shook his head at Guthrie's question. "No one seems to be paying any attention to us at all," he said. "They're used to tourists renting homes here. The owners of this house have been renting it out for years." They made their way to the front door while Stu went back to his work in the living room. "I check the alarm system several times a day," Kellerman went on. Guthrie believed him; he was nothing if not conscientious. "Had a bit of a scare yesterday, though," Kellerman continued. "A Springer spaniel got into the garden and watered everything in sight, including one of the sensors. It's a complete write off."

"It'll brighten up somebody's day back at the office when they see your explanation on the expense report," Guthrie grinned.

Kellerman nodded absently, his mind already on something else. "What about the arrangements for Saturday?" he asked. "You haven't told me what it is you want. If I'm to pick up . . ."

Guthrie laid a hand on Kellerman's arm. "I want you out of here before Saturday, Norman," he said quietly. "Nothing personal, but the less you know the better it is for everyone, including you."

Kellerman nodded earnestly. "I understand," he assured Guthrie, but there was a trace of disappointment in his voice.

The two men talked for a few more minutes, then Guthrie took his leave. He returned the car to the parking lot, and made his way by a circuitous route to where he had left the Mercedes. He was not followed; of that he was quite certain. He hummed tunelessly as he drove, pleased with the way things were falling into place. Tomorrow, Stauffer would call and give him the number; the magic number that would tell him which of the Chinese delegates was the American agent. And then the operation would begin.

It was three minutes to seven when McCrimmon pulled into the loading zone outside the Cascade Inn. Jacintha must have been watching for him because she came down the steps as he left the car. She smiled in greeting. She was even lovelier than he remembered. He held the door for her.

"I hope I haven't kept you waiting," he said.

She shook her head, and he caught the same ethereal hint of jasmine that had lingered in his senses since their earlier meeting. "You are very punctual," she told him. "I like that." She settled herself in the seat, and McCrimmon went round and got in the other side. He helped her fasten the seat belt, and his eyes met hers. He experienced the same indefinable sensation that he'd felt earlier when he'd taken her hand in his. He didn't understand the mystery of the chemistry that was taking place, but he did know that he liked it.

He pulled out into traffic, conscious of her eyes upon him. At six-foot-two, his head almost brushed the head liner of the car. His eyes were dark, deep-set astride a hawkish nose, the lines around them etched by years of squinting into a western sun. Lean and angular, his features tempered by the heat of prairie summers and the sting of winter snows, McCrimmon had about him an air of quiet confidence. He drove down the remainder of the block, made an illegal U-turn at the traffic lights, and started back up the other side of the street toward the bridge. The girl beside him watched the steady stream of people moving along the sidewalk, threading their way from store to store in a seemingly never-ending parade.

"Is it always this busy?" she asked abruptly.

"Believe it or not, it really isn't busy right now," McCrimmon told her. "This is pretty quiet for Banff. The real flood of tourists won't arrive until late June or early July.

Jacintha lifted her eyes to the peaks as they crossed the bridge. "They really are beautiful," she mumured, half to herself.

"People?" McCrimmon's attention was focussed on the road ahead.

"The mountains. They seem — oh, I don't know — magnificent, timeless, so untouched by the world around them, so detached . . ." She broke off and laughed self-consciously. "I'm sorry," she apologized. "I seem to be babbling on."

McCrimmon shook his head. "Don't apologize," he told her. "The mountains affect many people that way. I grew up on the prairies within sight of them, and they've always fascinated me. Sometimes I find a quiet spot and just lie there looking up at them. They have a way of putting things back into perspective." He glanced across at her and grinned. "Now who's babbling on?"

He swung the car to the left through the gates to the hotel and drew up in front of the main entrance. A young man in uniform hurried forward as they got out of the car, but stopped when he recognized McCrimmon.

"Oh, it's you, Bill," he said. His eyes went to Jacintha approvingly. "You want to leave the car here?" He was speaking to McCrimmon but his eyes never left the girl.

"If you don't mind, George. We'll be in the Rob Roy if you need the keys."

"No trouble at all," said the young man. "None at all."

"Thanks, George." McCrimmon steered the girl inside.

The table was in a quiet nook a little removed from the other diners, and McCrimmon gave silent thanks to Sylvia Graham. As he took his seat across the table from Jacintha, he again caught his breath. If he had thought her lovely earlier, he must have been only half awake, he decided. She was beautiful. She wore a simple, high-necked dress of textured cream. Her long, black hair lay softly against her shoulders; a single golden band adorned her neck. The warm glow of amber lights reflecting from the timbered ceiling caressed her face, accentuating the slightly oriental caste of her features. She was regarding him quizzically.

"I'm sorry," he apologized. "I guess I was staring. But you are very beautiful, you know."

The girl colored. "You are embarrassing me," she

said. "But I must admit you do it very nicely."

The wine steward appeared at McCrimmon's elbow, and, after some deliberation and gentle coaching from the helpful steward, they made their selection.

The mellow tones of a saxophone moved slowly up the scale, and other instruments came in one by one. "Would you care to dance?" McCrimmon asked, and received an affirmative nod. He took Jacintha by the hand and led her to the dance floor. She came into his arms as if she belonged there. Her hair brushed his cheek and teased his senses. The music flowed over them, around them, through them, and they moved across the floor as one. If the musicians had not decided to take a break after the fourth number, they might never have left the floor.

They had almost finished dinner when McCrimmon asked the question that had been uppermost in his mind since he'd met Jacintha. "Will you be staying in Banff long?"

The girl sipped her wine and appeared to consider the question. "A few days," she said at last.

A few days! Disappointment flooded through him. "Do you have to leave so soon?" He stared intently at the wine in his own glass. "I mean, I'm going to be tied up for a few days, but I'd like nothing better than to show you around." His eyes sought to capture hers, but Jacintha kept them firmly fixed on the table.

She slowly shook her head. "I'm afraid that's impossible, Bill," she said almost wistfully. "I borrowed my uncle's car, and I do have to earn a living. I'm sorry, but I must get back to Vancouver." She set her glass aside and drew a deep breath. "Now, enough about me. I don't know a thing about you except that you come to the aid of injured girls and take them out to dinner. Tell me all about yourself."

Before McCrimmon could reply, he saw Paul Cavanna approaching the table. The security chief halted beside him and placed a hand on McCrimmon's shoulder.

"I just had to stop by and see this very special date of

yours," he said genially. He looked across at Jacintha. "I hope you'll forgive the intrusion."

"Jacintha, I'd like you to meet a very good friend of mine," McCrimmon said. "Paul Cavanna. He's head of security here in the hotel. Paul . . . Jacintha Lee."

For a fraction of a second a startled expression shadowed the lovely features, then it was gone. Jacintha inclined her head in acknowledgment. "I'm very happy to meet you, Mr. Cavanna," she said.

"Please, Paul," he told her. "And it is my pleasure. I can see why Bill was so anxious to reserve a table here tonight. The hotel is honored."

Once more Jacintha inclined her head. "Everyone is being most kind to me today," she said. "Will you join us? We were about to have coffee."

Cavanna shook his head. "Sorry, I'd really like to, but I have work to do. It's been a pleasure meeting you, Miss Lee. I trust we'll meet again before too long."

"Thank you, but please call me Jacintha."

"Jacintha," he repeated slowly. "It's a very lovely name." With a nod to McCrimmon, he walked rapidly away.

"You have very charming friends, Bill," Jacintha observed.

"Paul's the best," McCrimmon agreed. "He certainly makes my job a lot easier." Coffee arrived and was served.

"You were going to tell me about yourself before Paul arrived," Jacintha prompted. "What do you do, Bill?" She sipped cautiously at the steaming coffee.

"Nothing very romantic, I'm afraid," he said. "Right now, I'm on special duty assigned to a seminar being held here in the hotel. I'm a sergeant in the RCMP."

The coffee was extremely hot, and it must have burned her throat, for she choked and could not seem to catch her breath. McCrimmon half rose from his seat, but she recovered quickly and waved him back.

"It's all right," she gasped. "I shouldn't have tried to drink it while it was so hot. Really, I'm quite all right," she insisted as he continued to look concerned. She smiled through watering eyes. "So you came to my rescue this morning only because it was your duty," she accused him with mock seriousness. "You weren't wearing a uniform, and you weren't driving a police car, so I didn't realize you were a . . ." She came to a faltering stop.

"A policeman?" He nodded gravely. "I'm afraid you've found me out," he acknowledged, matching his tone to hers. I'm duty-bound to help young women in distress; it's in my job description. It comes right after helping old ladies across the road."

"And do you always take them out to dinner afterward?"

"Only the beautiful ones," he said. His eyes held hers and the banter had gone from his voice.

She lowered her eyes. "You mentioned that you were assigned to special duty," she ventured, steering the conversation to safer ground. "What does that mean, Bill?"

"Oh, it's routine, mostly," he told her deprecatingly. "This one is an international seminar called GARS — Global Atmospheric Research Seminar. I work with the hotel security people, Paul's men, and other members of the force brought in for the occasion. I'm the liaison officer between the security team and the local force. After the seminar I'll go back to my regular job as a permanent member of the Banff Detachment. Not very exciting, I'm afraid," he concluded.

Her brows came together as she regarded him seriously. "But very important," she told him firmly. "You must be highly regarded by your superiors."

McCrimmon made a wry face. "That's not quite the way we look at it, believe me," he told her emphatically.

Jacintha picked up her cup and took an experimental sip. "When does this seminar start?" she asked idly.

"Well, the official reception is set for tomorrow evening," he told her, "although the actual work doesn't start until the following day. It's a sort of get acquainted cocktail party in Mt. Stephen Hall. I'll show it to you afterward if you like. It's patterned after a mediaeval banquet hall with a gallery running around three sides, and long, leaded windows that look out over the valley. I think you'll like it."

"I'd love to see it," Jacintha said. She set her coffee cup aside and glanced at her watch. "Perhaps we could see it now, Bill," she suggested. "I do have to be up very early in the morning, and I would like to see as much as possible before I leave. Would you mind very much."

Looking at her across the table, McCrimmon did mind. He minded very much. He had not anticipated such an early end to the evening; in fact he didn't want it to end at all. He tried to mask his disappointment.

"Would you like a nightcap before we leave?" he asked hopefully. "They have a nice little lounge on the next floor."

Jacintha shook her head. "I'm sorry, Bill, it's been a lovely evening, but I really must get back. Let's take a look at this mediaeval hall of yours, then I will have to go."

Two kilted elevator girls stood by the open doors of their elevators, chattering away like a couple of magpies. One, a short, plump, pleasant-faced girl, glanced at Jacintha and smiled. "Hi," she called cheerily. "Going up?"

Jacintha returned the smile and shook her head. "No, thank you," she told the girl.

"Okay," the girl said agreeably. "Have a nice evening."

McCrimmon regarded Jacintha curiously. "Do you know her?" he asked.

"Yes, in a way," Jacintha replied. "I bumped into her in a store downtown this afternoon. She's a friendly little thing; we just started talking."

"She probably thinks you're a guest."

"She probably does," Jacintha laughed.

They left the lighted hallway and stood at the

entrance to Mt. Stephen Hall. As McCrimmon had said, it was built in the style of a baronial dining hall. Twelve-candled chandeliers of beaten iron were suspended from the vaulted ceiling by sturdy iron chains. Matching candelabra adorned the walls. The mellow light reflected in the hand-rubbed sheen of dark refectory tables, and spilled in shimmering amber pools across the polished flagstone floor. It softened walls of textured stone, highlighted archways, glinted from the three-tiered leaded windows, and melted quietly into the shadows of the silent alcoves.

Jacintha turned her face to his, her fingers tightening on his arm. "Oh, Bill," she breathed, "it's beautiful!"

McCrimmon touched her face. His fingers gently traced the outline of her cheek. Sensuous strands of silken hair brushed against his hand. The closeness of her filled his senses.

Gently, she drew away. "I'm afraid it's time to go," she said softly. "It's been a lovely evening, Bill." She turned and moved toward the lobby.

He stood there for a moment, irresolute, confused by Jacintha's sudden desire to leave. He caught up with her in the lobby, barely acknowledging George's cheery 'Good night' as they made their way to the car. They drove in silence until, all too soon, McCrimmon pulled in before the Cascade Inn.

The girl turned toward him and laid a hand on his sleeve. "Don't get out," she said quickly. Her dark eyes held his steadily. "Believe me, Bill, I can't remember such a wonderful evening; I enjoyed it more than I can tell you. But I must leave. Please try to understand." She watched his face anxiously.

"I'm trying to, but . . ." he began, but again she stopped him.

"I won't be here very long, in Banff I mean, Bill. I think it would be best if we didn't see each other again. She leaned forward and brushed his cheek with her lips, then slipped out of the car and was gone.

McCrimmon remained there for what seemed to be a very long time. He couldn't understand what had happened. Somewhere along the line he'd blown it, but for the life of him he couldn't think what he'd said or done. Jacintha's actions made no sense to him at all. He rolled down the window and let in the crisp, cold air, drawing it deep inside his lungs, but, whether only in his imagination or in reality, the faint scent of jasmine lingered on. He started the car and nosed it into the late evening traffic, his mind still preoccupied with visions of Jacintha Lee. He turned right at the corner because it happened to be the easiest thing to do; he just wanted to drive and think for a while. He turned right again at the next corner, circling the block behind the Cascade Inn. The far edge of his headlights picked out a hurrying figure, and his brain registered the fact almost subconsciously. The figure darted between two parked cars and moved to the side of a yellow Datsun. He saw the flash of keys; the figure slipped inside and closed the door. Instinct made him continue past and pull in beside a fire hydrant near the corner. He cut his lights and waited.

The Datsun moved into second gear as it passed him, its driver too intent upon the corner to take the time to glance his way. McCrimmon's hands felt clammy as he gripped the wheel and watched the car turn right. He wasn't mistaken; his mind was not playing tricks on him. The driver was Jacintha Lee.

He tried to rationalize. There was no reason why the girl should not go out again. An appointment, perhaps. He dismissed the thought impatiently. She would have told him rather than running off without any explanation. Unless, of course, it was something she didn't want him to know about; that didn't seem to track either. Perhaps, like him, she just wanted to get out and drive, to think. He abandoned the thought. Why was her car parked back there on the street? Suddenly, he wanted to know where she was going. He dropped the car into gear and swung out to take the corner. A truck rumbling down the hill toward the traffic lights blew its horn. He barely stopped in time. The lights were red and the truck pulled up, blocking him completely. By the time the truck moved forward again, the yellow Datsun had disappeared. McCrimmon drove back to the Cascade Inn and parked. As he approached the desk, the man behind it looked up from the paper he was reading.

"Hi, Bill," he greeted McCrimmon. "What brings you here tonight?"

"Just routine, Tommy," McCrimmon said automatically. "Just want to check something out, that's all."

"Problems?"

The sergeant shook his head. "No problem, Tommy. I just need a little information."

"Sure, Bill." The man waited.

"I'm looking for someone by the name of Lee. Do you have anyone registered under that name?"

The man moved to the register. "How long have they been here?" he wanted to know.

"No more than a day or two. Could have checked in today."

The man shook his head. "No one here by that name," he said. "Got a Lang, a Livingstone and a Lucheski, but no Lee. You sure you got the name right?"

McCrimmon shook his head. "I'm not really sure of anything tonight, Tommy," he said. He made as if to leave, then turned back to the desk once more.

"You didn't happen to notice a young woman in here about ten minutes ago, did you?" he asked. "About five-three, slim, very black hair down to her shoulders."

Tommy's face broke into a broad grin. "You bet I did," he said. "Some doll, eh?" The grin faded and he looked anxiously at the sergeant. "She in trouble or something, Bill?"

"Did you see where she went?"

The man shrugged. "She just stood over there by the door for a few minutes," he said. "Went to the door and looked out a couple of times, then, next time I looked up, she was gone. I figured whoever she was waiting for must have picked her up."

"Could she have gone out the back way?"

"Why would she want to do that?" the man asked. McCrimmon remained silent. "I guess she could have," Tommy said dubiously. "If you go down that hall you can get out back."

McCrimmon nodded. "Thanks, Tommy," he said. "I owe you one. See you around." He made his way to the door.

"I don't suppose you'd like to tell me what it's all about?" the man behind the desk called after him. "No, I didn't think you would," he muttered, and turned back to his paper.

Chapter 6

McCrimmon pushed aside the remaining paper at his desk and leaned back in his chair. His mind kept returning to the night before. He had spent an hour cruising Banff, searching for the yellow Datsun without success, until, at last, he'd given up and gone home to spend a restless night. He'd tried, also without success, to tell himself that he was suffering from nothing more than a badly dented ego, and that Jacintha had just decided that she didn't want to become involved. He'd tried, but he couldn't ignore the fact that the girl had lied to him. Not only had she lied, but she'd taken some pains to make him believe that she was staying at one hotel, while in fact she was staying somewhere else. But where?

Of course, she could be staying at the Cascade under another name. Tommy was working the night shift, so he might not have seen her before, but why would she do that? And why would she park her car in the next street? His mind went back over the events of the evening. Was it just coincidence that Jacintha had choked on the coffee at the very instant he'd announced that he was a policeman? Was that what had prompted her to start looking at her watch shortly after that? He sighed wearily. Perhaps he'd been too long a policeman; perhaps he was too suspicious, but there were just too many questions. He didn't really have a choice, he told himself.

He made his way to the communications room where he picked up a memo pad and began to write. "Make sure that gets out right away," he told Mavis, the operator for that day. "I want the name and all particulars of the registered owner of a 'seventy-four or five yellow Datsun sedan. B.C. license plate SJC 496."

The girl scanned the memo without interest, and set it down beside the teletype machine. She poured a cup of coffee and offered it to the sergeant. He shook his head impatiently. "I don't mean after coffee," he snapped. "I mean *now!*" He turned on his heel and left the room. The girl's startled eyes followed him; it wasn't like Bill to act like that. She picked up the message and read it through again. There was nothing out of the ordinary about it, but if Bill said it was urgent . . . Her coffee remained untouched as she began to type.

When Quinn arrived at eight o'clock, McCrimmon avoided him and left the building. He drove to the Rundle Restaurant and brooded over coffee. It was ridiculous, he told himself angrily, that a girl he'd met only the day before could so monopolize his thoughts. He pushed her firmly from his mind and drove to the hotel.

The weather had turned colder, and ice had formed where yesterday there had been puddles in the street. Crystal-like frost sheltered beneath the trees, hiding from the probing forays of a pallid morning sun. The forecast called for scattered snow flurries, but McCrimmon cocked a calculating eye at the sky and made his own prediction. The cloud cover would burn off by noon and the rest of the day would be sunny and warm. And on that optimistic note, he left the car and went in search of Paul Cavanna and Inspector Wellington.

They spent the first part of the morning with the tour operators and the drivers. Because it was still early in the season, some of the regular drivers were not available, so it was essential that those who were new to the situation be made to understand the need for constant head counts, and adhering strictly to their schedules.

Lunch stops were usually the worst. Everyone settled in to enjoy the food and drinks; it was like pulling teeth to get them back on the bus. The same sort of thing would happen at the top of the gondola and chair lifts. The delegates would scatter and wander away, lured by breath-taking views of snow-clad peaks and verdant valleys. They would have to be coaxed and bullied into returning to the waiting bus. Unless, of course, it happened to be cold. A little nip in the air would help enormously.

The helicopter tours were something else again. No one seemed to know who had arranged them. Judging by the number of delegates who had signed up for them, they were by far the most popular of all the tours, but they were an added worry for the security team. The only good thing about them, as Wellington pointed out, was that once the delegates were airborne, they would have a lot of trouble eluding their guide.

The last part of the morning was spent with the GARS Coordinating Committee. Last-minute changes to the schedule, a speaker substitution due to illness, and a multitude of questions had to be dealt with. The Iron Duke fielded questions and complaints. They ranged from a formal protest by the senior delegate from the USSR about security, or lack of it, at the Calgary airport, to a female delegate who believed that she was being watched by someone with binoculars on Tunnel Mountain.

Wellington took note and duly recorded the official protest, then turned to the hotel floor plans. "What room is this lady in?" he inquired.

One of the committee members shuffled his notes. "She's in the north wing, front, on the sixth floor," he said. "I'm sorry, but I don't seem to have the room number."

Wellington shook his head in wonder. "That's got to be a distance of half to three-quarters of a mile at least," he said. He turned to McCrimmon. "Isn't there a viewpoint up there?"

"That's right, there is," the sergeant told him. "The buses stop there; it's one of the best places from which to photograph the hotel."

Wellington grunted. "We can't stop people from looking across the valley," he said. "Can't she be moved to another room?"

"We'll have a talk with the lady," Cavanna said. He made a note on the pad in front of him, then frowned as a thought occurred to him. "How did the lady know she was being observed?" he asked. "She must have damned good eyesight."

The committee member who had received the complaint grinned broadly. "She dragged me up to her room to show me," he said. "You wouldn't believe the stuff she's got set up there for taking pictures, including a telescope that must be five feet long."

"You mean a telephoto lens," Cavanna corrected.

"Hell, no, I mean what I said. "It's a telescope. I had a look through it. You can see clear down the valley with it."

Cavanna sighed. "We get all kinds," he observed. "I'd better send Bert. He's the fatherly type. Sounds like it'll be right up his alley." He glanced around the table. "Anything else?" Everyone shook his head. "Good," he said, "then I suggest we all go down and have some lunch."

The bellman led the way down the third floor corridor of the south wing. Tai Ling and Kuan Lo, trailing wearily behind him, barely heard the programmed recitation of dining hours, sauna, swimming, and all the capsulated amenities offered by the hotel. He stopped in front of room 340 and they waited while he opened it. Once inside, he set their cases down, checked the window and made sure they knew where everything was to be found. He hesitated expectantly. Kuan Lo stared dully at him, his mind befogged by travel and the violent wrench of changing time zones.

"Thank you, we can manage," he told the bellman

in excellent English. The man inclined his head and left
the room.

"It's customary to tip, I understand," Tai Ling
observed. "I suppose we should have done so."

Kuan Lo brushed the matter aside. "If we receive
exceptional service, it will be in order," he declared
pompously. "I presume he is paid some sort of wage for
carrying luggage. Tipping is an anachronistic custom
that permits our capitalistic friends to avoid their
obligations as employers. You'll notice that they seldom
refer to it when they speak of the virtues of their system."
His eyes twinkled as he regarded Tai Ling over the top of
his glasses. "Besides," he confided with a chuckle, "I have
very little money, and what I do have I intend to spend on
myself."

Tai Ling grinned in return. "So much for philosophies," he observed, and they both chuckled like
schoolboys on their first adventure.

Tai Ling stretched out on one of the beds, testing its
comfort. "Ah, that feels good," he sighed contendedly.
He slipped his shoes off and lay back again. "I didn't sleep
a wink in Vancouver," he told Kuan Lo. "I think I'll take
a nap before I do anything else. Do you mind?"

Kuan Lo shook his head. "If it will not disturb you,
I think I'll have a bath. Then I may have a sleep myself."

Tai Ling closed his eyes. "You won't disturb me,"
he said around a yawn. In less than five minutes he was
snoring gently.

Kuan Lo stepped out of the tub and toweled himself
vigorously. He opened the bathroom door and padded
silently to where his suitcase lay open on the bed. He
dressed quickly, watching carefully the rhythm of Tai
Ling's breathing. It was slow and regular; his eyelids
were relaxed and did not tremble. Satisfied, Kuan Lo
moved to the door and opened it. He attempted to set the
lock so that he could reenter without a key, but the lock
was old and could not be set to remain unlatched. He
picked up the key from the dresser and pocketed it; he
couldn't risk taping the latch.

The corridor was empty. Kuan Lo made his way toward the bank of elevators where a man and woman stood waiting. They glanced up as he passed but showed no sign of interest when he continued on. He looked for a sign, and found it around the corner leading to the west wing. The door to the service stairs was unlocked. Kuan Lo found himself in a dimly lighted stairwell of dingy green. His footsteps echoed hollowly as he started down the concrete steps, steadying himself against the steep descent by gripping the metal handrail. It was icy cold beneath his outstretched fingers. From somewhere below, he heard the clatter of metal pans, and the smell of freshly-baked bread rose to meet him. He descended two floors, and there, it seemed, the stairway stopped. A corridor led off to his right, to the kitchens he surmised, and a freight elevator stood open while two youths struggled with a heavy, metal cart that seemed to be firmly wedged between the doors. They saw him but paid him no attention. He turned to his left, found the door he sought, and gently eased it open. It led, he saw, into the carpeted hallway of the upper concourse above the lobby. He stepped out and mingled with the other guests moving toward a marble staircase.

Back in the corridor outside his room, Kuan Lo slipped the key into the lock and turned it carefully. He winced as the bolt slid back with a harsh, metallic click. He stepped inside the room and looked toward the bed. Tai Ling was propped up on one arm and was staring at him, his eyes not completely focused and still half full of sleep.

"Sorry, I didn't mean to wake you," Kuan Lo said, closing the door behind him.

"Oh, that's all right," Tai Ling said vaguely. "Have I been asleep long?"

Kuan Lo shook his head. "A few minutes, that's all." He motioned with his head toward the door. "I thought I heard someone knock while I was getting dressed, but when I went to the door there was no one there."

Tai Ling swung his legs off the bed. "I thought you

were going to have a sleep," he said, yawning. "You're dressed."

"The bath refreshed me," Kuan Lo said easily. "In fact, I was just thinking of having something to eat. What about you?"

Tai Ling thought about it, then nodded agreeably. It was understood that each was responsible for the other while they were outside their own country. If one of them should disappear from the other's view for more than a few minutes, an explanation had to be given in the daily report. It was a condition they took for granted and accepted. "I am getting hungry," he conceded, slipping his feet into his shoes.

"Good," said Kuan Lo, now quite certain that Tai Ling suspected nothing.

Tai Ling followed his former teacher from the room. He wondered why Kuan Lo had felt it necessary to lie to him.

At six o'clock that evening, when the American delegates were returning from supper in the Alhambra Room, they were confronted by a dozen young men and women chanting slogans. They carried placards that mutely echoed the slogans they were chanting. LEAVE THE WEATHER TO GOD, said one; STOP THE WEATHER WAR, said another. Cavanna's men moved in quickly, and when it was learned that the demonstrators wanted to present a petition containing 5,000 names of American university students demanding an end to what they termed weather manipulation, it was Cavanna himself who persuaded one of the American delegates to accept it conditionally. Fortunately, the young people were disciplined, and, once they were satisfied that someone would indeed study their petition, they melted peaceably away. But the incident was disquieting, and the security arrangements for the cocktail party were quitely reinforced.

The delegates began to arrive shortly after eight.

Each one wore an official name tag, and anyone who could not produce one was turned politely but firmly away. There would be a few complaints, but it was the only way to keep others from crashing the party. Cavanna's men mingled with Wellington's team, and almost every alcove in the galleries above seemed to be occupied by tall young men in quiet business suits who stood idly watching the gathering below. McCrimmon sat at the southern end, a vantage point from which he could see almost everyone except those standing along the southern wall immediately below him. The hall began to fill, and the murmur of many voices gradually swelled to a muted roar. Smoke from cigars, cigarettes, and occasionally a pipe, rose lazily toward the vaulted ceiling and drifted in layered patterns like mist above a marsh.

The minister, a short man with silver hair, dressed in a blue, pinstripe business suit, entered the hall from the northern end. He was accompanied by a taller man dressed casually in a leisure suit and multicolored shirt. McCrimmon recognized him as Doctor Roland Deacon, head of the Atmospheric Environment Service in Ottawa, and chairman of the seminar. The two men moved from group to group, chatting and shaking hands.

McCrimmon's attention was drawn once more to the far end of the hall where the Chinese delegation had, it seemed, arrived en masse. There were five members in all, but two of them immediately captured his attention. The first, the man in front and presumably the leader of the delegation, was squat and fat, and even from across the length of the hall, McCrimmon could sense that he was displeased. The second, in total contrast to the fat man, was a woman. Slight of build and extremely slender, she wore a simple gown of black. A small jewel glittered at her throat, but that apart, her dress was unadorned. Her hair was thick and black as ebony. McCrimmon was struck by the paleness of her face against that sea of black. Again, despite the distance that separated them, he could sense the impact of a vibrant personality. Except, perhaps, for the shorter hair, she reminded him sharply of Jacintha. Others, too, were very much aware of her presence. Heads swung round and courteous, formal bows marked her path. The fat man, McCrimmon noted, didn't like that at all.

A waiter stepped before the woman and offered her a drink. She inclined her head in gracious thanks and took one from the tray. The fat man waved the tray aside, and pushed his way beligerently through the throng, leaving the woman and the others staring after him. The woman said something to the other members of the delegation and, after a moment of hesitation, they each took a glass from the tray and moved to the side of the room. A few minutes later one of the delegates, a thin, ascetic-looking man with long, lank hair, left the others and eased his way through to where the fat man had literally backed the minister into a corner. The minister looked most uncomfortable.

The smoke was getting thicker and the noise was getting louder. McCrimmon leaned on the polished rail of brass in front of him and peered down through the thickening haze. A movement at the far end of the hall caught his eye. Suddenly, he froze. A girl, half turned away from him, was talking earnestly to a waiter. He saw her give him something. A slip of paper? or was it money? He couldn't tell from where he stood. She moved away and disappeared from view before he had a chance to see her face. The hair, even the dress looked very much like the one she had worn last night. But what would Jacintha be doing here? He shrugged the thought from his mind and turned his attention to the waiter.

The man had reentered the hall, and was threading his way through the press of delegates toward a point directly below where McCrimmon stood. He leaned over the rail and saw that the Chinese delegates, all five of them, were clustered there beneath him. He waited, curious to see for whom the note was intended; an assumption, he admitted to himself but a reasonable one under the circumstances.

The waiter had almost reached them when he appeared to trip. He lurched forward, dropping the empty tray as he cannoned heavily into the knot of delegates. Instinctively, their hands shot out to help him or fend him off as they staggered under the impact. McCrimmon's eyes narrowed as he saw the note change hands, but such was the confusion that he couldn't tell which of the delegates had received it. Something caught his eye and he glanced up just in time to see a movement beside one of the pillars on the west side of the gallery. Had someone else seen the exchange? The pillars blocked his view, yet there was something about the fleeting movement that made McCrimmon sure that whoever had been standing there had silently withdrawn. He looked down again.

The waiter was apologizing profusely. He picked up the tray and apologized again. The fat man snarled something at him, and the waiter flushed. He backed away, then turned and hurried toward the nearest exit. McCrimmon watched him go, determined to seek him out later. Perhaps it was none of his business; perhaps the girl he had seen was not Jacintha. Perhaps he was making a fool of himself. He continued to watch as the fat man elbowed his way rudely toward the far end of the hall. The others followed meekly. The Chinese delegation was leaving.

The man in the tan suit stirred restlessly and eased his shoulders away from the metal of the car door. It was getting cold again. He switched the engine on and let the warm air from the heater blow directly onto his feet. The luminous dial of his wristwatch told him that the time was 11:24.

His name was Jordan B. Olsen, a citizen of the United States. At least, that's what his passport said, and there were those in Denver, Colorado who would undoubtedly agree with it. He was a short, rotund man with pink, cherubic cheeks and thinning, sandy hair. Rimless glasses perched astride a small, straight nose, giving him an oddly dated look. Whenever he was nervous, as he was now, he polished them incessantly. He wished there had been more time. Moscow acted as if Banff were a suburb of Denver instead of over a thousand miles away. It was ridiculous to expect him to gather the kind of information they wanted in less than a week. He rubbed his glasses harder. Utterly ridiculous, and he'd tell his contact so. With that decision made, he settled his glasses firmly back in place.

The rear door of the car opened so abruptly that he jumped. A shadow slipped inside and the door snapped shut again.

"Don't turn around." The voice was low and harsh, grating unpleasantly on the ear, and with it came the acrid smell of tobacco that caught at Olsen's throat. He coughed but made sure he didn't turn his head.

"Are there any more passengers going to Lake Louise?" the voice inquired.

Olsen coughed again. "No, you're the only one," he managed to say. Already he was prepared to dislike this man. He remembered the rest of it. "Can I put your luggage in the trunk?"

"No, thank you, I sent it on ahead."

"Good," Olsen replied, speaking very clearly. "Then, if we start at once, we can be there just after midnight."

He heard a grunt, presumably of satisfaction, and the sound of rattling seat belts as the man behind him settled into the seat. "You have your instructions. Drive," the voice directed. "My name is Mayer. That's all you need to know."

Olsen switched on the headlights and set the car in motion. The lights of Banff thinned out and disappeared behind them as they crossed the railroad tracks and headed for the highway. He set the heater on LOW and rolled the window down an inch to clear the air. They drove in silence until they crossed the overpass and swung down to join the highway heading west. The tires hummed on the coarse-grained pavement, and the wind rumbled at the partly opened window.

The man in the back seat was square and compact. Heavy brows and grizzled hair gave him a fierce appearance, and yet there was an air of weariness about the man. He rubbed his knees with slow, deliberate strokes, welcoming the warmth inside the car. The night was cold and his joints were acting up again.

His real name was Malik, and, like Olsen, he'd been given little time to prepare for the job he was supposed to do. He smiled grimly to himself in the darkness as he recalled the unexpected invitation to dine with Kalenzetny at his *dacha* outside Moscow a bare three weeks ago. He remembered the awkwardness at dinner as they tried politely to rekindle the friendship they had known back in those early days of war and political upheaval. As comrades they had joined the KGB together, or MGB as the Ministry of State Security was known back then, and, as comrades they had taken basic training for almost a year. But then they'd gone their separate ways. He, with his gift for languages, was directed to field training school where he spent the next four years becoming someone else. Inured by the sights, the sounds, and the very stink of war, Malik had readily accepted the philosophy that the end always justified the means.

Kalenzetny had taken a different path, working his way through staff and diplomatic posts with diligence and zeal. Quietly, but steadily, he rose higher in the organization, pausing only long enough to sidestep the purges following Beria's execution before moving on again. Now, as Director of Operations, First Directorate, he held a coveted position. But the journey had been long, the climb extremely arduous, and there were younger men just waiting for the chance to topple him from power. Gaunt, emaciated, and with barely half a stomach left after several operations, Kalenzetny was grimly holding on. To him, the job was everything. Defying doctors' orders, he continued his twelve to sixteen hour days, drawing on reserves of strength that amazed his own subordinates and confounded those who tried to make him out an ailing man.

But was it worth it? Malik wondered. A *dacha* in a wooded glade close to those of members of the Politburo; imported furniture from Scandinavia, Utrillos on the panelled walls, crystal, damask, silver knives and forks. Was it *really* worth it?

But later, they had settled down with drinks in hand and Kalenzetny spoke of the reason for the invitation. In terse, clipped sentences, he gave Malik all the facts they had, which, when examined closely, were really precious few. But when Malik tried to probe for more, Kalenzetny cut him off with a wave of his hand, and dropped his bomb.

"You are expected to fail, Yuri Andreyevich," he said quietly. "Oh, not by me, although I must confess your chances are somewhat less that good. No, it is Shirov who wants to see this mission fail. Do you know Shirov?" he asked abruptly. "Head of E and V?"

Malik shook his head. "He must be new," he said. "The last time I had anything to do with Evaluation and Verification was when Chekev was in charge."

"You are behind the times." Kalenzetny swirled the drink in his glass, "Shirov has been there almost three years, now. He's young, he's clever, and he's ambitious. Ambitious as hell!" He drained his glass and set it aside. "But enough of that. The reason I asked you here tonight was because I wanted you to understand the background before you're officially assigned to the job tomorrow. There are things I can tell you here, as a friend, that I cannot tell you in my office." He smiled crookedly and their eyes met in silent understanding. Malik's eyes automatically swept the room, but Kalenzetny shook his head. "Believe me, it's clean," he said. He paused for a moment, then continued with what he had been saying.

"The information about the American sleeper, this deep-cover agent they apparently have in China, arrived at the Center five months ago. I know that for a fact. But, because it came through a known double agent, it was automatically suspect. As you know, it had to be verified and then actioned through committee. E and V just sat on it, giving it a low priority because they thought they had lots of time. Then, when they finally got around to doing something with it and discovered the connection with the nuclear submarine disaster last year, they had Military Intelligence swarming all over them." Kalenzetny rose, picked up his glass, and refilled it from the decanter. He raised an inquiring eyebrow in his guest's direction, but Malik shook his head, and Kalenzetny returned to his seat.

"Nikorayev was the one who was doing all the yelling. He's been trying to prevent the GRU from being swallowed up by us in the KGB, and he saw this as an opportunity. He took it directly to the Politburo, demanding that GRU be given this particular job since it was their submarine that was lost. The Politburo had to run that through committee, of course, but by that time E and V had decided it was too hot to hold, so they dumped it into Operations. Specifically, in my lap, and blaming the delay on the fact that the source was unreliable. The Politburo decided to play it safe, and ruled that since the double agent who passed the information to us in the first place was my responsibility, then I should be the one to run the operation."

Malik frowned. "So why does Shirov want to see the mission fail?"

Kalenzetny took a long pull at his drink. "Because, my dear Yuri, he wants my job. And Nikorayev will support him in return for Shirov's promise to support him in his bid to keep GRU separate. Of course, Shirov has no intention of leaving GRU alone if he's successful, but you can't tell Nikorayev that." He leaned forward and looked directly at his guest. "So, you see, Yuri Andreyevich, I have done you no favor." He raised his glass in salute. "But I wish you luck; my future depends upon you." He drained his glass.

And what of mine? The words were silent but insistent inside his head as Malik raised his glass and drank.

The motion of the car brought Malik back abruptly to the present. He tensed. "Why are you going so fast?" he asked Olsen.

"Just checking," Olsen told him. "There's been a truck behind us ever since we hit the highway."

Malik twisted in his seat. Two headlights bored through the darkness behind them. Three smaller yellow lights were set above the cab. The truck kept pace as Olsen increased his speed. "Drop your speed," Malik instructed. "We don't need a ticket."

"I don't like the look of it . . ." Olsen began, but Malik cut him off.

"He's mine," he growled. "A precaution, that's all." And a test for me, Olsen thought as he slowed. The lights behind maintained their distance.

"What do you have for me?" Malik asked abruptly.

Olsen shook his head. "Not much, I'm afraid," he confessed. "They didn't give me much time to . . ."

"Never mind the excuses," Malik cut in shortly. "What do you have?"

"There's an envelope on the seat beside you," Olsen said. He waited until he heard the crackle of paper and saw a thin ray of light appear in the rearview mirror as a penlight clicked on behind him. "His name is Norman Kellerman," he went on. "He's in charge of the Calgary branch of an oil consulting firm that goes by the name of Braun-Kellerman and Associates. Head office is in Tulsa; quite legitimate. Kellerman is local CIA." He heard a soft grunt behind him.

"All I can tell you is that he's made several trips to Banff over the past two or three months. What he did here, I don't know, but I can tell you that Banff is not on his regular route. His activities are usually tied in with the oil industry. The Fort McMurray Tar Sands, the new northern pipeline, the Pembina field, Cold Lake." He shook his head. "But not Banff," he ended emphatically.

The headlights swept across a never-ending line of trees as the car went into a cambered curve. Twin glistening points of light came hurtling out of the darkness. Olsen hit the brakes and swung the wheel hard over. The car slued across the center line before he managed to bring it back under control. A flash of white and dappled fawn slid past the car, and the deer was gone, swallowed up in the darkness far behind. Olsen muttered an obscenity beneath his breath and eased his foot off the accelerator. Behind him, he heard Mayer push himself back onto the seat from which he'd been catapulted when Olsen hit the brakes. He grinned to himself, and switched the lights to highbeam. The road ahead was clear.

"Is that all?" Malik had recovered his breath.

"That's it," Olsen replied cryptically. He'd learned his lesson. If Mayer wanted comments he would have to ask for them.

"Where's Kellerman now?"

"He may be right here in Banff," Olsen said, "but I don't know that for certain. He left Calgary a few days ago. I haven't been able to pick up anything on him, but he doesn't seem to be in any of his regular haunts."

Malik stuffed the photograph back into the envelope. "All right," he said. "We know they have to have time to debrief their man. If Kellerman has been visiting Banff, the most likely reason is to set up some sort of debriefing point. It has to be done here. They can't risk taking him too far away from the rest of the delegates." He was silent for a while, then, "Do you have any idea where it might be?"

Olsen shook his head. "You know how long I've been here," he said. "I'm a long way from my home territory."

"You think I'm not?" Malik said irritably. He lapsed

into silence for several miles. A viewpoint appeared ahead. "Turn around and go back to Banff," he ordered. Olsen slowed obediently, swung wide and made the U-turn. The truck was slowing as they passed it. Moments later, Olsen saw the lights appear in his mirror again.

"There can't be very many places suitable for debriefing," Malik ruminated aloud. "I think we'll have to talk to the real estate people about places that have been bought or rented recently. Hotels and motels are out; far too risky. No, it would have to be a house, off by itself somewhere. Secluded, hidden. Tomorrow, I want you to prepare several wallet-size pictures of our friend, Kellerman. Five should be enough." A lighter clicked and the car was filled with flickering light. Smoke billowed around Olsen's head. The light went out.

Olsen choked and lowered the window even further. Behind him, Malik shivered and massaged his knees. "Close the window," he said brusquely. "Are you trying to freeze me?"

Olsen sighed and rolled the window up.

Chapter 7

When McCrimmon arrived at the office the following morning, Corporal Quinn was already seated behind the sergeant's desk, the everpresent mug of coffee at his elbow. A half-eaten doughnut lay on a paper napkin beside it.

"Didn't expect to see you here this morning," he greeted the sergeant. "I thought you'd be up at the hotel."

"The Fowler case," McCrimmon reminded him. "It was held over until today. I have to appear in court this morning. I need the file."

"Help yourself," Quinn told him agreeably. "What's new at the hotel?"

McCrimmon sidestepped the question. "Any messages?" he asked.

The corporal took a teletype message from the HOLD tray and passed it across the desk. "Mavis is a little peeved," he told McCrimmon quietly. "She called the hotel three times yesterday and left a message for you to call back each time. You didn't call. She said you told her that this message was very important."

McCrimmon nodded absently and quickly scanned the message. The yellow Datsun was registered to a Joseph King, a contractor, aged 49, of 103 Palmington Cresent, West Vancouver. The car had not appeared on the stolen vehicles list. So, not everything Jacintha had told him was a lie. She'd said that she lived in Vancouver, and she'd told him that the car was borrowed. Perhaps this guy King really was her uncle. He folded the message and sat staring out of the window. But what of the incident he had observed last night? He hadn't seen the girl's face, but he was sure it was Jacintha who had given the note to the waiter. What was her connection with the Chinese delegation?

He needed more information. "How'd you like to do me a favor?" he asked the corporal.

Quinn broke off a piece of the doughnut and dipped it delicately in his coffee. "Like what?" he asked suspiciously.

"Get Mavis to send another message for me." McCrimmon waited until Quinn had his pencil poised. "This is a follow-up on the first message," he said, indicating the paper in his hand. "I want anything known on Joseph King of this address," he tapped the message in his hand, "and anything they've got on Jacintha Lee; age is early twenties, height five-four or five, weight about one-twenty . . ." He broke off as Quinn stopped writing and shook his head.

"Kilos, Bill, kilos, remember? All official transmissions must refer to weights and measures metrically," he reminded the sergeant. He pursed his lips as he looked at what he had written. "Of course, she could be a very large lady."

McCrimmon did some rapid calculations. "Fifty-five kilos," he ammended. "Jet-black hair, pale complexion, could be Eurasian. Believed to live and work in Vancouver or immediate vicinity. May be related to previous subject, Joseph King. Request present whereabouts of girl, if known. Inquiries about both subjects are to be discreet. Repeat, discreet. Got that?"

Quinn nodded and tore the page off the pad. One of the corporal's many talents was shorthand, and it never ceased to amaze McCrimmon when he saw Quinn's great hand flying across a page. His speed was phenominal.

Quinn frowned. "Isn't that the girl who called you the other day?" he asked. "The one you had a date with?" McCrimmon nodded. "What's the matter? She stand you up?" His lopsided grin robbed the words of offence, but he was so close to being right that McCrimmon squirmed uncomfortably. The grin faded from the corporal's face and his eyes grew serious.

"Mavis said you chewed her out, yesterday," he went on. "That's not like you, Bill. She was in here asking what she'd done wrong. Something's bothering you Bill; want to talk about it?"

McCrimmon hesitated. He felt a little foolish about Jacintha running out on him, and yet he wanted to talk to someone. He saw the real concern at the back of the older man's eyes. He told Quinn. Told him everything from the accident on the bridge to the note-passing incident in Mt. Stephen Hall. Quinn remained silent for a full half minute after McCrimmon had finished.

"That's it?" he said at last.

"That's it," McCrimmon said. "It isn't much, but I can't help feeling that this girl is setting me up somehow. I'm damned if I know why." He shook his head perplexedly.

Quinn continued to look thoughtful as he produced another doughnut from a bag sitting in the IN tray. "You really think she was fishing for information about the seminar?" he said. A quarter of the coffee-soaked doughnut disappeared.

McCrimmon frowned. "I didn't at first," he said, "but, thinking back, it seems so obvious. And yet I'm sure it came as a surprise to her when she found out I was on the force." He shook his head again. "It's not as if this particular seminar is all that important," he said, more to himself than to Quinn.

Quinn dunked the remaining part of the doughnut and bit into it. "You're kind of hung up on this girl, aren't you, Bill?" McCrimmon shot him a suspicious glance, but the corporal's face was still serious. He felt the color begin to rise in his face.

"She seemed so . . ." He shrugged and left the words unsaid.

Quinn swallowed the remains of the doughnut. "Well," he said pontifically, "there's no point in worrying about it now, at least until you see what kind of answer you get to this inquiry. You could be imagining the whole thing. The girl might have been genuinely interested in what you were telling her about the seminar. Maybe she just didn't want to get too involved." He shrugged. "After all, it was only the first date."

McCrimmon nodded, but it wasn't convincing. He rose to his feet. "You could be right, I suppose," he said dubiously. He shrugged the matter aside. "Now, how about the Fowler file?"

Quinn dug the file out of the desk drawer and handed it to the sergeant. "There is one thing I think you should do before you leave," he said, still holding on to the folder. "Go see Mavis and tell her you're not mad at her, will you? You know how upset she gets sometimes, and when she's upset, everyone has to tread carefully. Okay?"

McCrimmon grinned. "It's a deal," he said, "but make sure that inquiry gets out right away, will you, Quinn?"

"Just as soon as Mavis is happy again," the corporal promised.

Roy Guthrie left the hotel immediately after breakfast. The sky was clear, but, despite his belted leather coat, he found the weather cool. According to the morning weather report a cold air mass was moving south and east. Guthrie hoped it would pass quickly. He had more than one reason for wanting warmer weather.

With plenty of time in hand he didn't call for his car, but chose to walk instead. In typical tourist fashion, he carried a camera slung across one shoulder, and stopped every now and then to take a picture. It allowed him to see if anyone were interested in his progress. So far as he could tell, no one seemed to be. His step was light and easy. He felt good about his assignment. It was strange, he mused as he made his way across the bridge, it was always the little things that made the difference. The accidental meeting; the few words overheard; the curious incident observed.

Guthrie's fingers curled protectively around the cassette in his pocket. Such a small thing, so completely unforseen, yet so vital to his plans. It might even mean, he thought dispassionately, that one of his own people would not have to die.

Whether by accident or design, the Chinese delegation, together with their aides, sat in the front row directly facing the dais. In marked contrast to the other delegates who wore casual dress, they were all dressed the same in blue, high-necked Mao jackets with matching if somewhat shapeless trousers. The collar of Wu Tan's jacket splayed open, unable to contain the rolls of flesh around his bull-like neck. Like a grotesque Buddha, he sat between Sung S'u-mah and Yeung Chao, flanked by Tai Ling and Kuan Lo respectively. Smoke curled up from the cigarette in Wu Tan's hand. He used it like a veil, peering through it with slitted eyes at the people on the platform. From the corner of his eye he could see Yeung Chao's fingers plucking nervously at the buttons on his jacket. Yeung Chao did not like the change of plan. But, then, Yeung Chao wasn't in charge, was he? Yeung Chao had never had an original thought in his life, although, to do him justice, he was without peer when it came to bending someone else's brainchild to his own ends. But Yeung Chao was predictable; he would do as he was told; he would obey.

Wu Tan scowled contemptuously, and a woman on the platform who happened to be looking in his direction paled visibly and hastily looked away. He sucked wetly on the cigarette, and surreptitously stole a glance at the woman beside him. Now, she was quite another matter. Which was why he hadn't told her of the change of plan. He inhaled deeply and filled his lungs with smoke. Ten minutes more, he calculated. Ten minutes until the opening speeches of welcome would be concluded. Smoke dribbled from his nostrils. The woman on the dais shivered and drew her knitted shawl around her shoulders.

McCrimmon sat in court for an hour and a half before the Fowler case was called. A gray, mousey man approached the bench and said something the sergeant could not hear. The case was set over for yet another week, and McCrimmon was dismissed. He shook his head disgustedly and left the court. He wondered why he even felt surprised; it happened all too frequently.

He arrived at the Banff Springs Hotel just as the delegates were leaving the Alberta Room. The official opening ceremonies were over, but that it had been an unusual session was obvious even to an outsider. Animated conversations crackled like summer lightning among the delegates as they streamed from the room. Doctor Deacon, followed closely by members of his staff, pushed his way none too gently through the sea of people. His face was set, his lips compressed. He brushed aside the questions that rose on every side. McCrimmon went in search of Wellington. The inspector was on the telephone in his office. LaBelle, a Calgary corporal, was standing by.

"What happened?" McCrimmon wanted to know. "I hope it isn't as serious as it looks."

LaBelle, it seemed, was only too willing to bring McCrimmon up to date. "Everything was going real smooth," he said. "Dull as hell. Then, old Wu Tan, you know, the leader of the Chinese delegation, asked permission to read a prepared statement bringing greetings from the People's Republic of China. Well, after a bit of a flap because it wasn't in the programme, they agreed. Boy, were they ever sorry! Old Wu Tan spent the next few minutes blasting hell out of the Russians and the Western powers. He claimed that . . ." LaBelle paused and scratched his head. "Let's see, now, how did that go? Oh, yeah. He said, 'Not only are you threatening China on her borders, but you now propose, under the guise of weather research, to extend your surveillance and your threats to the skies above us.' " LaBelle looked pleased with his effort and McCrimmon smiled encouragement.

"He wanted to send Chinese observers to each of the launching sites to inspect the satellites before launch, and to have Chinese representation in the international monitoring programme set up to cover all phases of FIG, or whatever it is."

"FGGE," McCrimmon corrected. "Pronounced *Figgy*. It stands for First GARP Global Experiment. They intend to launch five satellites, among other things."

"Is that right?" LaBelle said. "How come you know about this stuff?"

"I took the time to read the literature they hand out," the sergeant told him. "What happened then?"

"Well, that's about when it started to get interesting," LaBelle said. "Several people tried to shout him down, but old Wu Tan just kept plugging right along. He never even looked up from his notes. Then, a couple of guys tried to get to the sound system to unplug it, but the Chinese had thought of that and had grouped themselves around it. The chairman made several attempts to rule Wu Tan out of order, but he might as well have talked to the wall. Have you seen that little Chinese guy? He's built like a brick shithouse, and twice as ugly. Nobody could move him." A faint grin hovered on McCrimmon's lips as he visualized the scene. That LaBelle had enjoyed it was quite obvious.

"Then, the Russians got up and walked out," the corporal went on. "The press finally woke up to the fact that they had front page news, and they began to scribble to beat hell. They needn't have worried; Wu Tan had press releases prepared for them. His guys were handing them out to anyone who would take them. They couldn't get to the phones fast enough. Man, you should have been there!"

Obviously, the corporal had been impressed, but it could only mean more responsibility for the security team, McCrimmon decided. "We'd better keep in touch with the chairman of the Activities Committee," he told Labelle. "In view of what's happened, some of the sessions may be changed or canceled altogether."

Wellington hung up the phone. "That's a damned good idea," he agreed. "Instead of standing there gossiping like an old woman, Corporal, get on it right away. And keep me informed."

The corporal made a wry face at McCrimmon over Wellington's head. "Yes, sir," he said stiffly. He turned smartly and left the room.

"You'd better stand by," Wellington growled at McCrimmon. "There's no telling what might blow up out of this." He turned back to the phone, but something in McCrimmon's manner stopped him from picking it up. "Well, what is it, Sergeant?" he snapped irritably. McCrimmon hesitated. He'd had more time to think about Jacintha while he waited for the Fowler case to come up, and the more he thought about the passing of the note, the more he was convinced that the incident should be investigated. Wellington's face was growing thunderous.

"It's just that I saw something rather peculiar at the cocktail party last night, sir," he said carefully. He went on to explain how he'd seen a girl give what appeared to be a note to one of the waiters, and how he in turn had slipped it to one of the Chinese delegates. The sergeant couldn't bring himself to tell Wellington that the girl might well have been a girl he'd dined with only the evening before. After all, he reasoned, it wasn't as if he was *completely* sure; he hadn't seen the girl's face.

"It may be nothing, sir," he concluded, "but since the Chinese delegation seems to be in the spotlight, perhaps it wouldn't hurt to have a word with the waiter."

Wellington nodded. "I agree. You should have reported this last night. Why didn't you?"

"I wasn't sure it was any of our business . . ." McCrimmon began, but the inspector stopped him with a scowl.

"I'll be the judge of what's our business and what is not," he said with finality. He turned back to the phone. McCrimmon was dismissed.

He made his way to Cavanna's office where he found both the security chief and Sylvia Graham working through their lunch hour. A pot of coffee and several packets of sandwiches were set out on a tray. Cavanna was talking on the phone, a half-eaten sandwich in his hand.

"Have some," Sylvia offered, indicating the tray. McCrimmon accepted gratefully. He poured himself a cup of coffee and selected a chicken salad sandwich.

"Thanks, I'm starving," he said. "Been sitting in court most of the morning." He nodded in Cavanna's direction. "What's happening?"

"You heard about the opening ceremonies, I presume?" the girl said. He nodded. "Well, as you might imagine, we've been getting calls ever since. Everything from a complaint by a visitor from Hong Kong who was jostled roughly by a group of Russians, probably took him for one of the Chinese delegates I should think, to explanations as to why we didn't have better control over the P.A. system. That, plus the fact that several tours will have to be rearranged so the Russians and the Chinese don't wind up on the same bus."

McCrimmon grinned sympathetically and helped himself to another sandwich. "Aren't you glad you joined Security?" he teased. "All that excitement and glamour."

The girl made a face. "All that typing and indigestion," she said tartly. "Anyway, what brings you here? Business? Or were you just looking for a free lunch."

"Food, what else," McCrimmon laughed, then became serious. "No, I'm afraid it is business. I wanted to talk to you about the waiters who were serving the drinks at the cocktail party last night. Do you have a list of them?"

Sylvia Graham shook her head. "No, at least not a separate list of waiters who are on duty for each party or meal. We do have a list of all members of the staff who will be associated with the seminar, but the actual assignments are drawn up by the food and beverages manager. You'll have to see him if you want information about a particular waiter." She regarded him quizzically. "What's it all about, Bill?"

"Maybe nothing," he told her. "It's just that I happened to see something during the party last night, and I'd like to check it out for my own peace of mind." He wiped his fingers on a serviette. "That reminds me, can I use your phone?"

The girl nodded. "I have a second line; you can use that. It sounds as though Paul may be a long time." She grimaced. "It doesn't matter what it is, whenever anything goes wrong in this hotel, everybody phones Paul." There was more than a little resentment in her voice. McCrimmon wondered if Paul knew just how much his secretary cared for him.

He dialed the number of the Detachment and asked for Mavis. "Do we have anything back on that inquiry yet?" he asked when the girl came on the phone. He opened his notebook and began to write as Mavis read off the message. It didn't amount to very much, but because the inquiry had been marked *Urgent*, — Mavis's idea, not McCrimmon's — the Vancouver police had felt obliged to send through what they had.

"Thanks, Mavis," he said. "I'll call you later." He set the phone down and finished off the notes, then sat back to read them over slowly. Joseph King had no record other than that of a solid, respectable businessman. Married, no children. Owned and operated *King o' the Mountain* landscape gardeners, with branches in Surrey, Pitt Meadows, and West Vancouver. The message indicated more to follow. There was nothing new on Jacintha. He snapped the notebook shut. Sylvia Graham eyed him curiously but refrained from asking questions.

Paul Cavanna dropped the phone into its cradle and let out a long explosive breath. He bit into his sandwich, then tossed it aside in disgust. "Dry as a bone," he said. "Toss me another will you, Syl?"

McCrimmon leaned across and passed Cavanna a couple of fresh sandwiches. "Trouble, Paul?"

"Oh, it's that damned woman up on six," Cavanna growled irritably. "Now she's being spied on by a gang of teenagers in a minibus."

"Why not just move her and have done with it?"

"She refuses to move," the security chief said. "Tell you the truth, I think she's enjoying all the attention. She's got poor old Bert climbing the walls. Let's change the subject, shall we? What's all this about a waiter, Bill? I heard part of what you said while I was on the phone." He tilted his chair back and began to munch on a sandwich.

"Probably nothing, Paul," McCrimmon said. It was beginning to sound like a recording. "Just something I happened to see at the cocktail party last night. It involves one of your waiters. I'd like to ask the man a few questions. Can you arrange it for me, Paul?"

Cavanna chewed thoughtfully, one eyebrow cocked in McCrimmon's direction. "How will it affect the hotel?" he asked.

McCrimmon smiled to himself. With Cavanna, the hotel always came first. He jealously protected its name and reputation. "I can't see it affecting the hotel at all," he said and hoped he was telling the truth. "It could have something to do with the seminar, but I won't know until I've talked to the man. It may prove to be none of my business, in which case I'll drop it, and gladly."

"This is one of the men who was on duty in Mt. Stephen Hall last night, eh?" When McCrimmon nodded, Cavanna picked up the phone and dialed a number. "Louis Peppard," he said when someone answered.

Sylvia Graham could contain her curiosity no longer. "Did I hear you mention Jacintha Lee?" she asked, indicating the notebook the sergeant still held in his hand. "Wasn't she the girl you took to dinner the other night? Paul told me about her." She rolled her eyes expressively.

Before McCrimmon could reply, Cavanna put his hand over the mouthpiece of the phone and said, "I saw your girlfriend again this morning, Bill. My God! but she's a beauty."

"You saw her? Where?"

"In the lobby. I don't think she saw me; at least, she didn't speak to me."

"You mean here? In the hotel?"

"Sure. She was . . . Oh, hello, Louis. Paul here. I'm looking for some information. Yes, that's right. It's for Bill McCrimmon. You remember him. Right. It's about one of the waiters who was working the cocktail party last night. He wants to know . . ." He broke off and listened intently, then turned a frowning face to McCrimmon.

"What does your waiter look like?" he asked.

"Smallish. Five-five or five-six. Slight build, dark complexion, and very black hair combed straight back."

Cavanna relayed the information into the phone, then said, "Hold on, Louis." He put his hand over the mouthpiece once again.

"Louis was about to call me," he said quietly. "A waiter who matches the description you have just given me seems to be missing. He's not a regular; that is, he doesn't live in. He's a local we call if we need extra staff. His name is Mike Minelli. He hasn't been home all night. His wife is worried sick."

Louis Peppard, the food and beverages manager, couldn't add much to what he had already told Paul Cavanna on the phone. Minelli was last seen in the kitchen sometime between ten and eleven the night before. Everyone assumed he had gone home. It wasn't until his wife phoned the beverage supervisor and asked if he had left that anyone knew he hadn't arrived home. Even then, no one had become alarmed. Minelli had been known to stay out late on more than one occasion, especially if the cards were running in his favor. But he hadn't stayed out all night for many years, and at 5:30 a.m. Mrs. Minelli had called the police.

McCrimmon, being on special assignment, had not checked the night log at the office. Even if he had, he would not have connected the missing person report with the waiter he had seen at the hotel. The report was treated routinely; just another over-anxious wife and a husband who had failed to let her know where he was.

"How did he get back and forth to work?" McCrimmon asked.

"He has a car. An old Dodge, I think it is."

"Where does he usually park it?"

"Probably over in the guest parking lot," Peppard told him. "They're not supposed to, but . . ." He shrugged. "They all know him over there."

"Has anyone checked to see if his car is still there?"

Again the manager shrugged. "I didn't," he admitted. "I just assumed that it would be gone. I can phone over and find out if you like."

McCrimmon shook his head. "Thanks, but we'll take a look ourselves," he told the manager. "Let Paul know if you happen to think of anything that might help us."

"I'll do that," Peppard promised. "You don't think

anything has happened to him, do you? I mean anything serious?"

"Don't worry, Louis," Cavanna said confidently. "He probably got cleaned out and doesn't want to go home and tell his wife. We'll find him."

McCrimmon said nothing as they made their way across the road to the parking lot, but he felt far less confident than Cavanna. A young attendent named Gerry came forward to meet them.

"Hi Paul, Bill," he greeted. "What brings you two over here?" His face became serious. "Nothing serious, I hope?" Cavanna explained, and the young man nodded. "Sure, I know Mike. Leaves his car here all the time. I always make sure he hides it way at the back because it looks so bad. I wouldn't want anyone to think it belonged to a guest. The rocker panels are all rusted out, and one of the windows has been broken for months. It's a wreck but it runs."

"Is it here now?"

Gerry shook his head. "No, I don't think so." He led the way up the slope toward the back of the parking area and his gaze swept expertly over the rows of cars. "No," he said positively, "it's not here now."

McCrimmon scratched his chin thoughtfully. "When does the evening man come on duty, Gerry?"

"Tony? Oh, he'll be here at four. "He was on last night, too."

"Good," McCrimmon said. "But I'd like to talk to him as soon as possible. Do you have his phone number?"

"Sure do," the young man said obligingly. He led the way inside the old, garage-like building and went into a small office in the corner. "Here it is," he said, running his finger down a list. "Tony Jordan." McCrimmon wrote it down as Gerry rattled off the number.

McCrimmon dialed the number but there was no reply. He dialed again, this time to the Detachment, and asked for Quinn. When the corporal came on the line, McCrimmon quickly brought him up-to-date. "I can't reach this evening man, Jordan," he told Quinn. "He was on duty until midnight last night . . ." He raised an eyebrow in Gerry's direction, and the young man nodded confirmation. "Yes, midnight," he repeated. "Have someone track him down, will you? Find out what he knows about Minelli's movements after he left the hotel. You should have a description of the car and the license number on the report Minelli's wife filed."

"What's going on, Bill?" Quinn asked him. "Is this guy's disappearance tied in with that girl friend of yours?"

"I'll explain it later," McCrimmon said, and hung up before the corporal could ask any more questions.

"Thanks, Gerry," he said to the attendant. "We'll be over at the hotel if you should happen to hear from Tony." The young man nodded and followed them to the door.

"Mike's not in any trouble, is he?" he asked anxiously. "I mean, he has been known to stay out before."

"Do you know where he goes when he does stay out?" McCrimmon asked.

Gerry shook his head. "Seems to me he has some friends downtown somewhere, but I don't know where. Mike doesn't win often enough to talk about it."

Cavanna and McCrimmon left the building and were making their way out of the parking lot when the sergeant pulled up short. Without a word to Cavanna, he started walking toward the far end of the lot. The security chief followed, curious to see what had caught the sergeant's interest. McCrimmon came to a halt in front of a yellow Datsun.

"Something wrong?" Cavanna asked.

"Jacintha's car," the sergeant said cryptically.

Cavanna looked puzzled. "What *is* all this about Jacintha Lee?" he asked. "Is there something I don't know about this girl?"

McCrimmon paced around the car. He tried the

doors. They were locked. "I'm beginning to think there may be a lot of things we don't know about Jacintha Lee," he said grimly. He turned to face Cavanna.

"Tell me, Paul, what was it you were going to say about her when we were in your office? You said you saw her in the lobby. When was that?"

Cavanna thought about it. "Eight, maybe eight-thirty," he said. "Why?"

McCrimmon shook his head. "I wish to hell I knew," he muttered. "I do know that I've been played for a fool, and I don't like it." He turned on his heel. "That girl is probably staying right here in the hotel," he said. "I'm going to check it out at the desk. Okay, Paul?"

"I'm just as curious as you are," Cavanna said. "Let's go."

The two men crossed the road and entered the hotel. A tall, thin girl with cropped fair hair greeted them. Her name was Iris. "Jacintha Lee?" she repeated when McCrimmon asked the question. She riffled through the cards. "Yes, here it is. Jacintha Lee, room 446. She's been here," the girl calculated backward, "four days. She's booked for ten."

McCrimmon did some calculations of his own. The date coincided with the end of the seminar. "Do you have an address?"

"One thirty-one B, Halcyon Apartments, Twenty-four twelve, West Eleventh Avenue, Vancouver. She has a car, a Datsun, license number SJC 496."

"No doubt about it," McCrimmon muttered. "Thanks, Iris."

"You're welcome," she told him. "What's she done, Sergeant?" The girl leaned on the counter and waited expectantly.

"Just a routine inquiry," he told her automatically.

"Just routine," she echoed. "I should know better than to ask. You and Kojak." The two men were about to leave when Judy came out of the office.

"Oh, Bill," she called. "I'm glad I caught you. Corporal Quinn just called. He wants you to call him back right away. Says it's important. You can call him from here if you like."

"Thanks, Judy," McCrimmon said. He made the call.

"We've found your man, Minelli," Quinn said without preamble. "But you're not going to like it. He's dead."

"He's what?"

"D-E-D — dead," Quinn repeated without humor. "They found him in his car about two blocks from home. The car was parked, the keys were in it, and Minelli was slumped over on the floor. Looks like he had a heart attack or seizure and couldn't make it home."

McCrimmon remained silent, his brow furrowed in concentration. Minelli's death was a strange coincidence. Very strange indeed. Not impossible, but . . . "Any history of heart trouble?" he asked.

"I've no idea," Quinn told him.

"When did it happen?"

"Don't know that either. I just found out myself when I began to make inquiries about Minelli. They told me that a guy by that name had just been found dead. The report came in at 13:12. Barr responded. Arrived at the scene at 13:27."

"Where's the body now?"

"At the hospital. Why?"

"I'd like to know when Minelli died," McCrimmon said. "I'd also like to know if he really did die of a heart attack."

There was silence at the other end of the line, then, "What are you suggesting, Bill? Do you know something we don't?"

"I'm not suggesting anything," McCrimmon said. "It's just that the timing is damned peculiar, that's all."

"What about the girl?" Quinn persisted. "What's she got to do with all this, Bill?"

"Look, when I find out, you'll be the first to know," McCrimmon snapped irritably.

"Yeah," Quinn drawled. "Perhaps it's time somebody asked her. That is, if she hasn't left town already. I can put out a . . ."

McCrimmon cut him off. "No need for that," he said curtly. "I know where to find her. Just leave that to me."

"Sorry I brought it up," Quinn said mildly. His voice hardened. "But, since we are both supposed to be working for the same side, it would be nice if you'd share your information with the rest of us, Sergeant. Where the hell is she, Bill?"

"Right here in the hotel," McCrimmon snapped, and hung up.

Cavanna eyed McCrimmon warily. "I gather Minelli is dead and you're not entirely satisfied that he died of natural causes," he said quietly.

"That's about it, Paul," McCrimmon agreed. He ran his fingers through his hair. "But, to be honest, I haven't a shred of evidence to go on. It's just that it's all so damned coincidental. Minelli apparently died of a heart attack while he was on his way home last night. He managed to pull his car over, park it, and switch the engine off before he died. Very strange." He cocked a quizzical eye at the security chief. "I think it's about time I had a talk with our Miss Lee," he said.

"What happened to 'Jacintha'?"

McCrimmon shook his head wearily. "Let it be, Paul," he said. "Just let it be." He turned away, then turned back again as a thought struck him. "There is one thing that should be done before I talk to her, though," he said. "Want to come along?"

Cavanna eyed his friend suspiciously. "What have you got in mind?"

"Minelli," McCrimmon said shortly. "I think we'd better take a look at his body. I've been assuming that Minelli and the waiter I saw last night are one and the same. I'd better make sure."

Cavanna nodded soberly. "I'll come," he said.

Constable Barr was still at the hospital when they arrived. He and Doctor Angleton, a tall spare man with a magnificently hooked nose and a clipped British accent, were helping each other fill out forms. The constable nodded deferentially to McCrimmon. The sergeant introduced Cavanna.

"We'd like to see the body," McCrimmon told Angleton. "I was looking for Mr. Minelli on another matter when I heard that he had died."

Angleton seemed relieved to find an excuse to leave the paperwork. He rose and led the way, leaving Barr to struggle with the forms. Minelli looked even smaller in death than he had in life, but there was no doubt that this was the same man who had delivered the note the night before.

"Can you give me an estimate on the time of death, Doctor?"

Angleton's eyes became hooded. "Between midnight and five this morning," he offered.

McCrimmon frowned. "That's a pretty wide margin, Doctor," he said. "Can't you come a bit closer than that?"

Angleton thrust his hands into the pockets of his white coat. "I don't think I'd care to at this time," he said carefully. "We'll know more after the autopsy, of course, but that will be done in Calgary. There are a lot of variables."

"For example?" McCrimmon prodded.

"Well, for example, I'm told that it is assumed the man spent the night in his car after he died," Angleton said. "The engine was turned off, so there would be no heat. The temperature went down to about -4°C, and it didn't get appreciably warmer until about midmorning. *If* Minelli spent the night in his car, we can be fairly certain that he died within the times I have stated."

"Are you suggesting he may have died somewhere else?" McCrimmon stared at Angleton.

"I wouldn't want to put it in exactly those terms," Angleton hedged. "But I'm not satisfied that the man did in fact die in his car under the conditions the constable has described."

McCrimmon and Cavanna exchanged glances.

"Would you explain that, please, Doctor?" McCrimmon said.

"I've already explained it to the constable," Angleton said with a trace of irritation. McCrimmon waited. Angleton regarded him sourly, then shrugged. "Oh, very well, if you insist. The constable told me that the man apparently realized he was in trouble while he was driving his car. He managed to get it to the side of the road and park it. All right, fair enough. It's possible." He paused and stood staring down at the body, once more annonymous beneath the sheet. "You'd think that a man who had the presence of mind to guide his car to the side of the road and switch off the engine would try to attract attention to his plight. Lean on the horn, for example, or at least leave the lights on."

"It may have been something he did automatically," Cavanna said.

"True, but I don't think he did." Again, Angleton paused as if he'd lost the thread of what he was saying. "You see," he went on at last, "the constable tells me that the body, when first discovered, was slumped over to the right of the steering wheel, head down, almost touching the floor on the passenger's side. The seat belt was buckled around his waist; it's an old model car, no shoulder harness, so the body was prevented from collapsing onto the floor or across the seat. A very natural position, I'm sure."

Angleton stopped speaking and whipped the sheet from the body. It was still fully clothed, but the clothing had been partly removed, then put back loosely. The doctor rolled the body on its side and pulled the shirt and jacket well up the back. He shoved the trousers down to expose the lower back.

"You see," he said, pointing to dark areas on the skin. "Post mortem lividity. The blood drains to the lowest parts of the body after death and discolors the surrounding areas." He paused once more, and this time McCrimmon was sure it was for theatrical effect. "This body," Angleton went on pontifically, "was on its back for some time immediately following death. If there is one thing I *am* sure of, it's that this man did not die and spend the entire night in the position in which he was ultimately found."

As the two men left the hospital and made their way to the car, McCrimmon's face was grim. "That talk with Miss Lee is long overdue," he muttered. "I'll drop you off, Paul."

Cavanna regarded his friend soberly. "Bill, she's a guest in the hotel," he ventured. "I'd like to come along."

McCrimmon shook his head. "No deal, Paul. This is none of your business. It's a police matter."

Cavanna snorted. "That's exactly what it isn't!" he snapped. "You've made it a personal matter."

A sharp retort rose to the sergeant's lips, but he choked it back. Paul was right, he conceded grudgingly. He was still smarting from damaged pride. So, Jacintha had lied to him; so what? It wasn't a crime. He told himself it didn't matter. The trouble was, it did matter. It mattered like hell! He drew in a deep breath and let it out slowly.

"You're right, Paul," he said. "Perhaps it would be best if you did come along." He swung the car into the hotel parking lot.

The carpeted corridor deadened the sound of their footsteps as the two men approached the door. McCrimmon thought he heard a faint sound from inside the room as he raised his hand to knock. The two sharp raps echoed dully down the hall. They waited. McCrimmon knocked again, straining to hear some sound, any sound that would tell him that Jacintha was inside.

"Not in," Cavanna said unnecessarily. "We can try again later." He began to move away but McCrimmon stopped him.

"Hold on a minute, Paul," he said in a low voice. "I'm sure I heard someone moving around inside. She's in there. I know she's there."

"There's nothing we can do about it if she doesn't

want to come to the door," Cavanna pointed out reasonably. "Even if she is in there, she could be having a bath. Let's try later on."

McCrimmon shook his head stubbornly. "The girl in that room may be the only one who can help us with our inquiries into Minelli's death," he argued. "I want to talk to her." He eyed the security chief speculatively. "You carry a passkey, don't you, Paul?"

Cavanna exploded. "For God's sake, Bill, let it alone! What the hell do you think this is? I can't go around opening doors for you even if you are a cop. Search warrants apply to hotels too, you know. And what's this about Minelli's death? You don't even know if there's anything wrong with it. He died of a heart attack, and, until an autopsy proves different, you haven't any right to go around questioning anyone." He turned on his heel and set off down the hall.

McCrimmon moved swiftly after him. He caught Cavanna's arm and spun him round. Anger flared in Cavanna's eyes.

"Wait. Paul, please wait," McCrimmon said earnestly. He thrust a hand through his hair as he searched for the words that would change his friend's mind. "Look, forget about the fact that I had a date with this girl," he said. "And forget about the way Minelli died. I'll admit, I don't know how he died, but you have to agree that it does look suspicious. Now, I do know I saw a girl pass a note or piece of paper to Minelli, and I know that Minelli passed it on to one of the Chinese delegates without the others knowing about it. I don't know what is going on, but it could have something to do with the security of this seminar. That's my concern and it has to be your concern, Paul." Cavanna was listening. McCrimmon hurried on. "I heard her in there. I know she's there. I need to ask her a couple of questions, that's all. Look," he went on rapidly, "at least let's get the floor housekeeper to take in some towels. We'll know for sure, then, whether she's in there or not. Maybe, somehow she knows it's me and doesn't want to face me. I don't know. What do you say, Paul?"

Slowly, the anger in Cavanna's face dissolved. "Okay," he agreed resignedly. "But that's as far as I go. If she comes to the door you can speak to her; but one step inside that room unless she invites you there . . ." His eyes glinted. "I'm warning you, Bill . . ."

"It's a deal," McCrimmon assured him. A few minutes later the two men followed a short, plump, gray-haired woman down the hall. She carried several towels over her arm. She stopped before Jacintha's room and knocked lightly on the door.

"Room service," she called. There was no response. She knocked and called out again, louder this time. Nothing. She looked inquiringly at Paul Cavanna and, after a moment's hesitation, he nodded. The housekeeper took a key from her pocket and inserted it into the lock. There was a sharp, metallic click, and the woman grasped the doorknob and began to turn it. Suddenly, the door swung inward.

The startled woman gasped but recovered quickly. "You ordered fresh towels, Ma'am?" she inquired. Without waiting for a reply, she thrust them forward. Jacintha Lee, her smoldering eyes fixed on McCrimmon, reached for them automatically. The woman fled.

Jacintha looked smaller than he remembered; then he saw that she wore nothing on her feet. A white bathrobe of terry cloth was wrapped tightly round her slender figure, and her hair cascaded in disarray around her shoulders. McCrimmon's thoughts flew swiftly to a moment in Mt. Stephen Hall, and the soft, subtle smell of jasmine. It was a fleeting lapse.

"I'm sorry to bring you to the door like that," he nodded in the direction of the departing housekeeper, "but it was necessary. We have to talk to you." He indicated Cavanna. "You remember Paul, I'm sure." The girl remained silent, but her eyes flicked to Cavanna and she nodded.

"Perhaps we could talk to you inside?" Mc-Crimmon ventured.

A violent shake of the head, then, "I'm sorry Sergeant," she said carefully. "It must have been you who knocked earlier. I was taking a bath. I didn't know who it was . . ." She trailed off and looked at each of them in turn. Her expression, McCrimmon thought, said 'Please believe me'.

The muscles of his jaw tightened. "I'm afraid I have to ask you a few questions," he said. His voice sounded unduly harsh even to his own ears. He tried again. "It really would be better if we could talk inside. We'll wait out here until you're dressed."

The girl's mouth set firmly and, again, there was that sharp, negative shake of the head. Her eyes sought McCrimmon's. "Please leave me alone," she said in a hushed voice. "I know what you must think of me . . ." She began to close the door.

McCrimmon cut in sharply. "It has nothing to do with . . ." He caught himself, but he could feel the color rising in his face. "It's not a personal matter any more," he went on. "This is police business. It concerns the note you sent to one of the Chinese delegates at the cocktail party last night." He was watching her closely. A shadow, no more, passed behind her eyes, but her expression did not change.

"I do not understand what you are talking about," she said, frowning as if puzzled.

McCrimmon sighed. "I saw you give the note to a waiter by the name of Minelli," he said patiently. "He passed the note to one of the delegates. Now, Minelli is dead. I have to know what was in that note, Ja— Miss Lee." Her eyes remained fixed, expressionless, but he saw the shock hit her despite her iron control. Her face grew pale and she had to moisten her lips before she could bring herself to speak.

"I don't know what you are talking about," she whispered huskily. "I sent no note to anyone, and I certainly don't know a waiter named Minelli." The color began to come back into her cheeks. "I'm sorry, but you must be mistaken. I cannot help you." She began to close the door once more.

McCrimmon took a pace forward and held it open. The girl's eyes flashed dangerously. "I've told you I cannot help you," she repeated icily. She turned to Cavanna. "You are in charge of hotel security, here. Are you going to let this man force his way into my room?" she demanded.

Cavanna laid a hand on McCrimmon's shoulder. "Sorry, Bill, but that's it," he said quietly.

McCrimmon's face hardened. "I'm investigating what may well turn out to be a murder, Paul," he grated. "Miss Lee may be able to help me. I'd appreciate it if you would allow me to do my job."

Cavanna's grip tightened. "Miss Lee says she doesn't know anything about it," he said evenly. "That's it, Bill." There was no mistaking the veiled threat in Cavanna's voice. The security chief would only be pushed so far. McCrimmon had pushed him to his limit.

The sergeant removed his hand from the door, but his eyes held those of the girl. "I'm going to get those answers," he warned. "One way or another, I'll get those answers." An expression he could not read touched her lovely features, and then the door closed. The lock snapped solidly into place as if to emphasize the barrier between them. Wordlessly, McCrimmon walked to the elevator, Cavanna half a pace behind.

The sergeant pressed the button. The image of Jacintha's face lingered hauntingly in his mind, and suddenly he knew the meaning of the expression he had seen so fleetingly.

It was fear.

Inside the room, Jacintha Lee walked slowly to the window and stood looking out with unseeing eyes. She shivered and pulled the robe tighter around her body. She heard a sound behind her but she didn't turn. A man stepped out from behind the bathroom door. The gun he held was made even more ugly by the bulbous silencer fitted to the barrel.

"That was very good," he congratulated. "Very good indeed." He slid the gun into an unseen harness beneath his coat, and settled himself comfortably in a bedside chair.

"And now we wait," he said. He pulled a paperback book from his pocket and began to read.

Chapter 8

The man behind the desk drew wetly on the fat cigar and blew out a cloud of smoke. Olsen coughed pointedly but the smoke continued to billow in his direction.

"This is a resort town, Mr. Olsen," the man said. "Half the people who live here rent out rooms or their houses at one time or another." He shrugged his rounded shoulders as if that ended the matter.

"I realize that," the man from Denver said patiently. "But I really feel I should make the effort to see Norman now that I'm here." Olsen frowned as if trying hard to recall something. "As I recall, he told me it was a secluded place, a little off the beaten track. I assumed he was talking about a house; he entertains you know, so it wouldn't be an apartment or anything like that. I wish I'd paid more attention, but I didn't know then that I would wind up in Banff myself." He shook his head ruefully. "As it is, I'll only be in town for a couple of days, Mr. Royston. I feel I should make some effort to stop by and say hello."

Royston shook his head dubiously. "I don't think we've handled anything like that recently," he said. "Mind you, a lot of people do their own renting and leasing, usually to people they know. A few work through agents in Calgary." His face contorted as if the thought gave him pain.

"I'd sure be grateful if you would check it out for me," Olsen persisted.

Royston regarded him through a blue haze of smoke. This guy just wasn't going to give up. He sighed and removed the cigar from his mouth. "Elaine?" he bellowed hoarsely. "Elaine? You out there?" A small, pinched woman with watery eyes appeared in the doorway. She blinked in Olsen's direction, then stood waiting patiently for Royston to tell her what it was he wanted. She looked, Olsen thought, as if she'd been waiting patiently for a very long time. Royston waved his cigar in the woman's direction. "How'd you like to tell her what you're looking for?" he invited.

Olsen repeated his story. A business friend by the name of Norman Kellerman had told him that he'd rented a place in Banff for several weeks. From the way he had spoken, Olsen had gained the impression that Kellerman had rented it through an agency; that it wasn't the usual cabin or chalet, but something more like a private house. Perhaps a little removed from the mainstream. Norman, he pointed out, preferred something secluded. Since Olsen hadn't expected to be in Banff, he hadn't pressed his friend for details. Now, finding that business had brought him here . . . He shrugged.

"If he ever found out that I'd been this close and hadn't tried to find him . . ." He shrugged again and the woman nodded understandingly.

"Kellerman," she repeated, frowning, "I don't remember anyone by that na . . . Oh, wait a minute. Was it some time ago? A couple of months, maybe?" She wasn't looking at Olsen. Her eyes were turned inward, scanning some invisible filing system.

"I think I *do* remember," she said with conviction. "Just a minute while I check the files." She disappeared into the other office and returned almost immediately. "Yes, here it is. Kellerman. He came in last February and we found a house for him. The owners will be traveling in the States until July." She looked questioningly at Olsen and he nodded encouragingly. She scanned the file again. "Occupancy May first, although Mr. Kellerman paid the rent from the end of February. I remember him now, such a nice man." She beamed at Olsen. "I have the phone number right here," she went on helpfully. "I could ring him for you if you wish."

"No, no, that won't be necessary," Olsen said hastily. "It would spoil the surprise, wouldn't it?"

"The house is called *The Firs*," the woman went on. "It's just off St. Julian Road." She moved to a large wall map and pointed to a spot a little below where Wolf Street joined St. Julian Road. "It's kind of old and surrounded by trees. I guess that's why they called it *The Firs*."

Olsen rose, now anxious to be on his way. He had been lucky, very lucky indeed. Kellerman might have used any name. Of course, if another name had been on the lease, Olsen would have immediately said that it was Kellerman's agent. Still, it was much neater this way; fewer questions.

"Thank you very much," he said. "You've been most helpful."

"Are you sure I can't phone or anything?" She was so anxious to please.

"Thank you, but no," Olsen told her firmly. "But I'll take the number down in case I need it in the future." He scribbled it in his notebook as the woman obligingly read it out. It seemed to satisfy her for she closed the file.

Royston struggled from his chair and ushered Olsen to the door while Elaine went back to her desk in the outer office, there to remain until the next bellowed summons brought her forth. Royston's cigar had gone out, but he stuck it in one corner of his mouth and thrust out a hand.

"Happy to have been of service," he said. "Keep us in mind if you're ever in the market for some choice property. We handle only the best, you know. How about a nice parcel of land just outside the park, eh? Good investment, you know. Nothing appreciates like land." He wasn't really trying; it was habit, sheer habit with Royston.

"I'll certainly keep you in mind," Olsen promised,

extending his own hand. They shook hands, firmly, professionally. Olsen moved off down the street, ignoring his car. He could pick it up later after Royston was safely inside again. Royston stood looking after him, then turned and made his way back inside. He wondered about Olsen. Sounded like an American, not much, but enough. Private investigator, maybe? One thing was for sure; he was no friend of Kellerman's

The telephone rang. He scooped it up. "I got it, Elaine," he said as he heard her answer. "Oh, hi there, Sam. Good to hear from you. You gonna pick up that piece of property in Canmore? It's a good deal, Sam . . ."

The prospect of a sale wiped any lingering thoughts about Olsen from his mind.

"It's on a quiet street and the house itself is almost totally concealed. There's a three hundred foot cliff behind it, actually the side of Tunnel Mountain, and high fences and trees on either side. I saw two men go around the side of the house. They weren't tourists and they sure weren't local residents." Malik stopped pacing, poured himself another drink, and motioned for Olsen to do the same. He accepted the invitation. Approving of Mayer's choice, Smith's Glenlivet, Olsen poured a generous three fingers.

"You're quite sure they didn't spot you?" Malik resumed his pacing.

Olsen shook his head. "Quite sure," he said. "I made one pass, walking. There are quite a few older houses in the area. A lot of people rent out rooms. If I'd been setting up this place I'd have put men in several upstairs rooms along the street. They'd have cameras and binoculars, and I'd have them photograph anyone who went near the house. They'd be in radio contact with the people in the house." He sipped his Scotch, rolling it around his mouth before letting it trickle down his throat. "There's no way we're going to penetrate a place like that except by frontal assault," he ended.

Malik stopped in front of him and eyed him sourly.

Olsen felt less sure of himself. "What about the waiter?" he asked. "Didn't he tell you anything?"

Malik's expression deepened into a scowl. "He didn't have time." he said. "He had the seizure just as they were driving off the parking lot. The fools brought him here . . ." He broke off in disgust and raised his eyes heavenward. "Oh, God, send me some professionals," he growled. Olsen wisely remained silent. Malik rocked back on his heels and squinted down at Olsen. "What about the Calgary end? Any sign of Kellerman there?"

Olsen shook his head. "I'm sure he's still in Banff. Most likely in the house."

Malik looked down his nose at the glass in his hand and nodded as if Olsen had confirmed his own thinking. "There isn't much time," he muttered. "He'll have to leave the house soon."

Olsen shot him a questioning look. "Why would he . . . ?" He stopped, wishing he'd kept the question to himself, for Mayer looked pained.

He sat down abruptly and thrust a broad finger under Olsen's nose. "Because," he said with the elaborate patience one might use on a particularly dense child, "the Americans must make their first move very soon. No later than this weekend. Do you know why?"

Olsen had no idea, but he chose to remain silent.

"They have to move soon because they have no more than a week to work with. If something goes wrong with their first attempt, they have to have time to set up a second try, an alternative plan." Malik drained his glass. "They'll do it this weekend," he said positively. "That's when the tour activities will be at their peak."

Olsen nodded, the light suddenly dawning. "And you think that whoever is in charge of this operation will send the local boy home before the real action begins," he said softly.

Malik looked vaguely surprised. "That's right," he said. "And that's when we'll pick him up." He sat staring at the empty glass as if trying to decide whether or not to fill it again. "He'll tell us exactly what we want to know," he said quietly. Malik shot a sudden questioning look at Olsen, and Olsen suppressed a shiver.

It was his turn to drain his glass.

There was a dank and musty odor in the basement, due, no doubt, to the uncemented root cellar at the far end. It was sealed off by a heavy wooden door, but with the arrival of spring and the warming of the earth beside the house, the smell had permeated the basement. The equipment, set up on a bench and trestle table beneath a blacked-out window, seemed to be dry enough. Roy Guthrie switched off the tape recorder and grunted his approval.

"So this can be operated manually from here or remotely from the control console upstairs?" he said.

Stu nodded. "That's what you asked for; that's what you've got."

Guthrie rubbed his hands together and looked pleased. "Excellent!" he said softly. The technician and Kellerman exchanged glances. Despite the confidence they had both projected, they were relieved that the trial run had gone so well. They went upstairs.

"Stu, I want you to return to your motel and stay there until you hear from me," Guthrie said. "Do whatever shopping you have to, and make sure you've got everything. I don't want you away from the phone for a minute. Okay?"

"How long will it be?"

Guthrie pulled at his lower lip as if giving the matter careful consideration. "No more than three days," he said at last.

Again Stu nodded. He didn't want to know more than that. He was well paid to stand by just in case the equipment failed. He'd only been called back once during the six years he'd been setting up audio-visual systems, and even that had proved to be the fault of the operator rather than the equipment.

"I'll be on my way," he said. He wasted no time, but put away his tools and test equipment in a portable cabinet and locked it, then left the house.

Guthrie stuck out his hand. "I guess that's it, Norman," he said. "I don't suppose we'll be seeing each other again, but I want you to know that you've done a good job for me here. I'll see that it's entered on your record when I get back." Kellerman returned the grip, pleased by Guthrie's praise. A word to the right man in Langley could do wonders for his career. Calgary was not exactly a conspicuous center of international intrigue; one could be overlooked very easily in such a place.

He grinned. "I'd sure appreciate that, Roy," he said, wanting to say more, much more, but afraid to in case Guthrie misunderstood. Already, Guthrie's eyes held that familiar look of preoccupation.

"I'll be on my way," he said. "Good luck in the operation." Guthrie nodded and followed him to the door. He watched until Kellerman's green Ford had disappeared down the driveway, then went back inside and picked up a walkie-talkie.

"Anyone show any interest in the two who just left?" he asked.

"Nothing. They're clean," a disembodied voice replied.

"Good," Guthrie said. "Keep watching the street." He began to review the hours that lay ahead.

Olsen, sitting in the passenger's seat of a three-quarter ton truck, shivered and pulled his coat around him. The sun had slipped behind the mountains and the temperature was dropping rapidly. A squall of snow blocked out the top of Cascade Mountain and drifted further down the wooded slopes, dusting the tops of evergreens with flecks of white. The man beside him yawned and lit a cigarette. His name, Olsen had learned, was Mike; a big, coarse-featured, hump-shouldered man who sat over the steering wheel as if it were a toy. Olsen coughed as the smoke drifted over to his side of the cab, but the man paid no attention. He sat staring straight ahead, waiting.

The portable radio mounted below the dash burst into life. "Light green Ford sedan, Alberta plates NBV 079, heading down Wolf, approaching Muskrat Street," a metallic voice intoned. The car crossed the intersection ahead of them as the radio went silent. Mike started the truck and dropped it into gear. Olsen picked up the microphone.

"Got it," he acknowledged. "It's Kellerman, all right. Stay parallel with us on Moose."

The radio crackled. "With you on Moose."

The truck swung around the corner into Wolf Street and came up fast behind the Ford. Mike hunched over the wheel and spoke coaxingly to the driver of the car in front as if he were sitting beside him.

"That's right, slow for the light," he muttered softly. "It's going to turn red. That's it. Watch for that pedestrian." He shot a look at Olsen. "Get ready," he ordered. "This is it."

"Here?" Olsen's voice squeaked with astonishment.

The big man merely grunted in reply. Olsen braced himself. Welded across the front of the dark red truck was a wide steel bumper made of quarter-inch plate. Rolled at the edges and ridged for added strength, it made a formidable weapon. The truck moved forward. The steel bumper of the truck slid over the decorative bumper of the Ford and pushed the trunk and tail lights some six inches ahead of where they were meant to be. If Olsen had not been prepared for the impact, he would have cannoned forward into the windshield.

The green Ford shot forward several feet and stopped. Kellerman's head snapped back against the headrest set just a shade too low, and felt the numbing hammerblow just below his ears. Even as his reflexes responded and his foot slammed down on the brake, he felt the car shoot forward several feet. The brakes grabbed, and he shot forward into the restraining harness of the shoulder belt. The idling engine died.

Dimly, his vision blurred by the double impact, he saw the grill of the truck in the rearview mirror. The numbing shock began to fade, and in its place came anger. He struggled ineffectually to free himself from the seatbelt. The lights had changed and a horn blared angrily as a car swept past the front of the Ford, now jutting well into the traffic stream of Banff's main street. With only a half-formed thought of getting his car out of the way of oncoming traffic, Kellerman turned the key. Two things happened simultaneously. The engine caught, and the door beside him opened. A man stood there, square and heavy-set and business-like. The gun he held looked as if it had grown out of the ham-like hand.

"Just turn the engine off and get out nice and slow, Mr. Kellerman," the man advised. "Hands up in front and come out easy."

Kellerman froze. If the man knew his name, this had been no accident. My God! he thought. I'm being kidnapped in broad daylight. His eyes remained fixed on the big man's face.

The gun flicked impatiently. "Engine off!" the man commanded menacingly.

Kellerman's hand reached toward the keys, then, without warning, changed direction and closed around the gearshift lever and slammed it downward. He desperately wanted a gear. Any gear. He floored the accelerator as the arm dropped into reverse. The car shot backward into the truck once more. The gunman leapt nimbly to one side, twisting like a cat away from the open door, but the edge caught his hand and the gun clattered to the street.

Kellerman pulled the gearshift lever further down, and the tires screamed. The car shot forward and the gunman, scrambling for his gun, was forced to jump aside again. Black, burning rubber laid a trail across Banff Avenue, and Kellerman twisted the wheel frantically to avoid a Cadillac trying to beat the lights. The Caddy rammed the already battered rear fender of the Ford and jolted to a stop. Antifreeze gushed from a shattered radiator while the driver slammed the steering wheel in helpless fury and screamed obscenities at the fast disappearing Ford. Twin tracks of burning rubber slued from side to side as Kellerman gunned the engine and fought the wheel to keep control. His only thought was to put distance between himself and the man with the gun. He took time to glance into the rearview mirror. The truck was less than a block behind.

As the Ford shot across Banff Avenue, the man called Mike had ducked aside, scooped up the gun, and started running to the waiting truck. He moved with lightning speed, and Olsen snatched madly for a handhold as the truck shot forward. The four-wheel drive engaged and he was slammed back in his seat. The corner of the welded bumper sheared the bumper and grill clean off the Cadillac, and the driver dropped his head against the steering wheel and cried.

While people scrambled madly for the safety of the sidewalk, Kellerman was trying to bring his dazed mind back into focus. He was running out of street and he had to turn either right or left. Instinct told him to avoid getting caught in traffic, and by turning left he would be forced back into the thickest traffic in town. He swung the wheel hard over and blindly made the right-hand turn on Lynx. He hit a pothole and the battered trunk flew up, blocking out his vision to the rear. Just two blocks down and he could find safety with the local police. He caught a glimpse of the dark red truck as the trunk flopped up and down behind him. His foot pushed harder on the pedal. The engine screamed, and he realized that the gearshift was still in first. He flipped it into second and left it there.

Ahead, a tanker truck began its slow maneuver, backing awkwardly from the pumps at the service station on the corner. An overalled attendant slouched belatedly into the road to check for traffic, and stood there gaping as the Ford flashed past mere inches from his nose. His frightened yell brought the tanker to a halt just as the truck shot through the narrow gap.

Olsen cringed as if by doing so it would somehow make more room. "This is crazy," he gasped. "You can't roar though town like this and expect to get away with it."

The driver kept his eyes glued on the road ahead. "We've got to get him now," he grated. "We can't allow him to get back to warn his people. If we lose him now we'll have to answer for it."

"But . . ." Olsen swallowed his words. There was nothing to be gained by arguing with Mike. Unfortunately, the man was right. Kellerman had been too quick for them. They had to catch him now. Olsen thought of failure, and Malik. He didn't like the combination.

The roar of car and truck burst on the quiet solitude of the Catholic church. The vicious snarl of engines broke against its walls of mountain rock and shattered there. The truck began to close the gap. But, with trunk lid flying, Kellerman could not see the danger.

Half a block ahead, the RCMP Detachment. A two-tier box of white and blue, its dab of Rundle rock a gesture, nothing more, to its National Park surroundings. But to Kellerman it was refuge. His eyes searched eagerly for a sign of uniforms outside, but none was there. Two cars stood empty in the parking lot. He raced toward the entrance, not knowing that the truck was almost on him. He swung the wheel and the rear wheels crabbed sideways, spinning, twisting, sliding . . .

A patch of gravel left over from the snow and ice of winter lay loosely in a pothole in the middle of the road. The clutching tires hit it and the car swung round to face the way it had come. The truck drove straight at it, cutting in front to block the entrance to the parking lot. Mike hit the brakes, and for an instant Olsen's eyes met those of Kellerman, and they both saw naked fear. The truck slammed sideways into the Ford. They sat there for perhaps two seconds facing each other, then reflexes responded once again.

Tires screeched and gravel flew as Kellerman hit the

gas again. He'd lost the gamble to find a haven and, even if the police had heard the noise outside, they'd be far behind by the time they got to their cars. He accelerated past the service station where now a group of gaping watchers stood. The trunk lid flapped up and down and he could see the truck was catching up again. He needed time; time to stop the car and lose himself among the stores and people. He cut left again and found himself on Wolf, fast approaching Banff Avenue where the traffic lights glowed red.

Behind him, the truck skidded around the corner. Olsen screamed into the microphone. "He's heading back on Wolf again. Where the hell are you?"

"Coming up to Wolf on Banff Avenue," the voice replied. "We lost track of you. We — "the voice rose to a high-pitched yell — "There he is. He's coming like a bat out of hell!"

"Cut him off! Stop him!" Olsen yelled back, his eyes riveted on the Ford ahead. He pressed the button of the mike again. "Alive," he yelled. "He has to be taken alive."

The lights again and people crossing. Startled faces flashed by the window as Kellerman zoomed into the intersection. The other side was clear.

He saw the white car coming at him from the left. In something less than microseconds his brain registered the determined eyes of the two men in it, and the microphone in the hand of the passenger. He knew they must be in contact with the truck. He skidded right and flung the car around the corner. He hit the gas and fired the Ford like a bullet down suppertime Banff Avenue. The white car followed close behind and the truck brought up the rear.

A girl, no more than seventeen, stood on the concrete median that ran the length of Banff Avenue. She looked directly at the speeding car, then, perversely, stepped off in front of it. Sweat poured down Kellerman's face. He felt the salty taste against his tongue.

"You stupid bitch!" he screamed uselessly, and

swerved toward the solid line of cars parked nose to tail the full length of the street.

Almost too late something clicked inside the girl's head, and the realization came that she was a hair away from instant death. She screamed and threw her hands out in front of her as if to hold back the speeding car. Her eyes flew wide with terror. The Ford brushed her dress as it slithered through. Shock shut down her overloaded brain and she fell unconscious to the road, backward by the grace of God, and out of the path of the white car and the truck.

Kellerman raced on, hard against the line of cars. Extended sideview mirrors on trailor-pulling cars flew off like shrapnel as the wider truck stripped them clean. They crossed the intersection with Caribou, thankfully with the lights on green. Only Buffalo to go and then the bridge. The choices clicked through Kellerman's mind. To cross the bridge meant dead ends, no matter which way he chose. He had to stay on this side of the bridge if he hoped to survive. And he had to stay in town. Once out on the open highway he wouldn't stand a chance. He didn't know what was under the hood of the truck behind him, but it was certainly bigger and more powerful than the Ford. He thought fleetingly of heading for the house, but dismissed the idea immediately. Perhaps the men behind him already knew about the house; they'd tried to stop him less than three blocks from it. But perhaps they didn't. Guthrie wouldn't thank him for leading them back to him.

The intersection was upon him. The white car was trying to come up on his left side. He swung the car in a screaming arc, hard left into Buffalo, and had the fleeting satisfaction of seeing the white car hit the median and bounce off. He hoped the wheels were wrecked.

The flash of red behind him told him that the truck had made it, then once again the view was blocked by the battered trunk lid. He pushed the pedal to the floor and began the climb toward the upper Tunnel Mountain

Road. The houses dropped behind. Slabs of chiseled rock rose high and solid on his left, while, to the right, the ground fell away sharply to the churning waters of the muddy river far below. Stunted trees dotted the steep decline; not much to slow your fall, thought Kellerman, should he lose control.

The climb grew steeper and gravel from the shoulder flew as he hurled the car around each sharper corner. He wished he had a standard shift, or better still, a front-wheel drive. The lid flapped down again and he could see the grill of the truck looming in his mirror. Across the river, the Banff Springs Hotel came into view. Far below, unguarded by a rail, Bow Falls thundered beneath a solid wall of spray. A lookout point where tourists stopped by the thousands every year appeared ahead. A hairpin bend, hard left and climbing steeply, the road hemmed in by rocks and trees on either side.

The truck had gained on the bend, and now it moved in tight behind. His head snapped back as it rammed him from the rear. A sardonic laugh burst from his lips as, at 68 mph, he swept past a sign marked 30 km/h. He wrenched the car around a right-hand turn. His tires spun and finally grabbed the coarse surface of the road. The way rose steeply and the potholes, gouged by winter frosts, grew larger. The thudding jolt of shock absorbers hitting bottom bounced him in his seat and made it all but impossible to hang on to the wheel. The trees closed in around him, and still the road continued to twist and climb. Patches of black ice and melting snow appeared. The sky was dark, the weather closing in.

There is nothing quite so awesome as the onset of a mountain squall. Like a sodden, woolen blanket, it cuts off light and muffles sound. Kellerman peered anxiously ahead as the storm closed in around the car; large, wet snowflakes drove against the windshield and cut visibility to inches. He braked, and felt the rear wheels slide. he snatched his foot away, then quickly pumped the brakes, sliding, slowing, straightening out again. He thumbed the windshield wipers on and held the car as close as he dared to the right-hand mountain wall, visible now only as a shadow darker than the rest. Off to his left lurked even greater danger, a plunge of several hundred feet beneath an observation point. Today was not a day for viewing.

The steering wheel jumped and twisted in his hands as if it were alive. The car lurched, rose and settled back, and something solid thudded hard beneath his feet. It banged along the manifold and then was gone. He slowed the car to a crawl, remembering too late the signs he'd seen a dozen times warning of falling rock. The swirling snow had obscured them, and he'd forgotten the treacherous, flaking slabs, rotted by the seeping runoff, that fall and shatter on the road. He prayed that this particular piece had not ruptured his gas tank.

He heard the trunk lid bang down, but he couldn't see the truck through the wall of snow. It couldn't be far behind. The driver was a pro, and the truck would hold the road better than the Ford. The windshield wipers thudded hard against the clogging snow. Kellerman had reduced speed to a crawl for fear of running off the road. He knew it well, but in this weather all he could do was inch along and hope the squall would be short-lived. Steam began to fog the glass, and he turned the heater to defrost.

As suddenly as it had come, the squall was past and the road ahead was clear. He put his foot down and the car responded. The road was dropping now. Down, down through short, sharp, treacherous curves, and down again. More rock across the road, spaced, it seemed, with malevolent design. The car bounced and slithered perilously close to the thrusting outcrops of rock that threatened to tear him from the icy road. He fought the wheel every inch of the way. Down into a hollow and up again to the top of a steep rise. And, at the crest, a bus.

The road was wide enough for two vehicles to pass with relative ease, but the planners had assumed that neither would be in the middle of the road. None had forseen that one might be doing close to sixty and accelerating. The bus driver spun the wheel, but years of ingrained caution on the mountain roads stayed his hands, for he was on the drop-off side, and nothing would persuade him to take the bus too close to the edge.

The green Ford shot by, its door handles cutting a perfect crease down the entire length of the bus. But it straightened out the car, and now the road ahead was clear. Wider, and all down hill, with shallower curves and trees on either side all the way to the junction where he could cut back toward the town and, with any luck at all, lose his pursuers once and for all. The lid banged down behind him and he risked a look into the mirror. The truck had made it past the bus and was gaining on him fast. And close behind the truck he could see the white car.

He couldn't risk more speed and even hope to make the left-hand turn at the crossbar of the T road ahead. He slowed to forty and braced himself for the tight left turn across a desultory stream of traffic coming up the hill from town. A space appeared and he careened around the turn. He almost made it. He would have, too, if it hadn't been for the backhoe working on the sewer line. The backhoe blocked the right-hand side of the road. A motor home, laboring up the hill from town, blocked the left.

Kellerman spun the car into an ear-shattering skid that flung the rear end round to slam against the backhoe arm, half buried in the trench. He clung to the wheel and hoped the car would stay upright. The backhoe operator was slammed against the side of his cab, and the steel hat he had put on not more than seconds before saved his life.

It was too much for the trunk lid. The impact flung it fifty feet away to land atop a stack of pipe. The engine of the green Ford died.

The driver of the motor home, a balding, whispy man of sixty, said "Oh, my God!" and slammed on his brakes. He came to a halt right in the path of the oncoming truck.

Mike hit the brakes and all four wheels locked tight, but melting snow and scattered mud from the trench had made the corner doubly treacherous. The truck took out the right, front corner of the motor home where a passenger would normally have been.

Kellerman heard the crash and saw the motor home bounce and shake. He guessed what had happened, and thanked whatever quirk of fate had put the motor home between him and the truck. He turned the key. The starter revved but the engine didn't catch. He cast around for a place to run, but he knew he wouldn't stand a chance if he left the car. He turned the key again in desperation. Lank, matted hair stuck to his forehead as the sweat poured from him. The wheel was slippery beneath his clutching fingers. The engine caught and roared. He slammed the gear shift into drive, and the battered Ford leapt forward. He took the only road left open to him, the back road to the highway, and too much open road.

Above him, for a frozen second, he saw the stunned imprint of the pallid face of the driver of the motor home. He saw the truck backing, tearing itself free from the tangled wreckage.

The road was fairly flat and straight, and he pushed the pedal to the floor. The engine whined to screaming pitch, and it didn't shift out of first until the needle climbed past sixty-five. He took the first curve at ninety and sizzled down the straightaway at a hundred-and-ten. The road was clear but narrow, and he had to make the best of it before it started to descend. A dying flash of sunlight caught the top of Rundle Mountain off to his right across the valley of the Bow. Fresh snow glistened, flashing like a lonely beacon, and was gone. The trees closed in around him. The needle moved closer to the right-hand side. And all he could see in his rearview mirror was the grill and hood of the dark red truck.

The road began to drop away to the left, curving sharply down, following the contours of the mountain. Two cyclists coming up the hill stopped to gape in wonder as the convoy roared past. Kellerman glanced in the mirror again. Now that the trunk was gone he had an unobstructed view, and his lips set grimly as he saw the flash of white some fifty yards behind the truck.

A sharp curve loomed ahead, and then another. Trails of burning rubber slashed the surface of the road, and gravel flew like bullets into space, peppering the tops of trees far below. Another curve, and now he was braking hard at every turn, accelerating pulling out. A warning sign said 20 km/h.

Again the brakes, pumping hard because he could feel them fading as the brake shoes grew red-hot. He heard the high-pitched whine as the truck behind geared down to absorb the sudden change of pace. A checkered sign gave warning of a sharp left turn. The two vehicles flung themselves around the corner at forty-five, an impossible speed on a road no wider than fifteen feet.

Kellerman almost lost control. The shoulder on the right disappeared below. The right, rear wheel raced freely in the space where solid road should be. He felt the sickening lurch that told him the car was about to slide that extra foot that would send him crashing down the mountainside. The sweat upon his face turned icy cold, and he had a senseless urge to scream.

And yet again, defying logic and all the laws of physics, the valiant, battered car found traction on the road again. A telltale streak of rubber left a silent tribute to the death-defying feat. He couldn't keep it up. His hands were sticky, slipping and sliding on the wheel, his muscles knotted with fatigue. How he'd stayed alive so far was beyond his comprehension. If he didn't slow the pace somehow, he'd do the job for his pursuers.

But still the truck came on, never letting up, pushing, prodding, trying to goad him into making that one mistake. But they didn't want him dead; they could have killed him back in Banff, and any number of times since then. Another jolt forced him to concentrate upon his driving. The road continued to descend. He pushed hard on the gas pedal, knowing he had to make the next three turns faster than the truck. He came out of the third one with tires screaming, bearing down on a narrow, iron bridge. Another warning sign flashed by, unheeded and unread. Beyond the bridge lay railroad tracks, Trans-Continental tracks linking Atlantic to Pacific; and just beyond, the highway, with traffic that was light but steady.

The raucous blare of a diesel train reverberated down the valley as Kellerman raced toward the tracks. The trees and the roaring of his engine had masked the rumble of the approaching train, but now he heard the growing thunder and saw the triple diesel engines pulling hard on the snake of loaded boxcars. Another strident blast hit him like a hammerblow as a startled engineer reacted to the sudden appearance of the car. Kellerman shot across the tracks, appalled at the closeness of the train. For one brief instant he felt relief; the train would surely cut him off from his pursuers.

But it was not to be.

A flash of red burst across the tracks mere inches in front of the leading diesel even as the Ford slashed across the path of a big blue Chrysler on the highway. The Chrysler's horn faded out behind him, drowned by the tortured scream of tires as he made the left-hand turn and gathered speed again.

The driver of the white car, bringing up the rear, had floored the gas pedal as he came hurtling off the iron bridge. He saw the others cross the tracks and gathered speed. The level crossing sign and the significance of the half-heard warning blasts registered too late.

The car roared out of the shelter of the trees just as the first diesel crossed the road not twenty yards ahead. The driver's foot slammed down hard. The brakes responded. All wheels locked.

Too late.

He spun the wheel. A tire burst. The car flipped half-way round and began to roll, its momentum carrying it straight ahead. It jammed itself between the second and third diesel engines, hanging there suspended, but only the driver knew. His passenger was dead, his head bursting like an over-ripe watermelon against the doorpost of the car.

The driver's brain still functioned, registering in slow motion the disintegration of the car around him. The engine block slammed backward and took away his legs, and yet there was no pain. He saw with awesome clarity the twisted wreckage sliding down between the massive, pounding engines, and he heard the piercing scream of metal as brakes slammed on too late. He caught a glimpse of trees and sky as the wreckage was dragged down between the engines. And he saw the massive metal wheel slice through the car just before it crossed his neck.

Kellerman had floored the accelerator when he'd made the turn onto the highway, but he couldn't hope to outrun the truck in a race to Banff. He wouldn't make it to the traffic circle. He had to get off the highway, and the only place he could do that was a hundred yards ahead.

The truck was gaining fast when he braked again, and it nearly overshot. He made the turn without a skid and stepped on the pedal hard. He heard the grinding whine of gears as the truck used them to advantage. He'd gained, perhaps, fifty yards, and if he kept to the middle of the road he might still have a chance. The road, a winding, peaceful route leading to Two Jack Lake and Minnewanka, was never meant for speed. It wound its way along the mountain ridges, rising steadily for several miles before descending once again close to the town of Banff.

The first stretch was fairly straight, the pavement good. Kellerman settled down to take the curves at twice the speed for which they had been engineered. Climbing, always climbing.

The corners became sharper, and black and yellow signs warned of winding road ahead. He cut straight across each corner, trying to gain a foot or two on each curve. He cut across a blind left turn around a bulging wall of solid rock, and barely missed a minibus coming down the other side. He felt a twinge of pity for the startled driver, then saw the truck was gaining on him once again. His foot was flat on the floor as he rocketed into the next tight turn.

A jagged chunk of fallen rock lay sharp and ugly in the road. He swerved too late and hit it with his right, front wheel. The steering wheel slammed hard against his thumb and broke it.

He heard the tire blow, and felt the car lift and begin to roll. He felt it slam against the unyielding face of rock. The glass around him shattered and, quite suddenly, it was quiet, and very, very still.

He heard the door beside him open, and he tried to turn his head to speak. He was very tired. He closed his eyes.

He didn't feel a thing when they pulled him from the car.

Chapter 9

Beneath the flat, uncompromising glare of the fluorescent lights, Quinn looked pale and hollow-eyed. That he was preoccupied was evident; a sandwich, dry and beginning to curl, sat untouched beside the phone.

"Got your message and came as soon as I could," McCrimmon said. "But you know how Wellington is. Tomorrow's Saturday, and we had to go over the security arrangements for every sight-seeing trip. I've drawn the helicopter ride," he ended disgustedly. He straddled the visitor's chair, picked up the sandwich, sniffed at it suspiciously, then threw it in the wastebasket. Quinn didn't even protest.

"Something to do with Minelli," McCrimmon prompted. "Is the autopsy report back?"

Quinn shook his head and let out a long, explosive sigh. "It's been one helluva day, Bill," he confided as he glanced at the clock. 11:25. "Sorry to get you down here at this hour, but so much has happened that I'm afraid I might have missed something. I've got that kind of feeling, know what I mean?"

McCrimmon nodded and waited for the corporal to continue.

"Minelli's body was sent to Calgary this afternoon, but they won't have anything for us until some time tomorrow. I checked about an hour ago just in case, but they'd packed it in for the night.

McCrimmon grunted. He'd hoped to have something earlier.

Quinn tilted back in his chair and stretched his hands above his head to ease his cramped muscles. "Had a bad one at the level crossing just off the highway on the back road to Tunnel Mountain," he went on soberly. "Two guys in a car hit a train. Wiped 'em out, and I mean wiped!"

McCrimmon nodded. "I heard about it," He said. "Have they been identified?"

Quinn scratched his head. "They're certainly not locals," he said. "Don't know who they'll turn out to be. It was a weird one right from the start." Quinn would not be hurried. He scratched his head again and linked his hands behind his head.

"As near as we can figure it, the whole thing started right here in the middle of town. A guy in a truck rear-ended a guy sitting at the lights over on Wolf Street. There must have been some kind of argument because they both lit out hell-bent-for-election; the guy in the truck apparently chasing the guy he hit. The first guy, the one who got hit, was in a green Ford; that's about the only thing the witnesses do agree on. The second guy, the one who hit him, was in a half-ton, three-quarter ton . . . whatever. From there on it's anybody's guess. Some witnesses tell it like it was a race; others say the truck was chasing the Ford. Anyway, somewhere along the line this white Plymouth, the one that hit the train, got into the act. Whatever they were up to, they roared all over town. Creamed the shit out of Arnie Goldman's new Cadillac. He's been waiting four months for that thing to arrive. First time out today." Quinn stopped and grinned crookedly.

McCrimmon's face began to crease. "Anyone hurt?" he asked, barely holding back the smile.

"Nope, not a scratch on Arnie," Quinn said. "But there ain't much left of the front of his car. No bumper, no radiator, no lights. Shaved right off."

The two men sat grinning at each other across the

desk as their imaginations went to work. Arnie Goldman was not one of their favorite people. Big, brash, beefy, and rich, that was Goldman; a man who thought money could buy anything he happened to want, including special consideration from the local police.

"He was kind of mad when we got there," the corporal went on. "But he was a helluva lot madder by the time we left. Three witnesses testified that he'd tried to run a red light and they had to scatter to get out of his way." Quinn shrugged, grinning broadly. "Didn't have any choice. We had to charge him."

"Oh, Judas!" McCrimmon groaned, but the smile remained on his face. "What happened then?"

Quinn thought for a minute. "Well, I guess the Ford and truck came around this way next, and doubled back right outside this building. Some of the boys heard them but by the time they got outside, the truck and car were gone. Damned near killed a girl over on Banff Avenue. Sideswiped a few cars along the way; tore up Buffalo and went on up Tunnel. Came close to creaming a bus; wrecked a motor home up by Douglas Fir Chalets, and bent a backhoe out of shape and shook up the operator."

McCrimmon regarded Quinn in amazement.

"After that, we're not too sure," the corporal went on. "It's obvious the Plymouth didn't make it across the tracks. It was lying third when two kids saw it down by the Hoodoos. They estimated the speed at close to a hundred, but they could have been exaggerating some." The Hoodoos, pillared sandstone formations carved by time and weather, were not far from the railroad crossing. The thought of cars racing down that twisting piece of narrow road, even at half that speed, sent involuntary shivers down McCrimmon's spine.

"The Ford and the truck made it across the tracks just ahead of the train," Quinn continued. "The Plymouth didn't. Jeez! What a mess!"

"What about the other two?"

Quinn shook his head. "That's one of the weird

things about this whole, screwy business," he said. "We know they only went down the highway as far as the turnoff to Two Jack Lake because they almost wiped out a guy and his family in a minibus part way up there. But after that they vanished. The guy in the minibus was so shook up he stopped. Both he and his wife say they think they heard a crash further up the road but they can't be sure."

"They didn't go and look?"

Quinn shrugged. "I guess the kids were shaken up and crying. The guy was scared, so he got mad. All he could think about was getting down here to yell at us for not patrolling properly to keep that kind of thing under control."

"You figure they went over the edge?"

Quinn scratched his head again. "I've had a couple of men up there searching the whole area," he said. "They found some broken glass not far from where the witness says he was when they almost hit him. And some chunks of rubber. Looks like a tire blew, but it was getting dark, so it's hard to tell whether or not there's more to be found up there. Not a sign of the car or the truck. Funny thing," he mused, "there's no dropoff for half a mile. I don't see how they could have gone over the edge."

"What have you got in the way of a description?" McCrimmon asked. "Plates? Make of truck?"

"The truck was red and the Ford was green," Quinn said. "And that's about all anyone can agree on. No license numbers; one witness said they were both carrying Alberta plates, but others weren't sure. No make or year on the truck. One said Fargo, another said Chev. The Plymouth, by the way, was rented in Calgary ten days ago."

"No accident victims reported? Hospitals?" Quinn shook his head.

"What about the two men who were killed? Have they been identified?"

Quinn made a wry face. "We have too damned much

ID on those guys," he told McCrimmon. "The stuff in their wallets matched Canadian passports they were carrying, and they look genuine as hell, but now we're not so sure. We found a key to a motel on the one we believe to have been the driver." He grimaced. "Poor bastard got his legs and head cut clean off." He shuddered at the memory.

"We found two more passports in their luggage at the motel, one U.S., the other issued in Argentina last month. The names in the passports were different, but the pictures were the same." McCrimmon sat up straighter. "Yeah, I thought you might find that interesting," Quinn said, "and there's something else you'll find very interesting. We found a piece of paper in one guy's pocket that had Minelli's name and address on it, and a sketch of the streets leading to his place, starting at Banff Avenue and Wolf. Minelli's car was left on that route. And then, of course," Quinn said very softly, "there were the guns."

If there had been any doubt about him having McCrimmon's full attention, there was none now.

"They both had guns," Quinn went on. "Czech, nine millimeter, short-barrel jobs with silencer attachments. Very professional. Certainly not the kind of thing the average tourist carries with him. I've alerted Security. They're coming down tonight."

McCrimmon whistled softly. "And I thought I'd had a hard day," he said. He eyed Quinn with new respect. "I'd say you've covered a hell of a sight more than most in the time you've had. I suppose the Security Service wants you to hold everything until they get here?"

Quinn nodded. "As a matter of fact, they put it just a little stronger than that," he grinned. "But I'm still looking for those other two clowns, Security or not. It's funny how they just disappeared like that."

McCrimmon glanced at the clock. "I agree," he said, "but I think you'd better get some sleep first." He yawned. "You've done enough damage for one day."

The telephone rang persistently. McCrimmon rolled over on his back and remained there, still half asleep. He listened to it ring twice more before groping blindly for the bedside extension.

"McCrimmon," he mumbled hoarsely.

"Bill, it's Paul." Cavanna's voice was low and urgent.

McCrimmon heaved himself up on one elbow and stared at the clock. The hands stood at ten minutes to five. He came wide awake. "Yeah, Paul. What's wrong?"

"I thought you ought to know," Cavanna said. "Your girl friend, Jacintha Lee, checked out of the hotel."

Confused, McCrimmon checked his watch. It showed the same time as the clock. "What the hell do you mean, checked out? It's ten to five in the morning."

"Believe me, I'm well aware of that," Cavanna said wearily. "I've been up since four myself."

"What's going on, Paul?"

"One of our guests came back about three-thirty, drunk as four boiled owls," the security chief explained. "He tried to drive his car up the front steps into the lobby. When our people tried to stop him, he threatened to sue everybody from the desk clerk to the combined board of directors of the CPR. And, because he happens to be the director of one of our leading corporations, the people on duty got me out of bed. By the time I got here, the guy had flaked out on the couch in the lobby. They have him safely tucked away for the night now, but he's going to have a hell of a head in the morning, I sincerely hope."

"What's that got to do with Jacintha?"

"Sorry, I'm tired and I'm rambling. One of the bellmen happened to mention that he'd sure had a funny shift. First there was this guest checking out at two in the morning, then this."

"Jacintha checked out at two in the morning?"

"That's who it turned out to be. Not many people

do that, so I was curious. Sure enough, it was our girl. I checked her room and the parking lot. The room's clean, the bed hasn't been slept in, and her car's gone." He paused, then added, "She didn't go alone, Bill." McCrimmon remained silent. "Some guy, I can't get any description except 'average', paid the bill in cash. Another guy, described as 'fairly tall, fair, but otherwise average', walked her to her car. The bellman says she appeared to be leaving willingly."

McCrimmon chewed his lip. He didn't like the implication of Cavanna's words.

"Sorry, Bill," Cavanna said, "but there's nothing more I can do. A guest left, the bill is paid in full. That's it, Bill, but I thought the least I could do was to let you know."

McCrimmon grunted wearily. "I know," he said. "Thanks for letting me know, Paul. I'll see you later on today. Oh, and Paul, don't let anyone into that room until I've had a chance to take a look at it, eh? I'll be down about eight."

"That much I can do," Cavanna said. "But I don't think you'll find very much. I'd say the room's been cleaned out very thoroughly." Suddenly, he yawned.

"I know just how you feel," McCrimmon said, and hung up.

The first sensation Norman Kellerman experienced as consciousness returned was pain. It pulsed with fierce insistence, like fire eating its relentless way through nerve and bone and tissue. He fought to stay unconscious, to return to merciful oblivion; but, perversely, his brain began to clear and the pain intensified. He arched his back in agony. Beads of sweat stood out across his pain-distorted brow. A searing bolt of pain forced his jaws apart. He screamed.

Inch by reluctant inch the pain receded until, at last, it settled like a wounded beast around his right leg, throbbing with every beat of his straining heart. He opened his eyes and blinked at the glare of the naked bulb directly overhead. Dimly, at first, and then more clearly, he saw the figures standing there, silent, impassive, like doctors at a bedside. They should be in white coats, he thought, and closed his eyes against the glare. He knew they were not doctors.

A vicious stab of pain made him gasp and his eyes flew open. The man closest to him leaned forward into the harsh circle of light. His face, it seemed to Kellerman, was made up of broad, flat, chiseled planes. A memory stirred, then slipped away again. The naked bulb accentuated coarse-woven eyebrows incongruously stuck on like strips of tangled fur above deep-set obsidian eyes. They observed without expression, probed without feeling from the darkened hollows beneath the beetling brows. Memory stirred more urgently. That face! It slipped away again as the man spoke.

"You are experiencing some pain, Mr. Kellerman," he said without inflection of emphasis. It was a clinical statement of fact that sent a shiver coursing through his body. He tried to move to hide the telltale sign of weakness, but he knew the watching eyes had seen it.

His mind was clearer now. The pain was centered in his leg. He remembered feeling it twist and snap when the car slammed sideways into the wall of rock somewhere up near Two Jack Lake. He remembered, too, being lifted into the truck. After that, only faint impressions. A man with rimless glasses, a hypodermic needle, a woman's voice asking if he was badly hurt. He felt again the arm around his shoulders and the fingers resting lightly against his throat ready to choke off any cry for help. The truck jerking back and forth, the huge hand on the gear shift, then nothing until the agonizing return to consciousness beneath the naked light.

Sweat ran down his forehead and into his eyes. He tried to wipe it away but his arm refused to move. He knew before he tried it that the other would be just as powerless. And something was happening to his senses.

Images that had been out of focus became sharp and crisp and clear. His hearing was acute; he could hear the rhythm of the breathing patterns made by the silent watchers gathered round him. There were four of them; he could hear them quite distinctly. And he could hear his own heartbeat like hammerblows inside his head.

He was lying on something that felt like boards, a table or a trestle; he could not tell. His arms were stretched and held in metal clamps above his head. His left ankle was also clamped, but he didn't want to try the right one for fear of bringing back the pain. And he was completely naked.

The face above him nodded as if in answer to an unspoken question. "I see you realize your position, Mr. Kellerman." The voice rumbled deep inside the throat, a harsh, menacing sound. It evoked an unreasoning sense of panic and his limbs began to twitch uncontrollably.

Again, the owner of the voice seemed to read his mind. "You have been given an hallucinogen, Mr. Kellerman. It heightens your awareness to a remarkable degree, and it is particularly effective in lowering your tolerance to pain." The voice took on an almost apologetic tone. "You see, Mr. Kellerman, we have so little time. You have certain information. We need it and we intend to get it as soon as possible. I regret the need for such painful measures, but I'm sure you understand my position." He spread his hands as if to say they both knew how the game had to be played.

A tremor started in Kellerman's right leg. Pain stabbed him again and he fought to control the palsy, but it would not be denied. It wracked him from head to foot and he arched his back in sweating agony.

The face above him smiled unpleasantly. "I'm afraid you're going to have to do much better than that," the man said with mock concern. "You see, Mr. Kellerman, your leg is broken and the bone is quite shattered at the knee. As you have discovered, movement is very, very painful." He paused to make sure he had Kellerman's full attention. "I'm going to ask you some questions. Each time you fail to answer them convincingly I shall be forced, reluctantly, you understand, to remind you of the condition of your leg." He leaned back until his face was partly in the shadows, waiting as if to let the words sink in. One of the other figures beyond the pale circle of light stirred as if in anticipation. The face appeared again, descending until the jet-black eyes were mere inches away from Kellerman's sweating face.

"Now that you understand the rules, Mr. Kellerman, let us waste no more time. Tell me, which one of the Chinese delegates is your spy?"

Tears flowed uncontrollably from his eyes as Kellerman shook his head and gasped, "I don't know. I haven't been told. I can't tell you anything. I . . ."

The shriek torn from his throat resounded in the narrow room. It crashed against the concrete walls and splintered into a million shards of brittle, piercing sound. His twisted, pallid face went ashen gray beneath the sheen of sweat. His mind sought feverishly for escape, but a tiny pinch of chemicals and the fiendish ingenuity of man completely blocked retreat. The pain washed over him in waves, and like the waves, receded. The tremors gradually subsided.

The man spoke again. "You see, Mr. Kellerman, I told you nothing but the literal truth. Please do me the courtesy of telling me the truth in return. I assure you, it will be much less harrowing for everyone." His hand moved to within an inch of Kellerman's shattered knee and hovered there. "I'm going to ask you once again," he said, enunciating each word slowly and distinctly. "If you do not tell me what I want to know, I'm going to turn you over to our friend, here. His name, for now at least, is Mike. You've already met him, although it's possible you don't remember. He is what you might call our resident expert on *persuasion*. Do you understand?"

As from a great distance, Kellerman heard the question. "Which one of the Chinese delegates is your spy?"

Like a giant seaslug emerging from the ocean floor, the chairman of the Chinese delegation pushed himself upright in bed and flung the morning newspaper to the floor. Sparks from his cigarette fell unheeded on the rumpled sheets and smoldered there awhile, then, one by one, went out. Wu Tan sat staring blankly at the wall. If headlines had been his goal, he had succeeded beyond his wildest hopes, for they were there, bold and brazen on page one, every scathing word he'd written for his press release.

But it was not, he knew, because the world was waiting breathlessly for news about an obscure weather seminar that his speech had catapulted him onto the front page; it was the second headline that shared the page with the text of his speech. He knew the item off by heart. Dateline, Peking.

SINO - U.S. TALKS BREAK DOWN

Citing the speech made by Dr. Wu Tan, chairman of the Chinese delegation to the Global Atmospheric Research Seminar currently being held in Banff, Canada, as "inflamatory, and calculated to embarrass the United States," Sherman Brubaker, U.S. Secretary of State, broke off talks in Peking today.

Prior to Dr. Wu Tan's speech, accusing the United States of spying on China, it was believed by observers here that an accord would be announced later on today. The talks were aimed at expanding trade, travel, and included a broad exchange of students between the two countries.

Members of Mr. Brubaker's staff expressed "surprise and shock" at Dr. Wu Tan's remarks.

Why? Why hadn't they told him? Wu Tan sucked at his cigarette only to find it had gone out. He flung it from him in silent fury. If only he had waited until Monday, the day originally scheduled for the speech. He groaned aloud and wiped his sweating forehead. If only he had waited; but, no, he had to bring it forward to show that he, Wu Tan, could single-handedly destroy the purpose of the seminar.

He fumbled for another cigarette and wished he had a drink. The smoke was dry and hot and burned his mouth. Just one drink. His eyes strayed to the telephone, but he stayed the impulse and dragged deeply on the cigarette. Make a strong statement, he'd told himself. Make it bold! The text the minister had given him was weak, too watered down. Even Yeung Chao had commented on it, obliquely, of course, as was his way. But, when he'd made the changes, Yeung Chao had expressed doubt and had urged him to return to the prepared text, to wait until Monday. And the more Yeung Chao had argued, the more convinced Wu Tan had become that *his* speech, *his* timing would be best.

The telephone beside the bed jangled harshly and made him jump. Wu Tan answered gruffly, expecting it to be the press again.

"One moment, please," a voice said in Chinese. "The ambassador is calling . . ."

Breakfast for the Chinese delegation was a dreary, tense affair. No one, it seemed, wished to be associated with them this morning, Wu Tan had seen to that, and they found themselves all but isolated in one corner of the dining room. They ate in silence, each preoccupied with thoughts he did not care to share.

Sung S'u-mah prodded at her grapefruit, her mind

still on the report she had received only minutes after the conversation between Wu Tan and the ambassador in Ottawa had ended. She knew precisely what the ambassador had said; knew also that Wu Tan's fate had not yet been decided only because Peking itself had not made up its mind. But when it did . . . She wouldn't like to be in Wu Tan's shoes. She stole a surreptitious glance at him. Certainly his appetite was unimpaired. He'd wheezed and grunted his asthmatic way through a mountain of scrambled eggs and toast, and then had ordered more. He looked up unexpectedly and caught her glance. He scowled and stuffed a piece of toast into a mouth already over-full.

Sung S'u-mah turned her attention to the grapefruit once again. And what of Yeung Chao? There was little doubt in her mind that he would be more than pleased by Wu Tan's misfortune. Indeed, he'd probably prodded him on in many secret, subtle ways. Even now his calculating little eyes darted in Wu Tan's direction as if hoping to see the fat man topple from his seat. Yeung Chao had visions of stepping into Wu Tan's shoes one day, and anything he could do to bring that day closer, he would do; of that, Sung S'u-mah was certain. But that might prove to be more difficult than he thought, for now the way was clear for her to move ahead. And, with the help of Wang Chen-yin, she could do it. The Department of Social Affairs, of which Wang Chen-yin was the undisputed head, had long desired to extend its influence in the scientific field. Perhaps they had been instrumental in prodding Wu Tan into . . . Sung S'u-mah thrust the thought aside. It was unwise to speculate even in the privacy of the mind.

Tai Ling, of course, was undoubtedly the better scientist; she'd have to give him that. But his career was already blighted, and he would prove no threat. She watched him now, his eyes fixed firmly on his plate, oblivious to the fact that his untouched eggs were, by now, completely cold. She knew the signs of old and wondered what was making him so nervous.

Her eyes shifted to Kuan Lo and, inwardly, she smiled. She knew his secret. She glanced back at Tai Ling's lowered head and wondered if he also knew, and was afraid. She decided not.

McCrimmon searched the room while Paul Cavanna looked on. Except for two slightly soiled towels and a partly used bar of soap, the room was devoid of evidence that Jacintha Lee had ever been there.

"Look at this, Paul," McCrimmon said as he closed the door of the bathroom cabinet. He pointed to the mirrored front. "Not even a smudged fingerprint. The whole place has been wiped clean." A muscle tightened in his jaw. "She's no amateur, I'll give her that," he said thinly.

"Either that or she has friends in the business," Cavanna agreed.

McCrimmon shot him a glance. "You mean her escorts? The ones she left with?"

"If they were 'friends'. "

McCrimmon remained silent, his eyes probing every corner until, at last, he seemed satisfied and moved to the door. "Thanks for letting me take a look, Paul," he told his friend. "I'd better get back to the Detachment. Quinn is being pushed pretty hard."

As they stepped outside, Cavanna laid a hand on McCrimmon's arm. "Look, Bill," he said quietly, "maybe it's none of my business, but what is it with you and this girl? You seem to be completely hung up on her. I've never seen you . . ."

McCrimmon cut him off. "You're right, Paul," he said evenly. "It is none of your business. Let's leave it there. Okay?"

Cavanna's jaw hardened, but he remained silent. They rode down in the elevator together, but they didn't talk again.

Corporal Quinn was on the phone when McCrimmon arrived at the office. He held up one finger to indicate he'd only be a minute, and gestured toward the open bag of doughnuts on the desk. McCrimmon shook his head and sipped cautiously at the coffee he'd brought in. It tasted of chlorine and mud. Spring-thaw water from Fortymile Creek. He choked but kept on sipping. It was an acquired taste.

"Thanks for letting us know," Quinn said into the phone. "I'll be expecting her." He dropped the instrument back in place. "Hey, Charlie!" he bellowed in the direction of the open door. "I'm expecting a visitor in a few minutes, a Miss Haggard. Bring her in, will you?"

"Will do," a voice replied.

McCrimmon persevered with his coffee. The chlorine appeared to be winning out over the mud. "What's that all about?" he asked.

"I think we've got ourselves a break," the corporal said. "A woman says she saw the green Ford and the truck up near Two Jack yesterday. That was Lou Harmon in Canmore; it's where the woman lives. He's sending her down to talk to us."

"How did you find her?" The chlorine was making McCrimmon's eyes water. He reached into the open bag and helped himself to a doughnut.

"We didn't," Quinn said, following the sergeant's example. "She called Lou. It seems that she saw the accident yesterday on her way home from work. She stopped and spoke to two men who were taking a third man away in the truck. According to her, he looked as if he'd been hurt pretty bad."

"Well, I guess it worried her, so she phoned Lou early this morning to see if he knew how the injured man was doing. When she described the accident and the location, he went straight out to see her because the description matched the APB we sent out last night."

"No sign of either vehicle yet?" The coffee was almost palatable strained through a mouthful of doughnut.

Quinn shook his head. "I don't understand it," he confessed. "From the way those tire tracks go into the side of the mountain, I'd say that car's got to be pretty banged up. There are chunks of rubber all over the place, and glass and green paint. It looks as though someone took the trouble to haul it out of there, but if they did I don't know what they did with it. It hasn't shown up in any of the garages in town, and I doubt if they'd haul it any further." He nibbled thoughtfully on the doughnut.

"Got any ideas, Bill?"

McCrimmon shook his head. "Let's wait until we've heard what this lady has to say," he advised. "You might try checking the road for stray pieces. If someone did haul it away, the odd part may have fallen off along the way."

"That's a possibility," Quinn agreed. "I'll get someone on it right away."

The muffled thud of booted heels sounded outside the door, and Charlie appeared. "Miss Haggard to see you, Corporal Quinn," he announced formally, ushering in a tall, thin woman with graying hair and pale blue eyes.

"Bring another chair in, Cha—Constable," Quinn said. He came around the desk to greet the woman. "I'm Corporal Quinn," he said, "and this is Sergeant McCrimmon. The sergeant has an interest in this case."

The woman acknowledged the introduction, then turned to McCrimmon who had also risen. "Are you a detective?" she asked.

He shook his head. "No, Miss Haggard, I just happen to be on a special assignment at the moment. That's why I'm not in uniform. Can I get you a cup of coffee?"

Miss Haggard favored him with a disapproving stare. "No thank you, young man," she said sternly. "Coffee isn't good for you, you know."

Charlie reappeared pushing a tilter chair ahead of him. The sergeant took it from him and closed the door. "Please have a seat, Miss Haggard," he invited. The woman sat gingerly on the very edge of the chair. The doughnut bag had somehow disappeared from the top of the desk. Quinn, looking every inch the policeman, sat waiting for them to settle.

"I appreciate your taking the time to come in, Miss

Haggard," the corporal said by way of trying to put the woman at ease. She sat bolt upright, her long, thin fingers clutching a huge soft-sided handbag as if she feared someone would try to take it from her. She nodded in acknowledgment, but said nothing.

"Could I have your full name and address?"

Miss Haggard gave it. "Will I have to give evidence in a courtroom?" she asked.

Quinn flicked a glance at McCrimmon and hesitated for a second before framing a reply. The woman was poised as if ready for flight. He didn't want to risk losing the only witness he had to what had transpired on the road to Minnewanka.

"We're not quite sure what happened here ourselves," he answered carefully. "We're hoping that you can shed some light on the matter. Perhaps, when we've heard what you have to say, I'll be in a better position to answer your question." McCrimmon made a mental note to chalk one up for Quinn. Somehow, it always surprised him that the corporal could be so diplomatic when he chose to be.

But the woman's reaction surprised them both. "Oh, I *do* hope so," she breathed. "I've never been inside a courtroom. What would you like me to say?" She settled back in the chair and looked expectantly at Quinn.

"Perhaps you could begin by telling us how you happened to be on the road up by Two Jack Lake last night, and what it was you saw there," Quinn suggested. "Just tell us in your own words and take your time. You won't object if I take a few notes, will you? Just to keep the record straight."

The woman shook her head. "Not in the least," she told him. "Do I have to sign a statement afterward?"

Another TV fan. "Quite possibly," Quinn said. "Now, then, Miss Haggard, how did you happen to be on that road last night?"

The woman tightened her grip on the handbag, took a deep breath, and plunged into her story while Quinn kept pace in shorthand. "Well, you see, I live in Canmore but I work in Banff. I drive in each day; I'm the cashier, that is, the *head* cashier at the new self-serve service station over on Banff Avenue, you know. I used to work in the office — that's before it became self-serve, of course — but Tom — he's the manager there — that's young Tom, of course, because old Tom — young Tom's father — died during the winter — do you remember that? He used to have the service station further down until they widened the road and he lost a lot of business, and that's when he decided to move to our new location. Well, he said — that's young Tom, of course — he's my boss now — that I could try working in the glass booth if I wanted to because there wasn't as much work to do in the office since we became self-serve. So I said I would try it for a month and see what it was like because it's such a change from working inside all the time and it gets very cold out there — the cold strikes up from the cement, you know, but Tom had a heater put in and it's not as bad, now. Of course, it's getting warmer, now, isn't it? I'm sure I don't know what it will be like next winter. I hope I don't have to leave there because I've worked for them for, oh, let's see, now — It was the year before they started putting the Rundle stone facing on the stores across the street . . ."

"Could we go back to yesterday and why you were up near Two Jack Lake last night?" Quinn interrupted.

The woman stared at him. "But I was trying to give you the background," she told him. "I was coming to that."

"The courts prefer to deal with just the relevant facts," Quinn said gently. "You were going home from work, I believe. What time was that, Miss Haggard?"

"Well, it would be sometime after six, I'd say. Pretty close to quarter past six. You see, I sometimes take that road home just for a change. It's a bit out of my way, but I live alone since Mother died, so it doesn't matter what time I get home — except to Victoria, of course — that's my cat — who has to be fed by seven or she'll simply tear the carpet to ribbons. I tried putting down a mat just inside the door — she always tears it up there — but she knew the difference, the little monkey. Mother never did like cats — wouldn't have one in the house, but Will Tupper — he lives just three houses down — he's retired now, of course, but he used to have a farm on the other side of the Indian Reserve — oh, must be eight or nine years ago — brought this little tiny kitten over on the Sunday, the day after the funeral — I suppose he thought it would be company for . . ."

"Miss Haggard," Quinn said patiently, "this may take some time, so perhaps if we could get on to what you saw yesterday?"

The woman nodded agreeably. "Of course," she said. "Now, where was I?"

"You were making your way home about six fifteen," Quinn prompted.

"Ah, yes, of course. Well, as I said, I was just taking my time and I'd passed the campgrounds up at Two Jack Lake when I came around the corner and had to stop suddenly for this truck. It was half-way across the road, pulling a car out of the ditch — well, it wasn't really a ditch, it's more of a slope that drops away from the shoulder of the road where they've blasted the rock away. The side of the car was all smashed in and there was glass and bits of tire all over the road. I assumed, at first, that the car had blown a tire and smashed into the wall. It must have been going very fast."

Quinn looked up from his notes. "You said 'at first'," he quoted. "Did something make you change your mind?"

Miss Haggard nodded vigorously. "That was just one of the peculiar things about the accident," she said. "You see, the lid of the trunk was missing, and the back of the car was all smashed in. It looked as if something had rammed into the back of it, and I wondered if that was why it had gone off the road. The lid of the trunk wasn't in the ditch and it wasn't in the back of the truck, and there was nowhere else it could be. I looked; I couldn't see any sign of it."

"We found it," Quinn broke in before Miss Haggard could begin to speculate upon what might have happened to the trunk lid. "It was some distance away from the scene of the accident. Please go on."

Again, Miss Haggard nodded vigorously. "I *knew* it wasn't there," she said, determined to have the last word on the subject."

"What about the people?" Quinn prodded gently. "How many were there?"

"Three, all men," the woman said promptly. "There was the driver of the truck, a big, surly man. I didn't like him at all. He had hair all over the back of his hands — I'm sure there must be *something* people like that can do about it. It's so, so *unnatural*." She shuddered delicately.

"What about the others?"

"Oh, yes, well, there was this other man — he wore glasses without rims — you know the ones I mean? You don't see them much any more, do you?"

"No, you don't," Quinn agreed. "Did . . ."

"I remember Harvey Travis used to have a pair," Miss Haggard mused. "You probably don't remember him — he used to run the bookstore before it was made into a restaurant — at least, part of it was. They had those funny little mother-of-pearl things that used to make little red marks on the side of his nose. He used to stick Band-Aids across the bridge of his nose — it used to blister, especially in the summer — but the glasses would slip down and he was always looking over the top of them."

"What did he look like?" Quinn broke in hastily.

"Harvey Travis? Oh — oh, dear me — no, of course not." Miss Haggard clucked her tongue at her own mistake. "You mean the man with the driver, don't you?" Quinn merely nodded, fearful of interrrupting her. "Well, let me see. He was older. He looked, oh, I don't know, sort of out of place in the truck, you know, more like a businessman. I guess it was because he was wearing a suit." She thought about that before going on. Apparently satisfied with her own explanation, she continued. "He had his arm around the third man, sort of holding him up. He — that is, the third man — was unconscious."

Quinn frowned. "Unconscious?" he repeated.

"Well, I didn't realize he was unconscious right away," Miss Haggard amended. "I thought he was drunk at first. It was only after I saw the blood on his face and clothes that I realized he must have been the driver of the car. Of course," she went on uncertainly, "I suppose he could still have been drunk. I was absolutely horrified."

Miss Haggard stared hard at Quinn and set her jaw determinedly.

"I'm not sure I understand," he ventured. "You say you were horrified?"

"Of course," the woman replied with some asperity. "I've taken First Aid courses, you know. You should *never* move a person under circumstances such as those unless you know exactly what you are doing. They could have killed that poor man. They should never have put him into the seat of that truck. I told them so."

"You told them so?" McCrimmon blurted out. He had been silent for so long that both Miss Haggard and Quinn turned to look at him.

"Yes I did, Sergeant," the woman said. "I got out of my car and went over to the driver. I asked him if the man had been hurt in the accident, and he said yes, he had. I told him they should not have propped him up like that, but he as good as told me to mind my own business." She sniffed and clutched her handbag even more determinedly.

"And then?" Quinn prompted.

"Well, the other man — the man with the glasses — told the driver to be quiet. He explained that they had been following their friend's car when it had blown a tire and spun out of control. He said that their friend was mostly shaken up, but they were taking him to a doctor to be checked over. When I asked him why they were taking up precious time with the car, he said that their friend had been most upset about leaving it, so they were going to tow it in for repairs. I didn't believe a word of it."

Quinn nodded encouragingly. He didn't want to stop her now.

"I think they had something to do with running that car off the road," Miss Haggard said darkly. "I've been thinking about it. The truck had scratches on one of the front fenders; they were fresh, too, you could tell that. I see a lot of cars and trucks come into the service station. Believe me, I've seen a few damages in my time. I could tell you stories. I remember just last year when John Sondegaard — he's the insurance adjuster, you know — came out to look at those two vehicles that hit head on out by the overpass — you probably know John; he works with the police all the time — where the young man and his fiancée were killed, and the woman in the other car was thrown clear without a scratch but her husband went through the windshield? Well, they brought those cars in to the fenced area behind the garage — it's been cut off by the alley now that we've gone self-serve, but . . ."

"I'd like you to concentrate on this particular case, if you will, Miss Haggard," Quinn said. His voice sounded slightly strained.

"But, of course, I'm coming to that." Miss Haggard looked faintly surprised that anyone could have doubted it. "As I was saying, I've seen a few damages in my time, and the back of that car was all smashed in as if something had given it a terrific wallop. There was no way that could have happened by hitting the rock wall."

The two policemen exchanged glances.

"And you should have seen that poor man. He looked terrrible. His breathing was irregular and he was mumbling something, but I couldn't make out what it was. The driver kept revving the engine. I think he was doing it on purpose just so I wouldn't hear what the man was saying." Miss Haggard stopped and shook her head as she recalled the scene.

"Please continue, Miss Haggard," said Quinn. "What happened then?"

"Well, I drive a station wagon," the woman went on. "It's so much more handy than the sedan we used to have when Mother was alive. Of course, she liked it, but when Finlay — he's the mechanic who used to work for Tom at the old garage — that's old Tom, of course — Finlay never worked for young Tom — they never did get on very well, those two. I don't know why." Miss Haggard paused to think about that, but Quinn cut in on her thoughts.

"You were saying that you drive a station wagon, Miss Haggard. "How, exactly does that . . .?"

"Oh, yes, of course, that's exactly it, isn't it?" she said earnestly. "You see, I offered to put the injured man into the back of my station wagon and take him down to the hospital myself. I was quite prepared to do that even if Victoria had to wait for her dinner and clawed the carpet, but they refused to let me do that. Finally, they just drove off up the road, pulling that dreadful car behind them. I've never heard of anything so ridiculous in all my life! It bothered me all the way home, and I kept thinking about it all last night." Miss Haggard lapsed into silence for several seconds. "I think they were *up* to something," she said at last. "If that man was really their friend, they wouldn't have bothered with the car, no matter what he said. Anyway, the car was completely off the road; it wasn't in anybody's way. It was still bothering me this morning. That's why I telephoned to find out how the poor man was." She looked searchingly at Quinn. "What *did* happen out there?" she asked. There was genuine concern in her voice.

"I'm afraid we're just as puzzled as you are," Miss Haggard," Quinn said. "And, until we find out more, I'd appreciate it if you would keep what you have told us to yourself."

Miss Haggard's eyes narrowed shrewdly. "I had begun to suspect as much," she said, lowering her voice conspiritorially. "It's a kidnapping, isn't it?"

"You see, now, why we have to proceed so very carefully, Miss Haggard," Quinn said, leaning across the desk to emphasize his words. "I'm sure we can rely on you."

"Oh, indeed you can. You can. Indeed you can," the woman breathed.

Quinn leaned back and looked at his notes. "You said they drove off *up the road*," he said. "Did you mean that literally, Miss Haggard? They actually went on up toward Minnewanka?"

"That's right," she agreed.

"Can you describe the car and the truck?"

The woman nodded quickly. "The Ford was dark green, but you know that already, don't you, because you have the trunk lid. It was a Maverick, four door, nineteen seventy-five or six, I'm not sure which. I couldn't see the license plates because the front one was right up against the back of the truck, and the back one was all mangled up. The truck was red, red and white really, if they tore off the plastic." She saw Quinn's puzzled expression. "The truck had very wide white stripes along the sides of the box, but they were covered up with some kind of stick-on stuff the same color as the rest of the truck. It had started to peel off at one corner, that's why I noticed it."

Miss Haggard stopped as a thought struck her. "Of course! That's why the license plates were covered with mud. The truck was disguised. The plates couldn't be read!"

"Can you tell me anything else about the truck or the two men in it?" McCrimmon asked. "It's important, Miss Haggard, very important."

The woman thought for a moment, started to shake

her head, then stopped. "I'm not very good at describing trucks and things like that," she said, "but I can tell you who's got a truck just like the one I saw. Simon Lomax — you must know him; his father works for the Parks Department — works over at the industrial park somewhere — Simon, that is — not his father. His truck is green and white, but it's the same make and model, I'm sure of it. Brings it in to gas up every few days. Does that help?"

"We'll check it out right away," Quinn told her. "And thank you, Miss Haggard. You've been a great help to us."

The woman looked pleased. "It's not the first time, you know," she said.

"I beg your pardon?"

"It's not the first time that my family's helped the police, you know," Miss Haggard elaborated. "Back in the 'fifties, when my father was still alive, they were making this movie up here with that blonde girl in it — I can never remember her name — and there was this man who used to come into town to . . ."

Quinn closed his notebook and sighed.

Norman Kellerman had never thought of himself as a particularly brave man. Throughout the training devoted to physical and psychological torture he had felt slightly sick, and had fervently hoped that he would never have to employ or be part of the techniques taught there. That seemed such a long time ago.

A bomb exploded inside his head. Sharp, stabbing, excruciating pain pulsed through his twisted body and fever gripped his throat. The rasping, retching, strangled sounds he heard were his own as he struggled to draw in air past his broken nose and swollen tongue. His eyes flew open wide, and were beaten shut again by the glare of light inches from his face. His tongue probed for moisture and encountered only broken teeth.

He could hear them, whispering in the shadows just

beyond the white-hot light. He breathed a silent sigh of utter resignation because he knew he could not fight them any longer. And he knew with equal certainty that he would die without revealing what he knew simply because that was the way Guthrie would want it.

He felt their hands upon him once again, and smiled. The body on the table was not his. He watched as from afar; he could see them down there with their instruments of torture. He saw the body writhe in agony, heard the screams wrenched from his lips. He turned away.

He neither saw nor felt the last convulsion.

Chapter 10

When McCrimmon arrived at the passenger loading zone behind the hotel shortly after one o'clock, he found an argument in progress. The tour dispatcher, a short, thin man with the dark, sad eyes of a wounded Bassett, was backed up against the side of a bus. Wu Tan stood in front of him, a pudgy finger stuck threateningly under the dispatcher's nose. The man appealed to McCrimmon for help.

"This delegation is supposed to be on the bus," he told the sergeant breathlessly, "but they refuse to go. They say they've made other arrangements, but I've had no such instructions. I still show them on this bus and . . ."

"Hold it!" McCrimmon said as the dispatcher's voice began to rise. "Slow down and let's see if we can sort this out." He moved in closer, forcing the fat man to give ground. The dispatcher slithered gratefully to one side.

McCrimmon turned to the leader of the delegation. "Now, have other arrangements been made?" he asked quietly. "And if they have, would you mind telling me what they are?" Wu Tan sucked in his breath and took the measure of McCrimmon.

"Perhaps I can help . . .?"

The words were spoken quietly but with an air of authority. McCrimmon turned to see the woman he had noticed at the cocktail party. She was even more striking at close range. He inclined his head. "Please do," he said. "The sooner we know, the sooner we can have everyone on their way."

Wu Tan had also turned at the interruption, and now he flung the woman a malevolent glance which she affected not to notice. He stood there glowering, panting as if he had been running hard. A dark band of moisture circled the fat man's collar, and the pungent, unpleasant smell of peppermint mixed with stale sweat impinged upon McCrimmon's senses. The fat man wheezed and choked but said nothing.

The woman ignored him. "It was I who made the new arrangements," she said evenly. "The other delegates, as I'm sure you must be aware by now, have made it very clear that they do not wish to be associated with us outside the seminar. I took the liberty of making other arrangements for the tour, with the approval of our chairman, Comrade Wu Tan, naturally." The fat man snorted and turned on his heel. He pushed his way rudely past other delegates emerging from the hotel, and went to stand alone beside one of the buses. The woman followed him with her eyes, but McCrimmon found her expression impossible to read.

"You must excuse our chairman," the woman said, turning back to the sergeant. "His task is difficult and his path is strewn with many obstacles. He is not, perhaps, at his best today." The apology, McCrimmon decided, was for the record, nothing more.

"And the new arrangements are . . .?" he prompted.

"A separate car to take us to the airfield and bring us back," the woman said. "And separate aircraft when we get there. We would not wish to cause out colleagues," her arm swept in a deprecating arc around the courtyard, "further distress."

"And you made these arrangements yourself?"

"With the full knowledge and approval of the seminar director of special events," the woman assured him.

McCrimmon held up his hands, palms outward.

"I'm sure you did," he said disarmingly. "It takes time for changes like that to filter down to everyone. Tell me, is there room for me in your car?"

There was a moment's hesitation before the woman answered. "I believe so. Why?"

McCrimmon turned to the dispatcher. "Look," he said. "I'll accompany these people on the tour. Charlie Hapgood is assigned to the tour with me, but that was assuming that everyone would be on the same bus. He can still cover the bus; I'll take the car. Will you tell him that?"

The dispatcher looked relieved. Buses were full; both drivers and delegates were becoming impatient. "Thanks, Bill," he said gratefully. "I'll tell Charlie right away." He almost sprinted from the group.

"You are very diplomatic," the woman said. A smile hovered just out of sight. "You are a policeman, are you not?"

McCrimmon smiled and indicated his civilian clothes. "Today I'm just a tourist like everyone else," he told her. "If there's anything I can do to make your trip more pleasant, please let me know." His face grew serious. "I hope you don't mind if I ride with you."

Wu Tan who had rejoined the group made noises as if he were about to speak, but the woman cut in smoothly. "It will be our pleasure," she assured him. "Your name is . . .?"

"McCrimmon, ma'am. Sergeant Bill McCrimmon, RCMP."

"Sergeant McCrimmon," she repeated. The way she spoke his name was so exactly like the way Jacintha had spoken it that it was uncanny, but he wasn't given time to dwell on that. "I am Comrade Sung S'u-mah," she told him formally. Quite suddenly she smiled. "But, perhaps you would be more comfortable with my academic title, Doctor Sung S'u-mah," she said. "I'm told that Westerners feel uncomfortable with Comrade." Before McCrimmon could think of a suitable rejoinder, she turned and began to introduce the others.

Wu Tan ignored the introduction, but McCrimmon was prepared for that. Yeung Chao, however, was also distant, and McCrimmon wondered why. But Kuan Lo and Tai Ling seemed to be cut from different cloth. They reminded the sergeant of two youngsters on an outing. Kuan Lo even had a bag of Turkish delight, a confection for which both he and Tai Ling had developed an inordinate fondness. He offered the bag to McCrimmon but the sergeant shook his head.

"Thank you, but not just now," he told the little man. Kuan Lo looked so genuinely disappointed that McCrimmon relented and took a piece. A long, black limousine drew up behind the buses.

"Ah, there's our car," said Sung S'u-mah. "The driver is punctual; that is good." She led the way across the loading area assuming everyone would follow.

McCrimmon, walking behind Wu Tan, became conscious once again of the fat man's labored breathing. He wondered how the man would fare in the helicopter. He made a mental note to have a word with the pilot before they left the ground. The last thing they needed at the seminar was for the leader of the Chinese delegation to have a heart attack.

The drive to the airstrip just outside Banff was uneventful. Even the weather was being cooperative. High, diaphanous clouds drifted lazily beneath a dome of blue, although the breeze that stirred the trees was anything but warm. His charges would appreciate the warmth of their bright blue, hooded parkas, the sergeant thought. It could get very cold at 10,000 feet. The car turned off the highway onto a graveled track that wound its way around the perimeter of the airfield, a patch of flat valley bottom that nestled in the shadow of Cascade Mountain, boasting little more than a tarmac strip and a brand new windstock snapping briskly in the stiffening breeze.

The helicopters squatted in ungainly fashion at the south end of the field. A red and yellow tanker truck was drawn up beside one of the larger aircraft, an umbilical hose connecting them. Beneath the trees on the west side of the field stood two large vans with aviation logos on the side. Drivers, pilots, and mechanics lounged beside them. There were seven helicopters in all. Five Bell 204s, sturdy, powerful ten-passenger jobs, dwarfing the two Jet Rangers, each capable of carrying only four besides the pilot. It was toward the Jet Rangers that Sung S'u-mah now pointed.

"I could not get another helicopter capable of carrying all of us on such short notice," she said, "so we'll have to split our party."

She had, McCrimmon noted, assumed complete control of the group, and no one, including Wu Tan, seemed inclined to challenge her authority. He wondered about that; wondered if she drew that authority from some other source. Chinese Security, perhaps? He resolved to treat her with cautious respect. The driver swung the car around and stopped some distance from the aircraft. Behind them, buses rumbled to a standstill and the passengers began to file out. The pilots left their place beside the trucks and moved to greet the aerial tourists.

One of the pilots, a solid, chunky man with graying hair, detached himself from the group and came toward the car. "Doctor Sung?" he inquired, looking from one to another. Already his professional eye was judging size and weight.

The woman stepped forward. "You are Mr. Krell?"

"Fred Krell," the man acknowledged. He indicated a lanky youth who had come up beside him. "And this is Jack Partridge. He'll be piloting the other chopper."

Sung S'u-mah nodded as if something had been confirmed. "I'm Doctor Sung S'u-mah," she said. "Are you ready to take off?"

Krell's eyes swept over the group and stopped at McCrimmon. "Are you all going?" he asked.

Sung S'u-mah looked inquiringly at McCrimmon. "You are welcome if you wish to join us," she said.

McCrimmon had the strange impression that she

was laughing at him behind those dark, expressionless eyes. "I *am* supposed to keep an eye on you," he said. "Thank you."

"It is our pleasure," Sung S'u-mah assured him seriously. "I suggest that you accompany our chairman, Wu Tan, since he is the leader of our delegation." She turned to the fat man. "You have no objection, Comrade?" Wu Tan wheezed and shook his head curtly. Again, McCrimmon wondered at the command the woman held.

"Then it is settled," she announced with finality. "Comrade Yeung Chao will accompany you, while we three" — she indicated Tai Ling, Kuan Lo, and herself — will ride with Mr. Krell." McCrimmon resigned himself. He was not looking forward to squeezing into the confines of the helicopter cabin with Wu Tan, but the woman was right; Wu Tan was the number one man, at least on paper.

The pilots led the way across the tufted grass to where the Jet Rangers stood. Sung S'u-mah, walking ahead of McCrimmon, shivered visibly as the chill wind gusted down the length of the valley, and drew the hood of her jacket over her head. The wind had icy fingers, and McCrimmon was glad of the heavy sweater he wore beneath his coat. When they reached the aircraft, McCrimmon stood aside to allow Wu Tan and Yeung Chao to enter first. The fat man wheezed and puffed as he clambered awkwardly aboard. His face was mottled purple by the time he'd settled in the seat.

As Yeung Chao climbed in after him, McCrimmon drew the young pilot aside. "I wouldn't go any higher than you have to with him aboard," he advised, indicating Wu Tan. "I don't want him having a heart attack up there."

The young man looked alarmed. "Maybe we'd better not take him up at all if he's got a heart condition . . ." he began, but McCrimmon stopped him.

"I don't know that he even has a heart condition,"

he said. "It's just that he has trouble breathing whenever he exerts himself. You carry oxygen, don't you?"

Patridge nodded, his young face still serious.

"Okay, then. I'll keep an eye on him. If there's any sign of trouble, I'll let you know. How high will you be going?"

"Oh, depends, I guess, on what they want to see. "Eight, maybe ten thousand feet if we go up around some of the peaks. There shouldn't be any trouble at those heights, but you never know for sure."

"I'll keep an eye on him," McCrimmon repeated. "Come on, let's get going."

The pilot still looked dubious, but the other aircraft were already warming up. The huge blades swept cold blasts of air across the field, and dust swirled about their heads. Partridge nodded abruptly to McCrimmon, waited for the policeman to climb inside, then took his own place at the controls. The engine coughed; the blades began to turn. McCrimmon strapped himself in. Partridge adjusted the earphones and listened. A base station acting as ground control had been set up in one of the vans at the side of the field, and he just caught the end of a transmission instructing CF-JXT, one of the 204s, to take off. He watched as the helicopter lifted off, circled the field, then made its way down the valley.

The rest of the 204s quickly followed. Then it was their turn. The engine roared; the rotars whined; they lifted off and, with nose well down, they followed the path of the others to the south-west. McCrimmon glanced back at Wu Tan. The ominous purple tinge had disappeared, and his color looked almost normal. Beside him, Yeung Chao sat pale and tense, his eyes riveted on the receding ground. Partridge caught McCrimmon's eye, and the sergeant gave a reassuring nod. The pilot returned the nod and took the helicopter up to 6,000 feet. The wooded slopes of Mt. Norquay rose steeply on their right, and they caught a glimpse of open chairs and gondolas moving slowly up toward the tea house and the lookout point beyond. Below them, winding back and forth upon itself, the Bow River glinted in the sun and led them west then north toward the glaciers and the river's source.

Back at the airfield, the second Jet Ranger was still on the ground. Clearance had been given for it to take off, but Krell had notified control that there would be a delay. Now, control was asking what the problem was. Krell pushed the mike button once again.

"AGY to control. We have a sick passenger aboard. Repeat, we have a sick passenger aboard. I think we should have a stretcher. Over."

Even as control confirmed receipt of the message, one of the vans left the shelter of the trees and came across the grass toward them. The driver had obviously been monitoring the open channel. The van stopped a few yards away and the driver got out.

Inside the helicopter, Tai Ling was protesting that he didn't need assistance. "It's just a stomach cramp," he assured them several times, but his face was deathly pale and he winced as another spasm hit him. "Perhaps," he gasped, "I had better sit in the car for a little while. But it's nothing. It will pass, I'm sure."

"It's all that rubbish you've been stuffing yourself with," Sung S'u-mah told him unsympathetically, pointing to the half-empty bag Kuan Lo was holding. Kuan Lo looked startled and shoved the bag deep inside the pocket of his parka as if to hide it.

"Whatever it is," Krell said, "I'll have to leave him behind. He turned to Tai Ling. "I'm sure you'll be better off lying down," he said. "There will be other flights later on; perhaps we can arrange for you to take one of those."

Reluctantly, Tai Ling nodded and allowed the pilot to take his arm and help him to the ground. Sung S'u-mah slid from her seat and took Tai Ling's other arm. Kuan Lo made as if to follow, but the woman stopped him. "We can manage," she told him brusquely. Once more,

Kuan Lo felt that he'd been reproved. He watched as they made their way to the waiting van, supporting Tai Ling between them. Krell held him upright while Sung S'u-mah climbed inside the van to help the driver lift the ailing man onto the stretcher.

Inside the van, Tai Ling lay quiet. His face was very pale. The driver checked his pulse and nodded to Krell. "He'll be all right," he pronounced. "Probably something he ate." He snickered as if he'd said something funny. While Krell and the woman returned to the helicopter, the driver closed the rear doors of the van and climbed back behind the wheel. He drove very slowly across the bumpy field toward the trees.

Strapped in once more, Krell checked his instruments and the engine roared into life. He picked up the microphone. "AGY to control. AGY to control. We are ready for takeoff. Over."

Then answer crackled in the earphones. "Cleared for takeoff, AGY."

Krell turned in his seat and looked at his two passengers. "Everything okay?" he shouted above the roar of the engine. Two heads nodded simultaneously.

Krell opened the throttle and they were airborne. As the helicopter swung in a tight arc across the field, the woman watched the van grow smaller and finally disappear beneath the trees.

The moving van lumbered slowly down St. Julian Road, its driver peering from side to side as if searching for an address. He slowed beside the narrow driveway leading to *The Firs,* then swung the nose of the van into the middle of the road. His helper jumped down from the cab and guided the van backward between the gateposts and up the drive. Guthrie stood at the window watching the helper dodge from side to side, guiding the huge van carefully to within five feet of the front door where it stopped. The helper immediately climbed back inside the cab. Guthrie glanced across at the man who was staring intently at a panel equipped with lights and switches and video monitors. The man looked up as if he'd felt Guthrie's eyes upon him.

"All clear," he said quietly. "All sensors operating and we have a condition Green."

Guthrie took a slim metal box from his pocket and pressed a button. Inside the cab of the van a similar metal box mounted beside the driver gave off a single 'bleep' and a small green light began to wink. The driver reached beneath his seat and pressed a switch. The muted sounds of hydraulic gear in operation could be heard behind him.

Guthrie had left his observation post, and now he hurried down the hall and opened the front door. The rear doors of the van were already swinging open, blocking out all vision from the side. From the top of the van, a metal plate, ridged like a corrugated awning, slid out horizontally until it touched the house. And last of all, a ramp dropped down to rest upon the topmost step leading to the front door. A square tunnel now extended from the van to the house. Guthrie moved forward, hand out-thrust to greet the first man out.

"I trust you weren't too uncomfortable, Professor?" he said as a tall, white-haired man with craggy features walked across the ramp.

A pair of blue, deep-set eyes twinkled as the man grasped Guthrie's hand and shook it firmly. "Not at all," he said. "I quite enjoyed it." Then he added, "But watch out for Sorenson; he's done nothing but complain about these 'cloak-and-dagger bastards' ever since we started. I think it has something to do with the way you people spend money." He theatrically cupped a hand around his mouth. "His latest request was turned down by the subcommittee, I understand," he said in a stage whisper.

"I'll watch my step," Guthrie grinned. "It's the first door on the right. Go ahead and take a seat. Your place is marked."

The white-haired man led the way and seven others

followed. Guthrie wisely avoided direct confrontation
with Sorenson. When the last man had left the van and
was safely inside the house, Guthrie pressed the button
on the metal box again. Inside the cab the light went out,
and a second 'bleep', longer than the first, signaled the
driver to throw the switch once more. The ramp and
overhead panel retracted and the doors swung shut.

The van moved off. Throughout the entire
operation neither the driver nor his helper had caught one
glimpse of the men they had delivered to the house.

Malik's voice shook with suppressed rage. "Well, find
out and call me back as soon as you *do* know!" He
slammed the phone down and turned to Olsen.

"It begins," he said softly. "One of the Chinese
delegates was removed from the helicopter just before
takeoff. Apparently the man was suffering from stomach
cramps. He's been taken to hospital."

Olsen's eyes glinted behind his glasses. "Which
one?"

Malik slammed his fist on the table. "That, my
friend, is the one small detail they neglected to find out,"
he growled. "Our man couldn't get close enough to see,
and no one at the airfield seems to know. He was taken
to hospital in a closed van, but it happened so fast that our
people were caught off guard. They failed to see the
transfer, or, at least, to understand its signficance, and
they failed to follow the van. Now all we can do is check
at the hospital to see who arrived there." The muscles
in his jaw worked. "The van could have made a dozen
stops along the way."

"What about the house?"

Malik scowled. "Completely covered," he said
disgustedly. "We can't get within a block of the place
without tipping our hand. It's happening and we just
can't get close."

Olsen wisely chose to remain silent. Malik paced the
room. He paused before the clothing taken from
Kellerman, and picked up what was left of the jacket. It

had been torn to shreds in the vain hope that something would be revealed, anything that might give them a lead. He flung it savagely to the floor and resumed his pacing.

"Get rid of these," he told Olsen, kicking the shredded clothing out of his way. "And give Mikhail a hand with Kellerman's body. Get it out of here." He continued to pace, shoulders hunched, hands behind his back.

"Where . . .?" Olsen began tenatively.

Malik swung round, eyes ablaze. "Do I have to do all your thinking for you?" he demanded. "Where do you think? Somewhere out there where he won't be found. There are thousands of square miles of wilderness all around us. Leave him for the animals. After a few days out there no one will recognize him. Just make sure he won't be found for at least a week."

He resumed his measured pacing. "After that," he muttered, more to himself than to Olsen, "it won't make the slightest difference."

A short distance away, some two miles west of the entrance to Banff National Park, a seemingly unrelated incident was taking place that was to have a profound effect upon the lives of several people.

A bear, old, scarred from many battles, and half blind with cataracts, snuffled his way through the long grass in the ditch beside the highway in search of food. His tattered, cinnamon-colored coat blended almost perfectly with the patches of exposed gravel that broke the contours of the bank. From across the road his quivering nostrils caught the scent of smoke and, faintly, the smell of frying bacon. He raised his head, testing the wind, saliva already dripping from his mouth in anticipation. His empty belly grumbled as the juices flowed. His head stopped moving, the scent now strong as an unsuspecting camper threw more bacon in the pan. The old bear snorted happily. He lumbered up the slope and burst upon the open road with surprising speed.

The driver of the yellow Buick slammed on his

brakes and spun the wheel hard over, but it was far too late. The pedal was barely half way down when the bumper hit the bear and bowled it over. It fell beneath the wheels; the car lurched sickeningly over the body and shot off the road into the ditch. It hit the graveled bank obliquely. The radiator wrapped itself around the engine block, and the hood tore loose like so much brittle cardboard. The driver was slammed forward so hard into his safety harness that, for a moment, he lost consciousness. He hung there, too dazed to know if he'd been injured, yet his mind still registered the fact that the bear, far from being dead, was struggling to its feet.

He watched in stunned amazement as the bear dragged itself away, one hind leg dragging as if broken or dislocated at the hip. It lurched across the ditch in front of the car and made for the shelter of the trees.

Tears started from the driver's eyes as he slammed both hands down on the horn in sheer frustration. "You lousy, stinking son-of-a-bitch!" he screamed futilely. He hit the horn again and again long after the bear had disappeared. He was still hitting it and screaming invective when someone scrambled down the slope and pulled him from the car.

The long, crenellated massif of Mt. Eisenhower disappeared behind them as Partridge turned the helicopter west. Consolation Valley stretched northward, its lakes still frozen solid at the edges. Ahead lay the Valley of the Ten Peaks, with Mt. Fay looming on their left, Mt. Babel almost directly ahead. Partridge slowed their forward speed so that they seemed to hang suspended between the two 10,000 foot peaks. He pointed to the north where a great pie-shaped wedge of ice and snow was encircled by a host of jagged peaks.

"The Valley of the Ten Peaks," he shouted above the engine's roar. "Wenkchemna Glacier and Moraine Lake." If the pilot hadn't pointed it out, it would have been difficult to tell there was a lake there. It was still frozen completely over and covered with snow.

By the time they reached Horseshoe Glacier, they were flying at close to 10,000 feet. Wu Tan continued to wheeze but his color was normal, for him at least, and both he and Yeung Chao seemed to be completely absorbed in the unfolding panorama.

The chairman tapped Partridge on the shoulder. "What mountain is that?" he asked, pointing ahead.

"Mount Temple," the pilot told him. "It's over 11,000 feet."

"Take us over the top," Wu Tan directed.

Partridge glanced inquiringly at McCrimmon. The sergeant turned to Wu Tan. "It gets pretty cold up there," he told him. "And, of course, the higher we go the more danger there is of icing on the blades."

Wu Tan's jet-black eyes stared at McCrimmon from behind folds of wrinkled fat. "I did not ask for your opinion," he said scathingly. He prodded Partridge with a stubby finger once more. "I want to go over the top of that mountain," he repeated. "Do it."

Partridge looked across at McCrimmon and shrugged. "It's his charter," he mouthed silently. The helicopter began to climb.

Under Wu Tan's direction, the helicopter slowly circled the top of the mountain. The altimeter stayed steady at 12,000 feet. The view in every direction was magnificient. Even the unemotional Yeung Chao broke into a spate of Chinese as he drew Wu Tan's attention to various features of the breathtaking landscape. Partridge nudged McCrimmon and pointed to the right where the three 204s were holding a line-ahead pattern about three miles further north and some 2,000 feet below them.

Wu Tan caught the gesture. "What is over there?" he demanded.

"More glaciers," Partridge replied. "Lefroy and Victoria. They are the ones behind Lake Louise. Would you like to take a look?"

Wu Tan grunted and, after a moment of indecision, Partridge took it for an affirmative answer. He set a northward course and gradually dropped his altitude to 10,000 feet once more. By the time they reached Victoria Glacier, the other helicopters had disappeared. Partridge flew low over the fresh layer of snow, its virgin surface blinding in the brilliant sunshine.

"There are goggles in the locker," the pilot told McCrimmon, indicating a box beside the seat. "Better pass them out or we'll have some very sore eyes tomorrow." He dropped his own into place.

McCrimmon gave each of the passengers a pair of the tinted goggles, then put on his own. Immediately, the dazzling whiteness beneath them took on shape and dimension. Long, sweeping slopes swept down to the very edge of rocky promontories, only to arc back up again and hang suspended in midair. It was hard to believe that beneath the soft, powdery surface of freshly fallen snow lay hundreds of feet of ice, inexorably scouring away the solid rock below.

"We'll go over to the edge so you can see the layers of snow and ice," Partridge said. They watched as the terrain suddenly dropped away and they were staring down at the frozen surface of Lake Louise far, far below.

Wu Tan's eyes glistened behind the shaded goggles. "Take us down the wall," he instructed Partridge. "I want a closer look."

Partridge maneuvered the helicopter to within about 300 feet of the glacier face, but that did not satisfy his passenger.

"Closer," he ordered. "Right up against the face."

"It's dangerous," Partridge told him flatly, but he edged the little craft closer just the same.

It was the first time McCrimmon had seen anything like it in his life. The afternoon sun shone full on the giant wedge of uneven layers of ice compressed to vitreous hardness rivaling the rock itself. The sound of the engine and the steady beat of the blades reverberated against the icy cliffs. A huge chunk of snow tumbled from the overhanging lip and plunged a couple of hundred feet before it bounced against the next protruding ledge, disloding first a trickle, then a flood of powdered snow. It fell like a waterfall, cascading in breathtaking slow motion down the almost vertical slope.

It gathered speed and force. Within seconds they were watching a full-scale avalanche. Huge chunks of frozen snow the size of boxcars bounced and tumbled down the sloping wall and burst outward into space. A thunderous roar almost drowned the helicopter's engine, and the four men watched in awe and wonder as the torrent disappeared beneath them, leaving a swirling spume of snow writhing in the air. Turbulence from the avalanche hit them just as Partridge swung the helicopter away from the face of the glacier.

It was as if the floor had dropped from under them. The little craft swung crazily from side to side, spinning wildly round the axis of its own rotor shaft. Partridge fought grimly with the controls while the blades above them clawed desperately for purchase. Ashen-faced, his passengers clung to their seats, watching with fascinated horror as jagged outcrops rushed up to meet them with terrifying speed. The altimeter swung wildly; it was impossible to tell how far they had dropped in the past few seconds.

Then, as suddenly as it had started, the buffeting stopped. The blades bit into the air and the four men were thrust deep into their seats as Partridge poured on full power. The controls began to respond once more and he was able to guide the helicopter into a shallow dive, gradually pulling out of their vertical descent. Trees and rocks seemed almost to brush the aircraft as they leveled off. McCrimmon let out a long, convulsive breath. Partridge glanced across at him, a sickly grin on features that were tinged with green.

"Now, *that* was *close!*" he said. "Too damned close for me. I won't be trying that again."

"You won't hear any objections from me," McCrimmon told him with feeling. He heard a sound behind him and turned to see what it was.

Yeung Chao had his head down between his knees.

His shoulders heaved. He was being violently sick into a plastic bag thoughtfully provided for just such an eventuality. The sergeant swiveled further round to see how Wu Tan was faring. He need not have worried. The chairman sat hunched forward, his eyes fixed on the settling snow at the base of the mountain. He seemed oblivious to Yeung Chao's retchings. He caught McCrimmon's eye and jerked his head in the direction of the mountain face.

"Good," he pronounced thickly. "That was very good. It was worth the trip."

Despite his companion's obvious distress, Wu Tan insisted that they complete the tour. They continued north, following the Alberta-B.C. boundary and the chain of seemingly unending glaciers. They crossed Kicking Horse Pass and continued on as far as Peyto Lake before turning east and picking up the river once again, a winding silver ribbon that would find its way, eventually, to the Atlantic Ocean. They were still some thirty miles from Banff when Partridge suddenly reached for the microphone.

"C-F Delta Foxtrot Bravo," he intoned. "Come in AGY." He pressed the earpiece closer to his head. "Trouble," he said cryptically in answer to McCrimmon's quizzical glance. He pressed the button again. "I read you AGY. Is anybody hurt?" He listened intently for some time, then said, "We can't be more than a few miles away, Fred. I'll switch to ELT and follow it in. Out." The helicopter banked and headed west.

"Krell has had to make a forced landing," Partridge explained. "He's stuck half way up Mt. Babel. I'm going to take a look to see if there's anything I can do." The young pilot was not asking anyone's permission. His partner was in trouble and that was quite enough to override any objections his passengers might voice. Surprisingly, Wu Tan remained silent, while Yeung

Chao stared stoically out of the window, no doubt convinced that the fates were conspiring against him.

"Anyone hurt?" McCrimmon asked.

"Fred's got a banged-up hand, and the others have a few bruises, but apart from that, they're okay. It sounds as if they were mighty lucky."

"What about the helicopter?"

"It ain't gonna fly, that's for sure," Partridge said.

The pilot switched channels and turned the volume up on the cabin speaker. An insistent, undulating, raucous sound filled the tiny cabin.

"ELT," Partridge said by way of explanation. "Emergency Locator Transmitter. It triggers automatically on impact. We can follow it to its source by the strength of the signal."

The sound grew stronger. Mt. Babel loomed ahead. Partridge switched to voice frequency and cut the speaker off. The single earphone crackled and he pressed it hard against his head.

"You're cutting out, Fred," he said into the mike. "Say again very slowly." He listened intently, then acknowledged the message and set the mike aside. There was a frown on his face as he turned to McCrimmon.

"He says we're below him," he told the sergeant. "He says he's on a ledge about a thousand feet above us and to our right. Keep your eyes open. We're going up."

The little craft began to climb, its forward speed reduced almost to nil. The trees thinned out beneath them and stark crags of jutting rock topped with snow began to appear. A wind-whipped veil of snow swirled angrily from the summit, blocking out the open skies above. Capricious gusts buffeted the helicopter as it slowly clawed its way up the forbidding wall. Yeung Chao, still deathly pale, was prompted to ask about the danger.

"There's always a wind around Babel," Partridge told him. "But don't worry about it; we won't drop like we did before."

His words did little to reassure his passenger. Yeung Chao groaned and wrapped his arms tighter around himself as if by doing so he somehow gained more protection. Wu Tan favored him with a contemptuous glance.

"There he is!" McCrimmon pointed upward and to the right.

Partridge followed the line of McCrimmon's outstretched finger, and stared into a veil of snow. He held the helicopter steady, as steady as he could against the powerful gusts. The obscuring curtain parted.

The Bell Jet Ranger, twin to the one they were in, was perched like a broken toy on a ledge that couldn't have been more than fifty feet wide and forty deep. One blade was broken off and nowhere to be seen. The rotor shaft was bent, and there was damage to the tail where it had slammed against the wall. One skid had given way on impact, so the fuselage sat tilted at an awkward angle of some thirty degrees or more. Three figures stood beside it waving madly. They appeared to be unhurt, although the woman seemed to be supporting herself against the side of the helicopter, favoring her leg, McCrimmon thought. His eyes swept the ledge, but there was no sign of the other member of the Chinese delegation. He wondered about that but kept the thought to himself. Perhaps Partridge knew something he didn't want to pass on to his passengers. Oddly, neither remarked upon it.

The ledge itself was carved into the living face of the mountain like some giant toehold, a notch in an otherwise unbroken face. Above it, sloping back toward the summit, was a layer of snow that must have been seventy or eighty feet thick. If it should be dislodged it would wipe the crippled helicopter and its erstwhile passengers right off the face of the mountain. Partridge nervously edged the helicopter away, not wanting to start another avalanche. He picked up the mike and cut in the cabin speaker.

"There had to be a better place to land, Fred," he said

with false jocularity. "You know I can't take you off there, don't you?"

They saw Krell lean inside the cabin and reach for the mike. His voice came through strongly so that everyone could hear it over the noise of the engine.

"Get back to base and get a rescue party up here," he instructed. "They can get a chopper to drop a rescue team about a thousand feet below us. They'll have to climb from there. It doesn't look too difficult unless the weather decides to close in. We'll have to spend the night up here."

"If we could get one of the big choppers to drop a sling . . ." Partridge began, but Krell's voice cut him off before he could finish, and they saw his angry gesture as he stood beside the open door of the crippled helicopter.

"Forget it," he told the young pilot. "We'd be wiped out by an avalanche before he had the sling lowered. Do it my way, Jack."

McCrimmon watched the wind send streamers of snow horizontally into space, and shivered. Krell and his passengers could freeze to death in a matter of hours if they weren't well equipped with survival gear.

It was almost as if Krell had divined his thoughts. "We've got enough food and water to carry us through a few days," he said. "The bags in the chopper will keep us warm enough." His voice cut out, then something akin to a wry chuckle came over the air. "I've sure as hell camped in better spots than this," he said. "But there ain't one of 'em could beat it for the view." Before Partridge could respond, McCrimmon asked a quiet question.

"*Can* they survive the night up here?"

Partridge nodded. "Oh, yes, they'll be all right," he said. "We carry the best survival gear. I'm not worried about that." He gnawed his lip and indicated the overhang. "It would be much simpler if a rescue team could go in from the top," he said, "but they won't dare risk it with that sitting there. They'll have to come up from below, and I don't care what Fred says, that's a tough climb. And if the weather changes . . ."

He didn't have to complete the sentence for McCrimmon to get the picture.

Partridge brought the helicopter down just short of the trees at the edge of the airstrip. The passengers from the 204s were filing onto the bus, completely unaware of the drama unfolding only a short distance away. While Partridge had concentrated on getting back to the airfield as fast as possible, McCrimmon had radioed ahead, giving the position of the downed helicopter and a brief report on the condition of Krell and his passengers. Knowing that he was using an open radio channel, he had asked the pilots of the 204s to say nothing of the forced landing to their passengers, and hoped that none of them had their cabin speakers on. Fortunately, they didn't, and they willingly followed his advice.

As the sound of the engine subsided, McCrimmon helped Wu Tan and Yeung Chao to the ground. Once clear of the decelerating blades, he guided them toward the waiting limousine, but Wu Tan abruptly stopped. He turned and planted himself in front of the sergeant.

"Tai Ling," he snapped curtly. "Where is he? I saw nothing of him up there, and you spoke of only three people when you were on the radio. Is he dead?"

Partridge came up behind McCrimmon. "No sir," he put in, "he's not dead. He must be the gentleman who was taken ill and left the helicopter before it took off. I heard it over the radio."

Wu Tan shot a thunderous glance at Yeung Chao as if, somehow, it were his fault. But that individual was still trying to cope with his own problems. His face was still quite white and he was shivering. Wu Tan swung round and fixed Partridge with a glittering eye.

"Why was I not informed?" he demanded.

"We were airborne before it happened," the young pilot explained patiently, "and there seemed to be no point in spoiling your trip for what would probably turn out to be little more than a stomach ache." He glanced around. "He should be in either the car or the van over there."

"I should have been informed," Wu Tan insisted petulantly.

"I'm sorry," Partridge said. There was an edge to his voice but he kept his temper under control. "If you will excuse me, I have a report to make so that the rest of your countrymen can be rescued." He turned on his heel and strode off toward the van housing the radio base station.

Wu Tan's eyes seemed to recede even further into the folds of fat, and he struggled to control his breathing as purple blotches appeared on his bulging neck. McCrimmon feared the man would have apoplexy.

"If he is not in the car, I want you to find him and bring him to me," Wu Tan said in a strangled voice. He turned and walked away without waiting for a reply. McCrimmon sighed and shook his head as he watched the broad, retreating back. As they neared the car, Yeung Chao darted ahead and opened the door of the limousine. He stood aside deferentially as Wu Tan forced his huge frame through the doorway.

Apparently Tai Ling was not in the car, for Yeung Chao looked back at McCrimmon and shook his head sharply. With a muttered imprecation, the sergeant made his way toward the vans where he found both drivers in the cab of one, listening to the radio.

"The little Chinese guy?" one of them said in answer to McCrimmon's question. "He passed out. I didn't know what was wrong with him so I took him into the hospital in Banff. Probably picked up some bug," he offered helpfully. "Looked like he had a fever to me."

"How long ago was this?"

"Right after the others took off."

"What did they say at the hospital?"

The man shrugged. "You know hospitals. They don't tell you nothin'."

Hunching his shoulders against the stiffening breeze,

McCrimmon made his way back to the limousine. He opened the front door and slid into the passenger's seat. He turned and faced the two men in the back.

"I'm afraid your man has been taken to the hospital in Banff," he told them. "We'll have to check with them to find out how he is."

Wu Tan stared at him for several seconds before speaking. When he did, his voice was deliberately offensive. "*We* will do nothing," he snapped. "You have clearly failed to keep me properly informed, or," he added ominously, "you have conspired to keep information from me." He waved a pudgy hand in a gesture of dismissal. "Leave us. Get out of this car. *I* will find out what has happened to our comrade, Tai Ling."

He was having trouble with his breathing again, and that seemed to infuriate him even more. "And as for you," he panted, "I shall contact your superior immediately upon my return to the hotel." His voice rose to a screech. "Get out! Get out of this car!" He fell back gasping.

The muscles in McCrimmon's jaw bunched and hardened, but he had no intention of letting this gross, boorish creature prod him into losing his temper. Instead, he pulled out a notebook, scribbled something in it, ripped out the page and handed it to the fat man.

"There's the name and number of my superior," he told him. "It might save you a little time." He opened the door and got out. "I'll keep you informed if I hear anything," he said. He closed the door and nodded to the driver. Whatever Wu Tan's reply, it was lost behind the heavy glass, but his distorted features were enough to indicate to the sergeant that it was something less than a fond farewell. As the car moved off, he made his way back to where the vans were parked. Partridge intercepted him.

"I'm on my way over to meet Chuck Drayton at the industrial park," he told McCrimmon. "The team will assemble there. They want me to guide them to the scene of the crash while the light is still good. They'll size up the situation and try to get a base camp established, then make their climb at first light tomorrow."

"Good," McCrimmon said. "I'll ride over with you, if you don't mind."

The flight to the industrial park where Drayton kept his own Jet Ranger took less than three minutes. McCrimmon recognized Drayton's truck turning into the compound as Partridge dropped the helicopter inside the high, chain-link fence surrounding the compound. By the time McCrimmon had ducked beneath the decelerating blades, Drayton was out of the truck and coming forward to meet him. He looked surprised.

"I didn't know this was a police matter, Bill," he said. "What's it all about?"

"It started out as a charter tour for the delegates from the hotel," McCrimmon explained. "I just happened to be in one of the other helicopters." He turned as Partridge came up beside him.

"Do you know Jack Partridge?"

Drayton nodded and extended his hand. "Weren't you with some oil outfit working out of Calgary?" he asked as the two men shook hands.

"That's right," Partridge said. "I still work for them, but they don't object to me doing a little free-lancing on my own time." His normally cheerful features took on a serious mien. "Fred Krell needed some help on this one, so he asked me to fly today. I sure wasn't expecting this."

Drayton turned and led the way to a small building in the corner of the compound. It served as an office, a workshop, storage room, and even an emergency hangar. "Don't think I know Krell," he said over his shoulder as he unlocked the door.

"He's new to Calgary," Partridge explained. "He's flown this area before, I guess, but I think he spent the last year or two in California."

They went inside and Drayton pulled a large-scale

map from a folder and spread it out on one of the benches. "Show me," he said.

Partridge studied the map for a moment, then traced one of the contour lines on the north-east side of Mt. Babel. "They're just about here," he said, jabbing the spot with his finger. "About eight thousand feet up on a very narrow ledge."

Drayton circled the spot Partridge had indicated with a pencil. "How in hell did he manage to get up there?" he wanted to know.

The younger man shrugged. "I don't know," he admitted. "His engine must have cut out and he didn't have anywhere else to go."

"On a ledge," Drayton mused. "Any chance that it will fall off?"

Partridge shook his head emphatically. "It's in there as far as it can go," he said. "It's safe enough, except, perhaps, from the overhang. There's seventy, maybe eighty feet of snow above them," he explained, "and a lot more on the slope above that, but it looked pretty solid." He glanced hopefully at McCrimmon, looking for confirmation.

"What about it, Bill? You were there; what do you say?"

The sergeant hesitated, not wanting to give Partridge cause for more concern than was necessary, but very much aware that Drayton needed all the information he could get.

"It withstood the noise and impact of the crash," he said carefully, "and it didn't show any sign of movement when we flew in close." He saw Partridge's face begin to relax, and he wished he could stop there.

But he couldn't. "The sun's been on it, Chuck," he went on quietly. "It *could* be solid, but it just may be that the only thing holding it up there is a crust about three or four feet thick. If it stays cold and freezes hard up there tonight they should be all right, but if the sun comes out tomorrow it could begin to soften." He drew a deep breath. "If the rescue team can't get up there before midday, and the sun is shining, I'd say it could be very touchy," he concluded. He looked across at Partridge. "Sorry, Jack, but it's better that they know the danger and be prepared for it," he said.

The young pilot nodded in reluctant agreement as he turned and studied the map once more.

"How soon can we start?" he wanted to know.

Before Drayton could reply, they heard the sound of another vehicle outside.

"That'll be Hans Lehman," he said. "He'll be leading the rescue team." He dropped a hand on the young pilot's shoulder. "He's the best there is," he said simply. "If anyone can get those people off that ledge, he can."

His voice took on a crisper tone. "Now, give me a hand with this gear," he said. "The sooner it's loaded, the sooner we can get up there."

Yeung Chao surreptitiously eased the window of the car open a millimeter at a time. His uneasy stomach craved fresh air, but Wu Tan detested drafts. Beside him, taking up most of the seat, hands clasped over his huge belly, the chairman sweated. Sweat ringed his thick neck and stained his collar; dark, wet patches spread outward from his armpits, and an acrid odor filled the car. The driver turned on the air conditioning.

But, despite his extreme physical discomfort, Yeung Chao was pleased with the latest turn of events, for Wu Tan was now in very deep trouble indeed. As chairman of the delegation, he would have much to answer for. It had been Wu Tan's decision, and his alone, to deliver the vitriolic address at the opening ceremonies instead of waiting until Monday as he had been instructed to do before he left Peking. And it had been Wu Tan's decision to change it, to 'put some backbone into it' as he had put it to Yeung Chao. Well, he'd certainly done that. Yeung Chao barely managed to suppress a snigger of satisfaction.

And now there was the matter of the crash that had

stranded Sung S'u-mah and Kuan Lo on the mountain. Not that Wu Tan could be held responsible for the crash, but it was just one more thing that had gone awry. The fact that he had lost track of one of his charges, one that had been politically suspect in the past at that, was a far more serious matter, and there would be a full investigation if the minister should hear about it. Yeung Chao decided that he could hardly leave something like that out of his report. But would it be enough? Why leave anything to chance?" Wu Tan had survived other crises; it was possible he would survive this one. It would be so easy to make sure. Yeung Chao hugged the thought to him and it warmed him.

"Stop at the hospital," Wu Tan told the driver as they crossed the bridge. The car swung left and made a U-turn at the junction of Spray and Mountain, and came to rest in front of the hospital.

"Well, get out and find out what is wrong with Tai Ling," the fat man ordered, prodding Yeung Chao viciously. "Bring him with you. I don't want him left with these people. I do not trust them." Yeung Chao scrambled out of the car and entered the hospital. He was gone for some fifteen minutes, and when he returned his features were carefully controlled. He returned alone.

"Well?" Wu Tan demanded. "Where is he?"

Yeung Chao slid into his seat and closed the door. "Tai Ling became very ill," he said carefully. "The hospital has limited facilities. It is a small hospital. They could not identify the cause of the problem, so when Tai Ling went into a deeper coma . . ." His voice cracked and trailed off.

Wu Tan's sausage-like fingers shot out and grasped Yeung Chao's jacket at the neck. He twisted the material until the younger man gasped for breath. "What have they done with Tai Ling?" he hissed, his face mere inches from that of Yeung Chao. A spray of spittle from his frothing lips struck Yeung Chao in the face.

"They sent him to Calgary," he gasped. "They said they had to. It was an emergency."

Wu Tan stared at his assistant, his mind already busy with the implications of this latest development. Slowly, almost offhandedly, he released his grip on Yeung Chao's collar and slumped back in his seat. He remained there for some time, staring off into the distance as if trying to see into the future. At last, as if awakening from a sleep, he roused himself and looked around. "Take us to the hotel," he told the driver wearily. He mopped his brow with an already sodden square of linen, but it made no difference. The sweat still came unheeded and unchecked. He stared out of the window with unseeing eyes. He seemed to have forgotten Yeung Chao completely.

But, huddled in his corner, Yeung Chao could not forget Wu Tan. Neither could he forget the indignities he had suffered at his hands. There was open hatred in his eyes as he made his decision. It was one that could be put off no longer.

Chapter 11

When McCrimmon telephoned the Detachment for someone to come and pick him up, Quinn came on the line.

"Can't you even go for a joyride in a chopper without screwing up?" he asked sarcastically. Then, more seriously, "They *are* going to be all right, aren't they?"

"No serious injuries," the sergeant told him, "but they're in for a pretty miserable night. There's no way they can be brought off until sometime tomorrow."

"It won't be any picnic up there," Quinn agreed soberly. "You can tell me all about it when I come to pick you up. Do you want someone to bring your car down from the hotel?"

"Thanks, that will help," McCrimmon told him.

"Right. See you in ten minutes." Quinn hung up before McCrimmon could reply.

Hans Lehman and his carefully selected team of Alpine specialists had arrived. Lehman, a stocky, taciturn man, was already studying Drayton's maps and listening attentively to Partridge as he described the position of the crippled helicopter. McCrimmon made a second phone call, this time to Wellington.

"I heard about the accident from the newsroom," the inspector told him. "You'd better alert the rescue team;

they can expect a flood of questions. Warn that young pilot, too. I'd like to keep this one low-key. I'm counting on assistance from your local people if necessary."

"You'll have it," McCrimmon assured him. "There is one other matter you should know about," he said. "One of the delegates by the name of Tai Ling is in hospital. Apparently he became ill prior to takeoff. No one thought to inform Doctor Wu Tan, head of their delegation, and he's pretty upset. He's not too fond of me, either. He'll probably be in touch with you first chance he gets."

Wellington grunted. "Then, he'll be even more upset when he hears that his man has been rushed to Calgary. Doctor Angleton phoned me. He didn't like the way things were going. Said his patient's pulse rate was much too high and he appeared to be going into shock. I guess they can cope with most things at the hospital, but Angleton was perturbed about the symptoms he was seeing." Wellington lowered his voice. "He wouldn't be pinned down, but I think he suspects poison as the root cause. I agreed that he should get the man into Calgary as fast as possible. One of your people went with him, and I've arranged for the Calgary Police to put a man on his room around the clock. I expect you to follow up on that as soon as you can. Okay?"

Poison! The word had an ominous ring, and even more ominous implications. But Wellington was waiting. "I'll take care of it," McCrimmon assured him.

"See that you do," Wellington said shortly. "And don't let the press get hold of *that* or we'll be all over the front page again."

"Believe me, you don't have to spell it out, Inspector."

Quinn arrived in his own car, a ten-year-old Chevy that looked better now than the day he bought it. It was his pride and joy, and there wasn't a man in the Detachment who didn't know within hours when another landmark had been passed. "Turned a hundred and forty thousand on the week-end," he'd say, and everyone would nod and suddenly find jobs that took them as far from Quinn as possible. To remain close was to hear again the seemingly endless saga of fine-tuning, synthetic oils, dramatic knocks at 97,000 (miraculously cured by a half turn on a pan bolt at 97,478), that invariably ended in a monologue on the assembly line products of today. But today his mind was on other things. He listened attentively as he drove McCrimmon back to the Detachment.

"Poison?" he echoed, matching McCrimmon's own reaction. "Why would anyone want to poison the guy?"

McCrimmon stared gloomily at the road ahead. "It could have been an accident," he ventured, "but since they're all eating together it seems unlikely." He shook his head. "I just don't know about that bunch. There's something odd about the whole lot of them. There's just too damned much activity around here since they came."

Quinn drove into the parking lot behind the building. "You're right about one thing," he agreed. "There's been a hell of a lot of activity around here lately, and none of it seems to make any sense." He switched the engine off and the two men got out of the car. "We got the autopsy report on Minelli this afternoon," Quinn went on. "Angleton was right. The body had been moved, and there were gravel grazes on the hands and one side of the head as if he'd fallen. Could have been in the parking lot where he kept his car. We're sending a gravel sample into Calgary for comparison tests."

"What about cause of death?"

"Ordinary heart attack consistent with the medical history of the deceased," Quinn said. "Of course, they can't tell us what might have triggered it." They went inside and made their way to McCrimmon's office. Out of habit, the sergeant went around the desk and dropped into his chair while Quinn settled into the one on the opposite side of the desk.

"There has to be a connection," McCrimmon

growled. "Minelli was passing something to one of the Chinese delegates; I'm sure of that. Then, very conveniently, Minelli dies. Minelli's name and address are found on the body of a professional hood who was killed while chasing someone else. The guy in the Ford may have been kidnapped, if Miss Haggard is to be believed, yet there is no missing person report." He shook his head helplessly. "And now," he concluded, "we have two Chinese delegates stuck on top of Mt. Babel, and a third one in hospital, a suspected poison victim."

Quinn made sympathetic noises. "We found the Ford," he offered helpfully. "I took your suggestion and had a couple of the boys walk the road. They found glass and tire tracks about a mile up the road. You couldn't see the car from the road. It had gone down into the trees. It could've stayed there for years without being spotted. Nothing much in it except some blood. Automatic transmission in neutral, and the tire tracks in the gravel at the side of the road had been brushed out. If our guys hadn't been walking, they'd never have spotted the tracks in the grass."

McCrimmon frowned. "Someone went to an awful lot of trouble to get rid of that car," he mused. "There has to be *something* about it that makes it important. What do you have so far?"

"Damn all, except that it's a rental out of Calgary like the Plymouth, but not from the same agency." Quinn stared morosely at a point above McCrimmon's head for several seconds, then said, "Oh, yeah, and there was a reply to your inquiry. It's on the desk there somewhere." He indicated a stack of papers beside the IN tray.

The sergeant shuffled through the papers, picked out the teletype and scanned it quickly until he came to the meat of the message.

Subject born 55 02 02 to Arthur and Mary Lee, San Francisco, California, U.S.A. Family moved Paraguay 1961 with Christian Service

Mission. Transferred Kuching, Malaysia 1965.

Arthur Lee died Malaysia March 1970, cause unknown. Subject returned with mother to San Francisco April 1970. Mary Lee died 71 03 16. Cause of death, pneumonia. Subject has no known living relatives.

Subject brought to Vancouver 71 03 26 by Joseph King, friend of subject's father, Arthur Lee. Joseph King applied for legal guardianship of subject 71 05 07. Awarded custody 71 10 13.

Subject attended Aston-Reed private school, Vancouver 1971-73. U.B.C. 1973-77. Grad. BA Fine Arts (Hnrs).

Present address 131B Halcyon Apts., 2412 West 11th Ave., Vancouver. Present whereabouts of subject - refer to message 78 05 19 478/334/17 VCR.

McCrimmon dropped the message on the desk and tilted back in his chair. "And that," he said dispiritedly, "gets us absolutely nowhere."

Quinn grunted. "I didn't find it much help either," he admitted. "And the Security Service," he went on, referring to the men who had arrived the night before, "won't even talk to me about the two guys who got killed. The CPR lawyers have been on to me several times. They think I'm holding out on them, so I've turned them over to the boys in the pinstripes. Let them worry about it."

Boots echoed dully in the hall outside the door, and a tall, thin constable by the name of Hall appeared. He had cropped, fair hair and the faintest trace of a moustache beneath a small, snub nose. He'd been trying to grow hair on his upper lip for at least two months. McCrimmon had seen more fuzz on a peach.

"Sorry to interrupt," Hall said perfunctorily, "but this could be important, Sarge. Corporal Quinn said to let him know if anything came in on that red and white truck."

Quinn glanced up sharply. "What've you got?" he asked.

Hall consulted a slip of paper in his hand. "I had a call from Cliff Bannister, Park Warden Service," he said crisply. "Came in at seventeen forty-one. One of his wardens spotted a truck matching the description we gave them up by the old fish hatchery out there toward the park gates. The wardens are in there looking for an injured bear that got creamed by a car this afternoon. Anyway, the chain on the gate across the road leading to the hatchery had been cut and wrapped around the gate to make it look as if it were still intact. When they got up to the hatchery they found the truck. Nobody in it but the engine was still warm. They backed off and radioed in for instructions. They figure whoever drove it in there could still be there."

McCrimmon was on his feet. "Tell Cliff to get his men out of there fast," he said. "They could . . ."

"I already told him that," Hall broke in quickly. "I also contacted Sam Holbrook on the highway. He was on his way in from Johnston Canyon. I asked him to cover the gate in case the truck comes back to the highway. There's no other way out of there." He suddenly looked anxious. "Was that all right, Sarge?"

McCrimmon nodded approvingly. "Better get back to the radio and warn Holbrook to stay well back on the Banff side of the gate. He's to call in if that truck reappears. Under *no* circumstances is he to try to stop it on his own. Got that?" Hall nodded and scribbled a note on the slip of paper.

"Are there any more wardens in there who haven't been contacted?"

Hall shook his head. "No, they're all out and waiting for instructions. They won't move until they hear from us."

"Good. Now, contact Canmore and ask them to bring up two cars to the park gates. They have a description of the truck, but warn them again that the men in it could be armed and dangerous. I don't want any heroics. Call the duty man at the gates and ask him to let us know if that truck goes through there before Canmore can get their cars into position. Make sure you tell him not to attempt to stop it. Oh, yes, and tell Holbrook that Quinn and I are on our way in the ghost car. Okay?

The young constable jerked his head in acknowledgment. "Got it, Sarge," he said crisply, and disappeared from view.

Wu Tan replaced the telephone with deliberate care. He slumped back in his chair and closed his eyes. He felt very tired. Beads of perspiration glistened on his forehead, and he could feel the soft, clinging wetness of his collar as it bit into the folds of flesh beneath his chin. He half raised his hand to unfasten the offending collar, but it fell back as if the motivating force had died before it could complete its task. His contact at the embassy had been polite. Cold, distant, and too polite. He had listened without comment while Wu Tan related what had happened to the members of his party, and at the end had made only one suggestion.

"The ambassador will no doubt require a complete written report confirming this conversation," he said without inflection. "May I tell him when he can expect it?"

The question irritated Wu Tan. Every word he had spoken would have been recorded as a matter of policy. But he bit back the angry retort that rose to his lips and glanced at his watch. Ottawa was two hours ahead of Banff. There was nothing he could do tonight. And, perhaps, by tomorrow there might be brighter news to report.

"I'm having some difficulties with the local police," he said. "They are withholding information, but," he paused as if considering, "by noon tomorrow," he said. "Banff time."

The voice at the other end of the phone seemed to hesitate as if about to disagree, but there was no hint of it in the next words.

"I'll tell the ambassador." The line went dead.

And that, Wu Tan knew, was not good. The nausea started again, faintly at first, then in stronger waves. His throat was dry. He couldn't swallow. He began to tremble. Was it never over?

Yeung Chao came out of the bathroom bearing a glass of cloudy liquid. "Your medicine," he announced. His voice sounded flat, almost deliberately devoid of expression. A nervous hand brushed back an errant lock of hair.

Wu Tan regarded the glass with distaste. "Take that filthy muck away," he said wearily. "I need something a lot stronger than that to restore my health." He stopped abruptly, surprised at what was in his mind. But the thought came boldly, not with the insidious stealth that had marked its coming before, and Wu Tan savored it. His mouth twisted sardonically, and his eyes fastened like claws on those of Yeung Chao.

"Fill that glass full of whisky and I'll drink it," he rasped. He laughed, a short, staccato sound that seemed to unnerve Yeung Chao, for alarm flared in his eyes and his hand shook violently. The lock of hair fell forward into his eyes again, but he made no effort to push it back.

"Oh, give it to me before you have it all over me," Wu Tan growled resignedly. "You can't even be trusted to carry a glass of medicine without spilling it." He took it from Yeung Chao and held it to the light.

"Poison," he pronounced. "That's what you'd really like to give me, isn't it Comrade?" His glittering eyes sought to hold those of Yeung Chao, but the other refused to look at his tormentor. Wu Tan grunted contemptuously, then flung his head back and drained the glass. He grimaced and thrust the glass at the younger man.

"Here, take it. See if you can carry it back without spilling it," he said. The laugh came again, higher this time as if he found the sally especially amusing. He heaved himself to his feet and thrust his face into that of

Yeung Chao. "Go on," he commanded. "See if you can carry it without spilling it."

But Yeung Chao didn't move. He stood there as if rooted to the spot, waiting, waiting for something to happen. His mouth moved but no words came out. He was shaking.

Wu Tan scowled and thrust out his arms to push Yeung Chao aside, but even as he did, the room began to sway and spin. He caught the edge of the bed as he fell, and felt the sinewy arms of Yeung Chao wrapped tenaciously around his chest. With surprising strength, Yeung Chao heaved the massive body onto the bed and stood there panting, looking down upon the face he hated.

"And now it's your turn," he breathed softly. The breath rattled in Wu Tan's throat; he seemed to be choking. Quickly, Yeung Chao seized a pillow and thrust it beneath the unconscious man's head.

"Oh, no, you're not going to get away that easily," he muttered as Wu Tan's breathing steadied. "I have plans for you." He bent and pulled a small case from beneath the bed, and from it took a small, wooden box. He set it with great care on the night table beside the bed, and opened it to reveal a glass syringe, two ampules of clear liquid, and several cotton swabs. The needle pierced the soft skin of one of the ampules, and he drew the liquid into the syringe.

"And now, you pig," he whispered softly, "you'll have your wish. You think you craved alcohol before? Just wait until you wake up!"

He tried to force up the sleeve of Wu Tan's jacket, but it was too tight. He mouthed a curse beneath his breath, then slid his bony fingers along the fat man's wrist. He found the vein and thrust the needle home. Yeung Chao straightened up and stood looking down at the recumbent form for a long moment, then picked up the telephone and dialed a single digit.

"Can I help you?"

"I'd like a taxi as soon as possible," Yeung Chao said. "I'll meet it at the rear entrance."

"You did say the *rear* entrance, sir?"

"Yes."

"It may be about ten minutes, sir."

"That will do." He had plenty of time.

Yeung Chao and the taxi arrived at the rear entrance at the same time. There were few people about. Two men were unloading what appeared to be linens from a van; a young couple walked hand in hand oblivious to everything except each other, and a squat, flustered-looking man had propped himself against the hotel wall while he struggled with a camera, light meter, and what was obviously a new set of instructions.

The driver opened the door, but Yeung Chao closed it firmly. "I'd like you to go into town and make a purchase for me," he said. The driver nodded non-committally. He'd had some strange requests in his time; there was little that would surprise him.

"I want you to bring me four bottles of whisky," Yeung Chao told him. "Bring them back here; I'll be waiting for you." He took money from his pocket, then stopped uncertainly. "How much will that be?" he asked.

The driver regarded him oddly. "Look, Mister," he said patiently, "you can buy all the liquor you want right here in the hotel. You don't have to send out for it."

"I'm well aware of that," Yeung Chao said stiffly. Did the man take him for a complete fool? "I prefer to do it this way. I intend to pay you for your errand, of course. Now, how much will four bottles of whisky be?"

"Rye? Scotch? Irish . . .?"

Yeung Chao recognized Scotch. "Scotch," he said.

"Anywhere from eight to ten bucks right on up to twenty five," the man shrugged. "Your choice."

Yeung Chao counted out forty dollars. "Get the cheapest," he told the driver. "I'll pay for delivery when you return. Now, please hurry."

The man regarded the money sourly. "Look,

mister," he said, "it's only fair to warn you. This is gonna cost you. I could be fifteen, twenty minutes in the liquor store, and the meter'll be running all the time." His tone implied doubt that Yeung Chao could afford such expense.

"You will be paid," he was told icily. "I shall be waiting here, never fear."

"It's your dough," the driver shrugged. "See you."

Yeung Chao waited until the taxi was out of sight before making his way back inside the hotel. There would be plenty of time to return to the room, check on Wu Tan, then come down again to await the return of the taxi. Not that he anticipated any problems with the chairman, of course; the drug should keep him unconscious for at least two hours. Yeung Chao allowed himself a taut smile. There was nothing to worry about. The drug he had administered directly into the bloodstream had been developed by Chinese scientists while searching for solutions to the problem of alcoholism. To them it was useless, for rather than help cure addiction, it served only to reinforce it. It had taken Yeung Chao more than a year to obtain two ampules without anyone's knowledge.

And there would never be a better time.

He and Wu Tan were the only delegates left of the original five. The others wouldn't return until at least tomorrow, and by then his purpose would be accomplished. Perhaps Yeung Chao might not have felt quite so secure if he had been able to observe the actions of the man who had been struggling with the camera and the light meter in the parking area. For, not only had he photographed Yeung Chao standing beside the taxi, but he had managed to edge close enough to eavesdrop on part of the conversation.

He was looking very throughtful as he followed Yeung Chao inside and went in search of a telephone.

As they were approaching the traffic circle outside Banff,

McCrimmon contacted Holbrook on the radio. "Any sign of the truck?" he asked.

"Nothing so far, unless they pulled out before I got here," Holbrook replied.

Hall's voice broke in. "Canmore has one car for us. That's all they have available right now. It'll be at the park gates in a couple of minutes. The truck hasn't left the park, so it's probably still up the hatchery road."

"Maybe they're hiding out up there," Quinn suggested.

McCrimmon shook his head. "There's only one way in and out of there," he said. "They'd be crazy to box themselves in like that."

They swung right at the circle and headed east along the highway. Before them stretched the broad, sweeping valley, a patchwork quilt of fresh spring greens against the serried ranks of darker evergreens marching up each ridge and disappearing down the other side. They reappeared again, higher and more distant, straggling lines inching their way in single file toward the topmost crags. Slanting evening sunlight touched the snow-clad shoulders of the Fairholme Range and turned them into gold. But neither man had time to dwell upon the view.

McCrimmon picked up the microphone again. "Tell the man from Canmore to keep on coming," he told Hall. "We may need him for backup."

"There's Holbrook now," said Quinn, pointing ahead.

"Still no sign of them," Holbrook's voice broke in.

"Okay," McCrimmon said into the mike as they passed Holbrook's stationary vehicle, "follow us to the entrance and plug it after we go in. Your backup should be here any minute now."

Holbrook raised a hand in acknowledgment as they went past, and his amiable voice came over the speaker loud and clear. "How come you guys get all the fun? I'm the one who got here first."

Hall's voice broke in once more. "Harper from Canmore is on the Seven Mile hill. He should rendezvous with you in less than five minutes."

Quinn and McCrimmon exchanged glances. "Rendezvous?" Quinn echoed. "What the hell are they teaching them these days?"

"Bilingual training," McCrimmon told him solemnly. "You should try it. You might even get extra pay."

"Balls," said Quinn succinctly.

"There it is. Turn in here," McCrimmon said.

Quinn slowed for oncoming traffic, then swung across the road into a narrow, graveled track now partly overgrown with weeds, and stopped. McCrimmon slid out of his seat and opened the gate that barred their way, then returned to the car. As the car moved cautiously down the winding track, Holbrook swung in behind them and blocked the gateway.

"Take it slow and easy," McCrimmon cautioned. "If these are the same men Miss Haggard saw, they could be dangerous. The two men who were killed at the crossing were carrying weapons. We'll have to assume these are too." He reached inside his jacket and eased the snub-nosed Smith & Wesson from its holster. He checked it carefully while Quinn inched the car along the narrow trail, eyes ever watchful as the trees closed in around them. They saw nothing for a couple of hundred yards, then, quite abruptly, they found themselves at the edge of a clearing. The abandoned fish hatchery stood alone and desolate at the far side, its windows boarded up against the weather. The red and white truck was standing in front of it.

Quinn stopped the car, blocking the exit from the clearing. He switched the engine off and both men rolled down their windows and listened. The chill wind surged restlessly through the tree tops; birds called and were answered; the ticking of the cooling engine sounded loud and metallic in their ears. With a nod to Quinn,

McCrimmon stepped out of the car and circled to the right, moving toward the truck. Quinn followed, moving to the left. Their eyes scanned the trees and the dilapidated building as they searched for some sign of the two wanted men.

Quinn checked the back of the truck while McCrimmon looked inside. There was nothing to indicate ownership. The glove compartment was clean; there wasn't a scrap of paper anywhere. McCrimmon moved around the front of the truck and ran his fingers over the scratches and dents on the welded steel bumper. There was a streak of green paint embedded in a crease in the left front fender, and part of the grill had been damaged. There was no doubt in the sergeant's mind that this was the vehicle Miss Haggard had described. They were moving to check the building when they heard voices. Someone was moving through the underbrush behind the hatchery. The two policemen flattened themselves against the wall, guns drawn.

Olsen came around the corner first, head down and puffing hard. He was saying something to the man behind him, a big man carrying a folded tarpaulin over his broad shoulders. Olsen was within fifteen feet of the waiting policemen when he realized they were there. His eyes flew wide and he opened his mouth to shout a warning just as Quinn stepped away from the building and out of McCrimmon's line of fire.

"Police!" he said. "Hold it right there."

The warning rising in Olsen's throat was cut off as a huge hand smashed into his back, hurling him forward into McCrimmon. The tarpaulin flew through the air and struck Quinn full in the face. He knocked it aside, but the big man had ducked back behind the building and was gone. McCrimmon sidestepped the falling Olsen and held his gun on him.

"Don't so much as move a muscle," he warned. The man lay on the ground, too stunned to move.

Quinn ran to the corner of the building and peered

cautiously around. A gun roared and he felt the wind of the bullet as it passed his cheek. Booted feet crashed heavily through the underbrush.

"I'm going after him," he called over his shoulder, but was stopped by McCrimmon's curt command.

"You're not going anywhere, Quinn," the sergeant said. "We'll do it right, with support. You go after him now and you'll get your head blown off." Quinn hesitated, still smarting from the ignominy of being caught off guard, but training and better judgement prevailed. McCrimmon handcuffed Olsen and pulled him to his feet.

"Keep an eye out for the other one," he told Quinn. "He could circle around and take a shot at us from the trees. For all he knows, we could be the only ones here. He may think he's home free if he can get us." He quickly searched his captive, but found no weapons.

"Jordan B. Olsen," he read from the driver's license. "From Denver, Colorado." He slipped the license back inside the wallet and returned it to Olsen. "Well, Mister Olsen, you have a little explaining to do. What were you and your friend doing in there?"

A shiver ran through the man but he remained steadfastly silent and stared at the ground. He seemed to be forcing himself to remain calm.

"Okay," McCrimmon shrugged, "have it your own way, Let's have a look at that tarp, Quinn."

The tarpaulin had unfolded when it fell to the ground, and now, as the corporal bent to pick it up, he saw the dark, damp stain in the middle of it. It was sticky to his touch, and the substance took on a muddy brown appearance when he rubbed it with his finger. His narrowed eyes swept the edge of the clearing.

"I wouldn't mind betting there's a body out there somewhere," he said quietly. "It's my guess that they were disposing of the driver of that green Ford."

Yeung Chao opened the bottle of Scotch and poured the

contents into the bathroom sink. He watched as the liquid disappeared down the drain, then rinsed the sink out thoroughly. He took the empty bottle back into the bedroom and set it on the bedside table beside a full bottle. He opened the second bottle and poured about four ounces into a glass, then held the glass to Wu Tan's lips. He raised the unconscious man's head and, little by little, forced the whisky into the slack mouth. Wu Tan choked as the raw liquid trickled down his throat. The effects of the drug were beginning to wear off.

Yeung Chao stood back and surveyed his handi-work. The first thing Wu Tan would see when he regained consciousness would be the Scotch. A third bottle stood, unopened, on the dresser, while the fourth was safely locked away in Wu Tan's suitcase where it would be found at the appropriate time. Yeung Chao rubbed his hands together. The stage was set. The rest was up to Wu Tan, although Yeung Chao was quite prepared to return and prompt the chairman should he stray too far from the script. With one last, careful look round, Yeung Chao slipped from the room via the connecting doors.

Wu Tan stirred. His mouth, his throat, his lungs, all seemed to be on fire. Each breath was like a furnace blast. He forced his tongue around his lips, and his brain registered a half-forgotten taste.

He opened his eyes, slowly, painfully at first because the light hurt them, then wider in astonishment as he stared unbelievingly at the bottles on the night table. He tried to think, to remember what had happened, but his thoughts refused to come together. Disjointed patterns flitted through his befuddled brain. He frowned hard in concentration, but his head only throbbed harder and he decided that remembering wasn't worth the effort. His eyes came back to the empty bottle. He didn't remember finishing it, but there is was. His throat was aflame. He reached for the bottle. It was cool.

He drank.

In the Embassy of the People's Republic of China, in Ottawa, a man with thin, graying hair combed straight back over a high, domed head, sat at an ebony desk, a telephone to his ear. His long, tapering fingers drummed lightly on the message just received from Peking.

A voice came on the line. "I'm sorry, sir, but there's no reply from Doctor Wu Tan's room. Would you care to leave a message?"

"No message," the man said incisively. "I will call later."

Malik scowled as he replaced the telephone. He sat back, fingers steepled beneath his chin as he digested the latest piece of information. Sung S'u-mah and Kuan Lo stranded on top of a mountain, Tai Ling supposedly in hospital, and Yeung Chao behaving very oddly.

That the Chinese delegation had been deliberately split up, Malik had no doubt. He detected the fine hand of the Americans behind the whole operation. Of course, he would have to verify that the two delegates were, in fact, stranded; that shouldn't prove too difficult. And he would have to keep an eye on Yeung Chao and Wu Tan to see what they were up to.

But his thoughts kept returning to Tai Ling. A shroud of secrecy cloaked the hospital. All that his man had been able to discover was that the man purported to be Tai Ling had arrived at the Banff hospital, only to be whisked off to Calgary under police protection. Strange, very strange indeed. Did the local police *know* what was going on? Or were they being used? The more Malik thought about it, the more he became convinced that the man now resting in the Calgary hospital was not Tai Ling. A switch had been made, perhaps on the way to the hospital, perhaps at the hospital itself. It didn't matter where it had happened; sufficient to know that it had happened.

That the crash on the mountainside had been stage-managed by the Americans, Malik didn't doubt for a moment. It accomplished several things. It took the ever-watchful Sung S'u-mah out of the game; it prevented Kuan Lo from looking in on his friend, and it served to focus attention on the plight of the stranded delegates rather than on Tai Ling's sudden illness. But that still left Wu Tan and Yeung Chao. Why hadn't they shown more concern? Wu Tan was in enough trouble at home without losing one of his delegates, or at least losing contact with him. Unless . . .

Malik dismissed the thought almost before it had formed. That there might be collusion between Wu Tan and Tai Ling was unthinkable. Now, if it had been Yeung Chao . . .

Suddenly Malik became very still. *What if Tai Ling were the decoy?* That would explain the whisky. It would explain why Yeung Chao found it necessary to bring it in secretly. *He was going to get Wu Tan drunk!* And with Wu Tan out of the way, for once he took a drink he would be finished, there was no one to watch Yeung Chao.

Malik rose from his chair and began to pace. Which theory was the right one? Which man was the American agent? If it were Tai Ling, then he was being debriefed at this very moment, probably at *The Firs.* If not . . . Malik shrugged resignedly. They could only watch and wait.

Chuck Drayton watched the Moraine Lake Lodge grow smaller as the helicopter swung wide across the river. The rescue party would spend the night there and start their climb at first light. They would be warm and comfortable in the lodge; far more comfortable than the trio huddled in the crippled helicopter high above them. Drayton's involuntary glance slid upward, searching for the ledge now deep in purple shadows as the light faded from the sky. A sudden gust of wind moved the helicopter sideways. He corrected for it almost without thinking. A thin veil of snow swept off the overhang and fell a thousand feet. The radio crackled and the voice of Lehman came in strong.

"We're all secure," he said. "Thanks Chuck. See you in a few hours."

"I'll be here," Drayton assured him. "Are you receiving us, Krell?"

Krell's voice came in fainter than Lehman's. "I can hear you but I didn't get the first part. We . . ." His voice cut out and a series of clicks rattled in Drayton's earphones.

"Are you still receiving me, Hans?"

"Loud and clear," came Lehman's reply, "but Krell is cutting out."

"Then it has to be his transmitter," Drayton said. A burst of noise came over the air. Evidently Krell was trying to talk to them but there was no voice transmission. Drayton routinely checked the ELT but Krell had turned it off to avoid unnecessarily alerting other aircraft in the vicinity.

"You're not coming through, Krell," Drayton said into the mike. "If you are still receiving me, press your transmit button twice."

Two distinct bursts of noise came through.

"Good, I got that," Drayton said. "The rescue team will start up at dawn. With any luck at all you should be off that ledge by noon. Good luck."

Two more bursts of noise sounded in the earphones.

Drayton put the nose of the helicopter down and sent it skimming down the long, tree-clad slopes. The light was almost gone from the sky and a speckled string of distant lights wound their way along the highway; travelers oblivious to the quiet drama taking place above them. Drayton shivered. He thought of the telephone call he had received earlier in the evening. Some photographer for a magazine wanting to hire him to fly in for some close-up shots of the stranded helicopter and its human cargo. He'd refused, of course, explaining carefully why it was impossible, but the man still persisted. Drayton had hung up on him.

He followed the moving lights below, thankful to be going home to a warm bed, even if it meant but a few hours of restless sleep. He breathed a silent prayer for all those who were not so fortunate.

Chapter 12

The house stood black and silent, almost invisible against the backdrop of ancient firs and rising mountain. The wind sifted softly through the tree tops like sand through brittle reeds. The two men who stood guard within the shadow of the house huddled deeper in their parkas.

A car went by the end of the driveway, slowing for the corner, then picked up speed and faded into the night. Somewhere close by someone plucked tunelessly at a guitar; a bird fluttered furiously and settled down again and all was quiet, except for the guitar.

One of the men touched the cold metal of his gun and felt reassured. He wondered briefly what was happening inside the house, then dismissed the thought as pointless. It was better not to know.

It was time to make the rounds again.

The air inside the room was thick with smoke from cigarettes. The eight men seated around the table had long ago discarded jackets and loosened ties; sound-proofing had its drawbacks. The white-haired man Guthrie had greeted as Professor was speaking.

"All right," he said, glancing through the sheaf of notes before him. "I'm sure you know what we have to do. I want you to start over again; go right back to the beginning and tell us the complete story just as if we'd never heard it before. Leave nothing out. If you remember something you left out the first time, include it. Okay?"

"I understand."

The disembodied whisper came from the speakers mounted above their heads. Despite the fact that they had been listening to it for hours, no one could have said with certainty whether its owner was young or old, fat, thin, tall, short, male or female. Such was the effectiveness of the electronic distortion so carefully designed into the system that it was impossible to identify the speaker.

"For the past ten years many of our scientists, mainly oceanographers and meteorologists, have been working on a secret project. The name of the project is, loosely translated, *Breath of the Red Dragon*. Each group worked separately within the parameters of its own specialized field. They were not told that others were working on the same project, neither were they told of the enormity of the undertaking. It was not until three years ago that the team was selected to work on the final stage of the project. That was when I first became aware of it.

"Very simply stated, the purpose of the project is to modify existing world weather patterns to the detriment of the USSR especially, and to some degree, that of the United States. Our activities were concentrated in two areas; one in the Pacific, the other in the North Atlantic. Since I am more familiar with events in the North Atlantic, I shall deal with it first."

The voice paused and the sensitive speakers faithfully echoed the distorted sounds of swallowing as the hidden agent drank from a glass of ice-cold water.

"Perhaps, for the benefit of those of you who are not familiar with weather patterns and their origins," the voice continued, "I should explain again that there are certain sensitive areas on the surface of the earth, or in this case the sea, where a very small change in surface temperature can produce a tremendous change in the flow of air at higher altitudes. Such is the case in the North Atlantic. I think by now you are all aware of the area of which I speak. It lies roughly four hundred miles south of the tip of Greenland, and it was in this area that our ships were operating last September when the Russian nuclear submarine blew up so mysteriously.

"But I'm getting ahead of myself. I should explain how we set out to accomplish what appears at first glance to be an impossible task; to change the world's weather patterns. As most of you know, studies have been going on for years into climatic changes caused by changes in direction of the jet stream in the upper atmosphere. In nineteen seventy-two, abnormally warm patches of water in the North Atlantic, produced naturally by an unusually mild winter, came in contact with exceptionally cold water off the coast of Greenland, resulting in a strong thermal updraft that both strengthened the jet stream and altered its course, diverting it far to the north.

"The jet stream developed a strong zig-zag pattern. Warm, dry air was carried across the North Atlantic and down across western Russia. A drought developed and their harvest failed. Other parts of the stream brought cold, wet weather to the British Isles and, eventually, to the eastern United States. On top of that, the low pressure area created over the eastern United States sucked in Hurricane Agnes, causing disasterous flooding and damage estimated at more than three billion dollars, the most costly storm in American history. Over one hundred lives were lost." There was a pause, then, "Several of you here tonight are, I'm quite sure, very familiar with the pattern of nineteen seventy-two."

One of the men at the table scribbled the figure 3 on the pad in front of him, then added nine zeros. He stared at it, fascinated, then proceeded to shade in the zeros.

"That, as I have said, was a natural phenomenon," the voice went on tirelessly. "Our task was to simulate patterns very similar to that. In short, to create weather patterns that would defeat China's enemies through a series of economic disasters and internal crises so massive that they would have time to think of little else. And no one could be blamed. It would be labeled as an act of God.

"We succeeded. At least, our technique was success-ful. You have only to look at the weather patterns for the past few years, the most impressive demonstration being, of course, the disasterous drought in the British Isles and Europe in nineteen seventy-six. Unfortunately, or fortunately, depending upon your point of view, manipulating the jet stream is not a precise science. It takes time to learn how to do it accurately. Even then, there are so many variables that it is virtually impossible to predict all the results."

The professor lifted his head and looked directly into the lens of a TV camera. "I think that is sufficient background," he observed, glancing around the table for confirmation. Heads nodded agreement, so he went on.

"Perhaps we could go to the mechanics of the operation," he said. "You mentioned eight ships, I believe?"

"There were eight ships in the matrix, Professor," the voice said equably. "There were, of course, two more. The supply ship and the dye tanker."

"Ah, yes, ten in all," the professor agreed. "Please continue. The composition of the matrix would be a good place to start."

"Very well." There followed the sound of more water being swallowed. Prompted by suggestion, two others in the smoky room reached for the water jug and filled their glasses.

The voice continued. "There were eight ships forming the points of an octagon. They were separated at the widest point by a distance of some twenty kilo-meters, about twelve-and-a-half miles. All the ships were old but extremely seaworthy, sailing under Liberian registry. Seven were freighters, the eighth was a tanker, empty of course, except for the ballast, generators, and the special electronic equipment associated with the master computer. As I say, they were old ships, but inside everything was new. They were fitted out with the very latest equipment, much of which first saw the light of day in the United States. Each ship carried extremely heavy-duty power plants and a computer-controlled navigational system."

One of the men at the table waved a hand at the TV camera. "When you say it was computer-controlled, I take it you mean the speed and direction of each ship was completely coordinated with the speed and direction of every other ship in the octagon. Is that right?"

"Quite correct. The lead ship, the tanker, carried the master computer. The others, sophisticated as they were, acted as slaves."

"I get the picture," the man said.

"Good. Please feel free to ask questions at any time, gentlemen, if I do not make myself clear."

Someone muttered, "Christ, it's hot in here!" and lit another cigarette.

The voice continued. "It was vital, not only to the success of the operation, but to the very survival of every ship in the matrix that its precise position be maintained with respect to every other ship because of the pinpoint accuracy needed for the laser beams, and the consequences of them missing their targets."

To the men seated around the table in what had been only a few short weeks before the living room of an elderly, retired couple, the words did not strike them as strange. They saw nothing bizarre in a situation in which a disembodied voice spoke quietly and calmly about changing the weather of the world; wreaking casual havoc on unsuspecting millions by tinkering with the basic elements that permitted life to exist upon their planet. They smoked, they drank, they scribbled notes, concentrating only upon how the information affected their particular studies. To them, it was little more than an academic seminar, the usual taped address merely replaced by the electronically distorted voice of a spy from the very heart of China.

The voice continued. "A newly-developed CO_2 laser was used. It is far more powerful than anything you have seen before. Five ganged generators provided the power, and the laser units beneath each ship were fed by fiber-optic cables almost a full meter in diameter. The beams were directed to every other ship in the matrix, that is to say, a laser beam went out from each ship in seven directions so that a full matrix pattern was formed between all the ships. Then, because the area to be heated was so large, and every ounce of energy had to be used, the beams were retransmitted, or reflected and amplified if you like, back and forth several times to form a tightly-woven grid. The secret of heating the water lies in the introduction of dye into the area of the ocean you wish to heat. Water, being relatively transparent, normally allows the laser beam to pass through it with little or no heating taking place. But, put an opaque dye in the water, and you suddenly have heat, tremendous heat.

"The ships cruised slowly back and forth over an area of some sixteen hundred square miles, linked by the matrix of lasers just as tightly as if they were linked by bonds of steel. Computers corrected for every wave, every roll. And the temperature of the water rose fractionally every day."

"How deep were your lasers?" The speaker was a pale, rumpled man with a bulbous nose.

A TV camera swung down and the lens stared blankly at him. "Fifteen fathoms beneath the hull," came the metallic answer. "Slightly deeper at the apogee of the water inside the matrix due to the curvature of the earth."

"Why so deep? I should have thought that you would want the heating to take place as close as possible to the surface."

"That would be the ideal situation," the voice agreed. "However, the water literally boils in the immediate vicinity of the beams. That depth was chosen to allow some cooling as the warmer water rose to the surface, and to avoid detection."

The pale man wrote something down on his pad and waved a hand to indicate he had no more questions for the moment.

"The tanker outside the matrix, the one carrying the dye, cruised back and forth ahead of the other eight ships," the voice went on. "The chemical used turns a deep green when it comes in contact with salt water, giving the water the opaqueness needed to heat it. The lasers burned up the dye, so little if any remained after the ships had passed. When observed from above, from a plane for example, the dye would appear to be just another shade of the ocean. It would cause no comment."

"But the ships must have been out there for weeks at a time," interrupted a man sitting next to the professor. "Surely ships traveling in formation like that would cause comment?"

"You must remember they were old, slow-moving freighters," the voice said patiently. "And they were several miles apart. Even if the pattern was observed by some passing plane, it was highly unlikely that the same plane would pass over that exact area often enough to notice the same phenomenon twice. No, we didn't fear detection from that source."

"But," the professor said quietly, "you would soon be out of business if the five proposed GAR satellites were launched, wouldn't you?" He cocked a quizzical eye at the TV camera.

"Exactly," the voice replied. "And that, of course, is why the leader of the delegation came out so strongly against the launching. The satellites would cover that particular area, and they have the ability to sample water temperatures. It would become impossible to operate undetected."

"What about other vessels in the area?" another man put in. "There had to be some traffic out there. Fishing boats. What about them?"

"There were many boats in the area," the voice said, "but they were shallow draft boats. In most cases we were able to continue operations while they were passing."

A young man with a military haircut broke his long silence. "But for some reason they failed to detect the Russian submarine," he said. "How did that happen?" He looked up at the TV camera and played a soft tattoo on his teeth with a wooden pencil.

"It happened when the supply ship came," the voice told him. "The power had been cut off during refueling. After the supply ship left, the technician in charge should have checked the scanner before powering up again. Either he failed to do so or there was a malfunction in the scanner. Apparently the submarine had entered the matrix during the refueling period." The voice seemed to fade a little. "You know the result," it said.

"You closed down operations after that, I presume?" It was the pale man again.

"Immediately. We made our way home by separate, predetermined routes."

"Leaving an underwater holocaust behind," the professor murmured. The voice didn't respond.

The man with the military haircut spoke again. "You said, 'We made our way home'," he said with the air of a man who has trumped his opponent's ace. "In fact, you have indicated in several of your statements that you were yourself there. Is that so?"

"It could be construed that way," the voice said. It offered no further elaboration.

The young man chewed on the end of his pencil. A high, nasal voice broke in on his thoughts.

"Now, let's get a handle on the kind of power you were using," it said dispassionately. "Just what kind of output are we talking about here? Let's start with the generators aboard the tanker . . ." The nasal voice droned on.

There was a general easing of cramped muscles.

Notes were thumbed, more water was poured. The professor tilted back in his chair and stretched. It was going to be a long night.

Wu Tan poured the last of the whisky from the bottle and set it carefully to one side. Like liquid velvet it glowed with a soft, amber luminescence as he lifted it to the light. He held it there, devouring only with his eyes the lambent gold shimmering in the glass. He lowered the glass and brought it to his lips, but did not drink. Instead, he savored the delicate aroma of the magical ingredients that seduced the senses and teased the palate.

He drank it slowly, letting the liquid linger in his mouth before allowing it to slide gently down the throat. A warm, lingering, satisfying glow penetrated beyond the surface membranes until every muscle, every nerve, every fiber surrendered to the all-encompassing embrace. Here, at last, he felt secure.

He could see, now, with amazing clarity the errors of the past; his errors, he admitted freely to himself, in listening to foolish doctors and psychiatrists who, in their ignorance, had insisted that his body needed no alcohol to function properly. What, after all, could they know of the chemistry of *his* body and *his* brain? He sighed as he looked back sadly down the long line of wasted years of needless torment; the years of total abstinence, believing their philosophies with all the fervor of the newly-saved. He felt pity more than anger at their abysmal ignorance.

A chemical imbalance, that's what it was. Wu Tan could see the words in his mind. He tried to mouth them but gave up when his lips refused to do his bidding. It didn't matter anyway. He knew. He knew more than all of them. A chemical imbalance . . .

A trickle of saliva slid down his chin and disappeared in the fleshy folds of his massive neck. And suddenly, with blinding clarity, he *knew*! So startling was the revelation that he struggled upright on the bed as if, somehow, it would give him a better vantage point.

But he knew. His porcine eyes narrowed and his massive head shook from side to side. He laughed, a guttural, staccato sound that broke into a gasping wheeze as he fell back on the pillow. He lay there choking on his own saliva until, at last, he heaved himself onto one elbow and the choking fit subsided. Tears ran down his cheeks, as much as from sheer blinding anger as from the choking fit. It was all so very clear. He dragged a rumpled sleeve across his face and wiped away the tears. He had to think, for now he had to be on guard against everyone.

How many had conspired to keep him from his rightful place? The minister? Certainly the doctors, but on whose orders? Oh, they had been clever; so very, very clever. 'You're an alcoholic, Comrade. You're sick, Comrade. We are here to help you. We will help you to be strong.' Oh, yes, he remembered; he remembered every word. A plot to destroy him. Him! Wu Tan!

His thick lips curled in contempt. Did they think they could trick *him*? He'd show them. Oh, yes, he'd show them. He'd hold them up to ridicule as he had once been held up before his peers. He'd expose them one by one for the charlatans they were. Yes, he, Wu Tan, would sweep them all aside. And the minister? Wu Tan's eyes narrowed to little more than slits as he thought about the minister. A public acknowledgment from the minister that he, Wu Tan, was the foremost scientist and scholar in his field would do to begin with . . .

How bold and clear his thoughts had become. Wu Tan allowed a few more drops to pass his lips and melt in his mouth.

The telephone rang.

Wu Tan frowned, unwilling to allow anything to interrupt this translucent flow of thought. It rang again. Carefully, very carefully, Wu Tan raised his glass and allowed the last few drops to trickle down his throat. The telephone rang a third time. He sighed a long, grumbling sigh and set the glass aside. He lifted the receiver.

"Yes?" The word caught in his throat and made him cough. Angered, he cleared his throat noisily and shouted "Yes? What is it?"

A thin, precise voice addressed him sternly. "This is Chung Yeng-tse," it said. "I have instructions for you. Where have you been? I have been trying to reach you for some time. You were told not to leave the phone until I called." The voice was decidedly peevish.

Wu Tan scowled. He was not accustomed to being addressed in such a peremptory fashion, even by an ambassador. A retort sprang to his lips but on an impulse he decided to be magnaminous.

"It was good of you to call, Comrade Ambassador," he answered politely, "but there was no need. I have matters well in hand. My earlier telephone call to you was merely to keep you informed of events. I am in no need of assistance." Wu Tan snickered loudly at the very thought of anyone being presumptuous enough to think they could assist him.

There was an astonished silence at the other end of the line, then, "Your new instructions come directly from Peking." Chung Yeng-tse's voice was icy. "They are as follows: You are to have two of your staff go immediately to Calgary where they are to remove Tai Ling from hospital and bring him back to your hotel. Once there, he is not to be allowed to leave his room, neither is he to speak with anyone who is not a member of the delegation. You, yourself, will remain in Banff until Sung S'u-mah and Kuan Lo have been rescued." The thin, reedy voice broke off abruptly, then went on again. "In the event that rescue becomes impossible, you will remain in Banff only long enough to verify that they are both indeed dead. You will then proceed to Vancouver by the earliest possible flight. Members of our Vancouver office will be there to assist you. Meanwhile, neither you nor any member of your party will discuss or give any reason for your departure from the seminar. An official statement will be issued from this office as soon as you notify me that you are about to leave the hotel. Your answer to any and all questions must be, *No comment*."

Wu Tan stared unbelievingly at the telephone. "What nonsense is this?" he demanded angrily. "*I* am in charge of this delegation, and *I* will be the one to decide when we will leave the seminar and this hotel. I . . ."

The ambassador's voice rose to screaming pitch. "I am Chung Yeng-tse," he howled. "The orders I am giving you come directly from Peking. You must obey! You must . . ." Wu Tan uttered a foul obscenity and hung up.

He fell back on the bed, scowling. He would show them; he would show them all. He dismissed the ambassador from his thoughts and reached for the glass. It was empty as were the bottles beside it.

His groping hand found the phone. More whisky, that's what he needed first. Then he could think . . .

Mikhail Velovich, the man known to Olsen as Mike, moved stealthily through the trees toward the sounds of traffic. He had been moving steadily eastward hoping to escape the net that he knew would soon be thrown around the area, but darkness was descending and he was having difficulty maintaining a straight course. The police couldn't hope to plug all the escape routes, but the sooner he was clear of the park the better.

A spasm of shivering hit him. He had left his parka in the truck when he and Olsen had carried Kellerman's body into the woods. It had been a mistake; one that could cost him dearly before the night was over.

He moved closer to the road until he could see the cars going by through the trees. There were fewer, now, their headlights boring tunnels through the thickening darkness. He edged closer. If he could cross the highway he could make better time because the searchers would be concentrating on this side. With luck, he would be outside the net and would be well clear of the area by the time they could mount a full-scale search. They couldn't do much until daylight and he would be gone by then.

More headlights appeared. A cavalcade of cars came down the long, sloping curve and made their way slowly eastward. He pulled back into the deeper shadow of a bush and watched the funereal procession with growing apprehension. As if by signal, they slowed still further, then stopped, spaced out along the highway about two hundred yards apart. Lights were switched to high beam and the road in front of him was bathed in light. A patrol car went past, and further down the road he saw another.

Mikhail moved deeper into the trees, drawing the darkness around him like a cloak.

It began to rain.

Hans Lehman awoke to the sound of a helicopter. It was dark. He looked at the luminous dial on his watch and saw the time was 3:42. He rose and went outside.

Gusts of wind funneled through the valley, driving fine particles of snow before it. They stung the face like sand, and Lehman had to shield his face as he searched for the source of the sound. He looked up to his left where he knew the survivors were huddled on the tiny ledge, but a thrusting corner of the mountain blocked his view. He squinted against the driving snow, but all he could see was the darker bulk of the mountain against a sky only fractionally lighter.

A light flared, a brilliant light behind the jutting crags. They stood out starkly in relief. A flare? A signal of some kind from the ledge? Lehman watched, oblivious to the sting of ice and snow. The light was bright and steady, not a flare. It was the snow that was making it leap and die. He watched for several minutes, then as abruptly as it had appeared, it went out again. The laboring beat of helicopter blades came fitfully through the storm as the wind switched directions, then it, too, faded and was gone. Lehman remembered the telephone call Chuck Drayton had received just before they had taken off. Some crazy reporter who wanted pictures; he'd offered Drayton twice his usual fee.

Lehman reached for the radio.

4:30 on a glowering Sunday morning. Gray, soggy clouds settled in the valleys, too heavy and too cold to rise until the sun came out to warm them. Windshield wipers thumped monotonously and defrosters were turned on and off as windows steamed up inside. The last lukewarm dregs of coffee were squeezed from thermos flasks, and men huddled deep inside their sodden jackets and stamped their feet to stir the circulation.

Quinn drove slowly past the stretched-out line of cars until he saw McCrimmon engaged in earnest conversation with a constable. The corporal parked his car behind the sergeant's, leaving the headlights on and pointing obliquely into the trees. He got out stiffly, stretched and yawned. The constable left McCrimmon and jogged across the road to where his own car stood, while McCrimmon walked back to meet Quinn.

"Brought you some coffee and sandwiches," the corporal said, holding up a flask. He unscrewed the plastic top. Steam poured from the spout, triggering hunger pangs that the sergeant had been trying to ignore for the past two hours. "Ellie made it fresh and ran it over," Quinn explained. "She figured we wouldn't last until breakfast without it."

"We'll be lucky to get breakfast at all this morning," McCrimmon observed, glancing up and down the road. He swallowed a mouthful of coffee and bit into a sandwich.

"Aaahh — thank God for the Ellie's of this world," he muttered appreciatively as he felt the warmth flow through him. He nodded in the direction of the departing constable who was now heading back toward the traffic circle. "We're taking the dogs in shortly," he explained. "They've been holding the west flank along the Minnewanka road, and the east flank along Carrot Creek.

With the rest of us strung out all along the highway in between, our man's got no place to go but up. And that," he concluded, "is one helluva climb."

"Too bad we couldn't have gone in last night," Quinn observed. "We could've been home in bed by now."

"We could also have been dead," McCrimmon said. "By the time we rounded up enough men from the three detachments and the wardens' service, it would have been too dark in there. We know this guy's dangerous; in fact he may be responsible for one death already. He can't travel far in the dark."

Quinn raised his eyes to the lowering clouds. "I wonder how those poor bastards up on the mountain are making out?" he said. "Last I heard it was beginning to snow."

"Some idiot was flying around up there in a helicopter a little while ago," McCrimmon said. "Hans Lehman reported it; figures it might have been the press. Some guy approached Chuck to fly him in for pictures but he refused. Lehman said he could see the reflection of a powerful light but that's all. He tried the radio but no one responded. He was madder'n hell. Right now he's praying that the vibrations set up by the helicopter haven't weakened the ice overhang." McCrimmon stared sourly into the plastic cup. "Chuck's on his way up there to check it out and make sure everybody's all right."

"Stupid bastards," Quinn muttered, biting into a fresh sandwich. His eyes scanned the peaks as if somehow he could see beyond the valley to where three people huddled together for warmth in the tiny cabin of the crippled helicopter.

"It'll be lighter higher up," McCrimmon observed. "They could be starting their climb already." He drained his cup, shook it out, and handed it back to Quinn. "Thank Ellie for me, will you?" he said. "That really hit the spot."

He walked to the car and picked up the microphone. "Charlie Three," he called. "Come in Charlie Three."

"Charlie Three here."

"This is Alfa Nine," McCrimmon said. "Are the dogs ready?"

"Ready, Sergeant."

McCrimmon glanced across the road to where the white trunks of the trees had been growing steadily ligher. Bushes that only moments before had been little more than indistinct shadows now gleamed wetly in the reluctant dawn.

He pressed the mike button. "Start checkoff, Charlie Three," he said. "And remember, keep the man on either side of you in sight at all times. We're going in."

A soft, stealthy, rustling sound brought Mikhail awake. He listened, trying to pinpoint the direction of the sound. It came again, a careful footfall, a pause, and then another somewhere off to his right. He opened his eyes and stared into a tangle of wet grass and twigs. He remembered trying to burrow beneath a bush in the dark as he sought desperately for protection from the rain and cold. Still listening hard, he moved with infinite caution.

Pain exploded everywhere as every muscle shrieked in protest. He clamped his teeth together to prevent himself from crying out, and felt the almost welcome warmth of blood when he bit his tongue. He held his body rigid; it was like a block of ice, and to move would shatter it forever.

The sound came again, closer this time. He cursed his frozen muscles and vainly tried to will warmth into his immobile body. A flicker, a movement out of the corner of his eye. Or was it just imagination playing tricks on senses dulled by the insidious cold?

He clamped his teeth together and forced his head around, wincing against the pain and blinking away the rivulets of water that ran into his eyes. He felt the hard metal of the gun pressing into his hip beneath him, protected from the elements but now quite useless to him in his frozen state. A mule deer stepped daintily into view, nostrils aquiver, ears flicking back and forth, alert to every sound in the dripping forest. It stood there poised, head up, testing, listening, its breath quite visible in the chill morning air. A tremor coursed through its glistening flanks as it caught the first faint hint of danger.

A violent shudder of relief wracked him from head to foot. Mikhail tasted salt and felt the warmth of tears coursing down his cheeks. He was crying with relief and cold. A thousand needles stabbed him as he forced himself to roll over and straighten out his legs. The startled deer leapt away and disappeared among the trees. He forced his hands together and rubbed them briskly, at first without feeling, then painfully as the blood began to flow.

He pushed himself to his feet, staggering like a drunken man until feeling began to return to his feet and legs. He almost wished it hadn't, for now he became aware of the sodden state of his clothes, and he began to shiver uncontrollably. Dank, gray mist pressed in on every side.

Mikhail compelled his reluctant brain to think. His watch told him it was 5:23, so more than six hours had passed since he had fallen exhausted beneath the bush, unable to go on, defeated as much by the absolute blackness of the forest as by the relentless chill that had sapped his strength and numbed his senses. He had become completely lost. By the time sleep had overtaken him, he was past caring whether they caught him or not.

But now, despite the miseries of the body, his brain was beginning to function again. The outlook was, to say the least, bleak, but it certainly wasn't hopeless. He didn't know how far he'd traveled in the pitch dark, but he was reasonably certain that he'd managed to maintain a north-easterly course. The ground to the north rose steeply, so if he continued to climb and move always to his right, he should move further from the highway and from his pursuers. With luck, he could move far enough to the east before the cordon could close, and from there he could make his way into open country.

His stomach growled complainingly. Mikhail cinched his belt tighter. He was no woodsman; his knowledge of edible plants was minimal, and he had no intention of making himself ill by eating the wrong ones. He could manage without food for a long time, and water wasn't going to be a problem, especially if the weather continued to stay like this.

Cautiously, he moved up the slope and to his right. The slope became steeper and he felt real warmth returning to his body and the stiffness eased. He pushed on, more confident now despite the odds against him. He'd been in tighter situations than this before, and he had one big advantage over his pursuers. He was prepared to be totally ruthless.

Mist deadens sound, but even if it didn't Mikhail wouldn't have heard the dogs less than a quarter of a mile behind him, for they had been trained to track in silence.

Sung S'u-mah moved stiffly in her seat and pulled the sleeping bag tighter around her shoulders. Beside her, with only the tip of his nose showing outside his parka hood, Kuan Lo snored gently. Sung S'u-mah smiled tightly to herself in grudging admiration. The helicopter creaked as Krell heaved himself erect and wriggled free of his sleeping bag. He pushed the hood of his parka back and cocked his head on one side.

"Chopper," he announced tersely. "Sounds like Drayton. We'd better get outside to show him we're still alive."

Inwardly she groaned. Cold, miserable, and exhausted, Sung-S'u-mah wanted only to sleep, but she reluctantly complied.

Krell leaned over and shook Kuan Lo roughly. The little man's eyes flickered open and stared blankly at the pilot, then recognition came. "Are they here already?" he asked in Chinese.

"The helicopter has come to see if we have survived

the night," the woman explained. "The radio doesn't work so we'll have to go outside to show that we're all right."

Kuan Lo nodded, now completely awake. His eyes searched her face as if he expected her to say more, but when she didn't he turned away and pulled himself free of his sleeping bag. Krell steadied him as he clambered awkwardly to the ground. Sung S'u-mah followed and they stood huddled beneath the threatening overhang with snow whipping at their faces. Oddly, the sky was almost clear above them. The snow was blowing off the mountain, but below, Consolation Valley was filled with thick gray cloud. To the east, Panorama Ridge was blanketed with freshly fallen snow, while even further to the east, like a giant painted backdrop, the crenellated battlements of Mt. Eisenhower loomed stark against the rising sun. Gusts of wind tugged at them as if trying to pull them from the ledge, snatching at their clothing and stinging their faces with particles of ice.

The helicopter came into view and they recognized it immediately as Drayton's. He circled some distance away, then took the aircraft higher, moving in a long, slow arc parallel to the contours of the mountain while he studied the fresh layer of snow that had settled on the overhang during the night.

"Wave to show you're all right," Krell said.

Dutifully, they complied. Then, as if the action had somehow released an inner tension, they flung their arms into the air and waved them madly, jumping up and down like children at a parade.

Drayton dropped lower, still staying well clear of the ledge, and waved back. The helicopter turned and dropped away, swinging wide around a buttress before disappearing from their view. They stared after it, straining to hear the sound as it faded into the distance, reluctant to sever the tenuous thread that connected them to the outside world.

The pale gray light of morning crept silently into the

room, bringing with it a coldness that robbed the still burning lights of their warmth. It stole across the carpet, sliding past the empty bottles, a single shoe, a discarded tie, and settled like a mantle on the mountainous figure slumped in the chair. Wu Tan stirred, his pudgy fingers still clutching the empty glass perched miraculously upon his massive belly. It rose and fell with each stentorian breath like an abandoned lifeboat on a rising swell. His disheveled shirt gaped open, torn aside when he had grown too warm, and pallid rolls of flesh spilled outward, threatening the very fabric of half-open trousers girdling the mighty paunch.

The TV set was on, left on throughout the night. An announcer read the morning news. The announcer's face faded from the screen and that of a troubled housewife took its place. Predictably, the volume doubled, and Wu Tan awoke to the screaming exhortation to avoid at all costs the perils of static cling.

He opened his eyes and stared blankly at the screen. Slowly, painfully, some semblance of consciousness returned. His neck was stiff and sore; his arm was wedged hard against the chair and had gone to sleep. His mouth was dry and full of fur, and his tongue felt several sizes too big. His eyes were bloodshot and refused to focus, and little men with hammers were working on his skull, goaded on to greater efforts by the shrill voices from the TV set.

He heaved himself erect and the glass toppled to the floor unheeded. His fumbling fingers finally found the switch. The voices died but the echo continued inside his head. He tried to swallow and almost choked on his own tongue. A drink. He needed a drink.

His wavering eyes searched the room and fastened on a bottle, then skipped impatiently to the next when he saw that it was empty. He pushed himself from the chair and sank to his knees, feeling desperately beneath the bed, praying that his outstretched fingers would encounter the smooth, cool glass of a bottle that had rolled there. A full bottle; even one with a few drops left in it, he didn't care, but there had to be a bottle. Nothing! Wu Tan struggled to his feet and lurched toward the bedside phone, stabbing blindly at the dial. He missed the #2 for room service and hit the #1 instead. The number rang and rang while the chairman's head throbbed with every ring. He felt an urgent stab of pain beneath his pendulous belly, a bloated bladder sending out alarms. He shook the telephone in silent fury.

The ringing stopped. A hesitant female voice that sounded very young said, "Dining room reservations. There's no one here at the moment except me. Reservations are not open until . . ."

"Whisky," Wu Tan growled, not listening to what the voice was saying. The word cracked in his parched throat. "Whisky," he shouted louder. "Send up whisky."

"I'm sorry, sir, but this is dining room reservations," the voice replied. "I think you want room service." Then, helpfully, "But it's Sunday morning, sir. I'm not sure if they . . ."

Wu Tan screamed an imprecation and felt that stab of pain again. A startled gasp came from the other end of the line and the phone went dead.

He dropped the phone and looked wildly round the room. His eye fell on the connecting door, the door that led to Yeung Chao's room. He lurched around the bed and grasped the doorknob, then pulled up short. Oh, no. That would be a mistake. Yeung Chao could not be trusted. No, he would not seek the aid of Yeung Chao the sly, Yeung Chao the cunning. He, Wu Tan, was far too clever to fall into that trap. He leaned his head against the door and ran his tongue over his swollen lips. They felt like sandpaper. He had to have a drink. If these stupid people would not bring him one, then he would have to go and get it himself.

He met no one in the corridor as he stumbled toward the elevator, quite oblivious to his state of dishabille. He was vaguely puzzled by the unevenness of the floor, unaware that he had lost a shoe, but his mind could only cope with one idea at a time. A drink. He must have a drink.

He reached the elevator without incident and pushed the button. He fell against the door and found it cool. He leaned his head against it and was convulsed by a spasm stabbing hard above the groin. Sweat ran down his face and settled in the flaccid folds of flesh around his bull-like neck.

The door slid back and Wu Tan almost fell inside. The startled operator stared dumbly at the apparition, her hand still holding back the door. Wu Tan gestured impatiently for her to close it and start it on its downward course. "The bar," he commanded hoarsely, wincing as the devils inside his head hammered harder. The girl, just a youngster filling in an awkward Sunday shift, remained immobile, her nose wrinkling at the noxious odor emanating from the half-dressed man.

"C-c-can I help you to your room?" she managed to stammer when she found her tongue.

"The bar!" Wu Tan roared, fixing the girl with a malevolent glare. When still she did not move, he seized her by the arm and thrust her from the cage. He fumbled with the controls until the doors closed and the elevator began to descend.

The pain hit him again. A throbbing, violent rending pain that made him gasp and double over. Tears ran down his face as he straightened up, and he willed the pain to go away. One thought and one thought only forced him on, for he knew with the complete conviction that is given only to a chosen few that all his body needed was alcohol to bring it into balance. Then, and only then, would mind and body be in perfect harmony and function smoothly once again. The elevator moved slowly. He hammered at the controls to try to speed it up. It stopped and he waited for the doors to open, then dimly realized that he had to open them from the inside. He cursed and fumbled with the unfamiliar mechanism and somehow got them open.

He burst like a bomb through a group of people talking quietly in the wide, heavily-carpeted hall, brushing them aside as if they didn't exist. He pressed on, trying to remember the location of the bar. His head, his loins, his whole belly were aflame. Dry, rasping, whimpering sounds rattled in his throat. He saw the doors ahead. He fixed his eyes upon them determinedly and forced his feet to take him there.

His body hit the doors like a battering ram, and they burst inward under his weight. He staggered ahead, then halted, swaying, trying to get his eyes to focus, trying to find the bar. Two hundred faces stared back at him, the whole room shocked to silence. It hung there like a movie halted in midframe, action frozen, speech forgotten, time itself suspended. This wasn't the bar!

Wu Tan stared myopically at the sea of faces, unable to comprehend, when, suddenly, as if a veil had been torn aside, they sprang into focus. Sharp and clear. Indelible. A woman, fork poised halfway to her mouth; a waitress in midstride; a pop-eyed little boy with jam around his mouth; gleaming cutlery and starched white tablecloths. A little girl with long blonde hair giggled nervously and was quickly shushed. Familiar faces from the seminar sprang out at him like goblins in a nightmare. Shocked, surprised, or openly amused.

Sweat started from his brow as comprehension dawned. The pain became unbearable. A despairing wail burst from his throat, and his body could withstand the searing pain no longer. He felt the flood of warmth, the fluid coursing down his legs, and the horror that he felt was mirrored in the eyes before him.

Chapter 13

A constable from the Lake Louise Detachment found
Kellerman's body. It had been dumped almost hap-
hazardly in tangled underbrush at the base of three
small trees. There had been no attempt to bury it. When
McCrimmon was informed, he wasted no time in having
it removed to the hospital. There would be little to be
learned by leaving it where it was, especially with a
manhunt going on in the immediate vicinity.

Angleton himself did the preliminary examination.
He looked shaken when he came out. "How can I get in
touch with McCrimmon?" he asked the constable who
had brought in the body.

"He's still out on the search but I can get a message
to him," the man said. "He's got a walkie-talkie."

Angleton shook his head. "This isn't something I
want everyone to hear," he said grimly. "Where's
Inspector Wellington?"

"Still up at the Banff Springs as far as I know."

Angleton went into his office and closed the door.
He picked up the phone and dialed the hotel. When
Wellington came on the line he wasted no time with
preliminaries. "You know about the body that was just
brought in, I presume, Inspector?"

"I've had a report," Wellington said.

"Did your report tell you that the man has been

brutally beaten and tortured?" Angleton snapped. "My God! Wellington, what in hell is going on?"

There was silence at the other end of the line while Wellington digested this latest piece of information. "Are you quite sure about deliberate torture?" he asked at last.

Angleton snorted. "Of course I'm sure. Whoever did it didn't exactly have a delicate touch, nor much time by the look of it. And you haven't answered my question."

"What does his face look like?" Wellington asked.

Angleton frowned at the phone. "I don't think I understand your question," he said.

"I mean are his features recognizable? Could someone identify him?"

"Provided they have a strong stomach," Angleton said thinly. "He should be cleaned up considerably before anyone is asked to do that."

"No. No, I don't want you to do anything to the body before it is sent to Calgary," Wellington said. "I want them to see it exactly as it was found. If there's any evidence to be found I want them to have every chance of finding it. You asked me what was going on. Quite frankly, Doctor, I'm damned if I know, but I'm sure as hell going to find out. Now, before the body is sent for autopsy, there's a woman by the name of Haggard, Miss Haggard, who will be along to try to make an identification. She's been asked to stand by. She should be there within the hour."

Angleton grunted acknowledgment. "It's going to be hard on her," he said. "Is she a relative?"

"No," Wellington said, "just a witness who may have seen this man before. It's important that she have a good look at him. I'd appreciate it if you would stay with her yourself."

Angleton grunted again. "I'll do what I can," he agreed.

"Let me talk to the constable who brought him in, will you?" said the inspector. "And thank you, Doctor."

When the man came on the line, Wellington said, "A Miss Haggard is coming in to see if she can identify the body. I'll be over there myself later on but I can't get away right now. I want you to remain with her throughout the identification and record anything she says. Anything, understand?"

"Yes, sir, I understand." The man hesitated, then, "It's not a very pleasant sight, Inspector."

Wellington grunted. "Can't be helped, Constable," he said, not without sympathy. "Help her through as best you can, but don't lead her into making statements. Let her make her own. I'll try to get there as soon as possible. After that, I want you to accompany the body to Calgary and make sure it is safely delivered to Doctor Freeman or one of his staff. Don't forget to get a signature. I'll be getting in touch with them myself later on. Got that?"

"Yes, sir."

"Good. Now, let me speak to Angleton again."

Chuck Drayton deposited the field rescue leader, a man by the name of Alan Dawson, and the winch crew by sling on a jutting knoll some 900 feet below the crash site at 5:47 a.m. It was as close as he could come to a point directly below the ledge. The climbing party, made up of Lehman, Gerry Bonner, and Cy Peterson, were deposited higher up the mountain on a cornice 600 feet below and some distance to one side of the stranded helicopter. They began the actual climb at 6:28 a.m.

They worked, for the most part, in silence. The mists in the valley lay like gray, amorphous shrouds, deadening sound and cutting them off from the world below. The quiet chink of metal, the cautious scrape of boots against the rock, a muffled grunt, and the rhythmic beat of their own breathing were the only sounds they heard. It was not, by Lehman's standards, a difficult climb. Short, stiff, pure rock faces with good ledges for the most part, but the melting ice of spring, covered by freshly-fallen snow, made hand and toeholds treacherous, and progress was painfully slow. They were held up for an hour when a promising route petered out abruptly, forcing them to retrace their steps and make an awkward traverse around a jutting buttress, a smooth, unbroken face followed by a wide, striated patch some eighty feet across where water had softened the rock to the consistency of pumice.

But, under Lehman's expert guidance, they inched their way steadily toward their goal, with Lehman in the lead and Bonner close behind. Peterson brought up the rear, trailing the nylon rope that would link them to the crew below once they reached the ledge. The sun broke through and warmed them, but its very warmth soon proved to be a mixed blessing. The probing rays caused hardened ice to melt and coat the rock with a film of icy moisture that numbed their fingers and made them insensitive to the texture of the rock.

Inch by inch they crept upward, making for the base of a narrow chimney that Lehman hoped would take them past yet another overhang, testing, probing, judging every hand and toehold carefully before committing their weight to it.

The face of the mountain darkened as clouds appeared from the west, scudding in a roiling mass across the sky and blotting out the sun. And with the clouds came wind and blowing snow right off the mountaintops, bitter, spiteful gusts that slashed with icy fingers at their faces and tried to tear them from their tenuous hold. Exposed, defenceless against the violent onslaught, they had no choice but to continue on. To remain clinging to the open face was but to court disaster.

They struggled on, Lehman leading them toward a narrow ledge, doubly cautious now in case one of the team should slip or be plucked from the face by the gale-force blasts. Ten feet away; five; then two. Lehman hung there, gathering strength for the final heave that would send him sprawling over the edge. Ice crystals blinded him as he sought to secure the safety rope, and the wind shrieked inside the chimney as he half dragged himself, half fell onto the ledge.

He struggled to secure the rope, the wind tearing at his very breath, sucking it from his lungs only to ram it back again as it switched direction. The rope was firm. He braced himself and took the strain. Bonner's head appeared, then he too fell over the edge. He lay there gasping, trying to get his breath. But there was no time. He struggled to his knees and bobbed his head at Lehman.

Together, they began to reel in the third member of the team.

Wu Tan slept. The doctor had gone, albeit reluctantly, for he was of the firm opinion that his patient should be in hospital. But Yeung Chao had been adamant, and in the face of his absolute refusal the doctor could do little else but leave. The room itself had been put in order and the empty bottles removed, courtesy of the housekeeper of the floor and some persuasion by Cavanna. Tempers had been smoothed; apologies had been made. But nothing would ever erase the memory of the disgraceful exhibition Wu Tan had made of himself.

It was 9:30 a.m., 11:30 a.m. in Ottawa. Yeung Chao picked up the phone and placed a person-to-person call to the ambassador. He was connected with unusual celerity.

"What is wrong out there?" the ambassador demanded before Yeung Chao had a chance to speak. "What is the matter with your chairman, Comrade Wu Tan? I tried to speak with him last night. Has he taken leave of his senses?"

"That is precisely why I have taken the liberty of telephoning you, Comrade Ambassador," Yeung Chao replied. "In view of the unfortunate, one might almost say calamitous events that took place here this morning . . ."

"Calamitous?" The ambassador's voice rose sharply as he echoed the word. Then, in a more moderate tone, but obviously under stress, he said, "Continue, please. I am listening."

"I would not wish you to believe me disloyal to our chairman," Yeung Chao began obsequiously, "but in view of his erratic behavior and loss of face . . ." He stopped, apparently overcome by the enormity of it all.

"Comrade Yeung Chao," the ambassador broke in impatiently, "you would be doing me a kindness and your country a service if you would simply relate, as briefly as possible, what has happened."

Yeung Chao sighed heavily. "As you wish, Comrade Ambassador," he said sadly. He took a deep breath and plunged into his story. "Last evening, after Comrade Wu Tan had spoken to you on the telephone informing you of the helicopter crash and Comrade Tai Ling's sudden unexplained illness, he appeared to be irritable and depressed. I'm afraid I attributed it to the unfortunate position in which these events had placed him; not, of course, Comrade Ambassador, that it was for me to judge. Naturally, I tried to help in any way I could, but I'm afraid he did not want my help. He became even more irritable and, I'm sorry Comrade Ambassador, but this is very difficult for me, he dismissed me, quite summarily I might add, and I went to dinner alone. I did not see him again last night, although I spoke to him through the door. It was locked, and when I called out to him to ask if he was all right or if he needed anything, he, I'm sorry Comrade Ambassador, but you did insist that I tell you, he became very abusive and flung some object at the door. He told me to go away and leave him alone. He actually *ordered* me to go. I did not see him again until about two hours ago."

Yeung Chao stopped as if overcome. He had to be prompted by the ambassador before he continued.

"It now seems that Comrade Wu Tan began to drink after I left. Quite heavily. There were a number of empty bottles on the floor of his room this morning. I—I do not know exactly how many . . ."

"So, he *was* drunk last night when I spoke to him," the ambassador broke in. "I suspected it, but with his past record I couldn't bring myself to believe it. After all these years it would be so utterly foolish."

"P-past record . . .?"

"You must have known that he was once an alcoholic," Chung Yeng-tse said testily.

"I—I had heard rumors," Yeung Chao admitted, "but I thought they were malicious lies put about by those who were jealous of Comrade Wu Tan's respected position. Perhaps, if I'd known . . ." There was a hint of accusation in Yeung Chao's voice.

"It cannot be helped now," the ambassador interrupted impatiently. "But I tried to reach you by telephone last night after I spoke to Wu Tan. Where were you?"

"What time would that be?" Yeung Chao parried.

"It was nine o'clock, precisely, your time."

Yeung Chao uttered an exclamation of regret. "My deepest apologies, Comrade Ambassador, but since I had an unexpected free evening after Comrade Wu Tan dismissed me, I took the opportunity to lead an impromptu discussion on the decadence of Western ideologies based upon what we have observed since we arrived here. I am very sorry to have missed your call, but I am pleased to say that all our members attended and entered into the discussion with enthusiasm. Later, after the discussion, I walked for some time trying to understand the problems of our chairman. His actions of the past few days have been puzzling, one might almost say irrational. But, of course, when we found the bottles of whisky concealed in his suitcase this morning, I began to realize . . ."

"Concealed? In his suitcase? Whisky?" The ambassador's voice hardened. "What were you doing going through his suitcase?" he demanded.

"The doctor who attended Comrade Wu Tan needed to know whether or not the chairman was taking any drugs or remedies. We checked the suitcase together to see if there were any pills. He had a heart condition, you know . . ."

The ambassador broke in again. "Doctor? What's all this about a doctor? Why did you bring in a Western doctor? Is Wu Tan seriously ill? Tell me at once. I want every detail."

Yeung Chao smiled to himself. He told the ambassador what he wanted to know. Every detail. When he had finished, there was an appalled silence at the other end of the line. When at last the ambassador did regain his voice, it was as if he had suddenly become very old.

"Give me your number," he said, apparently forgetting that he already had it. "Wait there. I will call you back within the hour."

The call came through forty-three minutes later. The ambassador had regained his composure. His voice was crisp and to the point.

"Since Comrade Sung S'u-mah is not available at the moment, you, Comrade Yeung Chao, are in complete charge of the delegation. You will not speak to anyone outside your party of the matters we have discussed. Should you be approached by members of the press or anyone else for that matter, you will make no statements. No comments at all, understand?"

"I understand," Yeung Chao said solemnly.

"You will place Wu Tan under close house arrest. He is to see no one, speak to no one other than yourself and one other, Shan Shi. He is, I am given to understand, an aide in your delegation. He can be trusted to keep watch over Wu Tan."

Yeung Chao ran a nervous hand through his lank hair. He had not been aware that Shan Shi was an agent of the Social Affairs Department. He recovered quickly.

"As you say, Comrade Ambassador," he said meekly.

"You will contact the authorities immediately and

find out how long it will be before we can expect the return of Sung S'u-mah and Kuan Lo. As soon as they are fit to travel, you will all proceed to Calgary where you will board the first available flight for Vancouver. Tai Ling is to be removed from hospital immediately. He will, of course, return with your party."

"I have no report on his condition . . ." Yeung Chao began, but Chung Yeng-tse cut him off brusquely.

"He is to be brought back immediately *regardless of his condition*."

Yeung Chao drew in his breath. "I understand, Comrade Ambassador."

"You will be met in Vancouver," the ambassador went on. "Arrangements will be made for you and your party to fly home as quickly as possible. Do you understand? Are there any questions?"

"I understand completely, Comrade Ambassador," Yeung Chao said. "May I express my sincere and deepest thanks for your confidence in me. I shall try to be worthy of your trust."

"The decision was not mine; it was made in Peking," the ambassador replied tersely. "There will be a full inquiry into this matter when you return. I suggest that you keep a full and detailed record of events. Inform me when you are ready to leave Banff. I shall expect to hear from you soon."

"It will be as you say, Comrade Ambassador," Yeung Chao said respectfully. He replaced the telephone only after he heard the ambassador hang up.

Yeung Chao sat on the edge of the bed and hugged himself. Literally. "I've done it!" he whispered. He fell back on the bed and flung his arms wide. "I've done it!" he shouted at the ceiling. Triumphant laughter echoed and reechoed around the room.

The mist that had wrapped him in its ice-cold blanket was lifting. Perversely, Mikhail wished it back again, for at least it had afforded him some concealment. He stumbled almost aimlessly from cover to less frequent cover, knowing that his pursuers could not be far behind. He had heard them, close, too close once, but had eluded them. Now, it seemed, there were more of them; he could hear them on every side, herding him up the mountain to where the cover thinned and snow still filled the crevices.

The ground rose sharply in front of him, its contours barren, wet and rocky. Foot-high clumps of weeds clung tenaciously to the graveled slope; no purchase there for weary hands and feet. His only hope lay to his right where the slope fell away, dropping into denser bush that offered sanctuary, however temporary. He stumbled, fell, and slid down the surface shale, ignoring cuts and scratches gouged by jutting twigs. He glimpsed a stream below and began to scramble down the wooded bank.

The bush beside him exploded. A huge, brown, bristling body hurled itself toward him, rearing high and, crazily, balancing on one hind leg. Blood-flecked foam dripped from yellow fangs, and pain-filled eyes followed every move Mikhail made as he tried to escape the charging bear. He tried to twist aside but the sodden slope betrayed him. He fell. A searing pain shot through his knee and it buckled under him.

The gun! "Oh, Jesus! Oh, Mary, Mother of God, help me now," he babbled incoherently as long-forgotten childhood prayers said in secret flooded back. He saw the gun a yard away. He rolled toward it and screamed with pain as his broken kneecap struck a jutting root. The giant body pivoted in a grotesque pirouette on its one good leg, and crashed down on top of him.

His dying shriek resounded throughout the forest as the mighty talons ripped away his throat.

Wedged as they were at the base of the chimney, Hans Lehman and the other two members of the team had no choice but to wait out the storm. The wind shrieked across the narrow cleft, hammering at their senses as if in spiteful frenzy because it had failed to pluck them from their precarious refuge. An hour passed before the veil began to lift. Clouds continued to tumble across the mountain, but the wind had lost its force and the blowing snow gradually subsided. Distant peaks began to reappear, and ragged clouds reluctantly divided to reveal the blue beyond.

Lehman wasted no time, pausing only long enough to radio to Dawson that they were about to continue their climb. "The chimney's about forty feet straight up," he told the rescue leader, "then it takes a sharp bend to the left. It looks as if we'll have to move to the outside. I'll let you know when we clear the top."

High above them, sheltered only by the thin walls of the helicopter cabin from the wind, the stranded trio shut their eyes against the sudden stab of sunlight. But with the light came warmth, welcome warmth upon their faces chilled almost to freezing. Buffeted severely by the wind, the crippled helicopter had shuddered and groaned at each fresh onslaught, and the icy blasts had found their way inside the cabin to turn their faces white with cold.

Yet now, with the sun full on them, the air inside the cabin was becoming warm. They shed their sleeping bags and opened their parkas to let in the warm air. Stiff and cramped from sitting huddled up, their movements were slow and clumsy as circulation painfully returned. Strangley, they did not speak. Their eyes slid furtively past each other's faces like strangers on a bus, moving on to stare into space or to steal a glance at the ledge, hoping to see the heads of their rescuers suddenly appear. They eased aching muscles and settled down once more to wait.

Once past the chimney, the rescue team found the going easier. A gully choked with detritus led upward to their right, making their ascent little more than a rock scramble, until it stopped abruptly at the buttress that stood between them and their final climb to the ledge directly overhead. It was grueling work. A short but dangerous traverse around the thrusting corner, then straight up the face, fingertip by tenacious fingertip, inch by inch, foot by hard-won foot.

Slowly, testing every toehold, Hans Lehman inched his way toward the ledge. He was thankful that the people on the ledge could not see him. Far better to rely upon his own time-tested skills than on the enthusiastic help of amateurs trying to help him up. The rock above him curved outward, forcing him to pause until Bonner could come up beneath him. Peterson followed closely, each man instinctively moving into the best position to boost Lehman over the jutting lip. Lehman swung outward, dangling for a moment like a puppet over the abyss. Bonner and Peterson moved swiftly beneath him, and seconds later Lehman sprawled safely on the ledge. The helicopter lurched as everyone scrambled to get out first, but he waved them back.

Krell understood. He held the other back while Lehman pulled himself to his feet and set about the task of pulling his companions up the last few feet. Two minutes later all three climbers stood safely on the ledge, and suddenly everyone was pumping everyone else's hand.

Sung S'u-mah embraced the leader of the rescue party with such fierce intensity that he could barely get his breath. Kuan Lo just stood there grinning as if his face would split. Huge tears coursed unheeded down his lined and weary face.

But Krell displayed no emotion at all.

While Peterson and Bonner set up the pulley system, anchoring it securely to the ledge by driving pitons into fissures in the rock, Lehman checked the condition of the survivors. He shook his head in amazement.

"The lady has a bruised leg, and the pilot has a couple of minor cuts on his arm, but apart from that they are all in excellent condition," he informed Dawson over the radio. "Not even a case of frostbite."

"Do you need any extra food or warm clothing up there?" Dawson inquired.

"Just the usual gear," Lehman told him. "We won't be needing the stretcher. They all say they prefer to go down by Grumminger seat." He glanced across to where Bonner was hammering in the last piton. "We'll be ready for the cable in a couple of minutes. I'll call you." Lehman was about to turn his attention to the newly-mounted pulley when another thought occurred to him. "What about the helicopter?" he asked. "It's just sitting here almost intact. Rotor's pretty mangled but the rest of it looks to be in fair shape. Any word from the owners?"

"Not a word," Dawson said. "They can't seem to find anyone who has any authority. Looks as if they've all gone away for the weekend."

While the cable was on the way up, Lehman turned his attention to the helicopter. The damage was remarkably light. One rotor blade was shattered, and the shaft was bent. The tail fan had buckled when it had slammed into the solid rock, but the frame and cabin were intact.

"I don't know how you managed it," he confessed wonderingly to Krell. "How did it happen?"

Krell shook his head slowly. "I hardly know myself, it happened so fast," he said. "We'd just been over the Valley of the Ten Peaks and I thought I'd show them the Fay Glacier. We circled the top of Babel, then dropped down to come around the east side. The motor just cut out on me. No warning at all. I was too far below the summit to land, and there was nothing underneath me for two thousand feet." Suddenly he grinned crookedly. "They tell you to set the blades and glide her in if your engine cuts out, but this was ridiculous. The engine fired a couple of times but cut out again. I saw this ledge, so when it fired again, I just pointed at it and ran her straight in. We were lucky."

"You can say that again!" Lehman said, shaking his

head. He turned to the task ahead of him. "Better get everything you want out of the chopper so we can send it down after you," he told Krell. "We can't do much about the chopper itself, so we'll anchor it down before we leave. Not that it's liable to hit anyone if it falls off," he grinned, "but we'd better make sure."

"I wouldn't spend a minute more than I absolutely had to up here," Krell said. "Leave the stuff; it's insured."

"It won't take long," Lehman told him. "Don't worry, you'll be safely down by then."

Krell shrugged. "It's your life," he observed. He began to unload the helicopter.

Once the cable was in place, the rescue equipment came up swiftly. Few words were spoken other than the brief commands to the base below. Each man knew his job and did it with an economy of time and motion that could mean the difference between bringing people off the mountains alive instead of dead. Bonner completed the last check and nodded at Lehman.

"All right," Lehman said, "we're ready to send the first one down. I'd better explain how the Grumminger seat works. All it is, really, is a piggy-back harness. The rescuer is strapped into the lower half of the harness, with arms and legs free, of course, while the person being rescued is strapped into the upper part of the harness. Their arms and legs are wrapped around the rescuer and secured firmly. There is no possible way that you can fall out, and the cable, winch, and pulley could lower an elephant if it had to."

"All right, a small elephant," he conceded, grinning at Sung S'u-mah's sceptical look. She regarded him blankly for a second, then returned the smile hesitantly.

Lehman continued. "The rescuer controls his descent by giving the team below instructions throughout the descent. You are both facing the mountain so you can keep from swinging into the face on vertical drops. When you come to a slope, the rescuer simply walks backward down it, supported by the cable. It's really a very simple and safe procedure."

"How can he use a radio while he is climbing down?" Kuan Lo asked. "He'll need both hands."

Lehman patted the helmet on Bonner's head. "There's a radio built into this," he told him. "He can hear the winch crew and us up here. He has a bone-conductance microphone built in so he can talk to us. He doesn't even have the inconvenience of a mike in front of his mouth." Lehman paused and looked around the little group. "Believe me, we haven't lost anyone yet. It is very safe, though, to be honest, it's quite a thrill if it's your first time, and I can assure you we wouldn't be up here if we had the slightest doubt about getting down safely ourselves."

The woman stared over the edge. "It looks so far down."

"I can still have the stretcher brought up if you'd rather go down that way," Lehman told her.

Sung S'u-mah seemed to hesitate, then shook her head firmly. "No, I'll go down on that seat thing," she said, indicating the Grumminger seat.

"Good." Lehman grinned encouragingly. "Now, who's first?"

"I believe," Kuan Lo said hesitantly, "you have a saying in the West about ladies being first?"

Lehman looked at him curiously. Perhaps it was the little doctor's accented English, but his words sounded sardonic and his eyes seemed to have suddenly become quite blank. If Sung S'u-mah had been apprehensive about the descent before, she showed no signs of it now. She inclined her head toward Kuan Lo almost as if he had paid her a compliment.

"Thank you," she said pleasantly. "I shall accept your kind offer." She glanced at Krell. "Unless, of course . . .?" She left the question hanging in the air.

Krell shook his head. "Go ahead," he said brusquely. "I've still got work to do up here."

"Of course," said Sung S'u-mah. She showed no fear as she allowed herself to be strapped into the Grumminger seat. Lehman checked the fastenings himself, then pulled her hood close around her face.

"I know it sounds pretty silly," he told her, "but try to relax. It makes it easier for you and it'll make it much easier on Gerry." She nodded without speaking.

Bonner settled the helmet more comfortably on his head, and spoke. "Are you ready below?"

The answer came back immediately. "Ready below."

"Do you copy, Hans?" Dawson's voice came clearly over the portable unit held by Lehman.

"I copy," he replied.

Bonner tested the tension on the cable. "Okay, I'm coming down," he said.

Lehman and Peterson eased Bonner and his human cargo over the edge. He took the strain and planted his feet firmly against the sheer face of the rock. Sung S'u-mah looked down and felt a moment of panic. The cable that had looked so substantial while they had been standing on the ledge suddenly looked thinner, like a cobweb glinting in the sun. Instinctively she clutched her rescuer tighter, and found out for herself why the Grumminger seat was so arranged. If her arms had not been strapped in place she would probably have strangled the man. She heard Bonner talking, and almost imperceptibly the calm assurance of his voice began to relax her. He talked constantly, and she had to marvel at the feather-touch of the winch operator far below them, somewhere out of sight.

They made rapid progress, the first two hundred feet being completely vertical. Bonner's arms and legs were spread like those of a human fly against the mountain face, preventing them from spinning as they descended. Then came a steep, jagged slope and that was much better because Sung S'u-mah could feel the solid tremor through her body as Bonner plodded methodically backward, supported always by the cable that now seemed to vanish into the clouds above. It was like going piggyback down a ladder, she thought, almost enjoying the experience when, abruptly, Bonner stopped and she heard him giving careful instructions to the winch operator. Her fears returned as she realized that they had come to the edge of the slope and from here on down they would be suspended over the edge of a bulge in the mountain. They began to move again, and were suddenly hanging free, yards away from the face.

They began to spin. Slowly at first, then more rapidly, descending all the time. The rock face disappeared and Sung S'u-mah found herself staring out across the valley. And then the rock face again. Three, four, perhaps five times they spun before starting to swing back the other way. She shut her eyes, fearing that she would be sick. She concentrated on Bonner's voice and drew comfort from it. The queasiness in her stomach subsided.

Warm air touched her face, and for the first time since starting the descent she allowed herself to relax, for warmer air meant a lower altitude. The spinning stopped and she opened her eyes. There, in front of her, was a solid wall of rock mere inches from her face. She wanted to reach out and touch it, but of course it was impossible.

The descent from that point on was slower but much easier, with Bonner simply walking backward most of the way. A short, vertical drop hard against the mountain face came next, then, quite suddenly, it was over. She heard other voices, and steadying hands reached out to support her. There seemed to be activity all around her. She felt someone tugging at the harness but no one seemed to be in any hurry to release her.

"Just stay put," a voice told her, "and we'll have you over to the lodge in nothing flat. Nothing to be afraid of. The worst is over. The chopper's here now."

She heard it then. The 'whap-whap-whap' of blades beating air, and she felt the blast of ice-cold air and stinging particles of snow and grit against her face. The helicopter hovered some fifty feet above them. A cable dangled from it and a man beside the winch held on to the end of it. Someone unclipped the Grumminger seat from the rescue cable, then snapped it to the ring on the end of the cable dangling from the helicopter.

"There's not enough room for him to land here," a voice shouted in her ear, "so you'll be carried across the valley underneath the chopper. Two minutes at the most. Nothing to worry about."

The man clapped her on the back, thumped Bonner on the helmet, then signaled to the helicopter. Sung S'u-mah heard Bonner talking again and realized that he was now in contact with the helicopter pilot above them. It was a short, dizzying, exhilarating flight, soaring across the valley some sixty feet below the helicopter, and Sung S'u-mah was almost sorry when it ended in a slow, inch-by-inch descent into the parking lot of the lodge. Voices, reassuring and calm. Hands, steady hands, kind hands stripped away the harness and suddenly she was free. She was on a stretcher, confined again, blankets tucked around her. She struggled to sit up. She wanted to thank her rescuer, but already he had gone; gone back to where the winch crew waited to hoist him up the mountain once again. Tears sprang to her eyes and tumbled down her cheeks.

"Are you all right?" a voice inquired anxiously.

The tension of the past twenty-four hours broke and she began to giggle. Tears streamed down her face and she giggled louder. She couldn't seem to stop.

Chapter 14

Jacintha shivered and drew the woolen cardigan tighter around her shoulders. "Couldn't we have more heat in here?" she asked. "It's freezing in this basement."

The red-faced man continued to watch the cassette rewind. "It's an old gravity furnace," he said over his shoulder, nodding in the direction of the squat monster that dominated the center of the basement. "The hot air rises, the cold air sinks. Unfortunately, we happen to be in the cold zone." The tape came to the end and he stopped the machine. He placed the cassette in a plastic case and scrawled a large R7 across it with a felt pen before stacking it with the others.

"What does the R stand for?" Jacintha asked idly, more to keep the man talking than for any other reason.

"Recorded," he told her. He indicated the cassettes in an open carrying case on the bench. "Those are the ones we didn't use. I always keep plenty of spares on hand just in case."

Jacintha picked up one of the cassettes and examined it closely. "It looks different," she said. "I've never seen a silver tape like this before."

The man nodded. "It is different," he said. "It's a special long-play tape, takes up no more reel space than the ones you buy in the store, but each cassette will give you a full two hours recording time, and it's virtually indestructible. We developed it in our own labs. It's far too expensive to market commercially."

"Do you do this kind of thing all the time?"

The man looked up and smiled, but he remained silent. He put another cassette on the machine and set it on REWIND. Then, very methodically as he had done throughout the whole procedure, he counted the cassettes marked R again. There were seven. A step sounded on the stairs. Roy Guthrie ducked beneath a furnace pipe and greeted them pleasantly. He stood watching the man at the bench for a moment.

"How soon can I have the tapes?" he asked, his eyes still on the cassette.

"One more to go," he was told. "Then I can get my equipment out of here. What about the ones upstairs?"

"The reels? They're already on their way," Guthrie said. "I'm taking these myself." He turned to go but Jacintha stopped him.

"What about me?" she wanted to know. "When can I leave?"

Guthrie stopped and appeared to consider. The sound of someone moving furniture came from the room above their heads. He cocked his head on one side, listening. "They're down," he said. His mind seemed to be elsewhere. "The news came in about an hour ago." Whatever was tugging at his mind, he dismissed it as he turned to face Jacintha and saw the questions in her eyes.

"Everything is all right," he assured her. "You'll hear it yourself on the next newscast, believe me."

Abruptly, Jacintha sat down on the stool beside the bench. Her legs felt wobbly as the tension drained out of her. "Then I can leave?"

Guthrie eyed her speculatively for several seconds. He's going to say no, she thought. He's looking for the right words.

"I see no reason why you shouldn't leave this afternoon," he said. "I think we understand each other?"

His answer took her by surprise. She should have

felt relieved but there was something, something she couldn't define just beyond the reach of her senses.

"May I — could I see . . .?" She stopped because Guthrie was shaking his head as she had known he would. He appeared to be genuinely sorry.

"I'll let you know exactly when," he told her. He turned and ducked around the furnace pipe and went back upstairs. The red-faced man slipped the last cassette into its container, marked it and put it with the others. He began to gather together his equipment and pack up the tape recorder.

Preoccupied with her own thoughts, Jacintha began to help. "Finished with this?" she asked, picking up the extension cord that trailed across the floor. The man nodded and she began to coil it up.

"Hold it a minute," he said, "I'd better untie it. I've got it tied to a post back there because the plug kept falling out. He disappeared behind the furnace, following the cord into the darkness.

It was the first time since arriving at the house that she'd been left alone. Without stopping to think where her actions might lead her, Jacintha grabbed a spare cassette from the carrying case and quickly scribbled R5 across the plastic holder. Her nimble fingers slipped the fifth cassette from the recorded stack and replaced it with the blank. She jammed the stolen one into the waistband of her skirt, easing it to one side so that blouse and cardigan concealed it, but in her haste the buttons of her blouse popped open and she struggled feverishly to do them up again before the red faced man came back.

"God, the dust that collects in these old houses," he said as he reappeared. "You can't move without getting it all over you."

She was still fumbling with the last button. Too late; he'd see her, wonder what she was doing. The button slipped into place and she looked up with fearful eyes.

The red-faced man was busy brushing the dust from his clothes, head bent, eyes intent upon his task. "I'm going to have to have these pants cleaned again," he complained.

"That's too bad," she said mechanically, trying to control her voice. Her heart was pounding as if it would burst. She bent to the task of coiling the extension cord again, eyes averted so he would not see the guilt within.

"Goddam furnace," he said without rancor. He started putting the cassettes away.

The small paneled room was warm and stuffy, and McCrimmon's eyelids were heavy. He would have liked nothing better than to close them and go to sleep, but there was work to do. A lot of work.

He forced his tired brain to focus upon the thoughts that seemed to want to slip away from him. "He must have walked right into that wounded bear," he told Wellington. "He was dead by the time we reached him; face, throat, and half his chest ripped away." He grimaced at the recollection. "The attack just about finished off the bear, too," he went on. "Good thing it did. It would have been rough going into the bush after a brute like that. They had to shoot it of course."

Wellington grunted. "Never did like bears," he said. "Can't trust 'em. What about ID on the dead man?"

"Driver's license, Social Insurance card, and a couple of credit cards all made out to Michael Vernon," McCrimmon said. "Canadian passport in the same name. We found it, together with over eight hundred dollars in a money belt under his shirt." McCrimmon consulted a small notebook. "A Timex wrist-watch, a pair of sun glasses, two receipts for gas for the truck, one on a Canmore service station, the other on a Shell station right here in town, so he's been around for a few days at least. A set of keys for the truck. The truck's registered in Vernon's name. Pocket knife, handkerchief, and a folded piece of paper in his shirt pocket that seems to be a list of expenses. It shows meals and accommodations for a period of six days in a motel unit in Canmore, but the last date was over a week ago. Either he hasn't been living there for the past week, or he hasn't filled in his expenses. I've got someone on it now."

Wellington nodded absently. "Another passport," he muttered, half to himself. "How many people do you know who carry their passports around with them?"

"I know what you mean," McCrimmon said. "The Security boys jumped on that one right away. They're digging into it now."

"Good," said Wellington surprisingly. He was not noted for his cordial relations with the Security Service. "They're the only ones with the resources to unravel this mess," he went on, "and it sure as hell is developing into a mess. Where's the body now?"

"On its way to Calgary," McCrimmon said.

"They're going to start wondering what in hell is going on up here," the inspector said sourly. "That woman, Miss Haggard, identified the other body as the man she saw on the Minnewanka road. She's quite positive despite the condition of his face. She'll make a damned good witness if ever we manage to put a case together." He placed his fingertips together and stared morosely at the sergeant. "Right now I'd just like to know what the hell is behind it all." He switched tracks abruptly. "Any more news about the condition of the people they brought off the mountain?"

"They've been taken to hospital for observation," McCrimmon said, "but it sounds as if they're all okay."

"Thank God for that, at least," Wellington said glumly. "That's the only good news I've heard today."

"Still having a bad time with the chairman of the Chinese delegation?"

Wellington shot McCrimmon a look that was hard to define. "The chairman of the Chinese delegation," he said ponderously, "will not be giving anyone a bad time for quite some time to come, if my information is correct. It seems that Doctor Wu Tan has a problem with alcohol. He managed to disgrace himself and his countrymen this morning in front of something like two hundred people. Doctor Yeung Chao has taken over his duties, and I gather the fat man will be kept under wraps until they leave, which will be as soon as possible now the other two are off the mountain."

"What about the other one?" McCrimmon asked. "The one who became sick; Tai Ling, was it?"

Wellington looked surprised. "Oh, yes, I forgot you wouldn't know about him, would you? He discharged himself from hospital this morning. Insisted on returning here against all advice. He's in the hotel now."

"That was a fast recovery," the sergeant observed. "Still, I'm glad it was no worse. I guess Angleton was wrong when he said he thought Tai Ling had been poisoned."

Wellington scratched thoughtfully at his chin. "Damned if I know," he muttered softly. "We'll probably never know. According to the Calgary doctors he was a very sick man when he left."

"Then, why . . .?"

The Iron Duke turned to stare at McCrimmon, fixing him with his cold gray eyes for several seconds before replying. Disconcerting to many, the stare was a mannerism McCrimmon had observed many times before. Wellington did it when he was preoccupied or puzzled.

"The new chairman, Yeung Chao, sent one of his aides to see Tai Ling in hospital this morning," he said abruptly. "He was refused admittance, of course, since Tai Ling was still considered to be very ill and poison was still suspected. The aide didn't make any fuss. He just went away, and half an hour later the hospital administrator received a telephone call from Ottawa telling him to let the man in and to allow Tai Ling to leave if he should want to do so. The call," Wellington said softly, "came directly from a minister."

McCrimmon pursed his lips in a silent whistle. To

stir up a minister in Ottawa on such short notice was next to impossible at any time, but on a Sunday morning? "I'm impressed," he said, not altogether flippantly.

"Once the aide gained admittance," Wellington continued as if McCrimmon had not spoken, "it was only a matter of minutes until Tai Ling was demanding to be released. The hospital authorities couldn't stop him and neither could the Calgary police. They called me to let me know what had happened, but there wasn't anything I could do by then."

"And you say he's back here now? Has a doctor seen him?"

Wellington shook his head. "Yeung Chao isn't allowing anyone near him," he said. "I tried to talk to Tai Ling when he arrived, but he scurried inside like a rabbit. He looked like hell but he was moving under his own steam."

McCrimmon rose and began to pace around the small room. "Do you think he might have made himself ill?" he ventured. "To get away from the others."

Wellington's eyes narrowed. "Are you suggesting that Tai Ling might have been trying to defect?" he said at last.

McCrimmon shrugged. "It's possible. It's happened before. Maybe he misjudged the dosage, made himself sicker than he intended, and went into some kind of shock. It would account for them dragging him back from Calgary that way."

Wellington thought about that. "It could have been something like that," he said finally, "but I'm inclined to think it has more to do with Wu Tan's performance this morning. Otherwise they would have brought him back from Calgary last night." His voice took on firmer conviction. "Yeung Chao informed me that the entire delegation will be leaving in the morning. They've been ordered home. He didn't say that, exactly, but I gather that's what's happened."

McCrimmon grunted. "He doesn't seem to give a

damn about his people, does he?" he said. "Here they are, barely down from the mountain and he wants them to take off for China."

"He's already been on to Angleton," Wellington said. "Told him he wanted his people back in the hotel this afternoon."

McCrimmon turned. "And . . .?" Wellington made a strange sound. If it had been anyone else, anyone else at all, McCrimmon would have sworn it was a chuckle.

"Angleton told him to get stuffed," Wellington said. "Politely, of course."

Tai Ling stared blankly at the ceiling, head throbbing dully, sweat glistening on his brow. He could smell the food on the table beside the bed and he swallowed hard to stop himself from being sick.

"You must eat," Yeung Chao told him, sloshing the soup around the bowl as if to tempt him. The bile rose in Tai Ling's throat and he set his muscles against it. "You must regain your strength," Yeung Chao coaxed. "You'll need it for traveling home tomorrow."

Tai Ling continued to stare at the ceiling. That's what was worrying Yeung Chao, that he might not be fit to travel. The newly appointed head of the delegation didn't want anything to go wrong.

The bile subsided. "Sung S'u-mah," he gasped, afraid to open his mouth too far. "I must see Sung S'u-mah."

Yeung Chao shook his head impatiently. "You cannot see her. She's in . . ." He broke off, remembering that Tai Ling knew nothing of the helicopter crash or that Sung S'u-mah was even now in hospital recovering from her ordeal on the mountain. She and Tai Ling had once been lovers, there might still be feelings. If Tai Ling became upset he might have a relapse, might delay their departure. Yeung Chao felt the prickle of sweat on his brow.

"She's in town," he amended. "I'll tell her you'd like to see her when she returns." He abandoned the bowl of soup. "Better get some sleep," he advised.

Tai Ling's eyes left the ceiling and sought those of Yeung Chao. "Soon," he whispered through clenched teeth. "Tell her soon."

"I have said I will tell her," Yeung Chao replied testily. He was becoming irritated with Tai Ling. The man represented a roadblock, and he was in no mood for roadblocks. "Sleep," he ordered as he turned away. "See that you get some food down him," he said quietly to the man who lounged beside the door. "He must be fit to travel tomorrow."

Shan Shi nodded mutely and closed the door softly behind Yeung Chao. He remained standing there beside the door, his eyes on the small figure in the bed. He, too, would be happy to see Sung S'u-mah again.

Tai Ling continued to stare at the ceiling without seeing it. The image fixed firmly in his mind was that of Sung S'u-mah's anxious face close to his, and of a blurred, yet somehow distinct figure standing behind her.

The last faint tinge of gold faded from the cotton-candy clouds as they melded into lumpish banks of gray. The rugged peaks stood black against the fading light in stark and somber silhouette. Shadows, black as ravens' wings, crept into deep, steep-sided valleys where rising evening mists already hid the river far below. The veil of night fell swiftly on the lonely road that led to Rogers Pass. No friendly wink of lights ahead. The salesmen and the early tourists had finished driving for the day. The big long-distance trucks that rolled right through the night had yet to reach this long and winding stretch of highway.

Jacintha gripped the wheel and flexed her arms to ease the stiffness settling in her shoulders. The monotonous hum of the engine and the warmth from the heater were beginning to make her drowsy. She rolled the window down and let the cold night air fill the car. The needle on the gas gauge still stood above the half-full mark, but she should have stopped at Golden to fill the tank in spite of Roy's explicit orders. She should have stopped at that viewpoint before she got to Golden. She should have explained to the two men in the yellow Chrysler that there were no gas stations for 150 kilometers between Golden and Revelstoke, and she didn't like the idea of setting out with only half a tank of gas. She should have . . .

Jacintha shook her head wearily and abandoned the imaginary conversation as she had so many times before. There was nothing to be gained by going over it all again. They had their orders; nothing she could say would change their minds. Her eyes flicked to the rearview mirror. Still there, not too close, but not too far back either. Roy's words came back again as they had repeatedly ever since she'd left the house. Over and over again like an endless tape.

"No stops until you get to Revelstoke," he'd warned her sternly. "Your motel is booked and paid for, and I want you there no later than eleven." He looked at his watch. "It's just turned seven now, you can make it easily."

"But . . ."

"No stops! Absolutely none!"

Suddenly he smiled, a shy, uncertain smile that transformed his face. "I'm sorry," he apologized, "but it is important that you do as I ask. If you don't agree, I'll have to insist that you stay until tomorrow. I'm sure you understand my position."

Already seated in her car, the tape cassette pressing hard against her ribs, Jacintha quickly nodded. She didn't want anything to prevent her leaving now. She didn't think she could take another night of fear. "I—I'll do exactly as you say," she said almost inaudibly. Her mouth was dry and her fingers trembled as she took the keys he handed to her.

"Good," he beamed. "I'm sure we understand each other perfectly." He paused as if uncertain about going on, then said, "There is one more thing I think you'd better know. After all, there's no need for you to worry needlessly. Two of my men will follow along behind you when you leave, just to be sure that no one follows you. I'm sure you understand."

Jacintha forced a smile. She should have known that Roy would leave nothing to chance now.

He stepped away from the car. "Drive carefully, my dear," he told her. "It's unfortunate that we couldn't have met under better circumstances." He sounded almost wistful. She was half-way to Lake Louise before the shaking stopped.

The cold night air cleared her head and stripped away the fear that had drugged her mind. Thoughts, half-formed, half-thrust aside, came flooding in. Why did Roy want her to be at Revelstoke by eleven? And, if it were so important, why had he delayed her departure until after seven? Why had he allowed her to leave tonight at all? It would have made more sense if he'd insisted that she stay until the Chinese delegation had left the country.

"*I'm to go as far as Revelstoke tonight. What about tomorrow?*"

"*You're free to do as you wish, my dear. Just don't forget our bargain.*"

What was going to happen tonight that made Roy so confident about tomorrow? Lights flickered across her face, a reflection of headlights in the rearview mirror. Nothing left to chance.

"Oh, God!"

She shivered convulsively. She rolled the window up but the chill that gripped her heart remained. Memories flooded in on her. Little things. Things that, at the time, had made no sense. The delays, the fussing about the car. So unlike Roy. Until seven o'clock.

Then it had been all business. "Stay in your car.

Revelstoke by eleven." *Revelstoke by eleven.* That was the key.

"Dear God, I hope I'm wrong," she whispered despairingly.

The lights seemed brighter now, not quite so far behind. She felt the panic rising, and brushed it angrily aside.

"He wouldn't dare!" she told herself aloud. He would, a voice inside her said. That was it! Roy didn't give a damn about her arriving at Revelstoke by eleven. He'd just used that as an excuse for the timetable, a timetable that would make certain she would be on this isolated stretch of mountain road after dark.

The lights were closer now, she was sure of it. She forced herself to stay calm. Wasn't there a lodge or something at the summit? She wished she'd kept track of distance since leaving Golden.

The accommodation book! The glove compartment. She undid her seatbelt and reached over for it, then realized she'd have to stop to read it.

The lights were getting brighter. She searched the road ahead for signs of other cars but she searched in vain. She fought the panic down. How far was she from the lodge? There had to be a lodge.

With sudden determination, she pushed the accelerator to the floor and the Datsun leapt ahead. It pulled away from the car behind and, as the lights grew smaller in the mirror, her confidence returned. She roared flat out into a curve and the lights behind her disappeared. Over a crest and down a long, sweeping grade, across a bridge and up the other side. Jacintha glanced anxiously in the mirror but the lights she saw were far behind. The grade increased and the car began to lose the momentum it had picked up no matter how she pressed the pedal to the floor. She had no time to check the mirror as the headlights of the Datsun swung out across the blackness of the valley, then abruptly swung back on the road again as she cornered tightly. The road twisted back and forth upon itself. Climbing, always climbing. But she could not ignore the light. It filled the car.

"I'm just going too slow on the hill," she told herself aloud. "It's probably not even them. It's some other car. He wants to pass, that's all." The lights behind flicked twice.

Thank God! It's not them. He's signaling to pass. Relief swept through her and, automatically, she pulled further to the right to let him pass. She was almost crying with relief. The car came level with her own. It was the yellow Chrysler. Yellow like the Datsun, almost identical, in fact. Somewhere, deep inside her, alarm bells reached a fever pitch.

Too late she tried to hit the brakes. Too late she realized that there was nothing there beside the road except a yawning chasm. And as the Chrysler swerved across her path she knew with awful clarity why the car was yellow. Who would notice yellow paint marks on a yellow car? If, of course, they ever found it.

The impact tore the steering wheel from her straining fingers. The headlights pointed into space, probing, finding nothing but infinity. The engine screamed as tires left the road, and the girl inside could feel it slowly start to somersault. She had the door half open when the metal crumpled all around her . . .

High above, the yellow Chrysler made a careful U-turn in the middle of the road and headed back the way it had come.

The half-ton truck drifted over the last rise before the road began the long descent to Moraine Lake, and the driver brought it gently to a stop. He killed the engine and the lights. Nothing stirred.

From the seat beside him he took a pair of powerful night binoculars and hung them around his neck. Next, from the glove compartment, he took a metal box no bigger than a pack of cigarettes. A telescopic antenna slid from its hiding place and locked itself securely.

He descended from the truck and placed the metal box carefully on the hood. Then, using the hood as a brace for his elbows, he focused the binoculars on the topmost slopes of the mountain two miles away across the valley. Faint as the outline was to the naked eye, the ridges jumped sharply into focus through the magic of the lenses. He began to scan them systematically.

He took his time. A rising moon, half-hidden by fast-moving clouds, laid silver strands along the topmost ridges, and twice he thought he'd found what he was looking for, only to realize that he was being fooled by tricks of light on snow. Something glinted dully in the right-hand upper corner of his field of vision. He moved the glasses a fraction of an inch.

A muffled "Ah!" of satisfaction escaped him as he recognized the ledge. Beneath the snow-clad overhang the moonlight probed the dark recess, and reflected back again from the windows of the crippled helicopter. He braced his left arm firmly and held the binoculars steady. Carefully, he reached out with his other hand and found the metal box. His thumb slid across the smooth surface until it found the small, protruding button. He steadied the binoculars until he had the ledge dead center, then pushed the button firmly.

The snow above the ledge convulsed, erupting outward, pale and glittering like a tiny silver nova in the moonlight. The overhang collapsed beneath the crushing weight of ice and snow, its rock support blasted into rubble by the charge.

He caught a glimpse of the helicopter as it disappeared beneath the avalanche, and then it was gone as if it had never been. Smaller overhangs broke loose, and soon there were a dozen streams of silver cascading down the north-east face of Mt. Babel. A sound like rolling thunder echoed and reechoed across the valley until at last it died away. A pall of dust and snow rose high above the valley floor and hung there like a cloud to mark the final resting place of the wreckage of the helicopter, buried now forever.

Chapter 15

Sung S'u-mah came suddenly awake. Despite the warmth and comfort of the bed she was cold and tense. For an instant she thought she was still on the mountain ledge, then memory returned and she opened her eyes. The familiar sight of the hotel room reassured her, but her thoughts returned immediately to the events of the day before and the strange behavior of Yeung Chao.

The journey from Moraine Lake Lodge into Banff was still nothing but a blur in her mind, but she remembered quite clearly the solicitous nurse who had helped her into bed at the hospital, and the tall, English-sounding doctor who had examined her later.

"You are in excellent physical condition," he had told her, "but you have been through a very traumatic experience. You need rest, complete relaxation; you're still far too tense. I'll have the nurse bring you a mild sedative. It will help you to relax. Best medicine in the world, sleep. By tomorrow you'll be as right as rain."

Sung S'u-mah nodded mechanically. "Were you here yesterday when my—my colleague, Doctor Tai Ling, was brought here? He had stomach cramps and . . ." She broke off as a guarded look came over Angleton's face. "Is anything wrong?"

"No, no, of course not," he said brusquely. "But, in answer to your question, yes, I was here. I sent him into Calgary for some tests and further observation."

Sung S'u-mah frowned. "I don't understand," she said. "He's not—not seriously ill is he?"

Angleton shook his head as if impatient to be rid of the subject. "This is a small hospital," he told her. "The cause of the illness was not immediately apparent. I just wanted to have other tests done. They couldn't be done here. Now, please try to relax. You need rest."

A few minutes later, Sung S'u-mah questioned the nurse who brought the pill, but it was obvious that she knew nothing of Tai Ling. Saturday was one of her days off. Within minutes of the nurse leaving, Sung S'u-mah had been asleep.

The sound of voices raised in anger roused her. At first, she tried to shut them out, irritated by the lack of consideration. She was so tired. She wanted only to be allowed to sleep, to be left alone, to sleep. The voices grew louder. She recognized one of them as Angleton's. The other belonged to Yeung Chao.

"These people have been through a very trying ordeal," the doctor was saying. "They need rest. Tomorrow we can talk about them leaving the hospital, but tonight . . ."

"There is no need to raise your voice, Doctor," Yeung Chao said waspishly. "I understand you perfectly. I understand your position here as a physician. You have a duty to your patients. But I, too, have a duty. I want Doctors Sung S'u-mah and Kuan Lo roused, dressed, and returned to the hotel immediately. Do you understand that?"

"I have a responsibility . . ." Angleton began, but Yeung Chao chopped him off in midsentence.

"You said yourself, Doctor, that they are not injured, that all they need is rest. They can do that just as well at the hotel where we are well equipped to attend to their needs. I would remind you, Doctor Angleton, that I am now the chairman of the delegation representing the People's Republic of China, and, as such, represent my country. If my two colleagues are not released immediately, I repeat, immediately, I shall inform my embassy in Ottawa that they are being held prisoner in this hospital."

An explosive sound came from Angleton, "Don't be so bloody ridiculous!" he snapped. There was a pause, then, "Now look here," he went on in a more conciliatory tone, "I don't know what you do in your country, but I would be much happier if I could check them over once more before they leave hospital. I'm sure that, given a good night's rest, I'll be able to recommend their discharge first thing in the morning."

When Yeung Chao spoke again, his voice was tight and deliberate as if he were holding himself in check only with the greatest effort. "My government has instructed me to have Doctor Sung S'u-mah and Doctor Kuan Lo returned to the hotel tonight in preparation for our departure first thing tomorrow morning," he said. "I have a car waiting. Please arrange to have them dressed and brought to me at once. Otherwise . . ."

Now fully awake, Sung S'u-mah strained to hear Angleton's reply. She felt faintly disappointed when it came.

"Very well," he said wearily. "But I insist upon a statement signed by you accepting full responsibility for the consequences. Then, and only then, will I allow my patients to be released into your custody." His voice faded as he moved off down the hallway.

Less than fifteen minutes later, Sung S'u-mah and Kuan Lo were bundled into a car and driven the short distance to the hotel. She had tried to protest, tried to reason with Yeung Chao, but the pill Angleton had prescribed had been a powerful one. She found it hard to concentrate. Her muscles were uncoordinated, and when she spoke the words seemed to trip over themselves. It was easier to give in. Ten minutes after she was back in her room at the hotel she was asleep again.

The telephone beside the bed jangled harshly, jerking her back to the present. Still groggy from the effects of the pill, she groped for it and answered.

"Sung S'u-mah?" It was Tai Ling. He sounded surprised.

She shook herself awake. "Yes," she answered thickly. "Are you all right?"

"I must see you! It's important!" Tai Ling's voice was harsh, insistent. "But not here. Not in the hotel."

Sung S'u-mah started to speak but Tai Ling cut across her words.

"Don't talk. Listen! They will be back any second. We are leaving for home later this morning. I must see you before then. I must see you alone. Understand? Meet me by the waterfall above the golfcourse in twenty minutes."

Sung S'u-mah struggled to a sitting position. Her head felt several sizes too large and the room swayed gently. "I—I don't—I'm not sure I can . . ."

"Twenty minutes!" he repeated.

"But . . ."

It was no use. Tai Ling had hung up.

Yeung Chao groped for the alarm clock, then realized it was the telephone that was ringing so insistently. He propped himself up on one elbow and squinted at the time. 5 a.m. He groaned. Who would want to speak to him at this hour?

The phone rang again. The ambassador!

He snatched up the phone. "Yes? Yeung Chao here."

"Ah!" There was a certain satisfaction in the monosyllable. "We have some business to discuss, you and I," the voice went on amiably. "Please be in room 446 in ten minutes."

He didn't recognize the voice but he pictured a big man. Probably European. "Who is this?"

"My name is of no importance," the voice said, "but

what I have to say to you is of the utmost importance. I suggest you come right away."

"I shall certainly do nothing of the sort," Yeung Chao snapped, about to hang up.

"Look in the envelope." The words stopped Yeung Chao. "Under your door. Ten minutes." The line went dead.

The envelope was there just as the unknown caller had said it would be, a square white patch against a dark carpet. Yeung Chao picked it up gingerly, afraid of what he might find when he opened it. The four photographs were very clear. The taxi driver taking the money; an enlargement of the license plate, and two very clear prints of the whisky changing hands. The bottles were hidden by the paper bags but it took no imagination at all to recognize the distinctive wrappings of the Alberta Liquor Control Board. A familiar knot returned to his belly, a knot he'd sought to obliterate by destroying Wu Tan.

He dressed hurriedly. Yeung Chao met no one as he traveled the dimly lighted halls and climbed the service stairs to the floor above. He made his way to the west wing and room 446. He knocked lightly on the door, acutely conscious of the early hour and the echo of the sound in the hallway.

The man who opened the door matched the voice on the telephone. Yeung Chao felt oddly pleased at his own acumen. The broad, flat planes of the man's face registered and the knot inside him tightened. The man motioned him inside and closed the door.

The room was similar to Yeung Chao's own but larger. The lights were on and the drapes were drawn. The man pointed to a straight-backed vanity chair while settling himself comfortably in the only armchair in the room. Yeung Chao hesitated, determined not to place himself at a further disadvantage by accepting the off-handed invitation, but he felt awkward standing alone in the middle of the room. He seated himself gingerly on the edge of the bed and retained the dubious advantage of height.

The man smiled mirthlessly. "My name is Malik," he announced. "It is my true name; there is no reason why you should not know it." He paused and studied his visitor openly, noting the tell-tale signs of nervousness. "You made a wise decision," he observed quietly. "But then, you are a prudent man, Doctor, at least most of the time."

Yeung Chao remained silent, eyes watchful.

Malik nodded as if he had expected that. He leaned forward in his chair, hesitated for a moment, then spoke very quietly and deliberately as if he'd decided to take Yeung Chao into his confidence.

"You see, Doctor, we each have something the other needs. You have access to information that I must have if I'm to protect the interests of my country, while I have something you need. I propose a simple trade."

Yeung Chao remained silent.

Malik sighed. "I am not just offering my silence as my part of the bargain," he went on carefully. "I am offering to help you achieve what you've always wanted. Recognition and power. Or," he concluded softly, "I can destroy you."

Malik lit a cigarette and blew the smoke in a steady stream toward the ceiling. Yeung Chao followed it with his eyes, his agile mind already seeking ways of turning the situation to his own advantage.

"What did you mean by 'what I've always wanted'?" he asked cautiously.

First hurdle down. Malik regarded his visitor through the curling smoke. "I mean exactly what I say. We can push you right to the top, the very top of your profession. And from there, who knows?" Malik spread his hands. "A ministerial post, perhaps?"

Yeung Chao's eyes narrowed. "You don't have that much influence," he said, probing. "How could you help me?"

Malik dragged deeply on his cigarette and allowed

the smoke to trickle slowly from his mouth before replying. "Time is short, Doctor," he said abruptly. "I don't have time for games. You and I both know that you won't even have a career if those pictures are circulated. For plotting the downfall of Wu Tan in such a manner as to embarrass and shame your country in the eyes of the world." Malik shook his head. "You will be executed, nothing less."

Yeung Chao shivered and brushed the lock of hair from his eyes.

"But, if you cooperate, I will not only withhold the pictures, I will give you the name of the traitor in your midst who has been selling information to the Americans. One of your colleagues. And that is only the beginning," he ended quietly.

"This information you want . . .?" Yeung Chao began hesitantly.

"Is already in the hands of the Americans," Malik said. "So, you see, it is no longer a secret. Specifically, I need to know what your people have been doing in the North Atlantic. And I need to know exactly what happened to our nuclear submarine out there last year. Your man gave that information to the Americans as recently as yesterday, I'm sorry to say."

"How can you possibly know that if you don't know what that information is?" Yeung Chao's voice had regained some of its confidence.

"Because we intercepted a message he sent out before he left your country," Malik told him candidly. "Every member of your delegation has been under close observation ever since you left Peking. Unfortunately, although we were able to discover the debriefing center, the Americans had it too well covered for us to penetrate. We did, however, manage to capture one of their agents."

Malik paused, allowing Yeung Chao to draw his own conclusions.

Yeung Chao found himself being irresistably drawn in. "Who?" he breathed. "Who is this traitor?"

Malik remained silent, a question in his eyes.

"I—I don't know all the details," Yeung Chao hedged.

Mailk nodded as if he'd expected that, but inwardly he breathed a sigh of relief. "But a bargain," he said firmly.

"A bargain," Yeung Chao said wearily.

"Good. The spy in your camp is one of your colleagues, I'm afraid. Tai Ling."

Yeung Chao's eyes narrowed dangerously. "But he is ill, very ill. I have seen him . . ." His voice trailed off as doubt crept in. "I suppose he could have been contacted in Calgary, but . . ."

Malik shook his head. "They were cleverer than that," he said. "Tai Ling never went to Calgary. A substitution was made, probably even before he reached the hospital at Banff. The man who went to Calgary was not Tai Ling. Tai Ling spent yesterday right here in town being debriefed by the Americans. Later, they switched again." Malik uttered the words with quiet conviction. That was the only way it could have happened he reasoned. There was no other explanation.

Yeung Chao's spirits soared. Tai Ling! Tai Ling of all people. Not that he had regarded Tai Ling as a serious threat to his own advancement, but he was afraid of Sung S'u-mah. Her position in the Social Affairs Department was unassailable. She was the one person who held both the qualifications and the power to defeat his bid for the chairmanship of the Revolutionary Committee for Meteorological Studies, North and Eastern Sectors. But if her former lover could be shown to be a spy for the Americans, it was but a short step to guilt by association . . .

Malik's voice broke in gently on his thoughts. It was as if he had read Yeung Chao's mind. "I can supply you with enough proof to destroy Tai Ling," he said. "And from there it is but a short step to demonstrate the complicity of Sung S'u-mah. She, after all, is the real stumbling block to your success."

Yeung Chao savored the thought. He would have

to be very careful, of course, but it could be done without anyone suspecting him. The important thing now was to get everyone home without alarming them. Once there . . . The idea seized his imagination. Why only North and Eastern Sectors? Why not Chairman of the Revolutionary Committee for the entire People's Republic? Sweat glistened on his brow as he considered the prospect. With this man's help . . .

"But first I must insist that we talk about the North Atlantic operation," Malik said. "There is very little time and there is a lot to be done." With luck, he thought wearily, he might still save Kalenzetny and himself.

Yeung Chao bobbed his head nervously. He would humor Malik, go along with him for now, but he would find a way to set himself free sooner or later.

"Of course," he said agreeably. "What exactly do you want to know?"

Back in his room at last, Yeung Chao slumped in a chair, completely drained. Malik, the skilled interrogator, had set a grueling pace. Not only had he demanded details about the North Atlantic operation, but he had insisted that Yeung Chao memorize recognition codes and contacts to be used upon his return to Peking. But, at last, even Malik was satisfied.

Yeung Chao closed his eyes, his thoughts already far ahead in Peking. It had not yet occurred to him that he had just exchanged one subservience for another, and almost willingly at that. This was Yeung Chao's Achilles heel, duly noted in the file that Malik held. He could not stand alone.

His thoughts turned to Tai Ling; Tai Ling the traitor. He smiled to himself as he savored the forthcoming downfall of Tai Ling and Sung S'u-mah.

A sharp, insistent rapping on his door scattered his thoughts. Annoyed at the intrusion, he pushed himself from the chair and crossed the room, but before he could reach the door the rapping started up again. Louder, even more insistent. He opened it, an angry question on his lips.

But the words were never uttered. Sung S'u-mah pushed brusquely past him and moved swiftly to the center of the room. Shan Shi, eyes averted, followed silently and took up a position just inside the door. Taken completely by surprise, Yeung Chao remained at the open door, indignation welling up inside. The woman was insufferable. The sooner they were back in Peking the better.

"Don't stand there like a mindless dolt," the woman snapped. "Close the door." Her jaw was set determinedly and Yeung Chao found himself obeying, albeit unwillingly.

"Tai Ling has disappeared," she announced baldly. "He telephoned me earlier this morning and asked me to meet him on an urgent matter. I went as quickly as I could but he did not appear. I waited, but still he did not come. He is not in his room and no one admits to seeing him." Her smouldering eyes held his accusingly. "Has he been with you?"

Yeung Chao shook his head impatiently. "No, no, of course he hasn't been with me," he told her, angered by the woman's aggressive stance. He swung on Shan Shi. "Why was I not informed of this before?" he demanded. "As head of this delegation . . ."

"As head of this delegation you were not in your room when you were needed," Sung S'u-mah broke in scathingly.

Blood suffused his face. "How dare you question my authority?" he howled. "I am the leader of this delegation. I was given that authority by Ambassador Chung Yeng-tse himself. It is my responsibility to . . ."

"Responsibility?" Her voice was low and filled with menace. "You dare to speak to me of responsibility? You who allowed Wu Tan to become so drunk that he not only disgraced himself and this delegation, but brought down shame and humiliation upon our country. You *dare* to speak to me of responsibility?"

"He was the chairman, then. He was in charge. I had no authority," Yeung Chao parried desperately. He could feel control slipping from his grasp and he groped for words to turn the tide. "It was not my place," he ended lamely.

Sung S'u-mah's eyes blazed. "It is everybody's duty to be vigilant!" she breathed, her voice tight with suppressed emotion. "I warned the minister before we left Peking. I told him that you were ambitious, not to be trusted; that you coveted Wu Tan's position as head of this delegation. And I was right!"

"You—you told the minister?" Yeung Chao choked. He sputtered to a stop, beside himself.

"It is on record," Sung S'u-mah confirmed relentlessly. "You didn't waste much time grasping for the leadership, did you? Perhaps you encouraged Wu Tan to drink, eh? Perhaps you arranged . . ." She gestured irritably, cutting off her own words, and failed to see the alarm in Yeung Chao's eyes. "But that is past. You will answer for it when we return home," Sung S'u-mah said brusquely. "The point is that Tai Ling has disappeared. Did you have a hand in that, also?" She continued before he could muster a reply. "It's a good thing I am now fully recovered and can take charge again."

Yeung Chao made one last attempt. "Peking has placed me in charge," he said defiantly. "I take my orders from . . ."

"From whom?" Sung S'u-mah's eyes held his unfalteringly. His own slid away. "I, too, have been in contact with Peking," she went on softly. "*My* orders come directly from Wang Chen-yin!"

Yeung Chao felt the touch of ice in his belly. "But—but the minister . . ." he faltered.

"The minister has been relieved of his duties," the woman said coldly. "His role in this affair will be dealt with at the inquiry when we return home." She turned to Shan Shi who had remained silent throughout the entire exchange. "You will continue your efforts to find Tai Ling," she told him. Her tone softened. "He sounded very upset when he spoke to me on the telephone; perhaps he has been taken ill or . . ." She broke off and shrugged away further idle speculation.

"Inquire through the authorities," she told Shan Shi, "but discreetly. We leave for home at ten."

Shan Shi inclined his head. "And if he has not been found by then?"

"You will remain behind until he is," Sung S'u-mah said without hesitation. "My first duty is to see that this delegation returns home at once." She looked directly at Yeung Chao. "I don't want to risk losing another member while we are in the West."

Yeung Chao stared at her sullenly. He wanted to scream at her. Wanted to tell her that her precious Tai Ling was a traitor, a spy in the pay of the Americans. That she too would fall, guilty by association. But how? How could he reveal what he knew without sowing the seeds of his own destruction? He choked back the words that would have stopped the woman in her tracks.

Chapter 16

Quinn and McCrimmon sat on opposite sides of the table in the general office working on their respective reports concerning the death of the man known as Michael Vernon. Wellington had assigned Corporal LaBelle to cover the hastily arranged departure of the Chinese delegation, an event the inspector viewed with more than a little relief.

"Call for you, Sarge," a constable said, cupping the telephone with a huge hand. "Want to take it here or in your office?"

"Who is it?"

"Sergeant Pender over in Golden."

"I'll take it here," McCrimmon said. He picked up the phone. "What's new in Golden, Stan?"

"Got an odd one for you, Bill," Pender said without preamble. "It's a girl. A girl by the name of Jacintha Lee. Ever heard of her? She says she's a friend of yours."

McCrimmon gripped the phone. "I know her," he said tightly. "How did . . .?"

"She's here in Golden," Pender said. "Been in an accident. She's damned lucky to be alive."

McCrimmon felt his throat constrict. "How bad, Stan?"

"Well, the doc says there are no bones broken, but she's got more damned cuts and bruises than she's got places."

"What happened?"

"She went off the road west of here. According to her she was forced off the road by another car, but we've only got her word for that. We haven't been able to get down to her car yet."

"The Datsun?" McCrimmon asked. It was all he could think of to say. "Was she driving the Datsun?"

"That's what she tells us. Like I say, she's luckier'n hell to be alive. She jumped on the first bounce when the car left the road. Good thing she did; the second bounce is two thousand feet further down. Must have knocked herself out because there were a couple of hours missing in her story. Anyhow, when she came to she crawled back up to the road. A trucker found her and radioed in for help." Pender broke off. "Bill, how well do you know this girl?"

"I—what do you mean, Stan? I know her . . . Why?"

"Well, it looks like we've got a problem," Pender said. "The truck driver tells us that she told him a pretty wild story about two guys in a car attempting to murder her. She was talking about being held in some house in Banff, all kinds of crazy things. But when she got here she clammed up tight. Won't talk to anyone here; she seems afraid of us. She says she'll only talk to you. Oh, yeah, she's got a tape recording, a cassette she's holding on to for dear life. Refused to let it go even while the doctor was examining her. She refuses to sleep or to take any pills or shots until she's talked to you. She's really spooked, Bill."

"Is she there? Can I talk to her?" McCrimmon ached to hear her voice again.

There was the sound of muffled voices as Pender spoke to someone in the room, then, "Sorry, Bill. She says she won't talk to anyone until she's back in Banff and can talk to you face to face."

He lowered his voice. "Bill, this kid is really scared. Hell, she's terrified of something."

"Can she travel, Stan?"

"Ordinarily, I'd say no," Pender said, "but in this case I think the sooner she sees you the better. The doctor says she's so damned determined to talk to you that we might as well let her come. He says she'll probably be sore as hell but if she's prepared to put up with it he's not going to try to stop her."

"Okay, Stan," McCrimmon said. "Get her over here as fast as you can. I'll be responsible for her when she arrives."

"Damned right you will," Pender told him amiably. "You want to let me in on this one? I've got to show something on my report."

"I'm not holding out on you," McCrimmon said, "and, so far as I know, she's not wanted for anything. You're in the clear unless you've got any charges pending."

"Nope. She's just another accident victim at the moment," Pender said. "I may want to talk to her again after we've had a look at the car, but until then she's all yours."

"Thanks, Stan."

"Let me know if anything comes of this attempted murder story, will you? She's got me curious now. Okay?"

"I'll keep you posted."

"Good. Oh, and Bill, we're charging the trip to K Division. Both ways. You guys in Alberta can afford it, and it'll save a hell of a lot of explanations. Okay?"

"Thanks a lot." McCrimmon grinned despite this new anxiety over Jacintha. "Just get her here fast, Stan."

It was ten minutes to eleven when the young patrolman from Golden ushered Jacintha into McCrimmon's office. Despite Pender's warning, the sergeant was shaken by her appearance, and so, obviously, was Quinn. Both hands were bandaged and her left arm was in a sling. A huge swelling beneath her right eye had almost forced it shut, and long scratches criss-crossed her cheek. More bandages covered her knees, and large blue-black bruises were beginning to appear on her shins.

She walked and held herself stiffly, and Quinn moved quickly to get another chair from the outer office, padded and with arms. McCrimmon came around the desk and, almost involuntarily, reached out toward her. He felt the cool tips of her slender fingers extending beyond the bandages curl tightly around his own. "You should be in hospital," he told her roughly. He turned to the patrolman. "What was Pender thinking about to send her . . .?"

"Excuse me, Sergeant," the man broke in hastily, "but it wasn't his idea. Miss Lee, here insisted . . ." He broke off with a shrug.

"Please, don't waste any time on me," Jacintha pleaded. "It looks much worse than it is. No, really," she said, seeing the obvious disbelief in his eyes. "Has the Chinese delegation left yet?" Her dark eyes searched his anxiously.

McCrimmon glanced at the clock. "About an hour ago if they left on time," he told her. "But what does the Chinese delegation have to do with you.?"

"You must stop them," she said earnestly. "They must be stopped before it is too late!"

McCrimmon held up his hand. "Hold it a minute," he said. "I'd like to know what this is all about first. I can't go around preventing foreign delegations from returning home, you know. What is it they're supposed to have done?" He walked around the desk and sat down. "Why don't you begin at the beginning?" he said. "It usually saves time in the long run."

She hesitated, then, "Could — could I speak to you alone for a moment?" Her eyes flicked to Quinn and the patrolman, then returned to his face. He reminded himself that this was the same girl who had lied to him, refused to talk to him when he had gone looking for her help, and about whom he knew absolutely nothing. He started to shake his head.

"Please, Bill," she said. "Please, it's important." Her eyes, dark and luminous in the pale, bruised oval of her face, refused to let his go.

The patrolman shifted uncomfortably. "If you'd like to sign for delivery, Sergeant . . ." he ventured.

"I think we could all do with a cup of coffee," McCrimmon said. "Would you mind, Quinn?" His eyes never left Jacintha's face. "And fix up the paperwork while your out there. Okay?"

Quinn hesitated. "Are you sure you want to . . .?"

"Yes," McCrimmon said curtly. "I'm sure Miss Lee could use a cup." Quinn shrugged resignedly and left the room with the patrolman.

"Now, then Jacintha," McCrimmon said, "what *is* this all about? What is all this about the Chinese delegation? And what have they to do with you?"

She sat staring down at her hands in her lap as if lost in silent reverie. He waited.

"I—I just don't know, Bill," she mumbled at last. "I thought that if I came to see you . . . I just didn't know who to trust . . ." She refused to look at him. "But now, I just don't know."

He lost patience. "Dammit, Jacintha," he exploded, "what *do* you want? You insisted on coming all the way back here from Golden; you wouldn't tell them anything and now you won't tell me anything. What in hell are you playing at?"

She continued to stare at her hands but her lip trembled visibly. She caught it between her teeth and slowly shook her head.

He threw up his hands. "Okay, that's it," he said. "I'm through playing games with you. I'm sending you into Banff hospital, and when you're well enough to answer questions I'm going to get to the bottom of this. You'd better believe I'm going to get some answers."

He stood up. Her head came up and he saw her face. Never had he seen such anguish and such pain. Her eyes were moist and tears trickled unheeded down her cheeks.

"Oh, Bill," she cried, "they're going to kill my father! Please, please stop them before it's too late!" She half rose to her feet and stood there swaying, arms extended in silent supplication. "Please, Bill," she whispered.

He came around the desk and caught her by the shoulders. She came into his arms and clung to him, trembling. He lowered her gently into the chair and fished around behind him on the desk for a Kleenex, found one and gave it to her without speaking. She wiped away the tears and drew in a long, shuddering breath.

"I'm sorry," she said at last, looking up at him. "I didn't mean to do that. I'll be all right now."

He watched her carefully as he returned to his seat and sat down. "I think you'd better begin at the beginning," he said quietly. "I don't know what this is all about, and I can't promise to do anything when I do know, but I'll help you if I can. That's the best that I can do. How about it?" They heard the clink of cups outside and Quinn's heavy boots sounded in the corridor.

"Can I still talk to you alone?" she asked quickly.

He shook his head. "I'm sorry, Jacintha, but you'll have to trust me about that. I'd trust Quinn with my own life. He'll have to stay and hear what you have to say."

Her eyes went to the clock. "What time do they leave from Calgary?" she wanted to know.

"Twelve thirty," he said. "You have lots of time. A phone call will stop them if it's necessary. It's the only way," he warned as he saw her hesitate. The door opened and Quinn entered with a tray of steaming mugs.

"You're sure they can be stopped?"

"Positive."

A long, drawn out sigh escaped her. "All right," she said, "but I'll really have to begin at the beginning if you are to understand." She closed her eyes as Quinn set the tray on the desk. She seemed to be gathering strength.

"My real name is not Jacintha Lee," she began quietly. "It is Shu Hua." A faint smile touched the corners of her mouth. "In Chinese it means Splendor of Modesty. My father was not a missionary as my papers state, neither was I born in the United States. I was born in Fukien Province in the People's Republic of China. My father is Kuan Lo, a member of the Chinese delegation."

He should have been surprised, but somehow he had been expecting something like this. He caught Quinn's worried glance. "I should warn you that you may be admitting to illegal entry into Canada," McCrimmon said, but the girl dismissed his warning with an impatient shake of the head.

"There are far more important things at stake than that," she said wearily. "After my mother was killed by the Red Guards, my father began to fear for our lives. You see, my mother was born in China, but of American parents. I was of mixed blood; no one knew what the Red Guards would do next. They were out of control. My father refused to leave himself, but he he arranged for me and my aunt, his sister who lived with us, to disappear. We were supposed to have been swept out to sea in a small boat and drowned, but we were actually transferred to a fishing boat which made its way to Hong Kong. Later, traveling with false papers, we made our way to San Francisco where friends helped us establish new identities."

Jacintha reached for the mug of coffee and sipped at it cautiously, wrinkling her nose at the strong smell of chlorine.

"My grandfather, that is, my mother's father, actually was an American missionary. His name was Charles King. He and my grandmother left the United States in 1932. They had one child at the time, a boy named Joseph, aged three. They had to leave him behind with my great-grandmother because conditions in China at that time wouldn't allow them to take him with them. They expected to send for him later. My mother was born a year later in China. She was barely one year old when her parents were both drowned in the great flood of 1934. By some miracle my mother survived the flood, and she was adopted by Chinese foster-parents and brought up as one of their own. In 1954 she married Kuan Lo. I was born in 1956.

"My mother's brother, Joseph, the one who was left behind, moved to Vancouver when he was just a young man. He became a Canadian citizen and has lived there ever since. My father managed to get word to him that we were on our way to San Francisco, and he came down there to meet us. He was in the process of trying to find a way to bring my aunt and me to Canada when my aunt became ill and died." Jacintha paused and looked down at her hands. "It was a terrible shock," she said huskily. "She was the only link I had to the world I had known. She risked her own life to bring me to safety. But, in a way, it made things easier. The authorities didn't question Joseph King's willingness to adopt the orphaned daughter of an old friend. They couldn't know, of course, that he was really my uncle."

"Why didn't your father come with you?" McCrimmon asked. "Surely, with your mother gone, there would be nothing to stop him."

The girl shook her head. "My father is fiercely proud of his country," she said. "He is a very good meteorologist, and China has so few really skilled professionals. They need such men desperately. He has always believed in the future of his — our country, and I really think that he believed there would be a day when I could safely return there."

A touch of sadness entered her voice. "I tried to persuade him again while he was here." Tears welled up and spilled over. She brushed them angrily away with her bandaged hands. "Last year my father sent word to my uncle that he was coming here to the seminar in Banff. He wanted to see me if only for a few hours. My uncle thought it would be too dangerous, I think more for me than for my father, because he feared I would be caught and deported."

Jacintha raised her eyes to McCrimmon's. "They have no children of their own," she explained simply, "and they treat me as their own daughter. But I had to come. I made arrangements to stay in the hotel through-out the seminar, but I had to get word to my father to let him know which room I was in. I didn't want him to inquire at the desk in case someone overheard him. And that's when everything began to go wrong." Her eyes were bleak and her voice dropped to a whisper.

"That's when you saw me give the note to the waiter. The waiter who died later on that night. It was my fault even if it was the Russians who . . ."

McCrimmon's head jerked up sharply. "Russians?" he echoed in a startled voice. "What have the Russians to do with all this?"

The girl composed herself with an effort. "I'm sorry," she said, "I'm not telling this at all well, am I?" Her eyes went to the clock. "Please be patient. I'll explain as best I can. The waiter delivered the note to my father, but it seems that everyone was watching. You saw me give it to him. The Russians saw him with it, but for some reason didn't get a good look at me. And the Americans saw everything."

She saw the question in McCrimmon's eyes. "Please, Bill, don't judge me yet," she said earnestly. "I'm not making it up, believe me."

McCrimmon sat back in his chair and said nothing — but it was obviously an effort.

"My father received the note and came to my room in the early hours of the following morning." Jacintha's eyes glistened at the recollection. "It was so wonderful to see him, to talk to him after all those years. We talked for hours." She pushed the memory aside with obvious reluctance. "It was only later that same day that I found out that the Americans had recorded everything we had said in the room, and . . ."

She broke off as she saw disbelief on McCrimmon's face. Even the unflappable Quinn was regarding her quizzically, distracted from the shorthand notes he had been quietly making. She raised her hands in front of her as if to ward off questions from the sergeant.

"Look, I know it all sounds crazy, but hear me out. I'm not making it up! This is real." She pointed to the bandages. "These are real; I didn't make this up and I didn't imagine the so-called accident."

McCrimmon held himself in check. "Go on," he said neutrally.

Jacintha picked up the coffee mug and held it awkwardly between her bandaged hands while she drank. She seemed to be trying to decide how best to continue. Quinn flipped to a new page and waited. She set the mug aside.

"All right," she said. "I'll have to go back a bit so you'll understand." She sounded very tired. "I didn't find out about all this until later, but I'll try to explain as best I can. It seems that one member of the Chinese delegation is a spy for the Americans, what they call a deep-cover agent, according to my father. He also told me that some of the meteorologists and oceanographers in China have been working on a very secret project that involves changing weather patterns, changes that can affect many countries. They can cause droughts, floods, storms . . ." She broke off at McCrimmon's snort of disbelief.

"Oh, come on, Jacintha, really!" He shook his head again. "I don't know what you expect to achieve by all this, but enough's enough. Why are you doing this? Why . . . ?" Words failed him.

The girl closed her eyes. Tears trickled slowly down her cheeks. McCrimmon eyed her narrowly. Despite the bandages her fists were clenched in what appeared to be sheer frustration. He glanced across at Quinn for his reaction. The corporal, too, looked puzzled, but finally he nodded almost imperceptibly and mouthed the words 'Go on'.

McCrimmon let out a long breath. "Okay, okay," he said wearily. "Go on. Let's hear it all."

Jacintha opened her eyes. "I can prove what I say,"

she told him quietly. "You'll need a tape recorder. I stole a tape from the Americans. It will bear out what I have told you."

McCrimmon nodded noncommittally. "Go on," he said, but it was quite apparent from his voice that he thought it a waste of time.

Determinedly, Jacintha again picked up the thread of the story, speaking very rapidly now as if to forestall further interruptions.

"The Americans were trying to set up a meeting with their agent, but they didn't want anyone else in the Chinese delegation to know or even suspect that such a meeting had taken place. They needed time, quite a lot of time, to debrief their agent. They decided to stage a diversion. My father and I happened to be exactly what they were looking for," she went on bitterly. "The Americans were watching everybody to make sure their agent was in the clear before they made contact, and that's how they happened to see me send the note to my father. They found out that I was staying in the hotel, and they sent flowers."

Quinn raised his head. "Flowers? Did you say flowers?"

Jacintha nodded. "I thought my father had sent them. There was no card, but who else could it be? They had a miniature microphone hidden in the flowers and they recorded everything that was said in the room."

Quinn dutifully wrote the explanation down. The girl frowned as if trying to bring events into focus.

"Somehow, I don't know how, the Russians knew about the American agent, but they didn't know who it was, so they were also looking for anything suspicious. They saw the waiter take the note, but they can't have identified me because they picked up the waiter when he left that night and tried to question him. At least, that's what I heard Roy, he's the American in charge, tell one of the others. Apparently, the waiter had a bad heart and he died before he could tell them anything." Jacintha looked at McCrimmon with pain-filled eyes. "I had no idea about any of this," she said. Her slender shoulders lifted and fell again in a helpless gesture. "I just wanted to let my father know where I was. It was my fault that the waiter lost his life, but I didn't know. You have to believe me, Bill, I didn't know."

That Minelli had died under circumstances that could be as Jacintha had just described was undeniable, and four other people had died in questionable circumstances since the beginning of the seminar. So far, there was little evidence to show that the deaths were in any way connected to the seminar itself, but something very unusual was certainly playing havoc with Banff's statistical average for unsolved homicides. And then, of course, there were the foreign passports. Maybe, just maybe Jacintha was telling the truth, or what she believed to be the truth. Maybe.

"You can't blame yourself for Minelli's death," he said quietly. She looked up, surprised by the compassion in his voice. "But there is one thing that bothers me," he went on. "How do you know all this? Who told you, and why?"

"The American called Roy told me. He was quite open about it because, as he put it, he needed our complete cooperation, my father's and mine. He pointed out that if either of us ever told anyone what we knew, he would see that I was deported and that my father's crime of sending me out of the country illegally would not go unpunished. What choice did we have?"

Jacintha's hands moved jerkily to her face. She was deathly pale. Her one good eye seemed huge and dark in the distorted oval of her face. Her voice faltered and fell to a whisper so soft that both policemen had to strain to hear her words.

"It wasn't until much later that I realized that he wasn't relying on blackmail alone to keep us both silent. It wasn't until last night that I realized he meant to kill us both."

Quinn had brought in a fresh pot of coffee. The hot liquid helped restore a faint touch of color to the girl's pallid cheeks, and she smiled, albeit wanly, to reassure them that she was going to be all right. McCrimmon regarded her anxiously. For a moment, there, he'd thought she would topple from the chair, but before he could move around the desk, Quinn was there with a steadying hand. She seemed to be recovering, now, but she was still deathly pale.

"You should be in hospital," he said shortly, if not unkindly. "You need rest and medical attention." He reached for the phone.

"No!" It was almost a shout. "Please, Bill, no." Her eyes flew to the clock. The hands were fast approaching twelve. "I'll be quick. There isn't much more to tell, but you have to believe me; you have to stop them from leaving Calgary." She didn't wait for a reply but hurried on. "They tried to kill me last night. So far, they don't know they failed. I'm sure they have a similar fate planned for my father. They could do it here, but I think they'll wait until he's back at home. It would be easier for them there. I'm the only one who can stop them."

McCrimmon's hand dropped away from the telephone. "You really believe that, don't you?" he said softly.

"Oh, Bill, I know it's true. That was no accident last night. They deliberately chose the spot and ran me off the road."

McCrimmon rose from his chair and stood looking down at the girl, steeling himself for what he had to say. "It's not quite as simple as you seem to think, Jacintha," he began quietly. "I know you've been through a lot and I understand the concern you must have for your father, but you must understand something too." Her eyes remained steady on his face. He wished she would look away. "If I go to my people and tell them that agents from the United States have tried to kill one person and intend to kill another, a member of a foreign delegation, how far do you think I'd get? Even if someone did believe me, and I don't think for a minute anybody would, what do you think they could do? Your father is a foreign national, a free agent as far as we are concerned. We wouldn't, we couldn't stop him from leaving the country. About the only way he *might* remain here is if he voluntarily seeks political asylum. Do you understand?"

The light in Jacintha's eyes seemed to die. She closed them as if to summon strength. "I understand," she said hollowly, "that you will do nothing to save my father from certain death."

The bitter accusation stung him. "If he would ask for asylum, then, perhaps . . ."

"He would never do that!" Jacintha's words cut across his own. "He doesn't agree with everything his colleagues are doing in China," she went on in a quieter voice, "but he knows that he is needed. He is highly respected in his field and he is convinced that he can do more for his country by remaining there. If he deserted China now he would be branded as a traitor, and his opinions, even his work, would be regarded as nothing more than echoes of Western propaganda. "No," she said with infinite sadness, "he will not stay here. Believe me, I have tried very hard to get him to stay."

The telephone jangled harshly. McCrimmon frowned. He had left instructions with Mavis to hold all calls. He picked it up. "McCrimmon," he said curtly.

"*Inspector* Wellington here." The Iron Duke's voice grated in his ear.

"Sir," McCrimmon said noncommittally. He was in no frame of mind to debate the finer points of protocol with Wellington.

"It seems we have yet another problem, Sergeant," Wellington said pedantically. Some of the edge had left his voice but he sounded very tired. "We have another body on our hands, an alleged murder, in fact."

McCrimmon sat down and waited for Wellington to continue.

"Tai Ling, one of the Chinese delegates, is dead. Two golfers found his body snagged in the brush along the river bank beside the golf course. From the condition of the body I'd say he went in above the falls. He's banged up pretty badly. Hard to say whether he was alive or dead when he hit the water, but the autopsy will tell us that."

"But, I thought they were all on their way to Calgary?" McCrimmon saw Jacintha lean forward, her eyes intent upon his face.

"He wasn't on the bus when it left here this morning," Wellington said. "I was there myself. I spoke to that officious little bastard who's taking Wu Tan's place, and he told me that Tai Ling was too ill to travel and would follow later. He told me that he's arranged for one of the aides, a man by the name of Shan Shi, to stay with him until he was strong enough to travel. It sounded plausible enough at the time, but when we tried to find Shan Shi after Tai Ling's body was found, he had gone. Checked out shortly after the others left."

"So he's your prime suspect if it turns out that the victim was murdered," McCrimmon concluded.

"There's more to it than that," Wellington growled. "Paul Cavanna had a report earlier this morning about someone being pushed into the river above Bow Falls. He spent some time checking it out, and it was only about an hour ago that we finally got together and realized we were working on the same thing from opposite ends.

"You actually have a witness?"

"That's right. The time's a bit hazy, but it was around seven o'clock this morning according to the witness."

McCrimmon's eyes automatically went to the clock. Over five hours ago! What had they been doing all this time? Why hadn't he heard from Paul? It was if Wellington had read his mind.

"We can't fault Paul," he said. "The witness gave

him a pretty wild story and he wasn't going to come to us with it until he'd checked it out thoroughly. It was only after he received a report from the club house on the golf course that he believed the story himself. Remember that woman on the sixth floor?" Wellington went on. "The one who's been driving Paul's people crazy with her stories about people spying on her from across the river? Well, that's our witness."

McCrimmon groaned aloud.

"She identified both victim and killer as Oriental. Since we had the photographs taken by Security on file, we showed her all the Oriental delegates. She picked out Tai Ling as the victim, and she picked out the alleged murderer."

"*From the sixth floor?*"

"No trouble at all," Wellington assured him. "If you recall, Paul's man told us she had a telescope in her room. He wasn't kidding. I took a look through it. You can read the date on a dime at half a mile."

"And the killer?"

"Doctor Sung S'u-mah."

"The woman?" McCrimmon said incredulously.

"That's what our witness says. She says she watched them meet. Tai Ling was there first; Sung S'u-mah came a few minutes later. They talked, then Sung S'u-mah hit him with something, she thinks it was a rock, and he fell down. Apparently he was only dazed because when she tried to dump him over the edge he tried to hold onto her arms. The woman struggled free and kicked Tai Ling very hard. Our witness was a little vague about where, exactly, but both Paul and I agree she probably kicked him in the balls. At least, that's where I told them to look when they do the autopsy. Tai Ling went over the edge and didn't reappear. Sung S'u-mah then ran off down the path toward the golf course. And that's when our witness called Paul," Wellington concluded.

There was silence at the other end of the line, then, "Right now, I want you to get to Calgary as soon as you can. I'm arranging for a warrant for the arrest of Sung S'u-mah and Shan Shi. I can't tie him directly into the killing, but witnesses in the hotel tell me that he was with her most of the morning, and one of the elevator operators heard her tell him to wait until the rest of them had checked out of the hotel before checking out himself. And," Wellington went on, "I want the whole damned pack of them held for questioning. I don't know what's going on, but it smells to high heaven of conspiracy, and I intend to get to the bottom of it. Get on it right away and report back to me after you've talked to Calgary. Have the members of the delegation held until you get there. If they give you any static, refer them to me, but make sure they hold the delegation."

"Right, Inspector," McCrimmon said. He was about to hang up when Wellington spoke again.

"Oh, yes, I almost forgot. We've identified the tortured man. He's an American by the name of Kellerman. Manages the Calgary branch of a firm of oil consultants with a head office in Tulsa. Only trouble is, the FBI suddenly went dead on us when we tried to run a check on his fingerprints. Draw your own conclusions, but I'd say he's not your average businessman." He hung up.

McCrimmon dropped the phone back into place and came around the desk, conscious of the questions in Jacintha's eyes.

"Tai Ling is dead," he said. "I guess we'll be holding the delegation in Calgary after all." He turned to Quinn. "Get onto Calgary right away and tell them we want the entire delegation held for questioning. If they want to argue they can take it up with Wellington. Afterward."

Understanding broke across her face. "Of course! Tai Ling! He must have guessed." Suddenly she pushed herself to her feet. "Now I'm more certain than ever that my father will be killed," she told McCrimmon. "They must be stopped."

"Quinn's taking care of that," McCrimmon said, but

right now you can give me some answers. What do you know about Tai Ling's death? Why was he killed?"

Jacintha met his probing stare with unflinching eyes. "I don't know who killed him," she said very quietly, "but I think I know why he had to die." Her face clouded. "Poor Tai Ling; he was just another pawn in their game. My father liked him very much. Was it Sung S'u-mah?" she said abruptly.

The crash of the telephone made them both jump. "The Chinese delegation left Calgary over half an hour ago," Quinn stated baldly.

McCrimmon glanced at the time. "Impossible," he said. "It's only 12:15. The plane doesn't leave until 12:30."

Quinn shrugged his massive shoulders. "Impossible or not, they've gone," he said. "There was an earlier PWA Edmonton-Calgary-Vancouver flight that was delayed by fog in Edmonton. It arrived in Calgary about three quarters of an hour ago. There were enough seats to accommodate the Chinese delegation, so they took it."

Dismay flooded over Jacintha's face. "Oh, no!" She breathed. The two words lingered in the air like the echo of infinite despair.

McCrimmon reached across the desk and scooped up the phone, speaking rapidly to Quinn while he dialed. "Get hold of Vancouver and tell them to hold the Chinese delegation for questioning about the death of one of their members and the disappearance of another member, a man by the name of Shan Shi. Specific warrants are being issued. And tell them I want someone who understands Chinese with them at all times. Give Vancouver a list of their names from our files, and tell them we are on our way. Under no circumstances are any of them to be allowed to leave, even if their embassy gets involved. Understand?"

He broke off and turned his attention to the phone. "This is Sergeant McCrimmon, RCMP," he announced.

"Is Ed Seymour there, please? Yes, thank you, I'll hold, but please hurry. It's very important." Quinn started out of the office, but McCrimmon covered the mouthpiece of the telephone with his hand and motioned him to stop. "After you've finished with Vancouver," he told the corporal, "get hold of Calgary and get us a connecting flight to Vancouver. If there are no commercial flights right away, get the RCMP plane down from Edmonton. Oh, and you'd better let Wellington know what's happened, after we've gone."

Quinn hesitated. "If I'm coming with you, how . . .?"

McCrimmon shook his head decisively. "Not you, Quinn," he said. "If she's willing to go, I'm taking Miss Lee with me. I'll need her in Vancouver."

His eyes sought and held Jacintha's. Gone, now, were the pain and fatigue, banished by the revival of hope. Her face was transformed. She reached out and touched his hand in silent gratitude.

Quinn shot him a worried glance. "I sure hope you know what you're doing," he muttered. Still shaking his head, he left the office.

A voice sounded in McCrimmon's ear.

"Ed? Bill McCrimmon," he said. "I need to get to Calgary fast. Can you have a plane ready in thirty, make that twenty minutes? There'll be two of us."

Jacintha was watching him, tense, expectant. God, but she was beautiful — bandgages, bruises, lumps and all. He wrenched his thoughts back to the phone.

"Thanks, Ed," he said. "See you at the airfield."

Chapter 17

The man whose credentials identified him as a member of the New China News Agency met them as they came off the plane. He conversed quietly with Yeung Chao and Sung S'u-mah, then led the way to a small VIP lounge overlooking the runways and the sparkling waters of the Strait of Georgia.

"I have arranged for a meal to be sent in," he told them. Apart from that, you will not be disturbed until your flight leaves in about four hours. I will return shortly before you are due to leave."

Kuan Lo sank wearily into the depths of a crushed vinyl chair. He watched as others made their choice of seats. The aides and secretaries drifted as if guided by some unseen force to the far end of the lounge, the end furthest from the windows. Wu Tan sat with them, his eyes still glazed from the effects of the drug he had been given before leaving Banff. Even as Kuan Lo watched, Wu Tan's head dropped forward on his chest and he drifted off to sleep. An aide assigned to him by Sung S'u-mah eased his collar open and listened carefully to the big man's breathing.

Predictably, Yeung Chao took the chair closest to the window where he now sat staring out with unseeing eyes. Sung S'u-mah sat a little apart. Her view commanded the entire room.

Kuan Lo closed his eyes, and his mind returned unbidden to the quesion that had bedeviled him for several days. He saw upon his inner eye his daughter's face, so beautiful, so full of life, so very like her mother. How wonderful to be so young and so terribly naive.

He cried out to her in silent agony. *Oh, my child, my lovely Shu Hua. Dare I hope that they will let you live?*

Yeung Chao nibbled at his fingernails. To be so close to the fulfillment of his cherished dream only to be thwarted by Sung S'u-mah was intolerable. There had to be a way to discredit her. But how? Behind her loomed the shadow of the omnipresent Wang Chen-yin, the man some said, albeit guardedly, was more powerful than the chairman. But Malik had told him not to worry. He had promised to take care of the threat the woman posed. After all, Malik needed him; it would be to the Russian's advantage to take her out of the game.

He shot a surreptitious glance in Sung S'u-mah's direction. She seemed so relaxed, so supremely confident.

Sung S'u-mah's eyes were closed, but she was anything but relaxed. She, too, was thinking about her place in the scheme of things, and the report she would be obliged to make to Wang Chen-yin upon her return to Peking. There would be a full-scale inquiry, of course, and she would have to answer for her part in the affair. But it would be Yeung Chao who would bear the brunt of the investigation. She could hardly be held responsible for events that took place while she was stranded on a mountaintop. Yeung Chao would find himself hard pressed, she decided.

He had failed to see that Wu Tan had taken to drinking again, and that would cost him dearly. He had failed to check on the whereabouts of Tai Ling until it was much too late, and he had failed to take even the most elementary precautions when Tai Ling returned. The record would show that it was she who had first raised the alarm and insisted that a search be made. The record would also show that it was she who had repeatedly

warned the minister that Tai Ling could prove to be a
security risk and should not be accredited to the seminar.
She had planned well.

The peremptory sound of knuckles on the door
roused her from her reverie. The door opened and a tall,
square man with a red complexion and sandy hair came
in. He wore a quiet gray business suit and a dark,
conservative tie. He was followed closely by a second
man, younger, thinner, Oriental. Police.

The elder of the two men consulted the piece of
paper in his hand and said, "Doctor Yeung Chao?" He
pronounced it 'Chay-oh.'

"Yes?" Yeung Chao rose jerkily to his feet.

The man in the gray suit smiled reassuringly. "My
name is Plant," he said. "Corporal Plant, Airport
Security detail. This is Constable Wong. We'd like a few
minutes of your time, if you don't mind, sir?"

The monotonous drone of the DC-9 lulled his senses and
made him drowsy. McCrimmon found it hard to
concentrate. Beside him, her head nestled comfortably
against his shoulder, Jacintha slept. One minute she had
been talking, the next she was fast asleep, overcome by
sheer exhaustion, her brain demanding respite from the
tension of the past few days.

The tape had been something of a disappointment.
Not because it failed to back up Jacintha's story — it did,
and very well — but because it would be completely
valueless in a court of law. There was nothing to indicate
when it was recorded, where, or to whom the various
voices belonged. The voice of the person being interro-
gated had been so distorted electronically that it would be
impossible to identify its owner. The only consolation
was that the Security boys would be delighted with it,
but they would roast him for holding it and not advising
them sooner. They had listened to it in the Cessna on
their way to Calgary, huddled over the portable tape

recorder with the volume turned up full in order to hear it above the noise of the engine. Jacintha had been so pleased to find it contained such specific information about the Chinese experiments that McCrimmon had to mask his own reservations about the value of the tape.

Quinn must have been very persuasive, for when they got to Calgary they found a waiting DC-9, a Winnipeg-Calgary-Vancouver flight that had been held for more than half an hour on some pretext or other. They were greeted by curious stares as they made their way down the aisle and took their seats.

For the tenth time in ten minutes McCrimmon looked at his watch. Still three quarters of an hour until they reached Vancouver. The NO SMOKING sign went on and a male voice announced that he was their captain. A weather advisory had just been received indicating that a mild weather disturbance moving in from the Pacific was causing turbulence over the western slopes of the Rockies. He advised the use of seat belts, the sign was already on, and assured them all that there was nothing whatsoever to worry about. McCrimmon, who was never truly happy in the air, wished the captain hadn't felt it necessary to add that. The voice of the captain was replaced by that of a stewardess who repeated an abbreviated version in French. McCrimmon shook Jacintha gently. She opened her eyes slowly and stared at him blankly until she realized where she was.

"How long have I been asleep?" she asked.

"About half an hour," he said. "Your mind just shut down. Sorry, but I had to wake you. I need some answers before we reach Vancouver." He held her eyes with his own. "Jacintha, I have to know the truth. You have to tell me everything you know about these people. Don't leave anything out. If you want me to help you save your father I must know everything. I can't afford surprises."

Suddenly she was wide awake. "Oh, Bill, you mean you will? You *do* believe me."

"Now, hold it there," he cautioned gently, "I didn't go as far as that. An awful lot depends on what you tell me in the next half hour."

She regarded him soberly. "All right," she said at last. "What do you want to know?"

"What makes you think that Sung S'u-mah killed Tai Ling?" he asked, watching her closely.

She was silent for a moment, then she said, "I think I'd better carry on from where I left off in Banff. It will be quicker that way."

"Okay," he agreed, "start from there."

She frowned in concentration, then began to speak very rapidly. He had to listen very hard to hear her words above the noise of the DC-9.

"You already know about my father, and that the Americans recorded our first meeting," Jacintha began. "Well, this man, Roy, the American, came to see me the following day. He played the tape. He told me that if I didn't cooperate with him he'd have me deported. He pointed out that while I might not suffer very much, after all, I was just a child when my father sent me away, my father would certainly be punished. He drew a very convincing picture."

"So you agreed to go along with him," McCrimmon said.

The girl shrugged. "What choice did I have? I was a prisoner in my own room. I didn't know at that time what it was they wanted. I wasn't left alone all day. They were still there when my father came again the second night. Once they explained the situation to him, he agreed to help them, to protect me." Jacintha turned and stared out of the window. "I think, perhaps, he knew then that they would kill us when it was all over."

"This Roy," McCrimmon said. "Was he in the room when I tried to talk to you on Friday?"

"He wasn't, but one of his men was," she said. "I didn't see Roy again until they took me up to the house early the following morning."

"That's when you checked out in the middle of the night," McCrimmon said. "It must have been shortly after your father's second visit. Is that right?"

"You knew about that?" she asked, surprised. "How?"

"Let's just say a good friend kept me informed," he said.

She looked puzzled for a minute, then her brow cleared. "Paul? That rather nice man we met at dinner?"

"Right," he said, "and he'd love you for that, but let's get on."

She nodded. "They took me to a house somewhere east, I think it's east, of Banff Avenue. I forget the name of the street, but I could take you there. Oh, the name of the house was on the gate. I saw it as I left. It's called *The Firs*." She stopped and shook her head angrily. "I was so stupid! I should have realized they they wouldn't let me see and hear so much if they really intended to let me go. But I thought they'd keep their word." She looked up at him. "I wouldn't have betrayed them," she said seriously. "I couldn't without destroying my father."

McCrimmon smiled thinly. "In that business they take no chances," he told her.

She nodded slowly. "I know that now, but at the time this Roy sounded as if he really regretted causing us so much trouble. He was so . . . so apologetic. I liked him," she said simply.

A gasp escaped her as the bottom fell out of the aircraft. They had hit the turbulence. McCrimmon's stomach clawed its way back into its proper place. The plane hit another patch of air that felt like washboard on a gravel road. A stewardess made her way down the length of the plane smiling fixedly at everyone. It didn't help.

Apart from the initial shock, the movement of the plane didn't seem to bother Jacintha. She waited for the bumps to subside, then went on with her story.

"The house was to be a debriefing center for their

agent," she said. "It was there that Roy first explained what it was he wanted me to do." She broke off and shivered at the recollection.

McCrimmon frowned. "But, why you? What could you do . . .?"

Another series of jolts hit the plane.

"Oh, I was the answer to a prayer," the girl said bitterly. "They had an alternative plan, but now they not only had me, they had a ready-made witness, a member of the Chinese delegation who would swear that nothing untoward had happened. And to make it even easier for them, my father was sharing a room with Tai Ling."

McCrimmon tried to ignore the queasiness in his stomach as they suddenly descended another fifty feet that wasn't on the flight plan. "I don't understand," he said. "What was it your father was supposed to do?"

"Just keep an eye on Tai Ling and make sure that he was given a drug at the right moment," Jacintha said. "You see, Tai Ling was to be the decoy. The whole idea was to split up the delegation so that it would be impossible to be certain about the whereabouts of any of the members at any given time. If suspicion had to fall on anyone, it was to be Tai Ling. He was to be the scapegoat.

"My father gave Tai Ling the drug in some candy just before they left for the helicopter trip. It seemed to work very well. Tai Ling got as far as the airfield before he complained of feeling ill. If it had taken longer to work, some reason would have been found to delay the flight. Krell, the pilot, radioed to the field van for assistance. It was driven by one of Roy's men. Tai Ling was supposed to pass out at that point, but that's when things began to go a bit wrong. Sung S'u-mah and the pilot helped Tai Ling out of the helicopter and into the van. He seemed to be unconscious by the time they got him there, but I guess he wasn't because that's when he opened his eyes and saw the two of us together."

McCrimmon frowned. "You mean . . . You were there?"

Jacintha nodded. "Yes, I was concealed in the van. Sung S'u-mah and I were dressed in identical clothes. Even our hair had been made to look the same. With the hood of our parkas up no one would know the difference even at a few feet. You see, that's when we changed places. She stayed in the van and was driven away with Tai Ling while I got into the helicopter. The only other passenger was my father, and Krell was Roy's man anyway.

"Sung S'u-mah is the American agent."

McCrimmon's open mouth closed with a snap as the plane rumbled across more aerial washboard. His mind was still too busy with the jolt Jacintha had just handed him to be bothered with the plaintive rumblings of a disgruntled stomach.

"But Tai Ling opened his eyes and saw the two of us there together," the girl continued. "It was only for a moment and his eyes were glazed, but Sung S'u-mah wasn't goint to take any chances on his waking up too soon. She had the driver give him a shot of something. She told him to put the needle in Tai Ling's leg so that no one at the hospital would notice."

McCrimmon thought about that. Perhaps, when Tai Ling regained consciousness, he had remembered seeing the two women together. He may have realized that he had been drugged and taxed Sung S'u-mah with it. Perhaps he had demanded an explanation.

Another thought thrust its way into his mind. "So Sung S'u-mah was being debriefed while you . . ." His stomach churned violently. "*You* were in the helicopter when Krell deliberately crash-landed on that ledge," he said. It sounded like an accusation.

She nodded mutely. "Oh, Bill, I was so scared," she confessed. "But Krell knew exactly what he was doing. He took us in there just as if he'd done it a hundred times before. In fact he wasn't satisfied with the amount of damage. He took a hammer to it to make it look more authentic."

"So that overhang *was* mainly rock," McCrimmon

said half to himself. "Young Partridge said it might be, but no one was prepared to gamble on it. But it was Sung S'u-mah who was brought off the mountain on Sunday." He stopped, remembering. "The helicopter Lehman heard during the night. The light up near the ledge. He thought some crazy press man had . . . Oh, my God, Jacintha!" His blood ran cold as he visualized the scene. You made that transfer at *night*?"

She nodded. "They gave me a pill that was supposed to calm my nerves," she said. "But it didn't seem to help very much. There was this big helicopter. Sung S'u-mah was lowered by a sling. It had to be swung to bring it in under the overhang. We all helped to pull it in and hold it while she got out." She shivered. "Then I had to get in and let them swing me out over that awful drop. If it hadn't been for my father . . ." She choked on the words and started to shake uncontrollably as she relived the terror of that night.

He slipped an arm around her shoulders and held her tightly. And, silently, the tears came.

McCrimmon rapped lightly on the door of the VIP lounge. Plant answered it and, after McCrimmon had identified himself, stepped outside and closed the door behind him.

"Any trouble?" McCrimmon asked.

Plant shook his head. "The little guy, Yeung Chao, got a bit excited but the woman had a few words with him and he shut up. I don't think he's got any fingernails left, but . . ." He shrugged. "I suppose you know there's only about an hour left before their flight to Tokyo?"

McCrimmon nodded. He was acutely aware that time was fast running out. As if to underscore the corporal's words, the PA system clicked on and a metallic voice reminded passengers bound for San Francisco that their flight was in the final boarding stage.

"Any conversations I should know about?" McCrimmon asked.

"No, they haven't said more than half a dozen words," Plant said. "The woman did make one telephone call, though — there's a phone in there — and no one told us they couldn't use the phone." He eyed McCrimmon warily as if expecting some reaction, but when none came, he continued. "Constable Wong took notes. It was in Chinese. He's inside."

"Send him out, will you?" McCrimmon said. "I'll be in in a minute." Plant reentered the room and the constable came out, notebook in hand.

"Were you able to hear the entire conversation?" McCrimmon asked him.

"No trouble," Wong said. "As a matter of fact, I got the impression that the woman wanted me to hear it." He consulted the book. "Time, 15:32," he said. "She said, 'We are being held in VIP lounge number 3 at the airport. There seems to be some misunderstanding about the whereabouts of Tai Ling and Shan Shi. Refer to my earlier report and notify appropriate contact. We seem to be awaiting the arrival of someone, RCMP I think, from Banff.' She listened for a moment, then said, 'No. Make it a code nine, extremely urgent. See that it is handled immediately.' "

"That was it?"

"That was it, Sergeant."

"No greeting? No names or identification of any kind?"

"I've told you everything I heard her say, Sergeant," Wong said. "But as I said, I think she knew I was taking notes even though she had her back to me. She spoke quite loud."

"Thank you, Constable," McCrimmon said. "Let's go back inside.

Sung S'u-mah rose quickly and crossed the room to stand before McCrimmon. "I hope you have a very good explanation for this unpardonable treatment," she said witheringly. "We have been held here as prisoners for more than three hours without explanation."

"Without explanation?" McCrimmon looked surprised. He turned to Plant. "Didn't you explain that we are investigating the disappearance of two of the members of the delegation, Corporal?"

"That I did," Plant assured him. "But the lady didn't seem to want to believe me."

"Of course I didn't believe you," Sung S'u-mah scoffed. "It is utterly ridiculous!"

"Ridiculous or not, it happens to be true," McCrimmon said equably. "Perhaps you would be so good as to tell me when it was that you last saw Doctor Tai Ling."

Sung S'u-mah regarded him levelly, her eyebrows drawn together in a slight frown as if trying to read his expression. "You are quite serious, aren't you, Sergeant?" she said at last. "Are you saying that something has happened to Tai Ling?"

"Suppose you tell me when you last saw him," McCrimmon countered.

Sung S'u-mah drew her brows together in a delicate line, apparently trying to recall the exact time. She rubbed her left arm gently as if it were cold and she were trying to restore circulation. "I haven't actually *seen* him since last Saturday," she said slowly. "He became ill just before the helicopter tour. But I did talk to him on the telephone. That was this morning, quite early. What is this all about, Sergeant McCrimmon? Has something really happened to him?" For the first time, her voice held a slight note of anxiety, an anxiety that was reflected in her dark eyes.

"Would you mind telling me the substance of your conversation?" McCrimmon said.

A quick frown of annoyance crossed the delicate features. "I really don't think it is any of your business, Sergeant," she said curtly. "It was quite personal."

"He was ill," McCrimmon reminded her. "According to Inspector Wellington, Doctor Yeung Chao told him that Tai Ling was too ill to travel today, but that he would be traveling home as soon as he was strong enough. How did Tai Ling sound when you spoke to him?"

The woman shook her head impatiently. "He sounded weak, of course. How would you expect him to sound? He has been ill. He still is ill, too ill to travel as you say; otherwise we would not have considered leaving him behind. You speak as if we had abandoned him. Shan Shi, one of our most senior aides, remained behind to look after him. Surely you have spoken to him?"

"He, too, seems to have disappeared," McCrimmon told her. "In fact he checked out of the hotel shortly after you did."

Sung S'u-mah's mouth set stubbornly. Her slender fingers unconsciously massaged her arm. "Impossible!" She said. "I don't believe you." She turned away as if disassociating herself from the conversation completely.

McCrimmon turned to Kuan Lo. "Doctor, I believe you shared the same room with Doctor Tai Ling," he said. "Is that correct?"

The little man inclined his head. "That is true," he agreed.

"And how was Tai Ling this morning when you left him?"

Kuan Lo rose to his feet and thrust both hands deep inside his pocket. "As my colleague said," he inclined his head in Sung S'u-mah's direction, "he has been very ill," he said carefully. "He had a fever and he was having difficulty keeping his food down."

"He was in bed when you left your room for the last time?" the sergeant persisted.

Kuan Lo's eyes flickered to Sung S'u-mah but she seemed to be lost in some private reverie of her own. "Yes, yes, of course," he said at last.

"What time would that have been?"

Kuan Lo shrugged impatiently. "I don't know exactly," he said tartly. "Does it matter?"

"I'm afraid it does," McCrimmon said.

The little doctor shot him a quizzical glance, then turned and stared out of the window. "Probably about nine o'clock," he said over his shoulder. "Yes, it would have been about nine." He turned back again. "That's about as close as I could come."

"You'd be prepared to swear to that?"

Kuan Lo bridled. "If it came to that, yes," he said testily. "But I fail to see why . . ."

McCrimmon turned to Plant, ignoring Kuan Lo. "On my way here I stopped at the office and explained matters to your Staff Sergeant," he told the corporal. "I think we can speed things up if I continue to question the others here while you take Doctor Kuan Lo to the office. I am not satisfied with his answers and there are one or two other matters which must be cleared up before the delegation can be allowed to leave for Tokyo. I will be down shortly. Perhaps by then his memory will have improved. Constable Wong can remain here with me."

Yeung Chao had been huddled over in his chair, nervously plucking at his lower lip. He had been holding himself in check with remarkable restraint, but this was too much. He jumped to his feet and literally screeched at McCrimmon.

"You have no right to detain us! No right at all!" His falsetto voice echoed around the room. "It violates international law! As a citizen of the People's Republic of China I protest this high-handed harassment of the members of this delegation. Your bullying tactics will be reported to our embassy, and I will personally see that charges are laid against you and you and you!" His finger stabbed at each policeman in turn. "You will be . . ."

"Be quiet!" Sung S'u-mah's words crackled across the room like jagged summer lightning. Yeung Chao stopped in midsentence, his mouth open in stunned surprise.

"You are on very dangerous ground, Sergeant," she went on softly. "I hope you know what you are doing."

"Just making routine inquiries, Doctor," McCrimmon said disarmingly. He nodded to Plant. "Please take Doctor Kuan Lo to the office," he said.

Sung S'u-mah stepped between Plant and the door. "I will not permit Doctor Kuan Lo to be taken from this room," she said quietly. "You have no right to force one of our people to go with you against his will." Her eyes blazed defiantly. "Either charge Kuan Lo with some crime or leave him alone," she said. "Once he has left this room you can do anything you like to him, and I refuse to . . ."

"I would prefer to avoid laying charges against anyone," McCrimmon broke in mildly. "We are asking for Doctor Kuan Lo's cooperation, that's all. And, as for holding him against his will," he went on deliberately, holding her eyes with his own, "the doctor will be permitted to return *whenever he chooses to do so.*"

Her eyes narrowed. Abruptly she turned away.

Plant took the doctor by the arm but Kuan Lo shook his hand off angrily. "I won't run away," he said with asperity. He marched out of the room ahead of the corporal.

McCrimmon heaved an inward sigh of relief. First hurdle over. He turned back to Sung S'u-mah. She was a striking woman by anyone's standards. The light from the big window glinted on her blue-black hair, and her chin was raised defiantly as she looked at him with smouldering eyes.

"As I said, Sergeant, I hope you know what you are doing," she said. "My colleague," she indicated Yeung Chao, "was quite right, you know. There will be very serious repercussions from our embassy. Are you willing to risk that?" The loudspeaker above their heads broke in with yet another departure announcement, and Sung S'u-mah folded her arms while she waited for it to finish, her fingers gently probing.

Without warning, McCrimmon seized her left arm just above the wrist and squeezed. Hard. The woman gasped and her face went white. She attempted to snatch her hand away, but, although he eased his grip, McCrimmon held firm. Yeung Chao charged forward, his face contorted with fury, arms flailing wildly. McCrimmon thrust out his other hand and fended him off.

Sung S'u-mah found her voice. "You will pay dearly for this indignity," she said through clenched teeth. She gasped as McCrimmon pushed the sleeve of her coat back to reveal a bandage from wrist to elbow.

"I'd like an explanation," he said.

Yeung Chao hopped from one foot to the other. Constable Wong moved between him and McCrimmon, but he, too, was clearly unhappy about the situation.

"*You* would like an explanation!" Sung S'u-mah exploded. "You are hurting me, Sergeant." She turned to Wong. "Constable, you are a witness to this unprovoked attack. Remember it well. I shall lay charges."

"Do you wish to remove the bandage yourself, or would you prefer me to do it?" McCrimmon asked. He made as if to do so.

"No!" Sung S'u-mah glared at him, struggling to regain her composure. "It was bruised and cut when we crashed on the mountain," she said grudgingly. "It—It was treated and bandaged when I got to the hospital in Banff."

"Good," McCrimmon said. "Then I'm sure you won't mind if I call the hospital and verify that, will you? It will only take a few minutes."

"Do what you like," she flung at him.

He nodded. "Thank you," he said, "but it looks as if it should be checked before you leave. Let's take a look at it, shall we? The airport nurse can put a new dressing on it."

"It's quite all right, thank you." Sung S'u-mah tried to pull the sleeve back in place but McCrimmon held firm.

"Hold still," he warned her. "It's coming off."

She opened her mouth to protest, then saw by his eyes that it would be useless. She clamped her mouth shut and watch grimly as he removed the tape and carefully unwound the bandage. It fell away to reveal four deep gouges that ran the length of her forearm. A trickle of blood oozed from two of them. They looked very new.

McCrimmon sighed. "You realize, of course, that even the waters of the river will not have removed the evidence from beneath Tai Ling's fingernails," he said.

Her eyes narrowed but she remained silent.

"Oh, yes," he said. "His body was found only a short time after he was thrown into the river above the falls." He shook his head as she began to protest. "There was a witness," he said almost gently.

A murmur went up from the aides and secretaries who had been sitting silently in the background like an audience spellbound by events in center stage. Yeung Chao's mouth fell open and he gaped from one to the other. His throat worked but no sound came out of his mouth. Sung S'u-mah stood very still, her eyes partly closed. She seemed to be making a super-human effort to bring her emotions under control. Then, quite deliberately, she began to rebandage her arm and smooth the tape back into place. She pulled her sleeve down and looked up at the sergeant with defiant eyes.

"You came here *knowing* that Tai Ling was dead?" she said. Her voice was barely audible. "And you are accusing *me* of having had something to do with it?"

"I am," McCrimmon confirmed. "And I must warn you that you need not say anything. There is nothing to hope from any promise or favor, and nothing to fear from any threat; whether or not you say anything. Anything you do say may be used as evidence."

The woman moved backward, her eyes still fixed upon the sergeant, and suddenly sat down as if her legs would no longer support her. He was surprised to see tears in her eyes.

"Tai Ling is dead?" she whispered. Her head moved slowly from side to side as if refusing to accept the fact. "And you think I had something to do with it? Oh, no! What possible motive would I have?" she asked helplessly. "Tai Ling and I . . ." Her voice caught in her throat and she looked down at her hands folded in her lap. "We were once very close," she whispered. "It was a long time ago, but . . ."

McCrimmon snorted. "And yet you didn't even bother to go and see him, sick as he was supposed to be, before you left," he reminded her. Her shoulders hunched and she covered her eyes with her hands, weeping silently.

"Watch them," he instructed Wong. McCrimmon moved to the telephone and dialed the number of the RCMP office in the airport. "Staff Sergeant Bentley," he said into the phone. Then, "McCrimmon here, Sergeant. Did the preliminary report from Inspector Wellington come through yet?"

"It did," Bentley told him. "He said to tell you there is bruising in the groin and lower abdomen consistent with the kick described by the witness."

"Good," McCrimmon said. "Perhaps you would call him back for me and ask him to have the medical examiner take a close look under the victim's fingernails for traces of skin and blood. If he finds them, I think I can match them for him."

"Right," Bentley said. "And I have a message for you from the young lady here in my office. She says to thank you. She's persuaded her father to make a formal request for political asylum in this country. I'm relaying the information up the line to the proper authorities now."

"Thank God!"

"What was that, Sergeant?"

"Don't let them out of your sight for one second," McCrimmon warned. "Their lives could be in great danger even now, Sergeant."

"I think I understand," Bentley said. "Let me know if . . . Hold on a minute." Bentley's voice became muffled as he cupped a hand over the mouthpiece and spoke to someone in the room with him. He came back on the line. "We just picked up the other man, Shan Shi, on an incoming flight from Calgary," he said. "He's here now, but he's not saying much."

"Good. Hang onto him. I'm going to need him later."

McCrimmon hung up and turned to Yeung Chao. "You were very anxious to say something earlier," he said. "When did *you* last see Tai Ling alive?"

Yeung Chao flicked his lank hair back with a nervous gesture. He didn't understand what was happening. Certainly some of the things he'd heard didn't make sense to him. But he did understand one thing. Sung S'u-mah was in trouble. There had to be a way to capitalize on that.

"Believe me, Sergeant," he said earnestly, "I know nothing of Tai Ling's death. Nothing at all!" He shook his head violently to emphasize the point. He licked his lips several times before going on. "It was Sung S'u-mah who told me that Tai Ling was missing from his room this morning," he said. "Naturally, I didn't question her word. She was backed up by one of her — one of her aides, Shan Shi. It was they who organized the search."

McCrimmon glanced across at Sung S'u-mah but she didn't look up.

"I was very busy, you understand," Yeung Chao continued. His confidence was beginning to return. "I had my orders to return at once to Peking. There was so little time. I had no choice but to accept Sung S'u-mah's suggestion that Shan Shi be left behind to look for Tai Ling. Naturally, if I'd had any idea . . ." He spread his hands.

"But you did tell Inspector Wellington that Tai Ling was too ill to travel, did you not?" McCrimmon said.

"I—I may have said something like that," Yeung

Chao admitted. "I had so many things on my mind, so many responsibilities, and Sung S'u-mah insisted . . ." He seemed to run out of words. He sat down abruptly.

"Are you telling me that one of your members was missing and you simply left an aide to find him without inquiring further?" McCrimmon said incredulously. "A man, who by all accounts, was very ill?"

"He—he wasn't *very* ill," Yeung Chao protested, "and it wasn't like that, I assure you, Sergeant. I know nothing about his death; you have to believe me. If Sung S'u-mah had . . ."

McCrimmon turned away in disgust. "Would you care to comment, Doctor?" he prompted, turning to Sung S'u-mah. "There seems to be more than one version of what transpired before you left the hotel this morning."

She looked up at him with bleak, pain-filled eyes. Her face was pale and drawn. Strands of straying hair clung to cheeks moist with tears. She drew in a long, shuddering breath and let it out again in a gesture of utter resignation.

"I—forgive me, Sergeant," she said in a voice so low he could barely hear it. "I did not want to tell you the *real* story . . ." She broke off and pulled nervously at her lower lip as if she were afraid she had already said too much. "I only hope my superiors will understand," she said hesitantly. "I only hope *you* will understand." Her voice grew stronger. She had made her decision.

"First, I must apologize to Comrade Yeung Chao. I did mislead him, quite deliberately, but only because I judged it to be in his own best interests. It has been a very difficult time for him." She inclined her head in the direction of a completely bewildered Yeung Chao. "As you are aware, Sergeant, I am an accredited delegate to this seminar. I hold a doctorate in meteorology, and I have taken part in several of the atmospheric research projects which were to have been discussed. But that was not the only reason for my being here. I was sent here to keep an eye on Kuan Lo." She smiled tightly. "I see you are surprised, Sergeant. I suppose I should go back a bit so that you will understand.

"You see, Kuan Lo has had a tragic life. He was married to a very beautiful lady named Ya-Feng; it means grace or elegance in your language. And they had a daughter named Shu Hua. Ya-Feng's real parents were Americans, missionaries who were killed when she was very young, and she was brought up by Chinese foster-parents as one of their own. They, that is her foster-parents, were Buddhists, and they brought her up in the old ways. Even after she married Kuan Lo she used to go to the temple with her foster-parents quite regularly. That's how she came to be there the day the Red Guards sacked it. Most of the people ran away, but she stayed to protect the only parents she had ever known. The Red Guards didn't harm the old people, but they set out to make an example of Ya-Feng."

Sung S'u-mah folded her hands in her lap and looked down at them. "They killed her," she said almost inaudibly. "They beat her and threw her around like a rag doll until she collapsed on the temple steps. Then they proceeded to kick her to death. No one was ever punished for the crime." She looked up at McCrimmon. "Every revolution has its excesses," she explained sadly. "It couldn't happen today."

McCrimmon's thoughts went out to Jacintha. If this woman knew, she must have known how her mother died. How her father must have been afraid for her. Sung Su-mah was speaking again.

"It was almost a year after Ya-Feng's death that Shu Hua was supposed to have been killed in a boating accident, but her body was never recovered. Kuan Lo withdrew from the academic world and nursed his grief. Everyone who knew him felt very sorry for him. But, a few years ago, he began to emerge. He began to take an active interest in his work. He threw himself into it and once again became the highly skilled and respected scientist that he had been in earlier years. He was welcomed back with open arms."

Sung S'u-mah folded her arms and looked off into the distance. "But something had made my superiors suspicious, and they began to investigate the disappearance of Shu Hua. They managed to trace her to Hong Kong, and from there to America. A woman, an aunt, I believe, went with her, but she died somewhere on the journey. There was a relative in Vancouver. The girl found her way there. From time to time Kuan Lo would communicate with her. That's how my superiors found out about it in the first place, I think. When delegates were being chosen to attend the seminar, it was only natural that Kuan Lo should be one of them. Regardless of anything else, he is still one of our leading meteorologists."

McCrimmon frowned. "But if you had such doubts about the man, why give him the opportunity to . . ." He shrugged and left the words hanging in the air. "Surely there was someone who could take his place?"

Sung S'u-mah shook her head. "It wasn't quite as simple as that," she said. "You see, there was some suspicion that Shu Hua might be working for the Americans, but we simply did not know. It was decided to allow Kuan Lo to attend the seminar, and that I should stay close to him to try to find the truth. I saw him make contact with his daughter in the hotel. I recognized her from the photographs I had seen. She was older, of course, but there was no mistaking her."

Sung S'u-mah looked directly at McCrimmon, her eyes unwavering. "I *will* admit to planting a listening device in Shu Hua's room," she said, "and I'm not sorry for that, distasteful as it was." Her chin came up defiantly as if she expected him to rebuke her, but the sergeant merely nodded for her to continue.

"I was appalled to find out that matters were far more serious than my superiors had supposed," she went on. "Kuan Lo was an active agent for the Americans."

She shook her head perplexedly. "I don't know how or when it started, and I don't know why. Perhaps he felt that he was striking back for the death of his wife. I really have no idea. But one thing was certain. He had deliberately sent his daughter out of the country with instructions to contact the Americans and tell them that he would work for them. Perhaps the woman, Ya-Feng, had planted the seed; she was an American, you know." Sung S'u-mah broke off. "He didn't want to leave his homeland, but he was prepared to betray every secret ever entrusted to him," she said bitterly.

"What did all this have to do with Tai Ling?" McCrimmon said.

Sung S'u-mah gathered her thoughts together. "You were right," she said at last. "Tai Ling was murdered. I'm sure of it. But not by me. Apparently, Tai Ling found out about Shu Hua; found out that she was alive and that Kuan Lo was meeting her secretly. Tai Ling is — was a simple man. He asked Kuan Lo for an explanation. He told Kuan Lo that he would have to report the matter, if not during the seminar, at least as soon as they returned home. Kuan Lo put him off, telling him that he would explain it all in a few days. He swore Tai Ling to secrecy. Poor Tai Ling. He didn't realize the danger he was in. Because he had once been Kuan Lo's student at the university, and because he respected him, he agreed to trust Kuan Lo for a few more days."

The woman shook her head sadly. "I wish I had known. Perhaps I could have prevented what happened. You see, Kuan Lo made one attempt on Tai Ling's life without any of us suspecting it. You were there at the time, Sergeant. It was at the airfield. Somehow, Kuan Lo persuaded Tai Ling to take a drug, probably in a drink or in the candy they were eating. We all thought it was a mild stomach upset, but it almost proved fatal. I stayed in the helicopter with Kuan Lo because I didn't want to let him out of my sight. But the drug only made Tai Ling very ill. He was rushed to the Calgary hospital for

324

treatment and that probably saved his life. It was while he was there, I think, that he realized that Kuan Lo had tried to poison him. He left the hospital, sick as he was, and returned to the hotel. He intended talking to me; we were once extremely close as I said earlier, but, of course, by that time we were stranded on the mountain. He was still very ill. He collapsed in bed and didn't tell anyone about Kuan Lo.

"Finally, early this morning, he telephoned me. He told me that he had to see me and that he was convinced that Kuan Lo had tried to kill him. He wouldn't tell me why, but, of course, I already knew. I went to his room and found him in a terrible state. He had a high fever and his behavior was extremely erratic. Kuan Lo was not there, of course. Tai Ling babbled like a child. At one point he didn't even seem to know me and I had to struggle with him to prevent him from running out of the room in his pyjamas. He was terribly strong despite what he had been through."

Sung S'u-mah looked ruefully at her arm. "That's where I got this," she said. "Of course, he didn't realize what he was doing. I managed to calm him and he became quiet and very rational. He told me more about his suspicions and the strange behavior of Kuan Lo. And that," she said softly, "was where I made a fatal mistake. I told him to get dressed while I went to find Shan Shi so that we could move Tai Ling into his room where he would be safe. I only expected to be gone a few minutes, but I couldn't find Shan Shi. It was, perhaps, fifteen minutes before we returned to Tai Ling's room."

She raised her hands and let them fall back into her lap. "He was gone," she said simply. Tears welled in her dark eyes. "We searched, Shan Shi and I. At first I thought Tai Ling had become impatient and had made his way to Shan Shi's room or mine, but then the truth began to dawn on me."

Her voice broke and she had to compose herself before she could continue. "We looked everywhere we could think of in the hotel," she said. "Both Tai Ling and Kuan Lo were nowhere to be found. While Shan Shi searched the road toward the town, I went down toward the golf course. I met some men down near the clubhouse, and they told me that they had seen a man and a woman helping another man down the path which leads to the falls." A wry smile twisted her features. "They couldn't describe the men," she said, "but they described the woman in some detail. There was no doubt it was Shu Hua."

"You followed them?" McCrimmon said.

"Yes, but I found nothing. No sign of them at all. It was early; there was no one about. Of course, I know now what must have . . ." She stopped and swallowed painfully. "I returned to the hotel because I didn't know what else to do. And that's when I saw Shu Hua. She was just driving out of the courtyard. I only caught a glimpse of her, but there was no doubt it was Shu Hua. No doubt at all."

Sung S'u-mah looked up at McCrimmon. "So you see, Sergeant, your witness saw Shu Hua struggling with Tai Ling, not me. It would be an easy mistake to make."

McCrimmon rubbed his chin. "And all this took place early this morning?" he said.

The woman nodded. "That's right."

"Can you tell me what kind of car the girl was driving?"

Sung S'u-mah frowned in concentration. "It was yellow," she said at last, then shook her head. "You have so many different kinds. There are so many I have never seen before. I'm sorry."

"It's not all that important," McCrimmon assured her. "I assume you found Kuan Lo shortly after that?"

"Oh, yes, we found him," the woman said. "He was having breakfast. Said he'd been there all the time. He acted very surprised when we told him that Tai Ling had disappeared."

"Did you accuse him?" McCrimmon asked.

"She shook her head. "No, of course not. We were due to leave for home in less than two hours. I didn't want anything to make him think we suspected him of having a hand in Tai Ling's disappearance. He will be charged with treason and murder when we arrive home, I can assure you. And, although I cannot speak for my government, I am confident that they will demand the return of Shu Hua to answer for her part in this affair."

The loudspeaker broke the ensuing silence. The disembodied voice announced that flight 401 would be leaving in thirty minutes for Tokyo.

Sung S'u-mah rose from her chair. "If it will be of any help to your, Sergeant," she said, "I will send you a written statement which has been witnessed and notarized as soon as I reach Peking. We must leave, now. I trust there will be no reluctance on your part to return Kuan Lo to us? It was one of our people who was murdered and he will have to answer for that. Once you have apprehended the girl, your part in this affair will be over. It will be an international matter to be decided between our two governments."

"You have been most helpful, Doctor," McCrimmon said. He turned to Constable Wong. "You have been listening closely to Doctor Sung S'u-mah's story, Constable?" he said.

The man nodded. "I have, sir."

"Good. Remember it because you will undoubtedly be called upon to give evidence." He turned back to the woman who was collecting her shoulder bag and handbag.

"Doctor Sung S'u-mah, I must ask you to accompany me," he said, laying a hand on her arm. "The explanation you have just offered is not consistent with the facts as we know them. You will recall that I warned you in front of witnesses that you need not say anything. You are under arrest. A warrant has been issued charging you with the murder of Tai Ling." McCrimmon spoke the words quietly so that no one other than the constable, Yeung Chao, and Sung S'u-mah herself heard him over the general background noise of the aides and secretaries gathering their handluggage together. Yeung Chao choked and abruptly sat down again. For her part, Sung S'u-mah merely frowned as if McCrimmon's words had caused her a moment of displeasure. She shook her head impatiently.

"You are being very difficult, Sergeant," she said curtly. "I have made every effort to cooperate with you, but now I must insist. May I take something from my bag?"

Constable Wong moved to her side.

"Very carefully," McCrimmon said. "Hold the bag out in front of you."

With steady fingers, Sung S'u-mah slid back the zipper on one of the pockets of the leather shoulder bag and carefully extracted a slim red book. McCrimmon recognized it at once for what it was and so, apparently, did Constable Wong. They exchanged glances as the woman proffered it to the sergeant.

"My passport," she said coldly. "You will notice that I have diplomatic status."

McCrimmon thumbed through it and noted that it had been duly and properly stamped upon her entry into Canada. There was no doubt in his mind that it was genuine. There was also no doubt in his mind that this woman was a member of the Chinese Secret Service, or Social Affairs Department as they preferred to call it.

He handed it back. "Ordinarily, this passport would grant you immunity from the consequences of crimes committed in this country," he told her stiffly, "but I don't think you can expect it to shield you from the charge of murder. Please come with me."

The telephone beside Yeung Chao rang. He jumped and stared at it but made no move to answer it. Constable Wong scooped it up.

"For you," he told McCrimmon.

"Set your handbag and shoulder bag on the floor in front of you," the sergeant told the woman. "Then go and sit over there." He indicated a seat several feet away. "Make sure she doesn't leave her seat," he told Wong.

Sung S'u-mah looked as if she might refuse, but apparently thought better of it. She set the bags on the floor and retreated to the chair McCrimmon had indicated. Behind her there was a hushed scuffling among the delegation staff, all craning to see what was happening. McCrimmon picked up the phone. The Iron Duke's familiar growl greeted him unceremoniously.

"Have you arrested that woman yet?"

"Just this minute, Inspector."

"What kind of reaction did you get?"

"She denied the charge and produced a diplomatic passport, pleading immunity on the strength of it."

Wellington's answering grunt was explosive. "She's going to get away with it, too," he growled. "I've just had a call. Hell! I've been called by everybody and his dog in Ottawa telling me to keep hands off. Doctor Sung S'u-mah does have diplomatic status and is so listed in Ottawa. I'm sorry, McCrimmon, but you're going to have to release her."

"Are you quite sure the people in Ottawa fully understand the situation, sir?" McCrimmon grated.

"Don't think I haven't argued until I'm blue in the face," Wellington said. He sounded utterly weary. "The woman is to be released immediately, Sergeant. That is an order. A copy of the order has been transmitted over the network and it should be in your hands in a few minutes. The man, Shan Shi, has a diplomatic passport also. I've instructed Bentley to release him."

McCrimmon glanced at the wall clock. "The plane doesn't leave for almost twenty minutes, Inspector," he said quickly. "Perhaps if we . . ."

Wellington's voice was harsh as he cut across the sergeant's words. "You have a direct order to release that woman," he snapped. "Do so at once and return home as soon as possible, Sergeant." He hung up.

That Sung S'u-mah had understood the substance of the conversation was evident. She rose from the chair, calmly picked up her bags and moved to the door while McCrimmon watched sourly. She stopped and turned. "Kuan Lo does not have a diplomatic passport," she said. "Am I to assume that he will be detained?"

"You can assume what you wish," McCrimmon said shortly.

She regarded him dispassionately. "I think you will regret your actions," she said calmly. "In fact I'm sure you will." She motioned to Yeung Chao. "Come along," she said as if to a child. "The plane is waiting."

He rose jerkily to his feet, started to leave, then had to run back for his briefcase. The others, including the somnambulent Wu Tan, straggled along behind. Shan Shi stood just outside the door. He was alone.

With an angry jerk of his head for Constable Wong to follow him, McCrimmon fell into step beside Sung S'u-mah as she headed for the concourse. "You can't carry it off, you know," he told her. Then, quite deliberately: "*Your cover's blown!*"

Her eyes were guarded as she glanced up at him. "It is a fact that I am about to leave," she reminded him. "And I urge you to forget anything you may have been told by others."

"That sounded like a threat," he said.

"Take it however you like." she replied indifferently. Sung S'u-mah stopped so suddenly that an aide following close behind almost cannoned into her. She flung open the flap of her shoulder bag and began to rummage around inside as if searching for something.

"Sorry," she apologized a moment later. "I thought I had left something behind."

It was Shan Shi's studied indifference that alerted McCrimmon. Two uniformed constables were making their way across the concourse ahead of them. If Sung

S'u-mah had continued on, their paths would have crossed. And between the two constables, looking very small by comparison, were Kuan Lo and Jacintha. *Sung S'u-mah thought Jacintha was dead!* Which, of course, was why she had felt quite safe in blaming her for the death of Tai Ling.

A dapper, sandy-haired man watched the tableau from the upper level. The appearance of Jacintha on the concourse had come as a shock to him also, but that was why contingency plans were made. Stauffer would be mad as hell, but . . . He folded his newspaper and nodded to someone in the crowd below, then made his way toward the exit and the waiting car.

The man with the raincoat over his arm seemed to materialize out of nowhere. The two shots a split second apart were barely audible above the high level of noise in the cavernous terminal. McCrimmon saw the astonished look on Sung S'u-mah's face as her small body seemed to lift off the floor under the impact of the bullets. She crashed backward into Yeung Chao and the two of them went down together. She was dead before she hit the floor.

Yeung Chao sprawled beneath her, dragged down by the weight of her body. His briefcase flew one way; pencils, papers, and the envelope of damning photographs flew another, spilling out. Shan Shi lunged at the disappearing gunman only to trip and go down himself when his feet became entangled with those of Yeung Chao.

McCrimmon leapt across the tumbled mass of bodies, his outstretched fingers grasping the trailing raincoat of the fleeing man. The man twisted around. The gun came up, exploded. He felt himself slammed backward even as the man slipped from his clutching fingers. He fell heavily on his side, and his head hit the floor with an audible crack! The lights above him darkened. Shan Shi was on his knees beside him. McCrimmon vaguely wondered why the man just knelt there, staring at something in his hand. The lights became brighter for a moment. It was a photograph. Shan Shi was staring at a photograph of Yeung Chao.

The lights faded and went out.

It had been raining for two days. McCrimmon leaned back against the pillows and stared disconsolately out of the window. Without thinking, he started to put his hands behind his head, felt the stab of pain, and dropped them to the bed again. The bullet was deflected upward by the rib it smashed, and lodged against his collarbone with sufficient force to crack it. Splinters from the rib drove inward and caused a massive haemorrhage. The blood, unable to escape through mangled bone and ruptured tissue, put pressure on the lung. Not surprisingly, the lung collapsed. Which was just one of the reasons why McCrimmon had spent the better part of two weeks in a private room of a Vancouver hospital with no one to talk to except his doctor, the nurses, and a physiotherapist who helped him with his breathing exercises several times a day.

And, of course, the two Security Service men who went by the unlikely names of Blackamoor and Sprout. Somber and unsmiling, they came as a set. They even looked somewhat alike and, perhaps because of that, always appeared in different-colored suits. Blackamoor favored brown; Sprout leaned heavily toward navy-blues and grays. They, McCrimmon suspected, were the other reason why his doctor had suddenly changed his mind about releasing him two days ago, and why there had been no visitors.

By the ten-day mark he was lapping nursing stations G, H, J, and K in just under six minutes. It worked out, he calculated roughly, to slightly more than half a mile an hour. He'd phoned Jacintha's apartment half a dozen times a day when he first got on his feet, but no one ever answered. He'd tried the number of Joseph King in West Vancouver and was told politely but very firmly 'There

is no Miss Lee at this address . On his third attempt he
was asked not to call again. On the ninth day he stopped
calling altogether. And, as for Blackamoor and Sprout,
they evaded every question that he put to them just on
general principles.

Footsteps paused outside his door. A knock,
perfunctory and demanding as someone entered.
McCrimmon groaned aloud. Blackamoor and Sprout he
didn't need.

"You look worse than this goddamned weather!"

"Quinn!" McCrimmon twisted around to stare
unbelievingly at the solid figure of the corporal dripping
water on the polished floor.

"By God, it's good to see you, Quinn."
McCrimmon started to swing his legs over the side of the
bed but the corporal stopped him.

"Just relax and let me set this down," the corporal
said. He cleared a space on the bedside table for a large,
square box tied with string.

"A little something Ellie sent you," he said by way
of explanation. "A triple decker chocolate cake?"

McCrimmon groaned with pleasure. He'd tasted
Ellie's chocolate cakes before. "Thank her for me, will
you Quinn? And give her my love."

Quinn draped his sodden raincoat over the back of a
chair and stood looking down at McCrimmon. "So,
how's it going, Bill?" he said more seriously, taking in
the bandages and the sallow skin. "We've all been kind of
worried about you, including, believe it or not, old
Wellington. He's been checking every day, but the
damned Security Service won't tell us anything. So, I
figured, with the weekend off, I might as well fly out here
and see what the hell was going on."

"Sure glad you did," McCrimmon said, more
pleased than words could tell. "But the worst is over and
I feel fine. I've been ready to come home for several
days." He brushed the subject aside impatiently. "But
what's been happening on the outside? No one tells me

much at all, although they did tell me that Sung S'u-mah is dead. What about the others? Yeung Chao and Wu Tan and . . ."

"Hold on, hold on," Quinn told him, holding up his hand. "One thing at a time. They're still looking for the man who killed Sung S'u-mah, but I don't think they'll ever find him. It was a straight assassination, no doubt about it; probably by her own people." He shook his head. "It's a bad business," he pronounced solemnly. "As for the others, they were allowed to return to Peking safe and sound. Well *sound* anyway, I don't know about *safe*. I suspect they'll be answering questions for a long time to come."

"What about Kuan Lo? Is he still here?" McCrimmon couldn't bring himself to phrase the question differently.

Quinn nodded once again. "Somewhere in the depths of Ottawa," he said, "though God knows what they're doing with him. State and Immigration are squabbling over jurisdiction as usual, but the Iron Duke seems to think that State will win.

"Remember Olsen?" he asked suddenly. McCrimmon nodded. "Son-of-a-bitch got out on bail," Quinn said disgustedly. "He disappeared two days later and no one's seen him since. Oh, and they found the house, *The Firs,* remember? Just the way Jacintha told us."

McCrimmon fiddled with the bed clothes. "Have you seen her?" he asked diffidently.

"A couple of times," Quinn told him off-handedly. "She was down in Ottawa with Kuan Lo. Security's been giving her a pretty rough time, I guess. They never seem to run out of questions; they're like a goddamned dentist's drill."

McCrimmon's eyes grew angry. "After all that girl's been through," he flared, "she's had enough. They're not dealing with internal matters now." His voice began to rise. "They'd better watch their step! They've got no right . . ."

"Hey, cool it, Bill," Quinn told McCrimmon placatingly. "She'll be all right. She's got a lot a guts. She'll be fine."

McCrimmon turned away. Rain splashed against the window. "You've seen her, Quinn," he said tightly. "How does she look? Are you sure she'll be all right?"

The corporal lumbered to his feet. "Why don't you ask her for yourself?" he said quietly. "She's waiting out in the hall. I told her it would be all right, but she wanted me to come in first to make sure."

He staggered back as McCrimmon almost fell off the bed in his haste to reach the door.

"For God's sake, Bill, you'll bust a gut . . ."

McCrimmon wasn't listening.